Amazing Disgrace

Amazing Disgrace

Catherine DiMercurio Dominic

Five Star • Waterville, Maine

First Edition
Second Printing: July 2006

Published in 2006 in conjunction with Tekno Books.

Set in 11 pt. Plantin.

Printed in the United States on permanent paper.

Library of Congress Cataloging-in-Publication Data

Dominic, Catherine C., 1970–
    Amazing disgrace / Catherine DiMercurio Dominic.—1st ed.
      p. cm.
    ISBN 1-59414-466-4 (hc : alk. paper)
    1. Women food writers—Fiction. 2. Italian American families—Fiction. 3. Domestic fiction. gsafd I. Title.
  PS3604.O464A84 2006
    813′.6—dc22   2006000059

For David, Margaret, and Grant

Acknowledgements

I am indebted to those individuals who have expressed their faith in my writing, especially my parents, Pat and Paul DiMercurio; my siblings, Michelle, Vickie, Vito, and Terese; the family I've gained through marriage, especially Rhonda, Nicole, Kitty, and Dave; Dr. Lillian Back; my friend Mari; and more than anyone, my husband David. Additionally, I'd like to thank a few others who helped me along this book's journey: Wendy, Lauri, Chris, Liz, Sherry, and Steve.

Chapter One

"Go," Nonna said again, her voice a hot whisper on my cheek. My grandmother's ancient Sicilian fingers, pinching at my arm, insisted that I rise from my knees.

Despite the chill in the air, a bead of sweat formed on my upper lip. As I slid across the worn wooden pew, I felt my mouth grow dry and I began breathing just a bit too quickly, reacting to Saturday confession at St. Benedict's the same way at thirty as I had when I was ten. I was cornered, caught. Once, I had seen a hand-lettered sign on the shoulder of the interstate. "Rabbits for sale. Pets or meat" it had read. Held hostage by that stark image now, I realized that there were two kinds of Catholics: those who were butchered by the faith, and those who were coddled by it, fattened on a diet rich with righteousness and the promise of salvation. Shaking my head as I rose, I looked down at my Nonna, plump, sturdy, and kneeling contentedly. She smelled like rosewater perfume and garlic. Usually, Nonna smelled mostly of garlic; the rosewater perfume was for Father Roberto. Rosary beads choked the woman's used-up hands as she murmured her prayers the old way, in Latin.

"Please, God," I mumbled as I shuffled to the confessional, closing the green velvet curtain behind me, "don't let me end up like that."

I knelt down, touched my forehead, heart, left shoulder, then right shoulder, chanting quietly, "In the name of the Father, Son, and Holy Spirit." To Father Roberto's hidden face, I said, "Bless me Father for I have sinned. It's been a month since my last confession." Then I rattled off a list of minor transgressions, none of which was *the* sin my grandmother was urging me to confess.

"Aida," Father Roberto intoned. Grimacing, I wished he'd respected the anonymity the screen between us was designed to provide. He could have at least pretended he hadn't recognized my voice. "For your penance," the gravel-voiced priest went on, "say two rosaries. And come to confession more often."

"Thank you, Father," I whispered. My gratitude was a falsehood. I'd have to confess that next time.

"And Aida?"

"Yes, Father?"

"Try not to cross your Nonna so much. It is difficult for her to bear," he counseled.

My mouth dropped open in silent disbelief and outrage. Struggling to compose myself before I slid open the heavy curtain, I stepped out of the confessional, cast my gaze toward the worn brown Berber carpet, and returned to the pew where my grandmother waited. She looked at me expectantly as I knelt down next to her, her black and white eyebrows lifted. I just nodded once in her direction and bowed my head, creating what I hoped was an illusion of contrition.

I breathed deeply, smelling my grandmother, as well as the cloying fragrance of incense. It made me want to gag, as it always had. Nonna's glass rosary beads clicked next to me, reminding me of my own penance. Instead of pulling out my own rosary, I stood up, kissed the scratchy white hairs atop my Nonna's head, and began to sidle out of the pew. She glared at me, whispering loudly, her words burdened by her thick Sicilian accent, "Aida, where are you going? What did Father Roberto tell you?"

"I have to go, Nonna," I mouthed. She thrust both hands upward, palms facing the heavens and growled something unintelligible in Sicilian dialect.

"Ciao!" I whispered as I blew her a kiss. Poor thing. It wasn't her fault she was a saint and I a near-pagan.

Stepping out of St. Benedict's, I was knifed by January's icy wind. I yanked my wool hat down over the wavy black hair that had refused taming earlier this morning. Of course I hadn't bothered trying much. After all, I was just going to confession.

My father's house, where Nonna lived as well, was two blocks away from the church, but I trudged six more to my little brownstone apartment building. I loved the old place, and the whole 1920s and '30s downtown neighborhood of Middleton. These several blocks, from the courthouse, past St. Benedict's, and all the way down to the old meatpacking building, which had been converted into an antique store and two upper flats, formed the heart of Middleton. From it, the rest of the Midwestern, middle-class town spilled across former cornfields in waves. Lots of people thought the city was a bit ordinary, but to me it was as cozy and familiar as an old handmade quilt, passed on for generations.

As a food writer for the local paper, I had spent more time exploring the city than most people ever bothered to. I knew that you didn't have to drive a few hours to Chicago to find an upscale wine bar with a gourmet dinner menu, because Bacchus had just opened up on the corner of First and Jefferson. I also knew that as a Sicilian, it was really hard to find authentic Sicilian food anywhere except at a relative's house, but you could get it at Nino's. It helped that Nino was a second cousin of mine, and I could always get a table. Residents of Middleton who only dined in the chain restaurants that were opening up on the outskirts of town were missing out on the phenomenal Korean place that was right next door to the old theater that had just been renovated. Tuesday nights you could watch back-to-back foreign films while sipping on really good espresso from the café in the lobby. That's why I loved my job. I had a chance to get people excited about where they lived, a chance to keep Middleton from becoming as middle-of-the-road as its name suggested.

Pushing open the door to my building, I climbed two flights up to my apartment. The exercise had warmed me, despite the fact that it was only twenty-four degrees outside. Walking into the butter-yellow kitchen, I put on a pot of coffee and then meandered to the living room, painted in the same, subtle creamy color as the kitchen, and flopped into what had been, in another life, my mother's favorite chair. Absently stroking the worn leaf pattern, I picked up the *Lonely Planet* travel guide to Tuscany, fantasizing about the trip I'd promised myself I'd take sometime in the next few years. Just as I was getting comfortable, the door bumped open.

"Birch? What the hell?"

"Hey, Love," he said casually, just as if we were still seeing each other. We had broken up, again, about two months ago. He crossed the room in a few short strides and kissed my forehead. His long and loose blond curls tickled my face as he pulled away slightly. I tried not to smile.

"Why do you still have a key? You can't just come waltzing in here anymore, just because we live in the same building," I scolded.

"Why not?" he asked, looming dangerously near. "You know it won't last. We'll get together again. We always do.

Hey, where were you so early on a Saturday anyway? I saw you walk up a few minutes ago."

"Confession."

Birch's eyebrows arched over his coffee-colored eyes in reply.

"She made me go."

"Nonna?" he asked.

I nodded.

"She made you?"

"She has powers," I replied, waving my hands in a mock-magical gesture. "You know that . . . You were watching me?"

"Oh, Aida. You'd be disappointed if I hadn't been watching you. Do I smell coffee?"

"Yeah, help yourself."

In a moment, Birch wandered back from the kitchen, cup in hand, and sat on the floor, looking up at me. We were both quiet. He sipped his coffee; I pretended to read my book. He was a hard person to ignore. He smelled like a summer evening just before it rained, and it always felt that way, too, when he walked into a room, as if some good, much-needed thing was just about to happen. And he smiled a lot. He had dimples and big beautiful teeth. Then there were those wild, golden, springy curls all over his head.

"Let's get back together," he said suddenly, quickly, grinning.

"What? No." I put my book down and leaned forward, resting my elbows on my knees, my chin in my hands. "Birch, what's this all about? We talked about this. On-again off-again doesn't work for us. Three years is too long to be playing that game."

"The only reason we're ever off is you. *I* want to be with

13

you. I always have. Why do you keep cutting me loose?"

I turned my face into my hands and mumbled into my fingers, "I don't want to talk about this right now."

"Why not? It's a good, brisk, honest morning. You've already confessed to Father Roberto. Now fess up to me."

"I sort of lied to Father Roberto. At least, I didn't tell him everything I was supposed to. Everything Nonna thought I was supposed to," I amended.

"What are you talking about?"

"Kind of a long story."

Birch shrugged. "So? Spill it. But you're not off the hook about you and me yet."

I sighed, pulled my fingers through my hair, then crossed my arms over my chest. "Well, the short version is that my brother asked me to be Joseph's godmother, and . . . I don't think I can do it."

"Why not? I don't understand. What did you say to Marco?" he drilled, his sandy brows knit together.

"I just tried to explain myself, which was hard, since there is so much I don't quite understand myself. There are just so many things about Catholicism that I've never felt comfortable with."

"But you go to church every Sunday. You go to confession, communion," he pointed out.

I nodded slowly. "I know. Haven't you ever tried really hard to convince yourself something is right, even though your gut tells you it's not?" I kept going, not giving him a chance to answer. "All my life I've felt . . . sort of anxious about the whole thing. But what the hell do I know? So I just kept going. I even took a class once. It was called 'Renewing Your Faith' or something like that. It didn't help much. I just keep going through the motions until something startles me into questioning mode again."

"And Marco's request did it this time?" Birch asked.

"Mostly, but . . . I guess it's also the time of year."

"You mean, because of your mom," he said, his gentle voice quieting a little.

I shrugged and my gaze left his face, turned toward the window. I noticed snowflakes beginning to fall. I looked at Birch once again. He was leaning forward, but thankfully he didn't reach out to me. I'm sure I would have started to cry if he had touched me. "Anyway, I think I'm finally admitting to myself that I've never felt peace or happiness in the Church. How can I stand up and profess beliefs I don't have and say I'll teach Joseph those same beliefs if something were to happen to Marco and Rosie? I don't think I can do it. I won't make a promise I have no intention, or even ability, to keep. That's what I told Marco. Nonna called me a heretic."

"And made you go to confession," he surmised. "God, Aida. I had no idea you felt this way," Birch said as he rose, setting his coffee cup on the floor. He stood there looking down at it, one hand on his hip, the other tangled in his hair.

Terrified of how surprised he seemed, I said, "Don't look like that, Birch. Don't you go being disappointed in me, too. I can't stand letting someone else down."

"Aida, I'm not disappointed in you. I'm just shocked, that's all. I don't think we ever talked about religion before. Not seriously." He started pacing about the room, talking almost to himself. "Maybe you should talk to Father Roberto again. Maybe you could talk to my Uncle Sean. He can help. He's easy to talk to. He—"

"Stop it!" I yelled. "Birch, just stop! I don't need you to fix this for me. It's my problem, okay? I have to figure it out for myself. Just . . . I don't know . . . back off, a little."

15

"You don't have to yell at me," he shouted in return. "I'm only trying to help!"

"I can't stop yelling. I'm Italian. And I don't want help," I continued loudly. I stood up, too, facing him, my hands alternately on my hips then flying up into the air. "You want to know why we broke up? I'll tell you, okay? You're too good for me, all right? You've got beliefs, faith. You stand for something. Everything you do says you stand for honesty, kindness . . . peace. You go to church, you believe in it, you run an animal shelter. And now you want to save me. But I'm not what you need. I'm not what you should have, Birch." I stopped for a moment to breathe and watched Birch's disbelieving face trying to recompose itself.

"Aida, I . . . you're wrong about me. You've got it wrong."

He moved toward me but the phone began ringing and I dodged him. I spoke quietly into the receiver then hung up and turned back to Birch. "It was Marco. He wants . . . I better go. We're done here anyway, right?" I asked as I started pulling on my boots.

"What? You can't leave now. No, we're not done! There's a lot I'd like to straighten out still." He sounded pleading.

"Come on, Birch. Let it go, all right?" I begged. I turned around, threw on my coat, hat, and gloves. "Lock up when you leave!" I hollered behind me. Stomping down the steps and out into the snow, I swallowed the lump that had gathered in my throat. How could I have just dumped all that on him and left? He didn't deserve it. There was so much I wanted him to understand.

"Aida!"

I looked up to where Birch was sticking his head out of my window, shouting down at me.

"Aida! I'm not going to leave this alone! I won't leave you alone!"

"Why not?" I called to him, truly mystified. I would have given up on me long ago if I were him.

"I'm Irish. We don't do that . . . And we yell, too, in case you hadn't noticed!"

As I turned my face into the wind, I couldn't help but smile a little in that frozen air.

I trudged around to the parking lot in back of my building, unlocked my dependable little black hatchback, a Volkswagen Golf, and carefully proceeded through the gathering snow to my brother's house, about ten minutes away. Marco and Rosie lived in one of Middleton's most charming areas. It was an older subdivision not too far from downtown. Their home was a Craftsman-style brick bungalow, complete with porch swing and, yes, a white picket fence around the small front yard. Aside from the fence, I had to admire Marco's good taste. As an architect, he knew a good house when he saw it. He had chosen a solid and well-kept home in a popular area and would make a mint if he ever decided to sell. Of course he never would. He was far too sentimental to sell the house he had lived in when he got married, when his son was born. I couldn't blame him for that.

My brother had already been out to shovel the front walk and sweep off the front steps. I knocked a couple of times on the oak door. It swung open in almost an instant, revealing my sister-in-law Rosie, all bundled up in trench coat, boots, hat, scarf, and gloves. She kissed me on the cheek. "Aida! That was fast. The roads aren't too bad, then? I'm just taking Joseph to my mother's for a visit."

"Hi, Rosie," I stumbled. I hadn't talked with her face-to-face for a couple of days, since I had told her and Marco that I couldn't be Joseph's godmother. I had expected a little more grudge-holding, but I should have known better. Ever the peacemaker, the diplomat, Rosie wouldn't be the one who ruffled any feathers.

Rosie picked up the handle of Joseph's car seat carrier and hoisted it up to hip level. "Say good-bye, Joe," she cooed.

"God, Ro. He's so quiet, I didn't even know he was in there." I peeked underneath the canopy and gave my drowsy two-and-half-month-old nephew a kiss on his little dark head. He was swarthy, like the rest of us—me, Marco, my Dad, all our cousins. We were all some shade of medium to dark olive, all had dark brown or black hair. Rosie fit in perfectly, although she was a little taller and less curvy than most Benedetto women, myself included. "Bye, Joseph. Auntie Aida loves you," I whispered. Rosie smiled, opened the door to leave, then shut it again as she turned back toward me. "Oh! I almost forgot. We need to figure out when we're going to get together to make the cannoli shells."

"Okay. I'll call you later after I check my schedule."

"Good. See you soon. And, Aida, whatever you decide about the baptism is fine with me. I know Marco's taking your decision a little harder than I am, but between you and me, there'll be no bad blood."

"Thanks, Ro," I said softly, leaning over to hug her.

We said our good-byes again, and as she departed, I closed the door behind her. "Marco!" I called as I passed the steps going upstairs. "Marc, I'm here!" I yelled again, entering their terra-cotta-colored kitchen.

"Stop shouting," my brother admonished as he strolled into the kitchen. "I was in the basement. You want coffee?"

"Sure. Thanks."

"Go make some," he ordered, scratching his stomach and inclining his head toward the percolator on top of the stove.

"Is that supposed to be Pop?" I asked him, raising an eyebrow. It actually was a pretty good impression of our father, but I didn't tell Marc that.

"Come on! It's dead on," Marco said, smirking crookedly as he began preparing the coffee. I sat down at the table and waited. As the coffee percolated, Marco placed sugar cubes and a pitcher of cream on the table and sat across from me.

"Thanks for coming, Aida. I just don't want this whole baptism thing hanging over us."

Nodding, I replied, "Neither do I. Anyway, I needed to get out of the apartment."

"So, I want to understand why you don't think you can be Joseph's godmother. We've always been close . . . always will be, I hope. I don't understand what's going on with you." Marco spoke slowly and patiently, a rare quality in our fiery family. Usually, when someone was upset or concerned about anything, the decibels rose and the pace of speech quickened to near-hysterical quality. I vowed to keep my head, to not get emotional and defensive. Unless he did first.

"Okay. First things first," I began, trying to order my jumble of instincts, reactions, and thoughts—everything that had brought me to my decision—into a list of cogent reasons that Marco would understand. "It's not . . . it's just that I simply cannot say those words, professing to believe things I don't. I mean, I thought I did, but now that I've stopped and actually started putting words to all the negative feelings I've had for years, I realize that my beliefs don't really correspond with doctrine very well. How could

19

I promise to teach Joe how to be a good Catholic?"

"But when did you stop believing? I just don't know where all this is coming from," he said, shaking his head. "What are you? An atheist now? Come on, Aida! All those years of church and catechism classes and confirmation and . . . and all of the sudden! I don't get it. What would Mom think? You're breaking Dad's heart, and Nonna's, too, you know. You're a stranger suddenly."

It hadn't taken long for Marc's patient questioning to turn into an emotional sermon. I lashed back, "Don't bring Mom into this, okay? I'm letting down enough living people. And of course you don't get what I'm going through. Catholicism works for you. You bought the whole package, you always have. I never have, Marc." I sighed, crossed my arms on the table and bowed my head.

"What do you mean?" He put his hand on my head. "Come on. Hey, I'll get the coffee, all right?" Marco said softly, vacillating between the hot-tempered, Church-loving Italian, and the protective big brother who saw me hurting.

When he came back to the table, I was sitting up again. I stirred two cubes of sugar and a lot of cream into the rich, black coffee. "Thanks," I said, as I sipped from the white ceramic mug. Taking a deep breath, I tried again to make Marc understand. "Do you remember that red matchbox car, the one with the flames on the side that you used to have when you were seven?"

"I had a lot of cars," he said.

"You don't even remember? You called it 'Spitfire.' See, this is what I'm talking about. You can't even remember the damn thing. I was tortured by guilt for years."

"What the hell are you talking about, Aida?"

"Spitfire. I took it to show-and-tell in kindergarten and lost it. I felt horrible. You were so mad at me, for a whole week. . . . Do you remember your first confession?"

Marco shook his head. "No, but I suppose you do?"

"When does that happen? Second grade, right? Well, the big sin I waited two years to confess to Father Roberto was that I lost that matchbox car of yours in kindergarten. That's a lot of guilt to be walking around with for two years when you're just a little kid. What kind of religion does that . . . to a child?"

"So that was one incident. Aren't you blowing it a little out of proportion?"

"It wasn't just one incident. The message I got all my life from church, from Dad, from Nonna, and even from Mom when she was alive, was that I was bad, a sinner, and I needed church and Jesus to keep trying to make me good. You know what, Marc? And I've been thinking about this since you asked me to be godmother—it starts with baptism. Right from the get-go we have to cleanse the baby of original sin. We're bad right from the start, apparently. I don't believe that, Marco. I just can't."

"Aida, that's the old thinking about baptism. Now it's more of a celebration, a welcoming of the baby into the Church family."

"God, listen to you. You sound like a priest."

"So that's something abhorrent to you now? Anyway, Rosie and I had to take a class," he said, explaining his knowledge of the "new thinking" on baptism.

"Look," I told my brother. "I'll bring the book I've been reading to Pop's tomorrow to show you. We used it for a class I took a few years ago and I pulled it out when you asked me to be Joe's godmother. It's supposed to be a 'modern' approach to Catholicism, and it talks about how even in the womb babies are tainted with original sin and experience 'human weakness' or something like that."

"Well, I'd be interested in taking a look at it, I guess." Marco paused to sip his coffee, then he placed the cup deliberately in a particular spot on the table. He sat back in his chair and looked at me. As he spoke, his hands turned his cup, as if he were tuning a dial on a stereo. Our father did that as well. It made me nervous, made me feel like I was being tuned out. "Look, Aida. I'm happy with being Catholic. Sure, I don't always want to get up for church, but I like that when I go, I feel closer to my family, and, yes, as corny as it sounds, closer to God. I listen to the sermon, I try to figure out how I can be a more caring father and husband and son. I pray. It makes me feel good. How can that be so wrong? So what if I don't agree with every single facet of Catholic doctrine? Who does? I don't think that makes me a hypocrite or a bad Catholic. This is the faith I was brought up in, it works for me, it helps me to try and be a better person, and I'm sticking with it. You should consider doing the same."

Folding my arms across my chest and jutting my chin out slightly, I asked, "Or what?"

"What do you mean, 'or what'?"

"Or I'll go to hell? Or my family will hate me? What? Why should I consider it?"

"Because it's good for you. No one is going to hell. No one is going to hate you, Aida. It used to work for you. Why give up on it now?" he demanded urgently.

"Aren't you listening to me at all, Marco? It never worked for me!"

"Then why the hell did you bother getting confirmed? You were in the eleventh grade, weren't you? You were old enough to make your own decision. Why did you wait so long unless on some level it was working for you and you knew it was the right thing to stay with it?"

22

"Mom had been dead less than a year. I felt guilty enough about that. And when I talked to Pop and said I didn't want to get confirmed he went into this huge speech about how he and Mom had failed. I couldn't handle letting him down."

"Wait a minute," Marco said, leaning toward me. "Why did you feel guilty after Mom died?"

"Oh, Marco, come on. You know what happened."

He shrugged. "What? You guys had a fight. So what. You weren't the first sixteen-year-old girl to argue with her mother."

I paused before I answered, recalling that morning. It had been early, but Mom was dressed already, busy getting breakfast ready. "We were fighting about curfew. I'd come home really late the night before," I began. "I remember thinking how unreasonable she was being. I was a good kid—no drinking, no smoking, no sex. But she didn't trust me at all. At least that's what I thought at the time. I called her a bitch, Marco. Can you believe it? She was never anything close to a bitch. But I said it, and she slapped me. She felt so horrible that she left right away to go talk to Father Roberto. Marco, maybe she wouldn't have gone if I hadn't said that to her."

"She went to confession a lot, Aida. She probably would have gone anyway. Hey," he said, gripping my hands, "it was a car accident. It wasn't your fault. And at least she got to talk to Father Roberto and cleanse her conscience before she died. No one blames you. You shouldn't, either."

Ripping my hands from his grasp and pulling my hair away from my face, I rose briskly. As I took a few deep breaths, my hands twisted through my hair again. "I don't know how we got so far off the subject. Look, I'm just going to go home. I'm lost here, Marco. All I want is for you, someone, anyone to empathize a little. Am I the only person who has ever felt like this? You said I was acting like a stranger. Well, you all just keep making me feel more and more strange." Spinning on my heel, I strode toward the door.

"Aida," he called after me. He caught up with me by the front door as I was jamming my feet into my boots. "It seems like this is more about Mom than the baptism," he said. "I didn't know you felt that way, so guilty. I wish you would have talked to me before."

"I'll see you at Pop's tomorrow," I told him, trying to behave normally. I kissed his cheek then turned toward the door.

"It wasn't your fault, Aida," he called to me as I walked to my car. Shrouded in failure, I found myself fighting back tears on the way home.

Up until a few days ago, when Marco and Rosie first asked me to be Joseph's godmother, everything had seemed normal, manageable, happy even. I loved my job, and most of my energies had been focused on making the food section of the *Middleton Daily Journal* the best part of the Sunday paper. I handled anything and everything related to food. I did restaurant reviews, provided recipes and cooking advice, I reported on new culinary trends and highlighted regional and international cuisine, offerings that could be found right here in Middleton. The paper touted me as some kind of expert because after graduating with a journalism degree from college, I had attended a culinary institute in Chicago. I had some credibility. I was earning it and using it to at least try and make a difference here.

Then this baptism thing infected my whole life, bringing years of religious doubt out of the recesses of my mind and into the open. The perpetual unraveling of my faith now screamed to be acknowledged, and as a result, my relationship with my family had become distressingly frayed. They wanted to fix me. I just wanted them to understand. Even Birch had failed to comprehend how I was feeling. And what was he doing, saying he wanted to get back together? I felt as if I had broken up not only with Birch, but now the church, too, and neither of my exes was taking it too well.

Arriving home with the better part of the day spent, I just wanted to make something to eat and take a bath. I parked the car, hauled myself up the stairs to my apartment, and unburdened myself of all my cumbersome winter vestments. It was only January and I was already sick of winter. Spring didn't come to Middleton for good until practically May. I sighed again. Forget eating. I needed a long soak in the tub more than anything. I started disrobing on the way to my bedroom. My sweater and t-shirt were in hand, and I had started to unbutton my jeans when I realized I was not alone.

"Birch? What in the hell are you doing here?" He was curled up on my bed like a puppy, and had apparently been sound asleep until I entered the room.

"Aida, you're back," he mumbled as he sat up.

Chapter Two

In defiance of his intrusion, I didn't bother to put my sweater back on. "Have you been here the whole time I was gone?" I asked through a sigh.

Rubbing his face with his hands, Birch shook himself and straightened up, regarding me more closely. "You look good, Aida."

"Thanks." I ought to, I added silently. I ran thirty to forty-five minutes, five days a week and preceded each run with a basic calisthenics routine. Being short and having generous breasts and hips meant that even an extra couple of pounds made me look dumpy. I had to work hard to avoid the little, round Nonna-look. "Anyway, you didn't answer my question."

"No, I haven't been here the whole time. I went down to the sanctuary to check on things. April is working with some abandoned kittens. We've got another cat who just gave birth, and April is trying to introduce the orphans to her, to see if she'll nurse them. Louis is there as well. He's got his hands full with a couple of dogs we rescued from being euthanized by the city's shelter. They've got some experienced volunteers with them, so I think everything is under control. I brought some paperwork home to work on."

I softened, distracted. "You spend so much time there, Birch. You need a break," I told him. He operated City Sanctuary, an expansive no-kill animal shelter owned by three wealthy and prominent local businesswomen. Five years ago they hired Birch, who had an MBA and a degree in veterinary medicine, to get the sanctuary in the black after years of mismanagement by their previous manager, one of the women's sons. In addition to overseeing the sanctuary's operations and hiring two full-time veterinarians, April and Louis, Birch was responsible for fundraising as well. The triumvirate, as Birch referred to his bosses, paid him a respectable salary and he received a decent benefits package. He also absolutely loved it there but was so devoted to the animals, I feared the toll the job took on him emotionally.

"I'm doing fine, Aida. Thanks for worrying about me, though. Look, the reason I came back is . . . well, we never finished our conversation earlier, and—"

"I'm sorry, Birch," my voice was rising in exasperation, "but I can't talk about religion anymore. I'm tired of trying to explain myself. God, you're as bad as my family!"

"I wasn't talking about that, although if you change your mind and want to talk to my uncle I'll set it all up for you. I should actually pay him a visit. It's been a month or so. You've met him before, haven't you?"

"A couple of times. But I have no interest in talking to him."

Birch went on, undeterred. "Well, let me know if you change your mind. Anyway, I wanted to talk about us," he said, walking toward me. "I wasn't just joking around before. I . . . Damn it, Aida. I'm so in love with you," he said, placing his warm, callused hands on my waist. "I want you to stop pushing me away. Let us be together. Stop seeing it as us starting up some old thing again. It's new. We're new."

Crossing my arms over my chest, I wished I hadn't tossed aside my sweater a few moments ago. I looked down at my brown socks. A hole was starting to form over the big toe of my right foot. "Are we, Birch?" I asked, my eyes still downcast. "The only thing that's new about me is that I've started being honest with myself about my faith. I'm tired of just going along with everything because that's what I've always done. And you . . . you don't need to be new. What did you need to change? Since I've known you, you've always been wonderful—good job, good heart, good family, good faith. It's not like I kept thinking, 'God, this guy's a jerk, what am I doing with him?'"

"Then what were you thinking?" he asked, grabbing both of my hands. "What? Was it all the crap you were talking about before? About me being too good for you? That's shit, and I'm not buying it. I don't care if you decide not to be Catholic anymore, Aida. It's a non-issue for me."

Suddenly I felt as if I had just run a marathon. I wanted to crumple into a little ball. I pulled my hands away from Birch's, moved to the bed, and sat down on the edge. I hoisted my heavy head up to meet his searching eyes. Taking a deep breath, I tried to sort everything out in an instant. I couldn't, so I just started talking. "I blame a lot on Catholic guilt, Birch. Did you know that I waited until I was twenty-two to have sex? And when I did it was because I thought I was going to marry John Vitale. I remember crying in Father Roberto's confessional about how I was regularly having premarital sex. I said a lot of rosaries before I realized that in my heart, I really didn't think that what I was doing was wrong, even if John never wanted to marry me in the first place."

"Thank God you got over that one," Birch said, smirking. "But what's your point?"

"Guilt, Birch. It's always coming back to haunt me, usually when I'm feeling pretty good about something. But rather than feeling contrite as I have most of my life, I've begun to just feel resentful. And especially now, with this whole baptism thing forcing me to really think about things. You know what I've figured out?" I raced ahead, not waiting for him to answer. It was all starting to make sense, now that I was saying it out loud and someone else was finally really listening. "I figured out that I'm not one of those people who think they don't deserve to be happy. I do deserve to be happy. My job makes me happy. I enjoy being with my friends. Before this baptism ordeal started, I was very happy just being with my family. Nonna can be a bit preachy, but she's pretty funny, actually. And my dad is doing better than he has in years. He puts on this gruff exterior to cover for the fact that he still misses Mom like she died yesterday, but he's sweet, and wiser than I often give him credit for. And Marco. He's always been my first best friend."

Birch opened his mouth to interrupt but I put up my hand to halt his words. "Let me finish. None of this seems to apply to you, Birch. I don't get to be happy with you. I don't let myself. There is something in me that is just terrified of us being together. I feel perfectly good enough for my own life. But I don't think I'm good enough for yours. And it's not just, 'Oh, Birch is a good Catholic and I'm abandoning the faith.' It's more than that. You care so much about things beyond your immediate world. You don't just go to work and save a few animals and come home. You live it and breathe it everyday. You're a vegan. Every aspect of your behavior is an *action* for the good of another being. You recycle. You pay attention to where your clothes are made so you don't exploit some little third-world kid. Birch, I can't be that good. I'm a food writer. I go to the new Italian restaurant opening up down the street and write about whether their veal is worth what they're charging. Veal, for Christ's sake, Birch! Why the hell do you want to be with me?" I fell back on the bed, spent, near tears. Reaching around, my fingers met with the soft cotton afghan my other nonna, Nonna Anna, had crocheted for me a dozen Christmases ago. It was all creams and browns and tans, and I pulled it on top of me. It smelled like Birch.

"You think you're the only one with Catholic guilt, Aida?" he asked as he came over to the bed, throwing himself next to me in a heap. I turned my head to look at him. He was staring at the ceiling. I watched his clenched jaw twitch as he chose his words. "You put me up on some kind of pedestal, but it's not that great up here, let me tell you. I'm a Catholic because my dad was in charge of my religious upbringing and I was terrified of disappointing him. Going to church with him was the only thing we ever did while I was growing up that made me feel even remotely close to him. I'm a good Catholic because my dad wanted me to be a good Catholic. I'm vegan because my mom taught me that it meant something to her and I found that it meant something to me as well. She taught me, in a way that Catholicism never did, that I was part of something bigger than myself. But no matter what I do, no matter how much I recycle or how much I donate to environmental groups, no matter how many strays I take in at the sanctuary, none of it makes me feel good enough, Aida. Not good enough for you, not good enough for me, not anybody.

"Who am I to think I'm doing enough? Who am I to be content with that when the world is such a mess? And on the other hand, who am I to think I can actually do something to help save any part of it? I'm either feeling guilty for being lazy, or for being arrogant. Do you want to know why I want to be with you? Because you *are* happy with your life, with your family, your friends. You are a good person and you somehow have the faith that that is enough. You say you can't be with me because of the things I do. And I want to be with you because of who you are."

Using the back of my hand to try and erase the tears from my eyes, I sat up and stared down at his face. "We are so fucked up," I told him as I laughed weakly.

"Of course we are. That's why we're perfect together. So can we just get on with it already?"

Silent for a few moments, I admitted to myself how much I had missed him. I did want us to be together, I always had. I just kept on witch-hunting for reasons why it shouldn't work. Maybe, if he believed I was good enough for him, maybe I could begin to believe it, too. "You won't blame me if I completely screw up your life?" I finally asked.

"Not as long as you offer me the same immunity."

"Okay," I told him.

"Okay? Really? Because we are going to have to do something about the veal thing. I can't just let that slide."

"You mean we get to try and change each other?" I joked.

"Just for the better."

Then I did what I had been longing to do for two months. Lowering my face toward his, I grabbed his curly blond head with both hands and kissed him hard. Then I whispered, "Hey."

"What?" he breathed.

"I love you," I told him.

"I know."

"But I can't have sex right now," I said. He stopped kissing me.

"Well, why not?"

31

"I'm sorry, but I'm starving," I said, sitting back on my heels. "I was just going to hop in the tub for a soak when I got home and then make something to eat. I haven't had a thing since toast before confession!" Birch just stared at me for about ten seconds before he started laughing. He had a big roar of a laugh that seemed to match the lion's mane he had for hair.

"I'm grateful you're a woman with big appetites," he said. "I just wish you'd reorder them."

"Tomorrow I will. I promise. You order some food. Whatever you want. I'll take a quick bath, okay?"

Birch sighed heavily. "Okay," he finally said. "But tomorrow, you and me. My place. Candles. The works."

Smiling, I couldn't help sweetening the deal in my favor a bit. "On one condition," I said.

Birch raised an eyebrow, frowning. "What?"

"Come with me to Sunday dinner at my dad's tomorrow," I bargained. It was always chaotic there. Usually the chaos had a pleasantness to it, a familiar energy that reminded us all about connections that went forgotten during the week. Tomorrow, though, there was bound to be tension, a certain level of animosity directed at me for my revolutionary refusal to accept the mantle of godmother. If Birch accompanied me, then I wouldn't have to endure it alone.

In reply, Birch rolled over, burying his face into Nonna Anna's afghan and groaned.

We arrived at my father's house at one p.m. Marco, Rosie and the baby weren't there yet. As we stepped out of my car, we could already smell the lasagna. Nonna must have cracked a window open in the small, steamy kitchen. The house looked the same as it had all my life. Dark red bricks rose up two stories. A wide front walk led up to the front door, but nobody ever went in the front door. My mom had always said the front door was for the president and the pope. Everyone else used the side door. It opened to a generous landing that accessed, via three steps, the kitchen or alternatively the finished basement where Marco had taught me how to shoot pool.

"Pop?" I yelled into the house. "Oh, hi, Nonna," I chimed as I shucked off my boots. I was hoping she had forgotten about my quick departure from church yesterday. From her perch at the top of the steps, she just nodded at me, and gestured toward Birch with a wooden spoon stained halfway up with tomato sauce. "So," she said. "You brought him."

"Birch," I reminded.

"I know who he is. I'm not senile yet." She pointed the spoon at Birch accusingly and spoke sharply. "I see you and your father in church every week. Why does your mother not come? And you," she said, turning the spoon on me, "where were you today? I didn't see you at mass. He came," she told me, gesturing to Birch.

"Nonna. Please. Can we at least get our coats off and come in?" I begged, avoiding her question.

"She's not Catholic," Birch answered. Sucking in my breath quickly I turned to glare at him. "My mother," Birch said to both Nonna and me. "She's not Catholic."

Nonna raised an eyebrow. "Then what is she?"

"She's just . . . spiritual. But not really religious."

"I'll pray for her, then," Nonna said as we came up from the landing. Finally exhaling, I mounted the stairs to hug Nonna and kiss her wrinkled cheek. Birch did the same.

"Now, Birch, go make yourself at home. Aida, stay," she ordered, pinching my arm. I watched Birch go into the living room before I turned back to my grandmother.

"Ouch! What's wrong?" I whispered loudly at her.

"You didn't tell me your friend was coming. I have nothing for the boy to eat. Lasagna with meat sauce. He eats no meat! *Non lo capisco.* I don't understand it. He's already skin and bones. You should have called me. What's the matter with you, Aida?"

I winced at her scolding, but could not defend myself. "You're right, Nonna. I'm sorry." Glancing around the kitchen and peeking in the cupboards and fridge, I smiled. "Don't worry. We'll manage. You've got salad, and bread, too, right? There, we'll put those olives out as well, and here's some linguine. I'll whip up a quick marinara for him. Hand me the garlic?"

"That's a girl, Aida," she said, pulling two cloves from the head of garlic and handing them to me. I had already turned back to my work but she took my chin in her cold, dry hand and turned my face toward her own. Her eyes were nearly black, just like my father's. "You're a good girl, Aida. You don't always make the good decisions, but you're a good girl. I'll go tell your father you're here."

"Thanks, Nonna," I said. I pressed my lips together. I sighed. She made me want to laugh and cry.

Before long, my sauce was simmering and I was at the sink cleaning up. Nonna had returned and was standing next to me, rinsing off dark green romaine leaves when my father walked into the red and white kitchen.

"Salvatore," Nonna greeted my father as he kissed her cheeks, which were flushed with the warmth of the kitchen.

"*Ciao,* Mamma. It smells wonderful in here," he said, reaching for the large wedge of parmagiano reggiano, the best Parmesan cheese, imported from Parma, Italy. The hunk of gold, for that's what it was worth around here, sat on the counter, waiting to be grated. Nonna slapped Pop's hand away.

"I'll go check on your friend, Aida," Nonna told me as she handed me the colander of dripping leaves. "Make a nice salad."

Nodding, I turned toward my father.

"Angelina," he said as his mouth split open into a grin.

It meant "little angel," and it was also my middle name. I turned from the sink and into his outstretched arms. "Hey, Pop," I said, kissing him. He was short and thick and strong. "How are you? You look tired."

"Oh, just fine, Angelina. Same. Same as always. We missed you at church today."

"Pop," I began.

"No, no, forget it."

I bit my lip. I would have preferred a lecture. I'd rather see a little of the old fight in him. "Is it . . . it's Mom, isn't it, Pop?" He always got this way, a couple of weeks before and a couple of weeks after the anniversary of Mom's death.

As he ran a hand through his thinning black hair, streaked with white only the slightest bit, I watched him scrambling for small talk, a way to ignore my question. "Smells good in here, no? Is your brother here yet?"

"No. Talk to me while I make the salad. Then we'll go rescue Birch."

Raising an eyebrow at me, Pop asked, "Birch is here? You're with him again, then?"

"Yes, Pop."

"Are you sure, Angelina? It never works out for you."

"Maybe it will this time," I said as I began to slice a red onion.

"Thinner," he instructed, watching my hands work. "With Birch, I don't know, Aida. He's a good boy. He goes

35

to church. He comes from a good family. Well, his father anyway. But maybe, he's too different. Too much of his mother's strangeness in him, no?" he asked.

"Damn it, Pop," I swore as I began cutting a tomato into small wedges. I kept my gaze upon my knife. "He's not strange. Neither is Glenda."

"Okay, okay. *Va bene*, Aida," he said in a tone of retreat. "Forget about it. And don't curse so much."

"Fine," I agreed, washing my hands and wiping them on a dishtowel already damp from the afternoon's work. "Let's go," I said as I tossed the salad with my hands before sliding the bowl into the refrigerator.

Pop and I walked into the living room to find Birch seated on the blue couch. The Sunday paper lounged in his lap, waiting for attention. The décor of the house had changed little since my mother had died fourteen years ago. She liked blue. The sofa and love seat were pale blue, as were the tiny flower buds in the wallpaper. Large oak shelves my father had built flanked the television, and were jammed with family photographs, cookbooks, books on the lives of the saints, the crime novels my father loved to read, and two bibles. You could sit just about anywhere in the house and be able to see religious items. In the living room alone, not counting the bibles, there was a picture of the Virgin Mary with the baby Jesus, a large crucifix, and a plaque by the front door that read "Bless this house, O Lord we pray. Make it safe by night and day."

Nonna sat in her rocking chair, crocheting something with bright red yarn, probably a sweater for Joseph. In her aging voice, as thin and crackly as onionskin, she was saying to Birch, "I disagree with you. I don't think that's what Father Roberto meant at all. But now, we can't ask Aida about it, can we?"

"Okay, Ma, okay. Let's save the church talk for later," my father told her.

Sitting next to Birch I asked my father, "Why? What's later?"

"I believe," Nonna said, putting down the finely stitched red yarn, "it's called an intervention. That's what they say on those shows on television anyway."

My eyes widened and I stared first at Nonna, then at my dad. "It's for your own good," he informed me. Turning my gaze to Birch, I found him trying not to laugh. "Did you know about this?" I asked him.

"No, Aida, I swear," he answered, trying to compose himself.

"This is no joke, young man," Nonna said, jabbing a crochet hook in Birch's direction.

Still standing, my father was peering out of the front window. "Marco's here, and he brought our special guest."

"It just keeps getting better," Birch whispered in my ear. We both got up to join my father at the window.

"Damn it, Pop," I said, watching Father Roberto climb out of Marco's minivan.

"Hey! I told you to watch your mouth in this house," he hollered.

"You don't have to yell. I'm standing right next to you."

Turning from the window and heading for the kitchen, he called out over his shoulder, "It won't sink in unless I yell . . . Marco! Come on in already."

Nonna rose and hurried to the kitchen as well. Sinking down into the rocking chair Nonna had just vacated, I buried my face in my hands, mumbling, "Oh, my God. What are they doing to me?" Birch, infuriatingly mute, simply put his hand on my shoulder. We listened to them all conspiring in the kitchen.

"What do you mean she knows?" Marco was whispering loudly. "I thought we weren't going to say anything until after dinner."

"I sort of let it slip," Pop said.

"Well, the cat's out of the bag now, so it doesn't matter. Let's eat. She's not going anywhere. Not before we eat," Nonna said.

Marco laughed. "You're right, Nonna. Aida wouldn't leave without her fair share of lasagna."

"I can hear you!" I yelled from the living room. Birch was laughing again. I turned on him. "What the hell is so funny?"

"Hey, is that Birch?" Marco called from the kitchen. His long strides led him to the living room in seconds. Marco stuck his hand out toward Birch and the two shook heartily before hugging. "Good to see you again."

"You, too, Marco."

"Where's Rosie and Joe?" I asked, suddenly noticing their absence. "Father Roberto," I greeted crisply, nodding in his direction as he and Pop entered the room.

Father Roberto was a tall man, thin and fairly attractive for an older gentleman. His hair was white, his jaw square, and his skin a warm olive hue. He smiled at me. "Hello, Aida. Birch, it's always nice to see you and your father at mass."

"Where is my only grandbaby? I don't see him enough, Marco," my father admonished.

"He seemed to be coming down with a cold, so Rosie decided to stay home with him."

Seemed fine yesterday, I thought to myself. She probably just didn't want to join this ridiculous intervention. They all were nodding with that oh-that's-too-bad look on their faces about Joseph. No one spoke for what seemed like an hour. From the kitchen, the timer rang on the stove. "Dinner!" Nonna announced. "Everyone, sit down. Come on, Aida."

I was never included in "everyone go sit down." Rosie wouldn't have been, either, if she'd been here. It really means "men folk go sit down." The women in our family always did all the cooking and cleaning up. And no one ever gave it a second thought, myself included. I didn't really resent it. Most of the time, I enjoyed the kitchen solidarity we shared. Wishing, as I often did, that my mother were with me, I sighed and followed my grandmother into the kitchen to help serve.

As Nonna placed Birch's plate in front of them, she explained quietly to him. "Don't worry; it's not an egg pasta, just semolina and water. Aida made your sauce, no meat, okay? The bread, too, has no eggs or milk. And we toasted some seasoned breadcrumbs in the pan with oil and garlic for the top of your pasta, since you don't eat the parmagiano, *va bene?* Okay?"

"Thank you so much, Nonna. I appreciate the trouble you went through."

"It was nothing. If I had known you were coming, I'd have more. Next time, make sure Aida calls, no?"

"I will, Nonna. I promise," Birch told her. Nonna smiled broadly, revealing her meticulously cleaned dentures. She and I finished bringing the food to the table, and finally sat down ourselves.

Dinner progressed fairly smoothly. Birch kept the conversation going with stories about animals at the sanctuary. He and Marco talked about college football. My dad and Father Roberto reminisced about "the old days" when the two of them, along with their friend Victor Alfano, had gotten into more trouble than you'd expect from the sons of three of the straightest-laced Italian families in the neighborhood. Father Roberto and my uncle Victor, who was now a lieutenant with the police department and whom we called "uncle" out of respect rather than relation, were my father's oldest friends, and I was pleased that he'd preserved these friendships after my mom died. I smiled at him, watching him laugh and argue good-naturedly with the old priest. And Nonna reigned over the whole affair, for the most part in silence. She noticed when anyone needed more water or wine or food and refilled glasses and plates discreetly.

As everyone mopped up Nonna's sauce with hunks of chewy bread, they lauded her cooking. "You've outdone yourself yet again, Fiametta," Father Roberto told my nonna.

"Oh, *grazie,* Father. It was nothing," she replied, her waxy cheeks blushing a little.

"And thank you for making something special for me on such short notice. The linguine was excellent," Birch told her.

"You should be thanking Aida for that."

Birch turned to me and smiled. "Thanks, Aida."

"I had a good teacher. Nonna taught me most of her secrets."

"Some," my grandmother said mysteriously as she rose and started collecting plates. I started clearing the table as well. Birch stood and began to help. I looked at him and shook my head, just as my father was saying, "Sit, sit."

"That's all right. I don't mind," Birch offered, as he had every time he had eaten here.

"You might not, but they do. Nonna only lets me in the kitchen to make the coffee. And I had to beg her for years to let me have that job," Marco explained.

Returning from the kitchen for another load of dirty dishes, Nonna said to my father, "Salvatore, take the boys and Father Roberto into the living room. Marco, I'll let you know when you can come and make the coffee."

"But I—" Birch began.

"*Andiamo!* Let's go," Pop said, placing an arm around Birch's shoulders and leading him from the room. Birch glanced back at me, shrugging.

"It's fine, Birch. Go."

Joining Nonna in the kitchen, we cleaned for fifteen minutes in silence before Nonna turned to me, up to her elbows in soapsuds and said, "Don't leave the Church, Aida. You must not."

"Nonna, you don't understand," I answered quietly, not looking at her.

"And I don't want to!" she shouted at me. "Everyone has some problem with the way things are. But you don't let it get in your way. You do your best. And you just keep praying. God will take care of you, Aida. You worry too much because you think too much. You always have. Have some trust, some faith." She wiped her hands on her apron, removed it, and walked away. I finished the dishes alone.

Taking a deep breath, I soldiered into the living room to meet the firing squad. Nonna was in her rocking chair, Pop and Father Roberto sat on the couch, Marco lounged on the floor in front of the television, and Birch was perched on the arm of the love seat, ready to flee. He rose as I entered the room and strode toward me. "Aida, I think I should leave now," he told me quietly.

I nodded. "That's probably best. Marco can bring me home."

"Wait a minute, wait a minute," my father said loudly, waving his hand in the air. "Nobody's going anywhere.

41

Birch, you're as good as family here. You should be here."

"And he's a good Catholic boy besides," Nonna joined in. Father Roberto nodded enthusiastically. I kept thinking he was going to jump up and ask for an "amen."

"Well, I . . ." Birch sputtered, his eyes pleading with me to rescue him.

"Sit down, make yourself comfortable," my father urged. Marco simply glared at Birch and me and ordered, "Sit. Both of you."

Shrugging, I made my way to the love seat. Birch sat down next to me and held my hand. I waited. No one said a word. Finally, I spoke up. "What? What do you want from me?"

"Just answers, Angelina. Why do you want to break this family with your stubbornness?" my father asked.

"I don't want to break anything, Pop." I tried to keep my voice even. "Look, I have some problems with the Church, okay? No offense, Father. You tried. You all tried to teach me. But what I learned just doesn't sit well with me."

"Oh!" Nonna shouted, eyes looking toward heaven. She clapped her hands loudly into a praying position then turned toward my father and said, "Gina never would have stood for this disrespect." She fixed her gaze on me, repeating the sentiment, "Your mother never would have stood for this."

"And what is it you've learned, Aida?" asked Father Roberto, ignoring my grandmother's outburst. His voice was soft, deep, mellow. He was always at his most serene when he was being judgmental.

"Honestly?" I began, immediately angered by his condescending tone. "Guilt. Apparently, I was a sinner before I was born and always will be bad, and I just have to keep going to confession and saying rosaries and asking God to help me be better, and thanking Jesus for dying for me. And if I do all that and don't enjoy anything too much—because I clearly don't deserve to—and keep praying for forgiveness and giving money to the Church and the missionaries, then maybe I'll get to go to heaven."

"Well!" Father Roberto said, and at the same time Nonna exclaimed, "Aida!" My father was just shaking his head. Marco glared at me. Birch squeezed my hand. The priest went on, "That is a rather exaggerated, unkind, and unfair portrayal of the Catholic Church, don't you think?"

I shook my head at him. Of course I didn't agree with him. He wasn't hearing me at all. I tried again. "Let's just start with baptism, then. Marco, remember that book I was telling you about? I brought it." I ran through the kitchen to the back steps where my coat and purse hung on a brass hook. Grabbing the book out of my bag, I marched back into the living room, calling out the title as I did so. *Christ Among Us: A Modern Presentation of the Catholic Faith for Adults.* We used this book for a class I took a few years ago. It was at St. Mary's, Father," I said, responding to his raised eyebrows. "You've never offered such a course. I pulled this book out when you first asked me to be Joe's godmother, Marco. Listen." Flipping through the pages as I stood in the center of the room, I found the place that I'd dog-eared and highlighted. " 'Infants being baptized should not be looked upon as if they were somehow interiorly evil, needing to be washed "clean" or "purified," ' " I quoted.

"See!" Marco interjected. "Not evil, not needing to be purified. Today baptism is a celebration, a welcoming of the child into the church community. Right, Father?"

The priest nodded, but I went on. "There's more. 'Rather, they are good and beautiful in God's eyes, and certainly free of moral fault,' " I read that part quickly to get to my point a little faster. Now, I held the book tightly with both hands and declared loudly, " 'But they share the inherent human weakness that we call original sin and experience what it is to be unloved, beginning in the womb, and will be unloving in return.' " I closed the book triumphantly, definitively, and surveyed the faces of my family as I returned to my seat next to Birch. Our hands found each other once again.

Marco spoke up first. "I'm sorry, Aida. But that doesn't affect me the way it does you. We're all born with original sin, even my little Joseph. We're human. We won't always choose the right path. That tendency is inherent within us all. Baptism says that everyone, Rosie and I, his godparents, and the whole church are going to help Joseph stay on the right path."

"That's a wise and accurate view of things, Marco," Father Roberto commended. My dad smiled at Marco, and Nonna grunted in agreement. Birch had not yet said a word.

I sighed. I clenched my teeth then bit the inside of my lip. We were all so lost. They were lost in their world and I was wandering in some place between their world, the one I had once inhabited, and some new, foreign place I wasn't even sure existed. I had no idea how to live in a world without Catholicism, and up until this moment, I hadn't really fully understood that by choosing not to be Joseph's godmother, I was actually severing myself from the Church all together. I don't think that's what I had intended, but that was where I now found myself. Looking up at my brother, I blinked away tears.

"I'm sorry, Marc. I love you. I have always, all my life, wanted to be like you. You're smart, you're beautiful, you always managed to stay in Mom and Dad's good graces, you took care of me and tried to keep me out of trouble. But no matter how hard I tried . . ." I paused. The tears had begun to stream from my eyes and I rubbed them away roughly with the heel of my hand. "I couldn't be like you. You're a peacemaker. Like Rosie. No wonder you guys are together. I wish I could accept everything as easily as you do. But I've never been able to take the easy comfort the Church offers. 'Follow the rules and you'll go to heaven. Come to church and you'll have all these people praying for you, with you.' I keep looking at the rules I'm supposed to be following and finding that while they might seem to be straightforward and moral and right, to me they are not.

"You want us all to help Joseph stay on the right path. And I don't believe that the path can be the right one if it says that even in the womb we experience 'human weakness,' that we bear original sin, that we will know what it is to be unloved, and be 'unloving in return.' That's not the path I want to be on, and I can't honestly say that I'd try to keep Joseph on it."

Marco and I looked at each other for a long time before he finally spoke. "I don't hold grudges, Aida. I'll always love you even if I don't understand you. But honestly, I'm shocked. This feels like it's coming out of nowhere."

"Angelina, how could you feel this way? That's not how we raised you," Pop said softly.

"No, it's not," Nonna chimed in. "You're making me ashamed."

"Perhaps, Fiametta, that is a bit strong," Father Roberto began. "Aida, look at me. Listen to me," he paused, waiting for my compliance, and I wearily raised my gaze from the floor to his face. Clearing his throat, he began again. "Some people, Aida," he inserted his trademark homily pause at this point, "some people are what I have come to regard as

45

spiritually blind. From all you have said today, I am convinced that you are one of those people."

"I'm not blind, Father," I said flatly, annoyed by his preachy metaphor.

"Child, let me finish, if you please. The spiritually blind are repeatedly shown the path to God, yet they do not see it. They are repeatedly offered the way to salvation, yet for some reason they reject it. Whether this failure is due to stubbornness or rather to some other inherent flaw, I do not know. What I do know is that I witness the ever-fruitless search that these people embark on as they try to make sense of things that simply do not always make sense.

"Faith is about accepting things that do not make sense, but the spiritually blind cannot do so. To the spiritually blind, to you, Aida, I say this: If you are blind then let Catholicism be your cane. If you cannot open your eyes and recognize the truth and have faith in it, then at least rely on your cane to guide you. Use it to help you along the path and maybe some day, because you have managed to stay on the path with the help of your cane, you may finally be able to see the path truly."

For a few long moments, the room was silent. I could think of no reply to the priest's sermon. My shoulders slumped. Maybe he was right. Birch's voice interrupted my thoughts. "An unexamined life is not worth living," he said.

"What?" Marco and I asked in unison. I was surprised to find Birch at last joining in.

"I think Socrates said that. I'm not sure, though. I'll have to look it up. At any rate, shouldn't Aida be applauded for her examination of her faith? Father?" Before waiting for him to answer, Birch went on. "And shouldn't we, instead of attacking her, allow her to keep digging, keep searching for some faith that she finds personally meaningful?"

"Thank you," I whispered without looking at him.

Marco spoke up again. "You raise an interesting point, Birch. I'm thinking of a compromise. Suppose we allow that a spiritual search, such as Aida's, is commendable. I don't think that's too much of a stretch," Marco said, getting to his feet and standing in front of me, "as long as that search always remains open to Catholicism."

"What are you getting at?" I asked, truly confused. Was he agreeing with me or not? And why?

"Well, I guess, as a Catholic, as your brother, I don't have a problem with you questioning your faith as long as you don't turn your back on it completely. Don't assume that because you have a certain set of problems with it that you must reject it entirely. Don't assume that because you have these problems with the Church now that you always will. And if you agree that this is a legitimate and fair approach to your own spirituality, I would agree that it is a legitimate and fair approach to Joseph's spirituality, should anything happen to Rosie and me."

I had been looking up at him as he spoke but now studied the room. Nonna's brows were knit together, but she nodded slightly as she considered Marco's argument.

"Well spoken," my father said, rising to join Marco and clap him on the back. "Aida was right. You are the peacemaker, aren't you?"

"Father?" Marco asked.

"Well, it certainly is not the traditional approach to the sacrament. But as long as Aida can repeat the baptismal vows, I would have no way of knowing how she would be interpreting them, whether she held those beliefs now, or felt that she at least might at some future date."

My mouth fell open. I turned to Birch in disbelief.

"Ah. A loophole, then. Not exactly what I had in mind," he said to me.

"Well?" Marco asked.

"Come with me," I said as I stood up and took my brother's hand. Leading him into the kitchen, I felt the weight of the stares of the rest of the group at my back. In the kitchen, I turned to face him. "Look. I think it was rather . . . shady of Father Roberto to extricate himself from spiritual jeopardy by saying he'd have no way of knowing my 'interpretation' of the baptismal vows."

"But?"

"But, that aside . . . I don't know. Maybe you have a point. I'll think about it, okay?" I told him, feeling sick to my stomach.

"Sure," Marco said, hugging me. "Thank you, Aida."

"Now, can you say my good-byes for me and tell Birch I'll be waiting for him in the car? I can't go back in there."

"No problem. That's what big brothers are for."

"Thanks," I answered, heading for the back steps. I sat down on the stairs and sucked back tears as I slid my feet into my boots. I didn't want to think about it. I didn't want to be open-minded. I just wanted to get out from underneath it all.

Chapter Three

Snowy and silent, the ride home dragged on much longer than seemed usual. The air inside the hatchback was thick with unspoken tension, and I was almost choking from claustrophobia by the time I parked in the narrow lot behind our building. At the door to my apartment, Birch hesitated. "Are you still coming up to my place? Or are you too pissed?" he asked. He lived one floor up, on the opposite side of the building.

"I'll be up in a little while. I just need a few minutes," I responded, glancing away from his face before I finished.

"Sure . . . Aida? What are you going to do?"

"I told Marco I'd think about it."

"I'm sorry. I was trying to stay out of things, and then I thought maybe I could help. I shouldn't have interfered. It wasn't my place."

Sighing, I looked into his eyes, saw the furrows across his brow. "Birch, that's not true. Look, don't worry about it. Everything would have gotten twisted around and mixed up whether or not you had said anything. I just don't know what to do. I love my family. I don't want to let them all down, I really don't. But it makes me sick to pretend to be fair-minded about Catholicism. I feel so much resentment. I feel as if I've been brainwashed all my life, and now I just want to deprogram."

"I don't get it, Aida. If you feel that way, why did you tell Marco you'd still think about being Joe's godmother? Why keep pretending that you are going to do this?"

Rolling back my slumped shoulders, I stood in front of him with my hands finding their way to my hips. Hadn't I just got done telling him that I didn't know what I was doing? I'd admitted that. He kept pushing and I felt myself gearing up for a fight I didn't really want. "I don't know, Birch," I finally said, a little louder than I had intended to. "It's a family thing, I guess."

Lowering his face to mine, Birch kissed my nose then rested his forehead against mine. "Well," he whispered, his breath warm on my cheeks, my mouth, "just remember. You're not in it alone, all right?" He drew himself away and as he ran his fingers through his hair he said, "Maybe you should talk to my mom. She's been teaching this stuff for years. She must have a ton of books she could loan you."

"What kinds of books?" I asked, leaning back against my door.

He braced himself against the door, facing me, one hand pressed against the wood on either side of my head. "Spiritual philosophy, histories of different religions, metaphysical poetry . . . she has everything. . . . Anyway, should we put all this religion business on the back burner for now? We have a date don't we?"

I nodded, smiling. "I'll be up in a little while."

"Hurry," he said, kissing me lightly on the lips before turning away and bounding up the stairs two at a time.

Closing the oak door behind me, I leaned my shoulder against it, closed my eyes, and pressed my cheek against the wood. For the second time today, I felt like laughing and crying at the same time. My family had intruded into what was for me—but not for them—the excruciatingly private matter of my faith. All I wanted to do was disengage from them, from the conventional notions of God and ritual and spirit. I wanted to lose myself, or at least, how it felt to be me right now. I wanted to extinguish all structured forms of thought and memory and be a little freer, for just a little while. Right now, Birch was my salvation.

After a quick shower, I dressed in a rush, throwing on a flowered silk shirt and a pair of worn out, comfortable jeans with a hole in the left knee. Grabbing a bottle of Syrah, I padded up the icy steps in my bare feet and knocked softly next to the brass 4-B on Birch's door. Toweling off his hair and wearing a white t-shirt and jeans, he admitted me with a grin. "Hey, 3-A. Nice to see you again," he said. That was my apartment number, 3-A. When Birch had moved in, he saw me coming out of my door, and he'd called me 3-A for weeks, even after I had introduced myself.

"Hi. Here. I brought wine." He took the bottle from me and I followed him to the kitchen.

After pouring us each a glass, Birch leaned against the counter next to me and we sipped our wine. "Aida," he began.

I put my fingers over his mouth before he could say another word. "You know, Birch," I whispered, my face just inches from his, "I'm just about all talked out for today." I took a long gulp from my glass and set it on the counter. Birch followed suit, then he held my face with both hands and kissed me. And oh, God, did I ever need to be kissed like that. I would have been happy to just die right there, kissing him.

Happily, I didn't, because what came next was even better. Stripping and practically tripping over each other through the living room, we tumbled into his bedroom. The walls were dark green, the curtains chocolate brown, and the bed was laden with the thickest, softest cotton blankets in all the earthiest of colors. Falling into that softness, my hands reacquainted themselves with his lithe body and lingered over the breadth of his shoulders, the squareness of his jaw. Across his chest, which still held the warm hues of last summer's tan, lay a small, flat gold cross on a fine-gauge chain. As long as I'd known him, he had never removed it. I felt the warmth of the metal between us as I breathed in his soapy scent. The length of my body was drawn toward his at even the slightest of his kisses. With great relief I tossed away all words and thought, forgetting my own name as I prayed his over and over in my head for the longest while until we were panting next to each other and melting back into our own selves.

"So, welcome back," he finally whispered hoarsely. I grinned at him as I wrapped myself in a fawn-colored blanket and watched him amble toward the bathroom.

My head was still spinning with color when I heard Birch call out to me from the bathroom, "Um . . . Aida?"

Reluctantly, I finally spoke. I had so enjoyed wordlessness. "What?"

"I . . . well it's just that . . . we appear to have a . . . condom breakage . . . situation."

Rolling over, I buried my face in the pillow. "Shit," I mumbled.

"What?"

"I said 'shit'!" I yelled back to him.

"Oh," came his reply as he found his way back to the bed. He cuddled up next to me, wrapped in a sage blanket. "It'll be fine, right?" he asked.

"Probably. I mean . . . I think so," I replied, wondering if sperm was meeting egg as we spoke. "I'm sure we're fine. When do you think it broke?"

"I really couldn't say."

I nodded. "Well, then. I guess we'll just have to wait and see." It was Birch's turn to nod.

After several quiet minutes, he finally found something to say. "Want to watch a movie?"

"Sure."

We ended up finding something on TV that neither of us had seen and falling asleep on his couch. When I awoke, it was six a.m. I kissed him good-bye. "Birch," I whispered, watching his eyes struggle to open. "I've got to go for a run and get ready for work."

Sitting up, he looked at me for a long moment. "What? Oh, right. I should get moving, too." He leaned over and brushed his lips against mine. Holding my face in his hands, he croaked in his wobbly morning voice, "Aida, no matter what happens, we're going to be together, okay?"

I couldn't reply. I couldn't even look at him. Closing my eyes, I buried my face in the crook of his neck.

"Aida?"

I breathed deeply for a moment, collected myself, and said as I rose, "I'll see you later. Call me when you get home from work." I kissed his sleepy mouth and let myself out.

What were the odds? I kept thinking to myself as I ran across shoveled sidewalks, my feet crunching over a few lingering snow patches. As I showered, blew my hair dry, and got dressed, I wondered, what were the odds that I could be pregnant because of one broken condom during the first time I'd had sex in months? People who were trying to get pregnant always knew the statistics about precisely when they could conceive, but I paid no attention to such things.

After applying a cursory amount of everyday work makeup, I proceeded to the kitchen and perused the contents of my refrigerator. Not much to work with. I missed Middleton's downtown open-air farmer's market. Three seasons' worth of fresh-from-the-earth bounty was a dream for anyone with a shred of culinary instinct. What really sounded perfect right now was a few stalks of the first tender asparagus of spring, served with a poached egg, some freshly grated parmagiano reggiano, and coarsely ground black pepper. Having none of these ingredients, I ladled thick vanilla yogurt from a local organic creamery over a sliced banana, and topped it with some maple walnut granola I had made last week.

Sipping hot coffee on the way to the office, I wondered if I should start drinking decaf, just in case. Did I feel different? "Stop it!" I admonished myself aloud. I couldn't be pregnant now. Now that Birch and I had really and finally opened up to each other about how we felt, I wanted our relationship to evolve naturally. I didn't want him to be rushed into thinking he had to take care of things if I were pregnant.

I traipsed up the slippery steps of my building and, turning toward the corridor that led to my cubicle, heard the familiar sound of clicking keyboards. Somehow, Sally and Jim, the sportswriters, always beat me to work. Yolanda, who covered music and entertainment, usually arrived a few minutes after I did, but today she, too, was already busy at her desk.

"Morning, guys," I greeted as I settled myself in front of my computer.

We exchanged brief summaries of our weekends, discussed some office politics, and then tried to get some work in before the Monday morning meeting with our supervising editor, Dwight Bukowski. The week looked pretty manageable. I had two new restaurants to review, and I had some research to do on Korean cuisine. There was also a stack of letters to sort through for my *Ask Aida* culinary advice column. I did have an assistant, an eager college student named Ken who started last month, who could do that. My editor also wanted me to start developing a new ongoing section that focused on "low-fat and fast" recipes. Where the hell was Ken anyway? Checking my voice mail, I learned that he had the flu. Maybe this week was going to be harder than I thought.

I hunkered down and started slogging through the letters and e-mails. Before long it was 5:30 and I realized I had scarcely moved from my desk all day, except to go to the meeting, and to run across the street to the deli where I ordered a bowl of vegetable soup for lunch. By the end of the day, I still had plenty of work to keep me stranded at my desk for hours, but I abandoned ship, packed up and headed home.

Seeing that Birch's car wasn't in the lot when I got home, I called the sanctuary once I had changed out of my work clothes into a t-shirt and sweatpants.

"Do you want me to wait till you get back to have dinner?" I asked him.

"Sorry, Aida. I've got my hands full right now. We're training some new volunteers, and my guy at animal control brought me a few pit bull pups from a fighting ring the cops broke up this weekend. Most of the animals had seen too many fights and had to be destroyed, but I've got three young ones who we can save."

"God, Birch. Be careful."

"No, Aida. They're really the sweetest little guys. Completely passive. I don't think they've ever seen a fight yet, but they were pretty badly beat up by the trainers who were trying to toughen them up. My vets and I are working with them right now. I'm going to be here a while yet. I'll stop by when I get home, okay?"

"Sure."

It was almost a relief, really. I missed him, but I also knew it was going to take a while for things to settle into a normal rhythm. We'd just gotten back together, and now we had this huge "what if" hanging over us already.

After throwing together a Caesar salad, I settled onto the couch to watch the news and eat my dinner. It was then that I noticed the blinking light on my answering machine. Pressing "play" I listened to my brother's message. "Hey, Aida. It's Marc. Just wondering if you've given any thought to the baptism thing yet. There are only three more weeks until they do the group baptism at St. Benedict's. The next one is not for a couple of months, and we really don't want to wait too much longer. Let us know as soon as you can, okay? We really don't want to be pushy, but we need to know, because if you don't do it, then we have to find someone else. Not that I want to do that. Talk to you soon. *Ciao.*"

"Christ!" I shouted at the answering machine. Hot with anger, I sprang from my seat and dialed the phone. "Hi, Marco. It's me. I got your message." Foot tapping a staccato beat on the floor, I tried to sound calm. "Hey, I'll do it, all right? You were right yesterday," I lied, forcing a swallow down my dry throat before I continued. "As long as I'm open to everything, including Catholicism, there really isn't a reason why I can't be Joe's godmother."

"Aida, that's great! Ro! She's going to do it," I heard him holler to his wife.

"Just let me know what I need to do."

"There's a brief rehearsal, right before the noon mass, and that's it," he explained.

"Fine. Good. I'll talk to you later then. Go ahead and let Pop know. *Ciao.*"

"Sure. Talk to you soon," he said before hanging up.

56

I tossed the phone down on my mother's chair and hurled myself onto the sofa, furious with Marco, and my whole family, really, for pushing so damn hard and with myself for giving up, giving in, giving them what they wanted, just for the sake of a superficial peace. What I really wanted to do right now was whip up some crème brûlée and devour a creamy bowl of sweet comfort. Instead, I whipped off my shirt, threw on a sports bra, and started doing push-ups. Running would have been more satisfying, but I was sick of running in the dark and in the cold, sick of winter in Middleton. Running was what I would usually do when I felt so agitated. It felt incredible, as if I were actually physically escaping all the bullshit in my head. I followed the push-ups with some sit-ups and a shower.

Later, when Birch stopped by around nine p.m., I was curled up in bed with the *Lonely Planet*'s guide to New England. I had about a dozen of these guides, but I'd only been to Chicago and New York.

"Aida?" Birch called after he'd let himself in.

"In here," I answered.

As soon as he entered the bedroom I could smell that he hadn't yet been home. "I'd love to join you," he told me.

"You smell like a kennel. There's no way you're getting in this bed."

"I know. It was a long shot." He slid down against the wall, seating himself on the floor, just inside the door of my bedroom.

"How are the puppies?" I asked him.

"We've got them pretty well cleaned up, stitched up and otherwise mended, at least physically. Not one of them has shown any sign of aggression toward us. They're all just a little terrified, but I think they're beginning to understand that what we want to do is help, not hurt. I think they'll be able to be pets one day, but we have to be really careful who we let them go to. People need some kind of understanding about these dogs." He stopped talking abruptly, ran his fingers through his hair. "You probably don't want to hear about all this right now."

"No, I do, Birch. I . . . I actually miss it there."

"You do? You had a rough time when you were volunteering."

"I know. It was so hard, seeing what they all had been through. And, well, I was scared of some of the dogs, too. We never had any pets growing up. You know that. I was just never quite comfortable with some of the animals. But I did get close to a few of them. Like that bloodhound. Remember her? She was so sweet. Molly, I called her. And then you get close to them and you start thinking, well, maybe if I moved to a house, with a yard, I could take some of these guys home, and then . . ."

"And then they get adopted and that's great for them but then you miss them horribly," he finished for me.

I nodded. Of course he knew what it was like. He lived it every day. I don't know how he did it. "Any favorites?" I asked him.

He smiled, tilting his head to one side. "Yes," he said. "I am completely in love with this husky, Sasha. She's a beautiful dog, Aida, just beautiful. She's kind of attached to me. Nobody could get near her at first. I'm sure she'd been abused. But I worked with her for a while and she finally started trusting me, and eventually showed everyone how sweet she can be. But she and I have some kind of special connection. I'll be sad to see her go. In fact, she did get adopted but they brought her back after a couple of days. Sasha wasn't getting along with the other dog in the house. When they brought her back, she got away from the guy, and Sasha ran straight to my office, licked my face and curled up under my desk. If there was anyone I'd bring home, if we could even have dogs here, it would be her. I think that's one reason why I stay in this building. If I had a house, I'd be bringing home dogs all the time. Anyway, How was your day?" he asked me.

"Marco left me a rather urgent message."

"About the baptism?"

I nodded.

"A little pushy, isn't he?" Birch asked.

"They all are. I told him I'd do it."

"What? Are you sure?"

"No. I was impulsive, angry. The only thing I'm sure of is that I'm exhausted. They're driving me crazy. I'm hoping that this will shut them up. The way I see it, it's not like I'm ever really going to have to be responsible for Joseph's religious upbringing. He'll still have a true Catholic godfather, Rosie's brother. And I can still try to guide him spiritually, if not religiously. So I'll say their little vows, buy him a children's bible, and not have to worry too much until it's time for his first confession. Poor thing," I added, remembering what the sacrament had been like for me.

Birch looked away, shook his head. "Aida, it's not like you. You'll never pull it off. You'll feel too guilty about lying to everyone."

Shrugging, I said, "I don't know what else to do, Birch. The baptism is in three weeks. What I'm envisioning for myself is not time-bound."

"What do you mean?" he asked, returning his gaze to my face.

"I mean, I'm not just planning on doing some reading and figuring out if I can still call myself a Catholic or not. What I really want is the freedom from Catholicism, or any

59

religion, really, to explore, to just be a spiritual person. I want to know what that feels like."

"You should talk to my mom, Aida, really. Your approach is sounding more and more like her own."

"You think so?"

As he nodded, I scooted to the edge of the bed and leaned forward. "Maybe I will call her. It would be so wonderful to have someone actually get what I'm talking about." I watched Birch's face flinch in reply. "Not that you don't," I quickly amended, but it was too late.

Springing from the bed, I was soon kneeling beside him. I picked up his hand and held it, feeling scraped knuckles under my skin. "I'm sorry, Birch. It's just that . . . I don't know. It seems like if you're completely happy with being Catholic, you can't truly understand how I feel. But you have been supportive. You haven't judged me the way my family has, and that means a lot to me."

"Why do you think I'm so happy to be a Catholic? I just told you the other day about my dad and me, about my trying to have some sort of real connection with him. That's mostly what Catholicism is for me. There are a lot of things I don't agree with, but I tend to just overlook them. I try not to think so much about doctrine."

"But don't you feel like a hypocrite? I mean, that's part of what I'm grappling with. I can't stand feeling that way anymore."

Hanging his head, he looked down at our clasped hands and shrugged. "Aida, I can't start dissecting things the way you do. I don't want to feel like I have to change anything where my religious life is concerned. I just want it to be uncomplicated, you know? Nothing else is. Can't I just go to church with my dad and be allowed to feel that he is proud of me, at least in this one context? Can't I just go to church, try to glean a little peace, a little insight? Why can't it be that simple?"

"Maybe it can for you. But if there are things that you take issue with . . . I don't know. It just doesn't seem like you to just sweep your concerns into a corner, out of sight," I replied softly. Birch stood up for things. That's who he was. He wasn't confrontational at all, but there was no confusion about the things that mattered to him.

"Well, I guess you don't know me as well as you think you do, then," he said, pulling his hand out of my light grip.

Now it was my turn to wince. What was I doing anyway? Trying to yank him away from religion with me? Leaning against the wall next to him, I sat silently. I drew my knees up to my chest, considering what to say next. I couldn't think of anything I wanted more than for us to understand each other. Perhaps it was selfish of me.

Taking a deep breath, I tried another approach. "Okay, Birch, look. I'm not trying to get you to abandon Catholicism. But don't you think we should try to comprehend the other person's point of view?"

"Of course."

"Well, I'm trying to understand your position and here's what I don't get. I know you don't want to upset your father. I respect that. I've seen him pissed off, and he's scarier than my dad. Remember that time he almost hit you?"

"Which one?" he asked, with a grim little snort.

"I don't know what you guys were arguing about. Probably the pub," I said, recalling that evening. Birch's dad, Will, owned a pub that had been in McFarland hands for generations, but much to Will's dismay, Birch had no interest in running the place. "We were in your folks' backyard, and he raised his fist like he was going to punch you right in the face."

"He does have a temper," Birch said, looking up at the ceiling.

"Anyway, if there are things you don't like about the Church, leaving is not your only option. Why don't you speak up, try and change things?" He sat up a little straighter and turned to me, waiting for me to continue.

Leaning toward him, I pressed on. "You're a vegan not just because it makes you feel healthier to abstain from consuming any animal products, right? Isn't it because you believe in the rights of animals to not be hunted, to not be raised as a food crop, to not be experimented on, and so on? You're an activist. These are essentially your vegan doctrinal issues. But look at all the vegetarians out there who are concerned primarily for their own individual health and not the larger ethical issues."

"Just like all the Catholics out there interested in their own spiritual health but not the ethical issues of the community they're a part of," Birch put in.

"Right. As an activist, don't you try to get other vegetarians, and people in general, to interest themselves with animal rights issues, issues that transcend their individual, health-related concerns?"

Birch nodded slowly. "So, within the religious context shouldn't I be doing something to motivate Catholics to be concerned about something more than their own salvation? Is that what you're saying?"

"Exactly," I replied, as I rose to my knees and began speaking more quickly. "It's not just about how you feel in church, and getting absolution from your sins. What about how the whole system is structured? If there is a shortage of priests, why not let women become priests? Why not let priests marry? Why does the Pope appoint everybody? Can't we elect our own religious leaders? The whole structure is so insufferably patriarchal."

"Okay, okay, slow down, Aida. I get your point. But I have no idea how to even start such a crusade within the Church. And I don't know if I even want to."

"Sure you do," I answered, speaking to both of his concerns. "You know how to get people thinking about things without coming off as a revolutionary. You're always so calm and laid back when you're talking about veganism, and your work at the sanctuary, but it does put thoughts into people's heads. Look at all the volunteers you've recruited for the sanctuary. Start some sort of religious study group and get people fired up. It's a beginning anyway. It's a way out of being a hypocrite."

"There is still the problem of my father, though, Aida. This would really put my relationship with him at risk," Birch replied.

"Maybe you can talk to him, let him know how you feel. He may be an inflexible hard-liner, but he's still your father."

"I'll think about it. You've given me a lot to think about actually. But what about you? Why are you bailing out instead of being the rabble rouser you're encouraging me to be?"

We were still both sitting on the floor, and I curled myself into a ball by his side, burying my face in my hands. "God, Birch, I don't know," I whined into the cuffs of my shirt. "I just have to get away from it all—the Church, its history, politics, complexity, all the guilt . . ."

I trailed off, thinking of the lifetime's worth of blame I had heaped upon myself, for losing a childhood toy, for driving away my mother, driving her to her death. I know that the assigning of that blame was my doing, but I couldn't help but fault the Church for creating in me an intense proclivity for self-censure. I had been constantly reminded of the fact that I was a sinner, had always been a sinner, and would always be a sinner. I was required to try to be good, but also admonished to understand that being human, I would more often than not fail in my effort. No one ever blamed me specifically for my mother's death, but the specter of general, all-encompassing condemnation had haunted me all my life. Being asked to welcome an innocent baby like Joseph into the "Church family" had ignited my examination, my acknowledgement, of what my own life-long experience with Catholicism had been like.

Choking back the sob that threatened to tear itself from my body, I felt Birch's arm's wrap tightly around me. Leaning against his chest, I could feel the cross he wore underneath his shirt. As I pressed my cheek against him, I inhaled the damp, musky odor of unwashed dog. Birch had come here straight from work; I had forgotten. "I'm sorry," I murmured.

"For what?" he asked softly.

"I don't know. Being like this, I guess."

"Stop it, Aida."

Rubbing my face with my hands, I sat up and studied Birch's own tired face. "Want me to make you something to eat?"

"No thanks. I think I'm just going to go home and shower. Can I come back here and sleep with you tonight?"

"Please do," I told him.

"Are you okay?"

I nodded. "Mm-hm."

"You know it wasn't your fault, right . . . about your mom?"

"That's what everyone says."

"It wasn't, Aida. What are you going to do about the

64

baptism? What are you going to tell Marco?"

I stood up, stretching. "I don't know, honestly. I am as reluctant to destroy my relationship with my family as you are, Birch." All he could do by way of reply was nod and hug me.

The next couple of weeks passed quickly. Birch had spoken to his mother; the soonest we could get together was the Saturday before Joseph's baptism. That didn't really matter to me. I wasn't meeting with her in hopes that she could help me make any decisions. I just wanted to find out how she went about pursuing a spiritual life outside of the structure of any organized religion. How did she make it matter? I didn't want to just feel like I was "getting out of" the Catholic Church. I didn't want to just quit something. I wanted to start something.

As for the baptism, my feelings were as mixed as ever. My sense of duty to my family was constantly on the verge of collision with my growing repulsion for organized religion, particularly the one that had been force-fed to me. What should have been a promise of religious sustenance from me to Joseph was instead a bland offer, devoid of nourishment, and grudgingly provided only because it was insisted upon by my family.

As the days passed, I plodded through my work, thoroughly exhausted lately, and I took little joy in my restaurant reviews, usually my favorite part of the job. Every time I sat down in front of a plate of food for which I usually drooled, I completely lost my appetite. Today I had walked out on a perfectly good plate of Aloo Gobi from the new Indian restaurant. I was disgusted with myself; maybe I was coming down with something. It was Friday, at around half past six, and everyone was still at the office, wrapping up their stories.

Yolanda called out to me from her cubicle, "Hey, Aida!"

"What?"

"Sally and I are going to McFarland's for a drink. You about done? Want to come?"

I stopped typing for a moment to think. Birch had already said he was going to be late at work, and, anyway, I needed a change of pace. "Sure," I replied. "I'll meet you guys over there. I just need a few minutes to finish this up."

About half an hour later, I was parking my car outside of Birch's father's pub. I hadn't seen Will McFarland for a few months and I wondered if he'd be here tonight. Birch's mom, Glenda, had always loved me and I couldn't wait to see her tomorrow, but Will, he was another story. I couldn't read him at all. Curt and gruff with me most of the time, he had occasionally enveloped me in a few solid bear hugs. What I found upsetting about him was his volatile attitude toward both Glenda and Birch. In the few years that I had known the family, I had seen him rage at his wife and son over things that appeared trivial to me. Then he would storm off and lock himself in his den, emerging sometime later cool and distant, but controlled. I was used to moodiness and yelling in my own family, but there was never any true rancor behind it all, and no one ever stayed angry.

Walking into McFarland's, I found my friends and ordered a pint of English ale.

"So how are you doing, Aida? You've been so quiet in your little corner lately. What's going on with you?" Yolanda asked.

"God, it's been a crazy couple of weeks. We haven't had time to catch up for a while, have we?" As I spoke, Yolanda and Sally shook their heads and I wondered where to begin. It wasn't like me to go so long without confiding in them. Outside of my family, they were my closest friends.

"Well, Birch and I are back together," I began.

"Surprise, surprise," Sally said.

Yolanda laughed and added, "Yeah, we figured that out a while ago. You're not too quiet on the phone, you know. How long is it going to last this time?"

I shrugged. "I don't know. It's . . . it feels different this time. We really talked about it, finally opened up about some things. I think this could be it."

"Really? That's great," Sally said, squeezing my hand.

Yolanda just raised an eyebrow. "You guys have been doing this dance a while. I give you three months before you split again."

"Thanks a lot," I said, trying to smile and not take Yolanda too seriously. She was right to be skeptical, based on my history with Birch, but the thought of us apart again made me feel sick. I took a gulp of beer, then carefully placed my glass back on the table, feeling my fake smile slide from my face.

"Hey, I was only kidding," Yolanda was saying. "Are you okay?"

I pulled my hair away from my face as I took a deep breath. "Yeah, I think so. I don't know. I've been feeling really . . . emotional lately. And tired. Maybe it's PMS."

"Well you've been working really hard, Aida," Sally said. "Plus, isn't it . . . that time of year?" she asked cautiously.

"What? What are you talking about?" Yolanda asked, then suddenly remembering, she said, "Oh, right. Your mom. I'm sorry, Aida. I forgot."

"That's okay. I don't think that's it."

"Yeah, must be the PMS," Sally said, gulping her beer. "You have been kind of bitchy lately," she joked. I couldn't help but laugh. Just then, Will McFarland strode over to the table. He was tall and muscular. Thick, wavy black hair had been tamed by some zealous barber who had shorn the locks a little too close to the scalp. This evening, he wore a broad smile as he greeted my friends and me. "Good evening, ladies," he called out as he approached us.

"Hi, Mr. McFarland. It's good to see you again," I said as I stood up and kissed his cheek.

"Likewise, Aida. I hear you and my son will be joining us for dinner tomorrow."

I nodded.

"We're looking forward to it. You girls have a good night. Next round is on me," he said with a wink. "See you tomorrow, Aida. And make sure Birch showers before he comes over. I don't want him smelling like a filthy dog at the dinner table! No manners, that boy," he grumbled as he walked away.

"Thanks for the beer!" Yolanda and Sally yelled after him.

They ordered a plate of nachos and chugged their free beer, but I hadn't even finished my first drink. The smell of the nachos made my stomach lurch. "Hey, you two. I'm going to get going. I'm just not feeling right. I feel so queasy."

"Really? Still? I thought a couple of drinks would take the edge off for you. Unless maybe you're coming down with the flu," Yolanda said.

"Or maybe you're pregnant," Sally laughed.

Managing a weak smile, I scooted off of my chair, gave them each a brief hug, and began the drive home. Mumbling aloud and counting on my fingers, I tried to calculate when my period was supposed to begin. "It should have started days ago," I whispered to myself. I was extremely regular, with a textbook twenty-eight-day cycle. Simultaneously, I recalled the broken condom incident and Sally's parting comment. "Oh, my God . . . I can't be . . . shit." I turned abruptly a few blocks from my apartment into the parking lot of a small, family-owned drug store. Glancing at the clock, I realized they'd be closing in about twenty minutes, at nine p.m. I inhaled through my nose and exhaled through my mouth a few times, then paced toward the door.

The store was small and I found the pregnancy tests in no time. Just opposite the pregnancy tests were cosmetics, and a tall, thin, aging redhead was perusing the lipsticks. She smiled as I approached. I got the feeling she was the chatty type, so I only nodded in her direction briskly, not making direct eye contact. I started examining the various pregnancy test kits, amazed that there were so many different ways to pee on a stick. I sighed audibly in frustration and immediately realized my mistake. The redhead had been waiting for just such an opening.

"A baby, huh? How exciting!" she said. She had the kind of voice that you actually wanted to keep listening to, a little low, and with the hint of an accent to it, but you weren't sure where she might be from. It was a quiet, strong, mellow voice.

"You think so?" I replied, trying to keep my tone light.

"Don't you?"

"Well, I'm a little not married and my family's a lot old-fashioned. They're going to take it pretty hard if I am actually . . ." I trailed off.

"Actually pregnant," she finished for me. "What about your boyfriend? Will he be excited? Oh, never mind. Don't answer that. Too personal, isn't it? I just wish my boyfriend were a little more old-fashioned. We've been together almost a year and I still haven't met his family. Anyway, don't you worry about your family. Sometimes people don't know they want something until they have it. They'll come around. This baby could be just the thing your family needs. None of my business anyway, is it?" She paused and held up two shades of lipstick. "Which one?" she asked.

I pointed to the more subtle shade.

"Why?"

"Understated, but seductive. He'll love it," I told her. Looking down at my own hands, I saw that I held a pregnancy test kit in each one. I presented them to the redhead. "Which one?"

She pointed to the one in my right hand.

"Why?" I asked her.

"It has two tests in the box. No matter what the first one says you won't believe it and you'll be glad that you can do it again."

"Well, thanks. Good luck with your boyfriend," I said, placing the box in my left hand back on the shelf.

"Same to you. And congratulations. I just have a feeling." With a wave of her hand, she turned and strolled down the aisle, stopping in front of the nail polish. I paid for my test and made my way home.

Ripping off my coat and boots, I fumbled with the packaging of the test, seeking instructions. "May be taken at any time of the day," it read. Good. I could do it right now. "As early as first day of missed period." Excellent, I thought. No time like the present. Perching on the edge of my bed, I re-examined the directions, determined to do it properly so that I could not second-guess the results, whatever they might be. I stood up, then flopped back down on the bed.

How could I be about to take a pregnancy test? This wasn't the way things were supposed to happen, not with me anyway, not with Birch. The last thing I wanted was for him to feel trapped, pressured. He *had* said, though, that he wanted us to be together, had always wanted to be with me. No matter what Birch felt, the fact remained that I could be finding out within moments that Birch and I were going to be parents. But, God, how could I possibly be someone's mother? I was closing in on the point in my life where I'd been without a mother for longer than I'd had one. What did I know about being a mother? And without my own mother to guide me, how could I learn?

I sat up again, marshalling my courage, commanding my feet to find their way toward the bathroom. After fumbling with the fly on my black dress slacks, I urinated obediently and tentatively on the stick, then placed it on several tissues on the counter next to the sink. With one backward glance, I returned to the bedroom to watch the glowing red numbers on my alarm clock. Nine-seventeen, it read. At nine-twenty I'd go in and find out. I'd read *War and Peace* in college, and I was sure now that it had taken less time to complete the tome than the eternity that was playing itself out in my room this instant. Just as the nineteen turned to twenty, I was racing to the bathroom, listening to the phone ring and hearing the answering machine pick up.

As I stared at the pregnancy test, I heard Birch saying, "Hey, Love. Are you there? Maybe you're in the tub. I'm just leaving work. I'll be there soon. I've been thinking of you all day. I want to talk to you about something."

Chapter Four

Transfixed, I stood rooted to the floor, gazing at two bright pink lines, only dimly aware of what Birch had said. My only thought was that he, in a way, was with me when I learned I was carrying his child. The rational part of me reasoned that tomorrow morning I would take the other test, just to be certain. At the same time, my heart skittered around in my chest like a puppy on wet linoleum. Finally looking away from the test stick, I caught my face in the mirror, slowly realizing that the dreamiest of smiles had unfurled itself from ear to ear.

I felt as if my world had suddenly expanded infinitely in every direction. Turning on the faucet in the tub, I stripped off my clothes then neatly folded the pregnancy test in tissue and placed it in the cupboard underneath the sink. Into the tub I tossed a large, bathtub sized "tea" bag filled with lavender. I then slid into the deep basin and waited for Birch to arrive. I had no idea how I would tell him. I wasn't sure how'd he take the news, but given the peaceful elation that had enveloped me, I had to assume that his reaction would be, at the very least, tentatively favorable. I couldn't tell him before we visited his parents tomorrow; I wouldn't want to tell them right away, and Birch was appallingly inept at keeping secrets. Then Sunday was the big baptism, and that didn't seem like a good time. Maybe Sunday evening, when we were finally alone again.

Just then, I heard the door slam shut. "Aida? Are you here?"

"In the tub!"

"Can I come in?"

"Of course, silly," I said as he was already entering the room.

"Oh, my God," he whispered slowly.

"What? What is it?"

"It's you. It's . . . you're positively gorgeous tonight. So tranquil."

I smiled in reply. "Want to join me?"

"Sure," he said, taking off his clothes and stepping into the tub across from me. He sat facing me, stretching his long legs out on the outside of mine. Happily, it was an older tub, roomy and deep.

"Oh, your dad told me to tell you to shower before you come tomorrow," I told him.

"My dad? When did you see him?"

"Sal and Yolanda and I went out for a drink after work."

"He spends too much time at the pub. It pisses my mom off . . . and what's with the shower remark? He's always hated the sanctuary," Birch grumbled.

"He was just joking around, Birch. He doesn't hate the sanctuary."

"No, you're right. He hates that he has no son to bequeath the pub to, since I chose to do something else with my life. What's worse is that he blames my mom as much as me."

"Well, that's not very fair of him. But, hey, let's forget about your folks until tomorrow, okay?" I asked, massaging his foot.

"Okay," he said, smiling.

The night was perfect. We thoroughly enjoyed each other, and I relished my secret, refusing to acknowledge all the fears that I had driven from my mind when I found out I was pregnant. There would be time enough for doubt and reassurance, panic and planning. But that wasn't what tonight was for.

We awoke late the next morning, snuggled together in defiance of the icy January morning, and shrouded in my brandy- and claret-colored bedding. My bedroom was richly draped with the shades of tawny ports and Chianti-hued reds. It was warm and elegant, without being fussy or fancy, and complemented the mismatched antique dresser, headboard, and wardrobe I rescued from a local resale shop and refinished in my father's garage.

Birch opened his eyes to find me gazing at him. "Hey, beautiful," I greeted him.

Laughing in reply, he brushed his lips against mine. "Look who's talking," he said quietly. He cleared his throat. "Aida," he said. "I . . . there's something I wanted to talk to you about. I mentioned it last night in my message, but, I guess you were already in the tub."

"What is it?"

"Well, I've been thinking about this for a while. I love you, Aida. I want us to be together. To stay together. I . . . I'm asking you to marry me, Aida." He said this all as he lay casually on his side, head resting on one arm while the other draped over my hip, just as if he were asking me if I wanted a cup of coffee.

I, too, was reclining on my side, facing him. Being only a little surprised by his direct yet breezy approach, I kissed him, rolled onto my back, and laughed a little. "Birch," I said, shaking my head. "Jesus, Birch, you should have asked me before I jumped ship."

"What? What are you saying? Are you saying no?"

"I'm saying yes and no. You have to know that I love you. I'm just not going to do a whole big church-and-priest-dog-and-pony-show-Irish-Italian-Catholic wedding deal. I can't."

"Well, don't you think I know that? I asked you to marry me, Aida. Not to have a wedding with me. We can have a tiny civil ceremony, or hell, no ceremony at all. We can stand naked in the woods and just promise to be together. I just want you to know that I'm playing for keeps."

The puppy in my chest somersaulted and I smiled giddily at him. "I am, too, Birch. I am, too."

We made love again, and before going out for breakfast, I took the second test. The results were the same as the first, and on our way to Birch's favorite restaurant, I contemplated when and where I might tell him. The restaurant was called the Om Café, the only place in town where Birch could actually have more for breakfast than dry toast and a paltry fruit plate. Their menu was all vegetarian, with about a dozen vegan selections for each meal. Every time I went in there, the place was packed.

"I never knew Middleton had so many vegetarians, Birch. Do you know them all?" I joked.

He smiled. "Yes, in fact I do. We're all part of one big club, you know."

The hostess who was waiting to seat us overheard our conversation and chimed in. "Actually, only half of our customers are vegetarian," she informed.

"Really?" I asked.

"Really. They just come because the food is good." She smiled at us and then looked intently at my face for a few long moments. "Don't I know you?"

"I've been in here a few times."

"No, that's not it. You're . . . I know! You're Aida Benedetto, right? 'Ask Aida' and all that? From the paper. Are you going to review the restaurant?"

I grinned and Birch laughed at me. I didn't often get recognized from the black-and-white photo that ran alongside my column, but I got such a kick out of it when I did. "Actually," I replied, still smiling, "I did a few years ago."

"Well, we just expanded our menu, and in the spring we'll be renovating the place. The owner just bought the building next door, so we're going to double our seating capacity. Oh! Your table's ready. So anyway, you should do a piece on us in the spring. The press would be great."

"I'll think about it. Thanks," I told her.

Once we were seated, Birch raised an eyebrow at me.

"What?" I asked, picking up a menu.

"Oh, it's Aida Benedetto!" he mocked. "Middleton's second-biggest celebrity."

"Second biggest? Who has me beat?"

"Channel Four's weather girl, of course."

"Karen Keaner? She's so . . . perky."

He nodded appreciatively. I shook my head at him and we ordered our breakfast. In about fifteen minutes, Birch was served a stack of whole-grain, vegan pancakes, which I was certain defied culinary science (I had to find out what they used in place of eggs), topped with bananas and maple syrup. I ordered two fried organic eggs from happy, free-ranging chickens (or so the menu assured), along with rye toast and blackberry jam. Once the food was placed in front of me, however, I realized my mistake. Eggs? What was I thinking? The sight and smell of them induced instant nausea, but at least now I understood why I felt so horrible.

"Aida? Are you all right?" Birch asked. "You look a little . . . pale."

I nodded. "Sure, I'm fine. Can you excuse me for a moment? I just need to find the restroom. Oh, and can you have them take the eggs away. I've had a change of heart about them." I tried to force a little laugh out of my throat. "Maybe your veganism is wearing off. I'll be right back."

I strode quickly to the back of the restaurant, found the women's bathroom, locked the door behind me, and retched into a thankfully spotless toilet. It didn't last long, but I realized suddenly how difficult it would be to do my job, to think and write about food all day long. Glancing at myself in the mirror, I raked my fingers through my hair, wiped my mouth with off with a damp paper towel, and returned to the table.

Later that evening, we were getting ready to leave for dinner with Birch's parents. Birch was reclining on my bed as I rummaged through my closet, looking for my favorite red sweater, the one his mother had given me for Christmas two years ago.

"So, what are we going to do?" he asked me out of the blue.

Alarmed, I stopped my search and stared at the back wall of the closet. "About what?" I asked, still not turning to face him. I hoped I sounded normal. Had he figured things out?

"About getting married."

"Oh, right." Heaving a sigh of relief, I found the sweater and slipped it on as I turned to face him. "I'm not sure." I sat next to him. "I like that the whole justice-of-the-peace thing is rather official, but it seems so cold, so sterile."

"Well, what about something like this. We do the city hall ceremony, get all the marriage license business taken care of, but then we'll get away someplace, just you and me, and we'll write our own vows to each other, and we'll have our own private celebration. And later, if we want to, we'll have some sort of party with our families."

I started picturing it in my head, envisioning us by the ocean for some reason, standing on a rocky outcrop over the churning waters, with a grove of pine trees behind us, wrapped in each other's arms and professing our love for one another. I nodded. "I like that. I don't know about the family part of it, but the rest of it is good. How do you feel about Maine?"

"In January?"

"Maine in January. By the ocean, on a rocky shore, with a stand of pine trees nestled behind us," I said, answering his first question and deliberately avoiding the second.

"You've got it all planned out, huh?"

"It just sort of came to me."

"An inspiration. That's the best kind of plan," he said, kissing me. "I'll find out what we have to do as far as City Hall goes. You get your *Lonely Planet* book and find out where we're going to go. Deal?"

"Deal," I replied quietly.

"Aida?" Birch asked. "What's wrong? Family stuff? I noticed you weren't too excited about the idea of a big family reception."

"It's just that . . . well, my family is going to implode when I tell them I'm not getting married in the Church, and . . ." as I hesitated, consumed with the desire to tell him about the pregnancy, Birch interrupted.

"My dad might just go ahead and disown me as well, you know."

Sighing, I answered, "He'll be fine. Your mom can usually calm him down. Anyway, we should get going. Your dad hates it when you're late."

"Shit. You're right. Come on."

We ran downstairs and hopped in his Jeep and headed for the McFarland house, running about fifteen minutes late. We were supposed to arrive at half past six. Will McFarland opened the door of the large colonial home, which stood proudly on the corner of State and McKinley streets near the north end of town. He looked at Birch and boomed, "It's almost seven o'clock already! Hi, Aida," he said, his voice still gruff as he leaned over to kiss my cheek.

Looking up at Birch, I watched the muscle in his jaw tense at his father's tone. Nevertheless, he reached out across the threshold and hugged his father, who clapped Birch stiffly on the back.

"Well, come on in, you two," Will said, softening as Glenda appeared behind him, placing her hand lightly on her husband's arm. We stepped inside and removed our outerwear in the foyer. The house was perfectly symmetrical. The front door and entryway stood exactly in the center of the front of the building, and the interior rooms balanced each other neatly on facing sides of a wide oak-planked hallway. It was a stately structure, casually yet tastefully decorated, and seemed to reflect equally the occupants' contrasting natures.

"Hi, Mr. McFarland. Hello, Professor Fallon. It's so good to see you again," I greeted. Birch's mother had changed her last name to McFarland when she got married, but she taught and wrote under her maiden name. Her bouncy blonde hair was pulled back neatly, and cheerful toffee-colored eyes sparkled as they fell upon her son.

When her gaze turned to me, she said, "Aida, if I've told you once, I've told you a thousand times. Call me Glenda. You look wonderful. It has been too long, hasn't it?" She hugged me closely. I always did prefer to call her Glenda, but I never did so in front of Birch's father, who had never invited me to call him Will. Glenda was embracing her son. "Hi, sweetie," she said, kissing both of his cheeks, then pulling away to scrutinize his appearance.

"Hey, Mom," he greeted with a smile, enduring her examination.

"You're looking fit," she told him. "A little thin, though. Been working a lot? I can't wait to hear about the sanctuary. How are the volunteers I sent you working out?"

"The three sorority girls?"

"I hope you didn't hold that against them. They are genuinely interested in animal rights and welfare. It came up during my lecture the other day. . . . Well, we can talk more about all that later, though. Drinks anyone? Aida, some wine?"

"Um . . . I actually had a little too much at the pub last night, thanks to your husband," I lied. "Maybe just some water."

"Will, you're going to go broke if you keep giving out free rounds to all the pretty girls," Glenda chided. He just winked at me and said nothing to his wife.

"Birch, come on into my office with me," Will grumbled. "I've got some plans for the pub. Some renovations I'm thinking about. I want to bounce some ideas off you."

"Sure, Dad," Birch replied, rather unenthusiastically. Will was always trying to find a way to convince Birch to take over managing the pub, and I suspected, as did Birch I think, that the renovation plans were simply another of Will's efforts to sway Birch's thinking. When Birch glanced back over his shoulder at me, I smiled encouragingly and watched him disappear into his father's study.

In the kitchen, Glenda began putting the finishing touches on dinner. While the vegan moussaka finished cooking, she prepared a salad.

"Can I help you with anything, Glenda?" I offered.

"No, that's all right, dear."

"Really? Nothing? You always used to put me to work."

"Well, there is one thing. Would you mind cooking Will's steak? There's another in the refrigerator for you as

well. Usually he cooks his own; he knows I can't . . . won't
do it. But if you don't mind . . . you are such a good cook.
He loved how you did the steak that once."

"No problem. It was just pan-fried with butter and garlic
and black pepper. My dad loves it like that. I'll just do one
for Mr. McFarland, though. I'm not really in the mood for
steak," I said, pulling the meat out of the fridge and un-
wrapping the white butcher paper. Two nice T-bones were
nestled inside, or what I usually would have thought were
nice T-bones. Now, the bloody meat made my stomach
turn. I managed to prepare it without gagging, though.
"So," I began, trying to take my mind off the smell of the
cooking meat, "Birch briefed you about the religious issues
I was hoping to talk to you about?"

"Yes, he did. I have a list of books for you that I think
you'll find helpful."

"That would be great," I said, and went on to talk a
while about the difficulties I was having with the Church.

"Aida," Glenda broke in after I had been rambling for a
while, "do you recall when you first began feeling uneasy
with the Church's teachings?"

Nodding briskly, I told her the story about my first confession and Marco's car. "But you know," I told her, "it
could be that I'm just a guilt-prone person. Maybe that's
my nature."

"Yet it was a feeling you often experienced within the
church setting, Aida. I wouldn't be so quick to discount
your early intuition about the relationship you had with the
Church. Do you remember anything else?"

"I do. There were lots of times during my religion
classes that I felt confused about what was being taught. Of
course I never said anything. I remember being maybe six
or seven years old and being instructed that on the one

hand, God loved me, and on the other hand, that God was to be feared. I could never understand that. Why should I be afraid of someone who was supposed to love me? If I made mistakes, wasn't he supposed to forgive me, not punish me? So what was I supposed to be afraid of? It never made sense," I trailed off, feeling again as if I was babbling nonsensically.

"It sounds as if you've been internalizing confusion and anxiety for a long while. Didn't you ever talk to anyone?" Glenda asked quietly.

"No! Of course not. I couldn't. It wasn't done. It isn't."

Glenda nodded slowly. "I understand. You have grave concerns about leaving the Church and diving into the murky abyss of philosophical spirituality. I wish I could offer some advice regarding your family, but that is not my area of expertise. But if you begin to start exploring alternatives to Catholicism, the main thing to remember is that you have to keep searching. Never assume you have all the answers. There are so many religions and so many philosophies that have valuable tools for approaching what is commonly called 'God.' I prefer not to even use that term myself. It's too steeped in myths of gendered individuality."

"So what do you call . . . it?" I fumbled, feeling like a student—an extremely ignorant one—in one of Glenda's lectures.

"Light, or spirit. A force, the universe. The Good, the Way, Truth. Many names have been ascribed throughout history. It's going to be hard, after years of extremely structured Catholic indoctrination, for you to relax your efforts to try and pin things down neatly into one word, one concept. Be open. Instead of using your traditional prayer forms, still try to connect with the universe, but make some attempts at meditation. I included two very good resources on meditating in the book list I compiled for you."

Sighing heavily, I bit my lip and turned my gaze downward. I always seemed to find myself staring at my shoes.

"Aida? What is it, dear? I've lost your interest already? I'm sorry. It's difficult for me to get out of 'professor mode' sometimes."

"No, that's not it at all. It's just that this is all pretty overwhelming." It was more than that. Who was I to think I knew any better than millions of Catholics—than my own parents? Maybe I should just keep trying to squelch my own negativity about the Church. Maybe I should have kept my mouth shut. I regretted having argued with Birch about hypocrisy. I knew nothing.

Glenda reached across the countertop and squeezed my hand. "Aida. It's all right. Remember this: You are not trying to solve a mystery; you are trying to recognize it, and your place in it."

"But I don't even know where to begin, Glenda. I don't even know if I should." I felt like one enormous shrug, as if my existence could be entirely encapsulated in that gesture.

"You'll start reading, exploring. And we'll keep talking, I promise. I'm thrilled that you have come to me, Aida. I've always felt that . . . well, that you and Birch were meant to be together. Maybe that's why I feel especially close to you, more so than anyone else Birch has brought home."

"Thank you for that," I said. I wanted to say something more, but felt more confused than ever before.

"Dinner's just about ready. Would you please go collect our men?" Glenda asked. Hazarding a glance at her face, feeling wretched and ungrateful, I was relieved to find that she was smiling at me kindly.

On my errand to fetch the men, I smiled a little, thinking how civilized Glenda was. In my family, no one was ever "collected." When dinner was ready, you shouted at the top of your lungs from the kitchen and everyone came running.

If Glenda's aura of calm civility stood in sharp contrast to the demeanor of my family, I was strongly reminded, as I approached the study, of a few similarities between Will and my own relatives. I stopped in my tracks as I heard Birch's dad shouting at him. "Goddamn it, Birch! When are you going to come to your senses? Look, if you were really serious about helping animals, you would have opened your own vet practice. You could have made something of yourself. You've been shoveling shit at that kennel for years now and what have you got to show for it?"

"What have I got to show for it? Dad, do you listen to me at all?" Birch retorted, matching his father's volume. "Do you know how many animals we've saved from euthanization? City Sanctuary is one of the most successful no-kill shelters in the Midwest. Our outreach and fund-raising programs are serving as models for small and large shelters alike, all over the country! A good portion of that success is due to what I've contributed."

"Get off your high horse, son. I need you at the pub. And if you want to do charity work you should at least try to help somebody worth helping."

"What are you talking about?" I heard Birch reply.

"Animals, Birch! They don't even have souls. Catholic doctrine makes that very clear. It's all well and good to try and keep people from abusing animals, but Birch, you put so much of yourself into trying to keep these creatures from being humanely put down. You're losing a lot of sleep over something that doesn't even have a soul. If you're going to be such a bleeding heart, at least you could have gone into social work or something. At least trying to make someone a better person counts for a little more," Will ranted.

"I don't believe you're saying that," Birch answered, embarking on his own tirade.

I glanced back over my shoulder toward Glenda in the kitchen. Her face was hidden behind her hands. Hesitating for only a moment longer, I stepped forward and knocked loudly on the half-opened door. "Dinner's ready, boys!" I shouted into the room. I'd broken up a few rows between my own father and Marco with the announcement of dinner.

They both realized, of course, that I'd heard them fighting, so it would have been useless for me to pretend I hadn't. I strode into the room as if I had some right to do so and saw the two men standing a few feet apart, staring at each other, taut, tense.

"Come on, you two. Break it up. I know you heard me. Food's on the table. Let's go." Almost in unison, they both turned to glare at me. I was very proud of myself for this show of bravado, and half expected a pat on the back or at least a smile. But Mr. McFarland just nodded in my general direction and strode right past me. Birch frowned and ushered me out of the study.

Once we were all seated in the dining room, it was Glenda's turn to try to smooth the ruffled feathers. She began chatting about her students, and then discussed a manuscript she was editing for a colleague.

While Glenda attempted to get Birch and Will's minds off of their fight, I fought to keep my nausea at bay. By taking small bites and chewing each morsel for a long time, I was able to consume the eggplant moussaka without too much trouble. Glenda was a fine cook. The food actually tasted delicious, but my stomach felt knotted and acidic. Gradually, my nausea began to ease, but I declined a second piece of the entrée and instead nibbled on some bread.

Apparently bored with her own monologue, Glenda tried to draw her husband into the conversation. "Will," she said. "I saw your brother today." Will's brother was Sean, the priest. He lived just outside of a tiny village called Elk's Run, the next town over, west of Middleton. Sean had a couple of cows, two horses, and a few chickens. He fancied himself a farmer of sorts, and his parishioners, Birch once told me, thought their farmer priest quaint and a little odd, but adorable.

"Really? Why?" Will queried.

"He wants to write a book about being a Midwestern priest in a rural parish and wanted to bounce some ideas off of me."

"Why?" Will asked again.

"Well, I have written a few books myself, dear. He wanted a few pointers," Glenda replied.

"No, I mean why would he want to write a book like that?"

"Well, it's not as dull, really, as it may sound. He's actually looking to do something Thoreau-like, except instead of Walden Pond, it's the farm, and instead of Thoreau's naturalistic spiritual philosophy, he of course wants to explore the ways in which one's Catholic faith may be enriched by such a setting. Anyway, he's a bit distracted."

"Why? What do you mean?" Birch asked.

I watched Glenda's smile widen. She had successfully teased both her husband and son out of their rancor and engaged them in conversation. "Well," she began to explain, "there's a pretty, middle-aged parishioner who has volunteered to type his manuscript as he dictates it. She seems to be quite smitten with him, and today I watched her very innocent attempts at flirtation with him. It was adorable."

"Glenda, don't be ridiculous," Will said. "Sean's vows are sacred."

"Well, he made no attempt to discourage her. And at any rate, it's just a harmless flirtation, is all."

"There is no such thing," Will claimed definitively. "A vow is a vow."

Silence gathered around the dining table like a dense fog closing in on a ship at sea. I watched Glenda stare wide-eyed at her husband before she brought her teeth down upon her lower lip. She glanced quickly at me before turning her gaze to her plate.

Birch cleared his throat. My eyes darted from Glenda to Birch. He looked at me for a long moment before leaning back in his chair and saying to the table in general, "Maybe there shouldn't be such a vow."

Jesus, I thought. Here it comes. Will really screwed up back in the study when he brought up the Church doctrine about animals not having souls. That's what Birch's look had been for, I realized. We'd had that discussion about hypocrisy and the Church and either leaving or fighting to change things. Birch was gearing up for a fight.

"What?" roared Will. Apparently still enraged from the argument in the study, he was ready for battle as well. "No celibacy vow? There's a reason for that vow, you know. A man has to be willing to devote his whole being to God, he has to—"

"But there's a shortage of priests," Birch interrupted. "A serious shortage. Allowing priests to marry would certainly attract more men to the calling, and there are certainly moral, dedicated married men. And why not open the priesthood up to women as well?"

"There's a reason for that as well, son. Maybe you should start paying closer attention at mass."

"Birch, Will, please," Glenda begged weakly. I heard her, but I don't think Birch or Will chose to.

"Oh, I've been paying close attention," Birch was answering his father. "Why can't women be priests? It's because that's what Jesus wanted, right? And we know because he only selected men as his apostles, at least that's what the Bible tells us. I won't even go into the prejudices and the political agendas of those biblical scribes. And back to that celibacy vow. There was an article—I think it was in the *New Yorker*—a while back suggesting that it is the celibacy vow that initially attracts pedophiles to the priesthood. It seems that—"

Before Birch could finish his sentence, Will's chair scraped loudly on the wood floor as he rose in one swift movement. "That's quite enough!" His face was nearly scarlet, and he slammed a thick fist onto the table, causing a clatter amongst the plates and some splashing of cabernet on the crisp white table linen. As I watched the deep crimson stain soak into the fabric, Will spewed his words out of his mouth. I felt his disgust seep into the air of the small room. "How dare you speak such blasphemy in my house? At my table?"

I had been monitoring the growth of the angry red splotches on Mr. McFarland's cheeks, but now I riveted my eyes to my plate, wishing I could be anyplace else but here. I heard Glenda choke back a sob, and listened as another chair—Birch's—slid backward across the oak planks. Glancing up, I watched Birch fearlessly face his father. "Dad," he said, in a voice that seemed calm and collected, "we may not agree on what the Church's problems are, but surely you can admit there are some."

"Sure, there are problems. But you don't question doctrine. You don't suggest that Jesus made a mistake and that it resulted in pedophiliac priests. Good Catholics, like the kind I thought I raised you to be, don't speak with such utter disrespect about the Church."

In another effort to diffuse the situation, Glenda spoke up again. "Will, he just has some legitimate concerns. Lots of Catholics do."

"This is none of your business, Glenda. You gave up your right to have any stake in this kind of thing, so stay out of it."

As I winced at the contempt in his voice, Birch turned to regard his mother. "What is he talking about?"

I didn't belong here, not now. I longed to find a way to discreetly escape, but guiltily remembered how Birch had held my hand through my family's intervention.

Glenda opened her mouth to respond, but Will's glare silenced her. Birch and his father were still standing, and now Birch took a step closer to Will. "She has as much right as you and I do to have an opinion about the Church," Birch defended. Glenda shook her head, but only I saw, as Birch was staring at his father's face.

"No she doesn't, and you've sorely abused your own right," Will growled.

"How can you say that? Just because I don't swallow everything the Church teaches without question? Maybe I did for a while, and maybe I haven't said too much before, but we should be able to have a discussion about our faith. Why are you denying me the freedom to speak my mind about all this?"

"McFarlands don't question the Church. Some things are accepted without question."

"Like the fact that McFarlands follow in the footsteps of their fathers? This is more about the pub than the Church, isn't it, Dad?"

"That has nothing to do with it. I'm talking about *faith,* Birch. Accepting the teachings of the Church, the instruction of the Pope without question. Faith. Now do you have it or not?"

"I can't just ignore these things any longer. I love being a Catholic. But I feel like it's time to start talking about the Church's more archaic doctrines. I can still be a good Catholic, and—"

"No, Birch, you can't," Will cut in. "You're not Catholic and you're no son of mine," Will declared with some finality.

"What? You're going to disown me because of this? Come on, Dad. Be reasonable."

Glenda's thin, pleading voice trickled across the room to her husband. "Will, please. Do not do this. Do not."

Will turned his face from his son to his wife. He looked at her for a long moment. The room was utterly bereft of sound. As his stiff shoulders slumped, Will tore his gaze from Glenda's contorted face and glared at Birch. "Birch, you're not my son," he stated again, more quietly now.

"Dad?"

"For as educated as you are, you're a little thick, aren't you? You're not mine. Ask your mother. I never wanted it to come to this. I could have even forgiven you about the pub. But there was only one thing of value I could ever really offer you, only one thing that I thought would matter, and that was my faith. And you threw it back in my face. You threw it away, Birch." With that, Will strode briskly from the room. Glenda flew after him, calling his name, leaving Birch and me in a riot of confusion.

Chapter Five

Birch was standing there, still gazing at the place where his father had been. His mouth was slightly open and his eyes were wide.

Slowly I rose and walked over to him. "Birch?"

He didn't reply at all. I stood in front of him and wrapped my arms around him, resting my head on his chest, trying to comfort him with my presence, because what could words possibly do at this point? For what seemed like a long while, he remained rigid, unmoving in my arms. But finally, he yielded, stooping over slightly to bury his face in my hair. He made no sound.

Glenda found us like that when she re-entered the room an eternity of minutes later. "He's gone," she whispered, her face streaked with tears.

Birch did not look up, not even when his mother placed her hand gently on his inclined head. Her fingers wove themselves into his golden curls, and I suddenly took a step backward, feeling embarrassed for her and horribly in the middle of something in which I did not belong. Only after my withdrawal did Birch raise his head. He looked at me, and then at her, and groaned, "Tell me."

"Birch, I should go. I'll call a cab, all right?" I said, my voice hushed.

"I don't want you to go," he stated. It was the first thing anyone had said in a normal tone of voice in the room since Will's departure. With the funereal silence broken in this manner, the whole context of the evening's drama seemed to shift. Will's enigmatic revelation seemed less like a biblical mystery and more like a typical family secret, however painful and embarrassing it might be, that waited to be explained.

"But wouldn't you . . . don't you . . ." I faltered.

"I don't want you to go, Aida," he repeated.

"Glenda?" I asked. Maybe Birch didn't want me here, but Glenda had a story to tell, and she might not want to do it in front of me.

"Truly, Aida, I'd prefer you to remain as well. You will certainly be able to offer Birch more comfort than I can right now. I have a feeling I'm about to become the enemy."

"Mom, I don't know what's going on, but you'll never be my enemy."

"Come then. Let's go into the family room and sit by the fire."

Abandoning the dining room, half-eaten dinners cold on the plates, we passed through the kitchen, across the hallway and into the family room, where Birch coaxed a healthy fire from smoldering logs. He and I sat next to each other upon tapestried floor cushions strewn near the hearth, while Glenda curled her feet underneath her in an upholstered chair opposite us. To anyone looking in from the outside, we would have resembled children huddled at the elder's feet for a fable.

For a few moments the room was drenched in pregnant silence, except for the popping of applewood in the fireplace. Glenda breathed deeply and gazed up at the ceiling, as if searching through old, discarded files in her memory, and finally began. "I was an undergrad at Berkeley, in my junior year. As you recall, Birch, I didn't meet your father until we were both doing our graduate work at Michigan.

He was getting his MBA and I was working on my Ph.D.

"At any rate, I'm at Berkeley, entrenched in my course work and participating in a student environmental organization as well. The group's leader is a graduate student, Thaddeus Peterson, and before long, we become involved. Well, I am instantly head over heels for him. I so admired him. He was a good man. He treated people well. He had a social conscience, and ambition, and was one of the most peaceful people I have ever known. But we both knew it couldn't last. We wanted different things. He wanted to travel the world, to see it, to save it. I wanted to settle down, find a professorship at a nice, respectable university, get married, and have children. We were together for only a year. I never stopped loving him. I just moved on. And years later I met Will and we fell in love and he proposed." She paused for a moment, gazing at the fire.

Turning her eyes upon us, she said, "All this talking is making me thirsty. How about you two? Can I get you something to drink?"

"No, thanks," I replied. Birch just shook his head. Glenda disappeared into the kitchen and I regarded Birch's face for a moment. Like his mother, he could lose himself in the flames. He seemed unaware that I was watching him. "Are you all right?" I asked.

"I don't know. I—" he stopped abruptly as Glenda returned to her former position. She had a beautiful face, with smooth, rosy skin, and a tumble of blonde curls to frame it. Now, however, a series of lines appeared upon her brow. I noticed a few droplets of water at the neckline of her blue blouse. I wondered if she had really gone into the kitchen to splash some cold water on her face.

After taking a few sips of water, she began again. "It was a long engagement, as I really wanted to complete my dissertation before we were married. Several months before the wedding, I got a phone call. From Thaddeus. He wanted to see me. We met for coffee. I had feared that seeing him again would agitate all those old feelings, but it seemed immature to tell him no. We were just two old friends from Berkeley, getting together for a cup of coffee because he was in town on business.

"As it turned out, he professed that his feelings for me still thrived, that he couldn't escape them no matter where he went or how determined he was to lose himself in his work. I told him, and myself, that we were two different people now; that our love was a good memory and we should leave it that way. He gave me his number, told me he would be in town for a month, and kissed me good-bye before I could protest.

"I tried to be strong and for a few days I successfully overcame my desire to see him again. In the end, however, I was not strong enough. Before long, my love for Thaddeus had been entirely rekindled," Glenda said in a voice hushed and a little hoarse from the sobbing she'd done earlier.

She paused for a long while, staring into the fire like a fortuneteller would peer into her crystal ball. "No, that's not the right word at all," she began abruptly. "Not rekindled, as my love for Thaddeus had never abated in the least. I had simply believed it wasn't possible for us to be together. And my love for Will had grown right up along-side my feelings for Thaddeus, like a sapling thriving near an ancient oak. It seems you can be in love with two people at the same time, or at least I could. They each brought out different elements in me, and I was loath to end things with either of them.

"I was forced to make a decision, however, when Thaddeus informed me that he had been offered a spectacular position, with a South American rainforest preservation organization based in Brazil. He wanted me to come with him. I agonized over the decision but eventually realized that I did not truly want to spend my life sacrificing my own dreams so Thaddeus could pursue his. I needed someone whose visions of the future more closely corresponded with my own. I needed Will. And just as I was working up the courage to confess to Will about the affair, I discovered that I was rather unexpectedly pregnant."

Here Glenda stopped again. As she drank deeply from her water glass, I noticed Birch staring intently at her. The lump that had been gathering in my throat thickened as I simultaneously realized where her story was going and that I had a strange affinity to Glenda and her past. While I wasn't seeing anyone behind Birch's back, I certainly knew what it felt like to be surprised by a pregnancy.

Before Glenda could take up the thread of her tale again, Birch spoke up. "So Thaddeus is . . ."

"Yes, Birch. You are Thaddeus' son, not Will's."

I exhaled slowly. She had finally said it. I kept my eyes on Glenda, afraid to turn and look at Birch. Hearing a ragged sigh, or maybe a sob, escape his lips, I reached for his hand but still did not look at his face for fear I would start bawling uselessly.

"But how—" Birch began, before Glenda interrupted him.

"Please. Allow me to finish," she said. "I told Will everything. His deep sense of betrayal, he told me, remained outweighed by his love for me, and had it not been for the pregnancy he would have taken me back without hesitation. But given the circumstances, he felt he had the right to make our union . . . conditional. We had previously agreed, given his staunch Catholic background and my unconventional views on spirituality, that our children would receive their spiritual education from both of us, and that as they grew to an appropriate age, would be allowed to make their own choices in this arena. Will had a change of heart, though. He said that given the . . .” Glenda cleared her throat and then continued, “the shameful way this child was conceived, if he were to raise the baby as his own he would also take it upon himself to ‘save’ the child, by raising him entirely as a Catholic, without any interference from me.

“While I found this thinking flawed, I was desperate not to lose a man I truly did love, despite our differences. And I knew, with a ferocious maternal instinct I hadn’t known I possessed, that I must create a settled, stable, and loving home for this baby. I also hoped that while I would not be allowed to actively participate in the child’s spiritual development, I would be able to quietly lead by example, so to speak. So I agreed to Will’s condition. And I think it worked out as well as it could have. While you have never expressed great curiosity about my beliefs, Birch, neither are you a Catholic zealot. You seem to have a sensible approach to your faith, and I see now that you possess as much of a desire to question the status quo as I ever have had. However, to your father—for it is Will who raised you, not Thaddeus—this must have been seen as another betrayal, heaped, years later, on top of my own.”

Feeling Birch’s hand release my own and clench into a fist, I braced myself for his anger. He rose abruptly and paced the room, caged by his own conflicting emotions. “How could he use me like that? And how could you have kept this from me for so long? And how . . .”

While Birch railed at his mother, a few things started to fall into place for me, and would for Birch as well once he calmed down. Now it made sense that Birch felt closest to his father within the cloak of Catholicism, and that Will positively bristled at Birch's choosing a career based in activism rather than in the family business.

Birch finally stopped shouting. Glenda had said nothing in her own defense, or in Will's, but respectfully endured her son's outraged onslaught. "I hope," she said quietly, "that you can find it in your heart to forgive me, and your father. Our motivations sprang entirely from love. You said earlier that you could never regard me as your enemy. I pray that you still find that to be the case."

Saying nothing to his mother, Birch turned to me. "Aida, I'll go warm up the car." He spun on his heel and I heard the door slam shut moments later.

I looked at Glenda, at an utter loss for words. "Aida, dear. Don't look so forlorn. You needn't feel torn. I don't expect your sympathy. Go to him," she said, rising from her chair. "He needs you."

With my thoughts in a pathetic muddle in my head, rationality having eluded me, I acted out of instinct alone. I walked up to Birch's mother, hugged her tightly, clutching her for a few prolonged moments. When I stepped back to look at her face, tears were flowing freely, forming tiny rivulets down her cheeks. In a futile effort, my fingertips tripped lightly across her damp skin, but of course failed to erase the effects of her pain. I left without saying a word.

Effective language, or any words at all, continued to evade me. Birch and I drove home in a silence that hammered on my eardrums. As we reached my door, I opened my mouth to speak, but before any thought had gathered itself into an utterance, Birch said, "Aida, don't. You don't have to think of anything to say. I can't put any words to the feelings I'm having now, so I certainly don't expect you to. I know I said I'd go to the baptism with you tomorrow, but—"

"No, no. Of course not. I wouldn't expect you to go, now, after all this."

"I'm just going to go check up on things at the sanctuary in the morning. I've got some new weekend staff I want to observe. And I want to check on Sasha. She hasn't been eating well."

I could tell he was trying to sound normal, to say things that one would normally say, instead of, 'Hey, guess what? My father's not my father after all. Turns out my mom slept with an old boyfriend when she and my dad were engaged.'

Finding myself nodding, I made myself stop, and stood on tiptoe to kiss his lips lightly. "You know that whenever you might need me, I'm always—"

"I know. Good night, Aida." With that, he strode up the steps and out of sight.

When I walked into my apartment, I felt a little lost. It was very late, and I had to become a godmother tomorrow. I needed to get to bed, but it was rather difficult to stop thinking about all that had happened. As I warmed some milk in the kitchen, I listened to the answering machine. "Aida. It's Marco. You'll never believe it. Father Roberto has the flu. The baptism has been postponed until next week. Hang in there. Maybe we'll see you at mass to-morrow."

A wave of relief flooded over me. I literally felt the tense muscles in my shoulders and neck loosen a little. Having been granted a much-needed reprieve, I could just lie in bed tomorrow and fantasize about escaping to the east coast with Birch. It seemed like days ago, rather than hours, that we had hatched the plan.

Curled on my mother's chair and sipping warm milk and

honey, the ultimate comfort remedy my mom used to make for me when I was a child, I wondered about Birch's biological father, Thaddeus. Did he even know about Birch? Glenda hadn't said. And where was he now? Then there was Mr. McFarland. Would he and Glenda split up? Could he possibly reconcile with Birch? Somehow I was certain that Birch and his mother would soon be speaking again. They had always been extremely close, and while she had deceived him, she had been, as she had said, motivated by love. Yet I could only imagine what Birch must be feeling. None of this would have come to light if he hadn't been so adamant about challenging his father on the problems with the Church.

Gasping, I sat upright suddenly, nearly spilling my milk. Did he view me as the genesis of this whole drama? After all, I was the one who had urged him to take a stand, to fight for change, telling him that his father would understand. "Christ," I grumbled aloud. It wasn't enough that I had to tear my own family apart. Now I was starting in on Birch's.

The damned Church kept tampering with my life, needling me with constant reminders of a childhood lived out in guilt and anxiety. And now that I had given my resentment a voice, I found that I heard the Church's reply as a low growl, warning me against abandoning the pack. I would be tempted back into the den through the familiar strategy of guilt, skillfully wielded by my family. And if I nipped at the heels of Birch, trying to get him to follow my wayward lead, punishment would be inevitable, for both of us. The Church would be recognized as the wedge I had helped drive between Birch and his father, and I would be blamed. Unable now to derive any comfort at all from the sweet warmth of my mother's milk and honey, I dumped the drink down the drain and threw myself into bed.

While I had vowed to spend the next day in bed, I awoke agonizing over the role I had played in the dissolution of Birch's family. After choking down some dry toast and orange juice, I threw on an old sweatshirt and jeans and headed for City Sanctuary, where I knew I would find Birch. When I arrived, it was nearly ten a.m. Birch had probably gone to eight o'clock mass then headed straight for the sanctuary.

Standing outside the front door in the bitter January air, I knocked as loudly as the wind would allow before it carried the sound into the distance. I should have phoned first. The sanctuary was closed on Sundays, and no one would hear me knocking, as they were probably all working with the animals in the back of the building, not in the front office area. I ran back to the still-warm car, which I had parked next to Birch's Jeep, and dialed his work number on my cell phone.

"Birch McFarland," he answered simply, his voice low and devoid of its usual warmth.

"It's me. I'm here. Come let me in. I want to talk to you."

"Aida, what are you doing here? Aren't you supposed to be at church for the baptism?"

"Father Roberto has the flu. They postponed until next week. Just come open the door, okay?" In reply, he sighed into the phone before hanging up. He didn't exactly sound happy to have me here. Returning to the front door, I was greeted by Birch's grim face, his raised eyebrows, and the loud barking of dogs emanating from the kennel area. Birch hadn't shaved and his eyes looked bloodshot. A large, blue-eyed husky was at his side.

"Morning," I offered, kissing him quickly. "Is this Sasha?"

He nodded. "Aida, I've got a lot of paperwork to catch up on. I don't really have time for a social call."

I knelt down and let the dog sniff my hand before I reached out to pet her. "You are a beautiful girl, aren't you?" I said to her. Still stroking her fur, I looked up at Birch and said, "I wanted to see how you were doing after . . . after last night." We were still standing in the drafty front office and I was shivering. "Can we go back to your office?"

He turned and marched toward the back of the building without another word. Sasha turned and trotted behind him, as did I. He wasn't making this very easy. Following his flannel-clad back to his small, warm office, I sat down in one of the two wooden chairs that faced his desk, behind which Birch had planted himself, with Sasha at his feet. He looked at me, and gulped some coffee.

We sat in silence for a few moments before I tried again, "So? Did you get any sleep? Have you spoken to your mother this morning? How are you feeling about all this?"

"No, I didn't sleep at all, and no, I have not spoken to my mother, nor will I for quite some time. I feel like shit about all this and I don't really want to talk about it anymore."

I gulped. "I'm sorry."

"What the hell are you sorry for? You haven't been lying to me for thirty years."

"I'm sorry that I was so adamant about you standing up to your father about your problems with the Church," I stated quietly.

"What? Is that what this is about? You wanted me to make you feel better, tell you it's not your fault?"

Biting my lip, I remained silent as Birch went on, barely able to keep his voice down. "You've come to the wrong place for absolution, Aida. This is not about you. I'm more angry with you for you coming to me now because you feel guilty than I was about anything else you think you did. Damn it, Aida! You've got guilt and love so mixed up in your head that you don't even know what motivates you half the time. Why are we even together? Is it because you love me or because you felt so guilty about breaking up with me without explanation so many times before? And what was the reason you finally gave me about why you kept dumping me? Oh, that's right—guilt!" he accused, leaning over the desk. He was shouting now. "You said that you thought I was too good for you, so I guess you felt guilty about being with me in the first place, right? Give me a call when you figure things out, Aida."

Sitting there, with my eyes wide and my teeth clenched, I endured his onslaught, shocked and confused. I heard Sasha whining under the desk, and watched as Birch leaned down to pat her head. What the hell had just happened? Tears flowed down my cheeks as I ran from the room and out to my car. I half expected Birch to follow me, to take it all back, but he didn't.

Once home, I curled up in my mother's chair, with Nonna Anna's afghan, and wept, feeling more alone than I ever had in my life. Who could I even talk to at this point? No one knew I was pregnant. How was I going to tell Birch now? How would I tell my family? Marco couldn't possibly understand, and while my girlfriends and I were close, I felt too raw and wounded to just call them up and reveal it all. My chest ached and I felt exhausted and sick and utterly disinterested in trying to do anything to make myself feel better. Pulling my knees to my chest and wrapping the afghan more tightly around my body, I thought about what Birch had said. He was wrong about why were together. I loved him. That I knew without a doubt. But I wasn't yet ready to confront his other accusations.

I fell asleep in the chair and woke up late in the afternoon, feeling as if I had forgotten something. After talking myself into a peanut butter sandwich, I hauled myself from the chair and into the kitchen just as I heard a rapid-fire knocking on my door. "Birch," I whispered to myself as I flung open the door. Standing there, however, was not Birch, but Marco, with furrowed brows and clenched jaw.

"Marc, what—?"

"What the hell's going on, Aida?" he shouted, pushing past me into my small kitchen. "No mass—okay, I guess I should have expected that, although I thought since you agreed to be Joe's godmother you'd start coming to church again. But to not show up for dinner at Pop's, to not even *call*, Aida. You just can't do that to Pop. Or Nonna. Especially Nonna."

"Damn," I said, more to myself than to Marco. I had slept through Sunday dinner at my father's.

"That's all you have to say for yourself? Did something happen with you and Birch? He wasn't at mass this morning with his dad. I wish he could get you to go to church, instead of you getting him not to go."

I covered my face with my hands, wishing Marco would stop talking. "Did you come here just to yell at me?" I asked him, ignoring his questions.

"I'm just saying you need to be a little more careful with Pop right now. The sixth is Friday, you know."

February sixth was the anniversary of my mother's death and it was less than a week away. "I know, I know. I messed up. Look, I'm sorry, all right? Birch and I had dinner with his family last night and there was a bit of a family feud, so to speak. I'm sure that's why he wasn't at mass. And I'm . . . I'm not feeling too well today. Not enough sleep, I guess."

"Now that you mention it, you don't look that great. Maybe you're coming down with the flu, too. Want me to go get you some chicken soup?"

Trying not to gag at the thought of the soup, I shook my head. "No, that's okay. I'm just going to make a sandwich and see if that settles my stomach at all."

"Remember how Mom always gave us ginger ale when we were sick?" Marco asked.

I smiled. "And even if it didn't help our stomachs, the bubbles tickled and always made us laugh. I remember."

"Want me to go get you some?"

"Actually, that sounds really good. Thanks."

He returned in a few minutes and I nibbled on my sandwich while we both sipped ginger ale. We talked for a long while about our mother. My heart ached a bit, thinking about her. "She always smelled like lavender, remember?" I asked my brother. "And she'd wrap those brown arms around us and hug us until nothing bad even existed anymore."

"She was strong, too. How did her arms get so muscular?" Marco asked, looking into his drink.

"Are you kidding?" I responded, smiling. "Rolling out fettuccini. Kneading bread dough. Heaving laundry baskets of wet clothes up from the basement and out to the clothesline. She had quite a daily workout."

"Yeah, I guess you're right. And her *sugu*. God, Aida. It was even better than Nonna's, remember?"

I nodded. My mother had many secrets, and one of them was how she made the *sugu*, the thick tomato sauce that topped our pasta every Sunday. She had taught me how to prepare it, but mine never tasted quite like hers. I think she always added a little something when my back was turned. "She'd put it on the stove before we left for church and let it simmer until noon. 'Anything worth having takes time,' she always said. I miss her so much, Marc," I told him quietly.

He nodded, frowning. "So we'll meet at church at nine-thirty on Friday?" Marco confirmed, getting up to leave rather abruptly.

"Right." We always took the day off to be with Pop on the anniversary. We would go to church and say a rosary, then walk across the street to the cemetery and spend some time there before heading back to the house to flip through old photos of her. "I'll see you Friday, Marco. I'm glad you came by."

"Me, too," he said as he kissed my cheek. "See you, Aida."

After I woke up the next morning and vomited yellow bile in the shower, I realized it was time to make an appointment with my OB-GYN. Opting to skip my morning run, I phoned the doctor's office on the way to work. I explained my situation, and the nurse informed me that the only available date for my first prenatal visit was Friday the sixth, at 8:15 a.m. Calculating that I'd still be able to make it to the church to meet my brother, father, and grandmother on time, I accepted the appointment, thanked the nurse, and turned off my cell phone before I began to cry. My first prenatal visit? How could I be going to my first prenatal visit at all, not to mention without the baby's father, whom I didn't even know if I was still together with, and on the anniversary of my mother's death?

I stumbled through the week, trying to leave my desk nonchalantly on my way to the bathroom to throw up every so often. I completed my work dutifully, but with an utter lack of passion or shred of enthusiasm. Whenever anyone asked me if I was all right, I offered the same lie I had told Marco, "I think I'm coming down with something."

I kept wanting to call Birch, but was still stunned by our last encounter. Having no idea how to find my way back to him, or if he even wanted me to, I felt banished and blind. But before I knew it, I had wandered into Friday morning and was on my way to Dr. Grace Rodriguez's office on the east wing of Middleton Mercy Hospital.

The waiting room, designed to calm anxious visitors with shades of mauve and dove gray, smelled vaguely of citrus cleanser. After greeting the receptionist, signing in, and sitting down, I realized I was the only one there, having taken the first available slot of the morning. Various parenting magazines littered the waiting room. I had never really noticed them when I had come to the office for my annual gynecological exams. Now, however, there was not a *Newsweek* or *People* in sight.

Birch should be here. I should have told him by now, I thought to myself. Just then, the outer door of the waiting room yawned opened, admitting a teenage girl, very obviously pregnant, and an older woman who was, I assumed, the girl's mother. They were holding hands as they entered and as I watched them, a slow, throbbing thickness gathered around my heart and crept into my throat and would not be swallowed down.

I had been missing my mother for fourteen years, for only a little less time than this swollen girl with freckles and a long blond ponytail had walked the earth, and I wanted my mother with me now more than I ever had before. I wanted her next to me, holding my hand, telling me everything would be just fine, because even though I wasn't just

106

sixteen, I was as alone as the moon on a cloud-filled night, searching through the dark for the glimmer of some companion. I was terrified in a way that only a mother would understand, and only a mother's reassurance could offer any comfort right now.

The girl's own mother must have felt my gaze upon her, for she looked up just then and her lips tightened. My eyes flitted away in an instant, and I thought I might melt with sorrow. Just the briefest of smiles from this stranger-mother could have loosened the mass in my chest, but my glance must have lingered too long; she must have thought I was passing judgment on her daughter. I stared intently at the floor, focusing on the gray carpet flecked with threads of purple and mauve, and waited another fifteen minutes for a plump nurse dressed in pink scrubs to call my name.

Hopping to attention, I fled the waiting room as the nurse led me to Dr. Rodriguez's office instead of the expected examining room. I shook the doctor's honey-colored hand and sat down across the desk from her.

"Aida," she greeted with a smile that reached her dark brown eyes, "I only just saw you in November for your annual exam, and you didn't mention anything about wanting to start a family. Is this pregnancy a bit of a surprise to you?" she asked gently.

I cleared my throat and nodded.

"I only ask because if you haven't been planning on getting pregnant, you might not have been preparing yourself physically . . ." She went on to talk about the prenatal vitamins she would be prescribing, and asking me about my lifestyle, if I exercised, if I smoked, things like that.

We talked at great length and she encouraged me to ask questions as she offered an overview of what I could expect with the pregnancy in general and with the care she'd be giving me. She asked about the baby's father, and I lied and said that I had told him and he was very happy and planned on coming to subsequent appointments. Following the office portion of the visit, a physical exam ensued, complete with urine and blood samples to confirm the pregnancy. I was given a due date in early October, a prescription for vitamins, and the instructions to come back in a month.

As I climbed into my car, I rested my head on the steering wheel, wholly overwhelmed. There was no time to sit and contemplate it all, however. The roller coaster ride continued. It was the anniversary of my mother's death, and I was already late for the rosary.

Having sped to St. Benedict's and raced up the front steps, I breathlessly slid into the pew next to Pop. Nonna and Marco were kneeling next to him on his right. Three heads turned to look at me. Marco raised his eyebrows, Nonna shook her head, and Pop sighed. Their disappointment was unanimous, even though I had missed only the first few "Hail Mary's." From my purse I extracted my glass rosary beads, the ones I had been given by my mother for my first communion, and began chanting the words of the prayers with my family. Our voices swelled together, tumbling gently about in the near-empty church. Half a dozen elderly men and women were scattered about the pews, mumbling their pleas to God softly under their breath. As I prayed I chastised myself repeatedly, knowing I had no business reciting a rosary.

After we had completed our supplication, we mutely exited the church, and it wasn't until we had descended the cement stairs that the group turned on me.

"Aida, why do you disgrace us this way?" Nonna asked.

"I can't believe you'd be late for this," Marco said.

"I try, Angelina," my father began. "I try to understand

you. But you . . . you only think about yourself. Do you remember what happened when you were younger, when you
showed such disrespect for the family? The belt is what you
would have gotten. You remember, don't you, Marco?"

"I'm sorry, everyone. I didn't mean to disgrace anyone. I
had a doctor's appointment," I tried to explain.

"Why? What's wrong? You don't feel good? You come to
me, Aida, and I will make you my special tea. And I can get
you in any time," Nonna told me. "No waiting."

Marco chimed in. "I know you haven't been well, Aida,
but come on. Today was the only day you could get in?"

"Hey, look at me," Pop ordered. He held my chin with
his large right hand, tilting my face upward and peering into
my eyes.

"What?" I asked him.

"You're right. Something's not right with you. I can see
it in your eyes. How do you feel? What did the doctor say?"

"She said it . . . it looks like a mild case of the flu."

"That's what she said, hm?" my father asked, still
grasping my chin.

I nodded stiffly, glancing up at a sky gray as pigeon, and
tried to cough a little.

"Humph," he sniffed. "There's something else," he announced. "But let's go to the cemetery. Aida, you can just
wait for us at the house if you don't feel up to it."

"No, no. I'm coming," I said, wondering to myself what
my father thought he knew, what "something else" he
sensed. We trudged across the street and meandered
through the cemetery until we found my mother's grave.
Pop brushed the snow off of the headstone with his gloved
hand, and we stood, statue-like, in a semicircle around the
shining protrusion of rose-colored marble.

I thought of the last time I had seen my mother, inflated

with embalming fluid, caked with more makeup than she'd worn in her entire life, and laid out in the navy blue suit she'd hated. I had picked out a floral, knee-length flirty dress she used to wear when she and my dad would go out on their monthly date. Once, when I was too little to know what he'd meant, my father told my mother she looked sexy in that dress. But he refused to let her be buried in it.

After Mom had been dead for about five years, Marco and I used to try and find women for my dad to date. We gave up before too long. Apparently, the thought of sharing his life with anyone but my mother was too excruciating for him to bear, even though what hurt us more than anything was to see him so lonely.

Hazarding a glance around our little throng of mourners, I saw that everyone's head was bowed, I supposed either in prayer or deep in memory. Marco's face still looked boyish to me, and I was thrust again into the pool of my own memory, recalling a summer evening when we were children and my mother and father let us sleep in our sleeping bags in the backyard. We were about seven and nine years old, and excited by the night under the stars but a little terrified as well. We'd heard a sound and had run to the back door, flashlights in hand, calling for our parents. It was my mother who came to our rescue that night. She brought out a blanket and curled up on the grass between my brother and me. She stroked our faces and hair lightly with her short fingers, rough from washing dishes and scrubbing floors, and sang to us. The tune was nearly the same as "Twinkle, twinkle little star," but the song was an Italian lullaby about a firefly.

"Aida," Marco's voice jerked me harshly from my reverie.

"What?" I asked cautiously, wondering what I'd done now.

"What were you humming?" he demanded.

"Was I humming?" I hadn't realized I'd made a sound.

"Yes. It was that song that she used to sing us. 'Luciola,' about the firefly."

"I was just thinking about that night when we slept in the backyard. I didn't realize I was humming. Sorry," I mumbled.

"No, no. Sing it," he begged.

"I . . . No, Marco." Pop and Nonna were pissed off at me as it was. I wasn't going to risk incurring their wrath further by singing a childhood ditty while they were intent on mourning.

"Do you know it? Can you sing it?" Pop asked me.

I nodded.

"Well, go ahead. Sing," he insisted. "It would make your mother happy."

I glanced at Nonna. Her face was unsmiling, but her expression was not the usual one of disapproval, so I cleared my throat, and began the short song. When I had finished, the three of them stood there staring at me. I looked down at my boots. "I know," I whispered. "I'm not very good."

"No, Aida, you're not," Marco said, "but neither was she. Your voice sounds just like hers when you sing. I never noticed before."

I looked up at him. "Really?"

Marco nodded. Pop's eyes shone brightly with tears. "It's true, Aida. It's true."

Chapter Six

I woke up early Sunday morning, the day of the baptism, wishing that Birch and I had made amends so that I wouldn't have to go through this day alone. He had not yet phoned, nor had we even run into each other in the hallway of our building. His car was gone in the morning when I left for work and when I returned home every evening. He was either working long hours or staying someplace else.

Maybe he had spoken to his mother and was staying with her. Having phoned him twice this week, I was greeted only by his answering machine, and I recorded the same simple message both times: "It's me. Call me." With visions of our child's life intermingling with memories of my mother's death, the majority of my rational thoughts were fairly well strangled. Being without Birch tortured me. Yet even though Birch had expressed a vitriolic frustration with me, I possessed only one shred of trustworthy instinct, and it told me that Birch and I were not over. That was the only comfort to be found on Sunday morning, although I still sought it elsewhere, in the least likely of places.

St. Benedict's at eight a.m. in February was cold as a tomb and just as unwelcoming in every other regard. Outside, swollen charcoal clouds had eclipsed the sun for days, and not a single ray of sunlight pierced the church's stained-glass windows.

Easing into an icy pew near the back of the church, I knelt down and tried to pray, but sat back on the wooden seat of the pew when words failed me. My second thoughts about agreeing to be Joseph's godmother had nestled themselves firmly in my mind since I had first acquiesced to Marco, and they now served as silent chaperones, reminding me of their presence when I began to commit acts of outrageous hypocrisy, acts as seemingly innocent as prayer. Every time I began to pray, I prefaced my entreaty with the familiar, habitual address "dear God," and instantly began to question my own beliefs. By praying "dear God," I was automatically accepting that God was not only an individual, but one who was willing and able to receive and consider my forthcoming petition.

My heretical tangent was interrupted by the opening hymn, and I rose with the small congregation gathered for the ridiculously early mass and watched Father Roberto glide down the aisle in his white robes. Despite my concerted efforts to be fully conscious of every aspect of the mass that morning, I found myself responding and kneeling and sitting and standing, purely out of habit, along with the other lambs in the herd.

The hypnotic spell of the mass was broken, however, when the congregation began its profession of faith. The group, led by Father Roberto, began mumbling, just as they did every week, "We believe . . ."

I chanted the first two words of the prayer with the faithful throng and finally woke up, stopped speaking, and listened, as if for the first time in my life. In a soft, deafening rumble, everyone prayed on, ". . . in one God, the Father, the Almighty, maker of heaven and earth, of all that is seen and unseen . . ." they continued, and my eyes widened, a quiet reaction belying the quick, hot anger burning in me at the thought of being told for thirty years that there was only one acceptable conception of God, and it was an entirely male, powerful, controlling, rigid notion. I could no longer profess to accept it.

The sleepy congregation fumbled along with their creed. "We believe in one Lord, Jesus Christ, the only Son of God, eternally begotten of the Father, God from God, Light from Light, true God from true God, begotten, not made, one in Being with the Father. Through him all things were made. For us men and our salvation he came down from heaven; by the power of the Holy Spirit he was born of the Virgin Mary and became man. For our sake he was crucified under Pontius Pilate; he suffered, died, and was buried. On the third day he rose again in fulfillment of the Scriptures; he ascended into heaven, and is seated at the right hand of the Father. He will come again in glory to judge the living and the dead and his kingdom will have no end."

Wait a minute, I interrupted silently. That never seemed right to me. I believed in the historical Jesus, but couldn't quite buy into the notion that he was God, or the son of God. Weren't we all infused with divinity? Maybe the man Jesus was simply more in touch with his own divine nature, more aware of it than most people, making him easily recognized as a man of peace. Was he to be worshipped, though, or rather learned from, like numerous other men and women, secular and religious, who preached peace in their lifetime?

As these thoughts trespassed through my consciousness, the praying went on, "We believe in the Holy Spirit, the Lord, the giver of life, who proceeds from the Father and the Son. With the Father and the Son he is worshipped and glorified. He has spoken through the prophets. We believe in one holy catholic and apostolic Church. We acknowledge one baptism for the forgiveness of sins. We look for the resurrection of the dead . . ."

That was another thing, I thought. Life after death. I had never been able to decide what would be worse: remembering your life after you died, or forgetting it. It would be just as torturous to the person who died, I thought, to lose the people you loved, those who were still alive. Didn't my mother miss me as much as I missed her? Then again, how horrible would it be to forget the wondrous connections we had when we were alive? It seemed wrong, somehow, to no longer be aware of the love you experienced on earth.

"And the life of the world to come. Amen," everyone chanted.

As the praying individuals ceased their communal declaration, the streaming subtext in my mind that rose up to challenge each statement in the creed finally ran out of subversive comments. I had been taught at some point that saying "amen" at the conclusion of a prayer was the equivalent of affirming "I believe," and as the collective voice of the people in church that morning stated quietly their amen, I found myself shaking my head. The peaceable period at the end of their sentence was, for me, a harsh slap across the face, first stunning me and then propelling me into motion, finally into motion.

Quickly, quietly, I fled from the church, literally, figuratively. There might be true beliefs tucked away beneath those words, but they were shrouded by thousands of years of Roman Catholic politics. Hadn't I always thought so? Hadn't I clung to the mystery behind the words, rather than the words themselves, hoping that it was goodness and an earnest search for truth that mattered more than popes and bishops and priests and missionaries, striving to control people, to claim to know what's best for them, grasping for money, power, souls?

It had always been the shadowy form of the unknown that had meant something to me, not the outward, rigid structure. I couldn't lie about so many things, not to myself, not to my family. And not to my own child, I realized now.

What I needed to do, as the mother I would soon become, was to stand for something, to stand for truth, and honesty, and individual, personal faith. I couldn't do that with my heart while my mouth spoke droves of lies. Suddenly it didn't matter if it felt overwhelming and more than a little wrong to question everyone who had ever loved me. How would I ever teach my daughter, or my son, to stand up for what she or he believed in, or at least to figure out what that was, if I wasn't even willing to brave that storm myself?

Father Roberto had told me that I was spiritually blind, that Catholicism could at least offer me a cane. But I wanted more. I didn't want to just tap about in the night, eking out a false faith. People say that when you are blind, your other senses become more finely tuned, that you become able to perceive things that other people cannot. If I was blind, as Father Roberto had said, I would seek to develop my other senses. I could stretch taut my spirit, try to touch things more deeply with my soul. Let the blind priest have his cane. I wanted more.

On snow-covered streets, I drove with great urgency to my father's house, preparing my announcement in my head along the way. I called Marco, talking over his confusion, insisting he meet me at Pop's right away. Next, I dialed Birch's number, and heard the answering machine pick up.

"Birch, if you're there, please pick up. This is so important, please, Birch . . . Okay, if you get this message, meet me at my dad's as soon as you can. It's urgent. Please. I don't know what's going on between us, but we have to—"

"Aida?" Birch's voice cut in. "I'm here. What is it? Is everything all right? You sound panicked."

"Oh, thank God, Birch. You have to meet me . . . Birch? You weren't going to pick up, were you?" I asked, choking back tears. I was at a stop sign, and even though the way was clear, I did not cross the intersection. Thankfully, there was no one behind me.

"Aida . . . I don't know. It just seems like we both had a lot of things we needed to work out individually. Being apart for a while just seemed like the right thing to do after everything that happened."

"Did you really break up with me? Do you still feel that way?" I asked him quietly.

"I don't know. I thought I did, but . . ."

A horn honked behind me, forcing me to move forward, and interrupting Birch's hesitating thoughts. "Damn!" I swore, as irritated with the driver behind me as I was with Birch. I crossed the intersection and continued across the road toward my father's house. "Look, Birch," I said a little too loudly. I took a deep breath, trying not to yell. "I know you've got a lot to think about right now, with everything that has happened with your parents. I'm hoping that some of the frustration you directed at me was really about them, even though I can see why you were angry with me as well. But can we put it all aside for right now? Please come to my dad's. You need to be there," I insisted.

"Okay, Aida, but why?"

"They cancelled the baptism last week because Father Roberto was sick. It's supposed to be today, and I can't go through with it."

"Oh, no, Aida. Marco's going to—"

"Birch, there's more to it than that. And I . . . I need

117

you," I finished lamely. I hated to sound so desperate. I hated to need.

"I'm on my way. I'll see you in a few minutes."

It was shortly after nine o'clock by the time I stood in front of my father, my brother, and my grandmother in the living room. I was pacing. The men were seated on the blue sofa, and Nonna was in her rocking chair by the window.

"Angelina? What's this all about, now? You've got us all worried sick," my father told me.

"Please," I replied. "I just want to wait until Birch gets here."

"Is this about the baptism?" Marco asked. "What does Birch have to do with it?"

I said nothing, but noticed that Nonna was watching me. One eyebrow arched over a dark, murky eye. After a brief knock on the back door, Birch rushed into the living room and stood in front of me, scanning my face for clues. "What is going on?" he asked.

"I think you should sit down," I told him. Obediently, he posited himself upon the arm of the love seat and looked at me, waiting. Gazing at his dark brown eyes, his sandy brows, furrowed with concern, I softened.

"Speak, child! We're waiting," Nonna shouted at me.

Breathing deeply for a moment, I gathered myself, searching for inner strength I hoped I possessed but had never really recognized. Across from me, hanging on the wall, was my mother and father's wedding photo. Looking at her, knowing that she was pregnant with Marco at the time, I smiled inwardly, remembering when Marco and I, he twelve and I ten, had actually done the math.

"Well?" Marco yelled. "What is it? You're backing out, aren't you?"

"Hush, son. Let her speak," my father chided.

"Yes, Marc. I am backing out."

"I knew it!" my brother whispered furiously.

Ignoring his outburst, as well as the sad disappointment in his eyes, I continued. "I went to eight o'clock mass this morning, hoping for some sign that I was doing the right thing. You all know how I've struggled with this baptism, so that shouldn't surprise any of you. But when we all began reciting the profession of faith—and I know how badly this hurts you all, but I have to explain myself—I realized just then how many things I'd be lying about, speaking baptismal vows for Joseph. And . . ." I paused to swallow, to breathe before baring the whole truth to their angry, accusing eyes, to their pinched, dark brows, to their tight lips and flaring nostrils. ". . . I don't want to lie about such important things. I know you all think I'm becoming an atheist or something. It's not true. But I don't believe in things in the same way you all do. Pop, I know you and Mom did the best you could with me, did everything you thought was right. You had no way of knowing this, but it was so incredibly not right for me," I told my father, my tone pleading.

"Catholicism is right for everyone!" Nonna shouted at me. "Was it too hard for you? To follow all the rules? Too bad. Jesus suffered for you." Her face was twisted with rage, her dark eyes glaring at me through slits in her wrinkled, olive face.

In the wake of that fury, I could only sigh. It was impossible to try and make her understand. But surely my father could make some concessions for me. "Pop?" I squeaked.

"Angelina. I am more sad, disappointed, than I am angry with you. But your Nonna is right. Who do you think you are, to question God's word? Be good, Angelina. Be Catholic. Don't do this to us," he said, still seated on the sofa. His shoulders were rounded, his hands extended out to me.

"Pop," I stated flatly, a little more ungently than I had intended. "I hate being Catholic." I heard Nonna suck in her breath, saw Marco shaking his head, watched tears well up in Pop's eyes. I had to get this over with, I thought as I turned toward my brother.

"Marco," I said, facing him directly, "I'd make an awful Catholic godmother, as much as you want things to be different. But . . ."

Again I paused, again I surveyed their expressions. They were taking it horribly, and I wasn't even finished. My father's head was bowed; I could no longer see his eyes. Marco was glaring at me, openly fuming, waiting for his chance at rebuttal. Nonna sat quietly, shaking her head. Finally, I turned to face Birch. His jaw was set, but his eyes revealed none of the disappointment I saw in my family. "But, Birch," I began anew. "I promise you, I'm going to be a good mother."

"What?" he asked, cocking his head slightly to the side as if he hadn't really heard me.

"I'm going to be a good mother," I repeated. "To our baby."

"You're . . . ?" His eyes flew to my abdomen and back to my face.

As I nodded, he sang my name and scooped me up in his arms and twirled me around the room, oblivious to our audience. "Oh, God, Aida," he said when the room stopped spinning, burying his face in the crook of my neck. "Why didn't you tell me sooner? Never mind. We'll talk about all that later," he said, kissing my neck, my forehead, then my lips.

"Aida Angelina Benedetto!" My father hurled my name at me, shattering my joy.

I stepped back from Birch, realizing abruptly that there was a stunned and angry mob ready to tear me to shreds. "You disgrace this house!" my father ranted. "First with your hateful words against the Church, then by not granting your brother his wish for you to be godmother to his first-born son, and now . . . now this. Pregnant. You are not married!" he bellowed, emphasizing every word. "You never stay together long enough to even talk about it, it seems. And forget that he's not Italian. I can live with that. But now he's not even going to Church anymore. He wasn't there last week. I saw his father, but no son. Are you pulling him down with you? Did your mother and I teach you nothing? And your poor Nonna, who tried so hard to mother you after your own saint of a mother died. Look at the shame you cause your grandmother! And your mother is rolling over in her grave, I'm sure of it."

My father cut short his speech in order to shoot a murderous glare at Birch. "And you? What have you done to my daughter? You are supposed to be the man, the strong one. You are supposed to marry her and take her to church and baptize your baby."

Before Birch could open his mouth or even formulate a reply, Marco interjected loudly, "So when *is* the big wedding?"

"What?" I whispered.

"The wedding? St. Benedict's is beautiful in the spring. You won't be too far along by then. No one will even know."

"He's right," Pop declared.

"Wait a minute," I began. "Birch and I have talked about this." I looked up at him and he was nodding at me, confirming that our plans about our union were still the same. "We're not going to have a big church wedding.

121

Just a small ceremony at the city hall."

"That counts for nothing!" Nonna spat, standing up and walking slowly toward us. "That counts for nothing in God's eyes."

As if fueled by his mother's righteousness, my father nodded vehemently. "She's right, Angelina," he said in a low, angry growl. "I have had enough, you insolent, ungrateful daughter. Now it's time to listen to your father. I don't care if you're thirteen or thirty. Good daughters listen to their fathers and I have been patient with you long enough. You *will* be godmother to Joseph. You *will* get married in the Church. And," his voice had risen to a full yell by now, "you *will* have *your* baby baptized! You will not disgrace your mother's name! You will not bring shame on this family! Or you will no longer be a part of it!" he roared, standing only inches from me now, so close, in fact, I could feel his hot breath on my face. He still smelled of his morning coffee.

Birch took a step forward and a little to the side, moving himself slightly between my father and me. "Mr. Benedetto, please. You have a new grandchild on the way. Can't we all talk this through?"

"Are you going to marry my daughter in the Church, in front of God and our family? It's your duty, as a Catholic. As a man."

"I'm going to marry your daughter whenever and wherever she wants to get married. And if she doesn't want to get married, I'll still be with her, always. Our promises to each other should be good enough for God, and for you," he said evenly, coolly, looking my father unflinchingly in the eye.

Marco and Nonna were standing just behind my father, flanking their general. And I knew now it was time to retreat, and possibly, never to return to this battlefield. Before I fled, however, I wanted to make something clear to my attackers. "This is *not* what Mom would have wanted. She would never have disowned me. She would have understood. You called her a saint, but she was just a woman, just like me. Pregnant and unmarried."

Before I realized what had happened, my cheek and lip were stinging from the blow of the back of my father's right hand. He wore a ruby-studded pinky ring that had been his father's, and it had sliced into my lower lip. Blood trickled down my chin, and I put first my tongue, and then my fingers to the wound to staunch the bleeding.

My father had never struck me like that before. He used to bend Marco and I over the couch and crack us with his black leather belt a couple times a month for acting up in church, but he had never backhanded me across the face before. More than anything, I was stunned, but not more so than anyone else in the room, it seemed, including my father. Everyone looked at the blood on my face, and I stared down at the crimson wetness on my fingers. With my left hand, I grabbed my father's right hand, the one that had hit me. I turned it palm side up, and I smeared the blood from the fingers of my right hand onto his open palm.

Birch put his arm around my shoulders and I could feel him shaking. He escorted me outside, and I left my father standing there with my blood on his hand.

Birch hustled me to his Jeep. It warmed up rather quickly after he started the engine. Still parked outside my father's house, Birch examined the cut on my lip, dabbing at the blood with some tissues from the glove box.

"It's not that bad," he told me. "We'll get some ice on it

when we get home. I'll drive you back, then take a taxi back here and get your car, okay?"

I nodded in reply, still paralyzed with the shock of what had happened.

"Are you okay, Aida? I mean, of course you're not, after all that, but . . . is there anything . . . I'll just get you home," he fumbled.

Swallowing blood, I nodded again. Once we were home, Birch tucked me in on the couch with my afghan, made me some chamomile tea and gave me a washcloth with a few ice cubes folded up inside. Then he left again, to go get my car. All I could do was sit there and replay the whole scene in my mind, wondering how anything I had said or done had merited the punishment I had received. I simply was trying to do what I felt was right. Hadn't I acted with personal integrity? And now, as a result, I had no family.

Wincing, I placed the ice pack on my face as Birch walked back into my apartment. After removing his outerwear, he sprinted to my side, checking the wound.

"Well?" I asked.

"The bleeding has stopped. Your lip is pretty puffy, and you're going to have a nice bruise."

"No. I meant, what happened when you came for my car? Did you talk to them? Did he say anything?"

"No, Aida. I thought about knocking on the door, but I really had nothing to say. All I wanted to do was punch your dad's damned face."

"Why didn't you?" I mumbled.

"I didn't think you would have wanted me to."

I shrugged in reply. I didn't really want him to strike my father, but it made me feel defended to know he had thought about it. "I'm glad you didn't hit him. But you could have said something to him. I wouldn't have cared."

"So, now what?" he asked me.

"We're both orphans, I guess, unless you've patched things up with your family."

He shook his head. "I don't even know where to begin. My mother has left me a lot of messages. She said my dad came home to pack a suitcase. I guess he's living in the studio above the pub."

We were both silent for a while. Birch huddled up next to me on the couch. Before long, he asked, "How are we supposed to just do normal things, like eat, and work, now that everything is so different? I mean, God, you're pregnant, Aida. And our families . . . All I want is for us to be alone together, to regroup, to just be us. I have so many questions for you, when you're ready, about the baby. I want to know when you found out and how far along you are and how you're feeling and have you been to the doctor yet and—"

"Hey, slow down," I told him, pulling the blanket tighter around my body. "Tomorrow. Tomorrow, we should both call in sick. Everyone at work thinks I have the flu anyway. Do you think you can take the day off? We'll talk about everything, figure out how we can get away, maybe even to Maine, like we talked about."

"Really? Do you still want to go? What about city hall?" Birch asked, still leaning against me.

"I say we skip it for now. We have time. It's a technicality. It can wait. There is so much to discuss, about the baby, and about you and . . . everything. What are you going to do, Birch? I don't know about you, but *I'm* not willing to let your mother go. She gave me this list of books to read, and we were going to talk about spirituality, religion. And she's going to be a grandmother, besides! Are you going to tell her? And don't you want to find out more about Thaddeus? Your mother didn't even say if he knew about you or not."

"Aida!" he cut in. "I'm sorry," he said when I frowned. "I didn't mean to shout. It's just that—you're right. We have a lot to figure out, and I have so much to hash out with my mom. But she betrayed three people with her decisions. I just don't know if I'm ready to see her again yet. And as for my dad, it doesn't seem as if he wants anything to do with me anymore. I don't know what to make of that."

"Sorry," I whispered.

"Why?"

Shrugging, I said, "I didn't mean to push. Everything with your parents . . . it's really none of my business. It's just that . . . it would be great to have a mother in my life right now. I guess that's a little selfish of me, considering what you must be feeling."

"No, it's not. Aida, if we're going to be together—and we always were going to be, baby or not, despite my idiotic behavior last week at the sanctuary—then we have to embrace each other's family, even if they've pushed us away. No matter what is going on with my mother and me, you should feel like you can go to her. And . . . we have to tell her."

"I'm sure it'll go better than my announcement to my family," I said, trying to force my bruised face to smile.

"Don't," he whispered, picking up the soggy ice pack and placing it on my mouth again. "We'll figure things out tomorrow—how soon we can get away, when to tell my mother, everything, all right?"

Sighing heavily, I nodded.

"Hey," he said, pulling me close. "I promise you, Aida. Everything is going to be fine. And you know what else?"

"What?"

"I'm going to be a good father."

"I know, Birch. I know."

"So? When? When is our baby going to be born?" he asked, placing his hand on my still-flat abdomen. As I didn't have much of an appetite, and vomited on a semi-regular basis, I hadn't gained any weight yet. Happily, the vomiting was abating, although now it had been replaced by a constant feeling of nausea.

"Early October," I answered.

"October, huh? A fall baby. Have you been to the doctor already?"

"Friday was my first appointment. I'm sorry I didn't tell you sooner. I really wanted you to be there. But we'd just had that weird thing at the sanctuary. I tried to call, but, it seemed clear that you didn't want to talk. I was just . . . confused, I guess. And just so you know, we're together because I love you, not because of any stupid guilt thing. I might have a lot of guilt issues to work out, but not where you're concerned. Not anymore, Birch."

"I know. I'm sorry. And . . . Friday? Aida, that was the anniversary wasn't it? You had the first baby appointment on the anniversary of your mom's death? That must have been horrible. I'm so sorry I wasn't there. I was an ass. I shouldn't have let—"

"Stop it," I told him, leaning over to kiss him. "You'll come to the next one."

"Okay," he replied quietly. "Hey, the day's half over and I haven't seen you eat a thing. Did you at least have breakfast? Are you hungry? Shouldn't you have something?"

"I haven't had a bite all day, Birch. But the good news is that I haven't thrown up, either."

"Has that been happening a lot? That's normal, right?"

Nodding, I told him about how I'd been feeling, and together we wandered into the kitchen. He made salad, and warmed up some bread in the oven. I carved a hefty portion of Parmesan to have with my dinner, and it all sounded good.

I actually wanted to eat for a change, but the salty cheese and salad dressing stung the raw wound on my lip. As I tried to work around this difficulty, we talked mostly about the baby, and it was such a relief to me that he knew now, that he was ecstatic about the prospect of being a father.

"You know, Aida," he was telling me, "it's not entirely how I pictured things happening with us. I didn't think we'd be talking about babies this early on, but I did always envision us as parents eventually. I believe we're more ready than we think we are."

I smiled in a small sort of way, then cringed, feeling the cut on my lip spread painfully open a bit. "I hope so, but I suppose it really doesn't matter, does it? He's coming whether we're ready or not."

"He? Do you have some kind of maternal instinct that it's going to be a boy?"

"I don't know," I said, shrugging. "It just came out."

"So where's he going to live? Your place or mine?" Birch asked with a smile.

"I guess we should talk about moving in together, shouldn't we?"

Chewing his salad greens, Birch nodded. "We have a lot to talk about . . . Aida? Did you really mean everything you told your dad?"

I looked down at my plate. I had been wondering when he was going to get to all that. "Yes," I said quietly.

"You said some pretty inflammatory things."

"What was the worst?" I asked him, leaning back in my

chair. My tongue toyed with my lacerated lip, and I tasted the metallic flavor of blood.

As he shrugged, Birch said, "Well . . . it was hard to hear that you *hate* being Catholic. I mean, I know you feel a lot of resentment and all that, and that there are doctrinal positions you don't agree with, but, I guess I didn't really realize the extent of your . . . bitterness," he finished tentatively.

Pausing a moment as I regarded the tight line of his mouth, the angle of his bowed head, I began, "You can handle it," I told him. He lifted his gaze to my face. "I'm just like your coffee . . . dark and bitter," I joked sardonically. Birch sat back in his chair, his mouth half open as if he were preparing a retort but could think of none. Rising from the table and clearing our plates, I felt my pulse quicken at the notion that he was judging me for feeling bitter.

After setting the plates in the sink with a purposeful clatter, I looked over at him, saw him watching me with his full lips pulled down at the corners. Damn him, I thought. I would *not* be cowed into feeling badly for my attitude toward the Church.

Grabbing a mug from the cupboard, I poured a cup of the strong coffee I had set to brew just before our meal. Without taking my gaze from his face, I raised my eyebrows as I placed the mug in front of him. "Enjoy," I said before I spun on my heel and strode into the living room.

Chapter Seven

Later that evening, Birch called April and Louis to tell him he wouldn't be in the next day, and I left a message at work as well. As I soaked in the tub with Birch, I realized that being pregnant hadn't abated my desire for him in the least, nor had being angry with him. Apparently, the feeling was mutual. Limbs tangled around each other, we climbed out of the tub and stumbled into bed, dripping with bath water, laughing and panting.

With the bed damp from our hasty post-bath love-making, we decided to go upstairs to Birch's apartment to spend the night. Snuggled up in his soft cotton sheets, I wondered if I could live here. Would there even be room for a baby in either of our apartments?

"Birch, where are we going to live?" I asked as he entered the bedroom carrying two steaming mugs of cocoa.

"I hope soy milk is okay," he said.

"It's good," I said, sipping the warm drink and wrapping both hands around the hefty mug. "So, what do you think?" I prodded.

Birch climbed in bed next to me and propped himself up with a couple of pillows. "I think we should start out fresh," he said. "Besides, our apartments are too small, don't you think?"

As I nodded, I replied, "But I do love this building. I'll hate to leave it. This is where we met. We've been here a long time. This," I said slowly as the revelation dawned on me, "this is where our baby was conceived."

"I know."

We were both silent for a long while, considering our options. Finally, between sips of cocoa, Birch announced, "We'll start looking for a house."

"What? A house? Buy a house?" I hadn't even considered the idea before now. I assumed we'd just find a bigger apartment.

"Sure, why not? Are you worried about money? I've lived frugally all my life. I'm prepared for this. Don't worry," he told me.

"It's not that I'm worried. I've got money saved, too. It's just . . ." I couldn't finish, and I didn't know why.

"Cold feet?" Birch asked with a smile.

"Well, no," I faltered, flushing.

"Get over it, Aida. We're together. We're going to be a family. And we're going to need a house. Soon. We don't have any more time for your little second thoughts about us, if that's what's going on."

"It's not," I protested weakly.

"It is. I can tell. You've dumped me enough times for me to know what leads up to it. This is not the first time I suggested we move in together. You were wishy-washy about it before when there was just two of us, last year, and I said I wanted you to move in with me, and then a week later, you said it wasn't going to work out, we weren't going to work out. Well, guess what, Aida? We *are* working out. I think you know that, and I think this retreating act has just become a habit with you."

I put my empty cup down on the side table and looked into Birch's searching eyes. "I want to be with you. I swear it. I love you. If I seem reluctant about the house, or . . . retreating, as you said, it's just that . . . God, Birch. What the hell do I know about being a mother? So we're going to buy a house, and move in, and get the baby's room ready, and

131

then, come fall, I'll be required to do this job that I have no training for, and I can't just call my mom on the phone and ask for help like most other first-time moms out there. I never dreamed of what it would be like to go through this without her."

Birch put his arms around me and kissed the top of my head. "We'll figure it out, Aida. Just like everybody else does. I don't know much about being a father, either, you know. I've got one dad I thought I knew, but look how he's behaving. He left my mom, he walked out on me as well, apparently, because I didn't agree with him about the Church. And I've got another father who may not even know I exist. Where does that leave me? All we can do is struggle through on our own, together. I'm not going anywhere. You don't have to do this by yourself."

I was nodding against his shoulder, and as I toyed with the cross that lay across his bare chest, I tried to believe him.

"You know what else?" he said. "We'll tell my mom tomorrow, okay? You'll at least have one mom in your life to talk to about things."

"What about you? Are you going to talk to her about . . . everything?"

Birch paused for a few moments before replying. "I don't know. You know how I am. I guess I retreat a little, too, when I don't know how to handle something. But . . . she's my mom. I suppose I should allow that she was doing what she thought best, but I don't think I agree with what she did."

"But you don't have to, Birch. You don't have to agree with her, and you don't have to understand her in order to keep having a relationship with her."

Birch tilted his head a little to the side as I paused. "You don't think so?" he asked.

"No," I replied. "She's not an employee, or a volunteer at the sanctuary, someone you recruit and train specifically to do things your way. Don't you think she deserves a little more sympathy from you?"

"Well, what about you? Are you going to sympathize with your family?" he asked accusingly.

"I'm not going to start behaving the way they want me to, if that's what you mean. But that's not what I'm talking about. I don't agree with how they handled things. But if they welcomed me back with open arms, you can be damned sure I'll come running. You don't turn your back on family. My dad and brother and Nonna shut me out, not the other way around."

"But you're not going to go running back first, are you, Aida? You're going to wait for them to come to you. Who is turning her back on whom?" he asked. He had set his mug down on the nightstand and was lying on his side, propped up on one elbow. From his comfortable and casual position, he attacked me, and I rose to my knees and lifted my voice in my own defense.

"Damn it, Birch! He hit me. For telling the truth. And you want *me* to be the one to make amends?"

"Of course not, Aida. But don't give me a big self-righteous speech about how unconditionally important family is just because I'm still pissed at my mom for lying to me for thirty years."

"Self-righteous?" I sputtered. "I . . . I . . ."

"Forget it. Let's just agree that we both have legitimate reasons for keeping our distance from our families right now. That's reasonable, don't you think? Can we get some sleep now?"

Glaring at him, I marched to the bathroom to brush my teeth. When I returned to the bedroom, the light was off,

133

and Birch was stretched out on his side, with his back to me. I hated just dropping things. I hated that he had called me self-righteous. I stood there, glaring at his back, considering returning to my own apartment.

While I was too irritated with him to just curl up next to him and sleep, I also realized that his baby was inside of me and I could no longer turn my back and run away whenever we had some sort of conflict. Disagreement could no longer be viewed as an indication that things weren't going to work out between us. Sighing loudly, I grudgingly accepted that I was just going to have to work harder, to dedicate myself to being part of something larger than myself, to realize that I was part of a new family, my own family. I walked slowly to the bed and stood next to it.

"Aida? Come to bed. Don't go," Birch said as he rolled over to look at me.

Without a word, I crawled in bed beside him. He spooned himself behind me and threw his arm around my waist. "I wasn't going to leave," I whispered into the darkness, listening to Birch breathe.

"Okay," he replied as he moved my hair aside and kissed the back of my neck. "Okay, Aida."

The meek light of a February dawn peered tentatively into Birch's bedroom on Monday morning. Birch snored lightly by my side, and I sat up slowly, assessing my body's current reaction to pregnancy. My stomach, as usual, felt slightly acidic, but I was not sick. Swinging my feet from the bed to the floor, I realized with a small shock and great delight that today, I felt strong. Thinking of the baby, I experienced a thick energy coursing through me like sap. Maybe the feeling was at least due in part to the small victory I had achieved last night, when I had resolved to stay when flight seemed the more comfortable option. To celebrate my sense of well-being, I decided to go for a run.

Rolling back into bed, I kissed Birch lightly on the forehead, and whispered, "Hey, sleepyhead. I'm going to run. Want to come?"

His eyes fluttered open. "What? I don't know. You're hard to keep up with. And you don't let me talk."

"Haven't you ever heard of 'companionable silence'? Anyway, I'll go easy on you. The path through the woods shouldn't be too snowy. It gets plowed every so often and packed down by everyone pretty well."

"Okay," he mumbled. "I wouldn't be able to sleep anymore anyway. I worry about you running on the snow and ice. What if you fell? What about the baby?"

"Don't worry. I'll be fine. Meet me downstairs in ten minutes."

After changing into my winter running clothes and doing a few push-ups, I ran downstairs and was leaning against the brick building, stretching my calves when Birch emerged from the front door. We started out at a brisk pace, headed for the wooded path through the park. The cold air prickled in my lungs and I breathed deeply, savoring the smell of fresh air.

As we entered the park and set off for the woods, I glanced at Birch and smiled. He ran often and could easily keep up with me, but he didn't always enjoy my longer runs of over an hour. Once into the trees, we found that the path had been plowed recently, and was only covered by last night's few inches of snowfall, which crunched beneath our feet. I loved that sound, and looked over at Birch to say so, but when I opened my mouth to speak, he put his finger to his lips, whispering "Shhh," mocking my "no talking" rule. My mouth twisted into a smile and I led us on a path that meandered through oaks, elms, and pines.

Birds and squirrels darted in front of us, and I felt a little like an animal myself, trotting through the wintry woods. Actually, I realized just then that there was something about being pregnant that made me feel strongly animalistic, instinctive, protective, warm-blooded and wild, primal.

"Slow down!"

Suddenly I realized Birch was shouting at me and found that I was nearly sprinting toward an enormous pine tree heavy with snow. I slowed to a jog and waited for Birch to catch up.

"What are you doing?" he asked breathlessly.

I stopped at the pine and turned to face him. "I don't know. I guess I was just lost in thought. I didn't realize I had picked up so much speed." Our breath hung thickly on the air between us, and the sun made the snow sparkle like starlight. "I'm not going to be able to do this like everybody else, Birch," I panted.

"What are you talking about, Aida?"

"I don't know how to explain it. I mean, I like my doctor well enough, I suppose. But I feel like a dog or a deer or something. I just want us to hole up by ourselves someplace, alone, in the woods to have this baby."

"I'm not sure that's altogether safe," he said, smiling at me.

"You've delivered puppies. You could do it," I replied, mostly joking.

"Hell, I even delivered a calf once, but I think I'll leave this to the professionals."

"What—in a cold hospital, with drugs and IVs and masks and strangers? Hospitals terrify me."

"Of course they do."

"What do you mean by that?" I asked him, breathing

quickly and sweating beneath my layers of clothing.

"Where was the last place you saw your mother alive?"

I covered my face with my hands, nodding. "You're right," I whispered between my fingers. "That's why I'm panicking, isn't it?"

"Look, Aida," Birch said, pulling me towards him and wrapping his arms around me. "Maybe we have to be in a hospital and maybe we don't. I mean, people still have babies at home. I saw it on TV once. Maybe that's for us and maybe it's not. But even in a hospital we don't necessarily have to have the whole drug thing. And maybe we can find someplace where we actually feel a little comfortable. Hell, I'm sure, with all my mom's connections, that she knows someone who knows about natural childbirth and all that."

"Really?"

"Sure. We'll find out about everything. We'll ask your doctor. We'll keep all our options open, okay?"

He kept saying we, but I was still getting used to the idea that we were in this together. "Birch, I know how much you want to be a part of all this, but . . ."

"What do you mean, 'want to be'? I *am* a part of it, whether you want me to be or not. I guess I just assumed you wanted me to be. Don't you?"

I stamped my feet in the snow a little, feeling my muscles stiffen slightly with inactivity. "Of course I do, Birch."

"Then what is it?" he prodded.

"It's going to sound pathetic."

"Try me."

He was staring at me so earnestly, wide-eyed and innocent. He didn't know what it was like to experience the death of a parent, or anyone close to him. I was glad that he had been spared that pain, but it meant that a great chasm

137

existed between us. In an incredibly significant way, he just couldn't understand me.

"It must sound like everything comes back to my mother's death. I mean, Christ! It's been fourteen years. But I guess since she died, I've just always found it easier not to count on people too much. At least not for the big things."

"Why not?" he pushed.

I hesitated, looking down, watching my running shoes imprint the snow as I stomped my feet to keep warm.

"Why not?" Birch repeated. "Come on, Aida. Because they might not be around when you really need them?"

I looked up at him, licking my lips, offering only the briefest of nods.

"Damn it! You can't live your life afraid that everyone around you is going to suddenly die or otherwise abandon you! Who knows what could happen, to any of us, to me, to you? I'm not going anywhere! I'm here! With you, right now. That's what we've got to work with. Now *stop* trying to push me away. I don't know what God, or the universe, or whatever you and my mom want to call it, has planned for me. But what I intend is to always be with you. *Let me in.*"

"Don't you know I want to? Don't you know I'm trying?" I pleaded.

"I do know. Just don't stop trying. Don't keep overthinking it and looking for ways to complicate things. It's simple. Here we are. We love each other. Got it?"

I struggled with a smile, attempting to reassure the both of us. "Got it," I said quietly. "Can we go now, Birch? I'm freezing."

"Yeah, let's get moving."

We jogged the rest of the way home, silently, until we

were trotting up the stairs toward my apartment. When we arrived at my door, we found Birch's mother knocking on it.

"Glenda," I gasped, at the same time that Birch cursed under his breath. I glanced at his face. We had agreed that we would call her today, tell her about the baby, so I wasn't sure why he had reacted that way. Maybe he just hadn't prepared himself mentally for seeing her again.

"Aida! What happened to your mouth?"

My hand flew to my split and slightly puffy purple lip. I had been doing my best to try and ignore it. I hadn't yet thought of what I would tell people. "I . . . uh . . . it's nothing really."

"It's my fault. We were out for a run in the woods, and, as usual, she was half a mile ahead of me. I called out to her to wait up, and when she turned to glance back at me, she tripped and fell."

"What a klutz, huh?" I said, grateful for Birch's quick thinking. It was a plausible enough story.

"Oh, my. It must have been quite a fall. You might want to put some ice on it," she told me, before rushing at Birch and hugging him. "Birch, I've been trying to contact you, but you haven't returned my calls. Please don't cut me out of your life. I know I've made tremendous mistakes. But I'm still your mother."

With his hands on his mother's shoulders, Birch cleared his throat then bent down to kiss her forehead. "I know, Mom. Come on in. Let's talk."

Once inside, I invited Glenda to sit down. Birch and I stood in the kitchen and gulped down water, thirsty from our run. Warm and damp, the sweat was now starting to cool on my body.

"Why don't you go shower," Birch told me. I nodded in

reply, and as I excused myself and headed for the bathroom I heard Birch clanking around in the kitchen, putting on a pot of coffee for his mother.

Relieved to give Birch and Glenda time alone, I thought how polite and restrained Birch was being with his mother, trying to distance himself from her. Seeing her, I guessed, was making it extremely difficult for Birch to nurse his sense of betrayal. They had always been close, their adoration mutual. As hurt as I knew he was by her recent revelations, it would take a Herculean effort for him to actually push her out of his life.

When I returned to the kitchen, they were sitting at the table together, talking softly. I sat down next to Birch and noticed that neither of them was drinking the coffee Birch had put on before my shower. As Birch turned his gaze toward me, I frowned slightly in his direction before turning to Glenda. "Can I get you some coffee?"

"Oh, yes, thank you, Aida."

Before I could get up, Birch was rising from his chair. "I'll get it. Aida, are you having some as well?"

I nodded. "With lots of milk."

"I know."

"No. More than usual. So," I began, turning to Glenda. She was regarding me intently, head tilted to the side. "How are you doing?" I asked her.

"We were just talking about my dad," Birch said as he sat down with mugs of coffee for Glenda and me.

"He wants to separate," Glenda explained, her thin fingers tracing imaginary patterns on the worn oak table.

My eyes widened. "Really?"

"He said that it had all gone wrong. We made too many mistakes."

Birch toyed with the empty water glass in front of him.

"It's my fault," he said. "If I hadn't attacked the Church like I had, he wouldn't be doing this."

"Birch, that's not true," Glenda soothed.

"No, you're wrong. You don't understand the kind of relationship that we had. The only times in my life where he ever reached out to me, extended himself emotionally, had something to do with church. He feels like he's failed if I'm not a good Catholic. And I proved to him last week that I'm not a good Catholic."

"By his definition, at least," I added. "But what has that got to do with your parents, Birch?"

"Nothing at all," Glenda interrupted. "This is between Will and me. It has nothing to do with you."

"Don't the two of you see?" Birch moaned as he rose and began pacing the small kitchen. "Mom, you said it yourself. You told me that Dad would only agree to marry you and raise me as his own if you agreed not to interfere with his raising me as a Catholic. You said he wanted to save me, and that my questioning the faith seemed like betrayal to him." Having halted in front of his mother, Birch leaned forward and rested his hands on the table. "His marriage to you was predicated on my Catholicism, a faith I threw back in his face. If I'm not going to let him save me, then it was all for nothing."

"All for nothing?" Glenda whispered. "Do you really think that is what your father feels? Don't you suppose that he loved me just a little?"

I cringed, trying to hide behind my mug. Birch was out of line. His mother was hurt and angry enough. What was he doing?

"I don't know, Mom. I really don't. You two never seemed very much in love from my point of view. There was always so much tension between you two."

"We had our moments, but we have always loved each other. I understand how difficult all this must be for you, and why you would want to lash out at me, but—"

"Maybe you always loved Dad, but how do you think he felt, knowing how much you loved someone else at the same time! You chose the safe route, with Dad."

"I chose the safe route for you, Birch, for us, for our family."

"Whatever the reasons, you loved Thaddeus, too, and of course Dad knew it." Birch turned away from his mother and paced the small space in front of the table, muttering, almost to himself, "I can't believe you were sleeping with someone else while you were engaged to Dad."

Glenda bowed her head, tears streaming down her cheeks, but didn't reply.

Her silence spurred Birch on, and he stopped pacing to plant himself rigidly in front of Glenda once again. "Why didn't you just go with him, Mom? Why did you have to ruin Dad's life, too? Didn't you know him at all? He's all about loyalty. Did you really think he'd ever forgive you? He *did* marry you because of me. He wanted to take something bad—me, a bastard—and turn it into something good—a Catholic. He wanted to turn this horrible situation into a family. And he made it work for a good long while didn't he? Until I destroyed it. I knew how rigid his beliefs were. I should have kept my doubts to myself, worked through it all without . . ." Birch grew quiet and turned away from us. He wandered to the living-room window and gazed out at the icy street below.

Glenda and I caught each other's glance. I mouthed silently to her "Do you want me to go?" and pointed to the door. She shook her head vigorously. So I remained seated, mute, helpless, until Birch turned around and stalked back toward his mother. Apparently he wasn't finished with her yet.

"Does he even know about me?" he shouted at Glenda.

"What?" she asked, her voice quavering.

"Thaddeus. Does he know about me? You never said whether or not you had told him you were pregnant."

"I wrote to him after Will and I were married, just before you were born."

"You are such a coward," Birch spat.

"Birch," I said quietly, trying to soften him.

"No, Aida. She is. She didn't have the guts to tell Thaddeus right away, to give him a chance to fight for her, for me. She waited until he wouldn't have any choice except to respect the choice she had made for him, for all of us."

Glenda swallowed, then looked up at her son. "I was protecting you."

"From what? From my real father? You were protecting yourself. You were scared of having to make concessions. You said it yourself. You didn't want to sacrifice your dreams so Thaddeus could have his. That's what people do, Mom! People who love each other make compromises. Maybe he would have been willing to sacrifice some of what he wanted for you, for me, but you never gave him that chance. And you didn't give Dad a chance to find someone he could really love, someone who would be loyal to him. Maybe now he'll get that chance."

"You're right, Birch. I did make a horrible mess of things. I was young, and scared, too. I don't know."

"What man wouldn't want to know he was about to become a father?" Birch railed. I winced. Perhaps that was meant for me, as well as for Glenda. "How could you wait to tell him? What did he do when you told him?"

"He named you," Glenda offered quietly.

"What?" Birch whispered, finally unclenching his jaw.

"He wrote me and asked that if you were a girl, you be named Willow, and if you were a boy, that you be named Birch. Trees. That's what he did. He saved trees," Glenda spoke in subdued tones, her mouth twitching into a sad smile. Then she bent down and opened the large hemp knapsack at her side. "One of the reasons I came looking for you today was to give you these," she said, pulling out a pile of envelopes tied together with string.

"What's all this?" Birch asked, reaching out for the proffered bundle.

"Letters from Thaddeus. We corresponded while you were growing up. I sent him pictures of you, told him about all of your new skills, your dreams, your adventures. Remember that time, I think you were nine or ten, and you wanted to camp out in the backyard? Your father didn't want you to. I think he thought you were too young or it was too cold or something. So you crept out at night and climbed into the apple tree in the backyard. You actually fell asleep, and fell out of the tree in the middle of the night. You broke your arm. Thaddeus loved that story, but I remember him writing that he wished he'd been around to teach you how to sleep in a tree properly. Anyway, he told me to give you the letters when I thought the time was right."

"Did Dad know that you two wrote to each other? And what did he think of my name?" Birch asked.

"He thought the name was my idea. I knew he wasn't pleased, but you got a good solid saint's name for your middle name. He could live with 'Birch Michael,' I suppose. And if he did know about my pen pal, he never let on. Maybe . . . maybe you're right, Birch. Maybe he thought that as long as he had you, that was enough.

Maybe he felt that he'd lost me before we were married anyway."

"Did he?" Birch asked.

Glenda sighed. I thought she looked as beautiful as ever, and so young for her age. I watched her brush a few curly wisps of hair away from her face with both hands, and I knew the answer before she spoke it. "I . . . I love your father. That is, the father you've known all your life. All I know of who Thaddeus is now has come in the form of sporadic letters over the years. Any love I still have for him is really just for the memory of him." She took a long drink from her mug, swallowing the last of what must have been cold coffee by now. Birch looked away from her, then moved slowly toward the sunbeams bursting through the living-room windows.

Knowing what it was like to only have ever truly loved one man, I wished fervently that Glenda would seek Thaddeus out once again, to remake what had been broken. It probably wasn't fair of me to wish that, but Birch's family as he had known it seemed to me irreparably splintered. From what Glenda had said about Thaddeus, he seemed to me to be the kind of man Glenda should be with: earthy and idealistic, like Birch. Will was gruff and often rough, and had shown himself to be narrow-minded, cold.

Reaching once more into her knapsack, Glenda retrieved a small stack of books and placed them on the kitchen table. "And these are for you, Aida. Just a few of the best books to help you on your spiritual journey. There's an introduction to world religions, an overview of spiritual philosophy, a collection of poetry with spiritual and metaphysical themes."

"Thank you, Glenda," I said, and then I glanced toward Birch. We still hadn't told Glenda our news. I called out to him softly, apparently breaking into his thoughts. I watched him shake his head a little before he looked at me and returned to my side.

"Mom," he began. "I'm still trying to figure out what to make of all this. I'm sorry if I was so . . ."

"Please, don't apologize, Birch. You have every right to feel as you do, and to express yourself as you did. Just, please, keep talking to me about it, about anything. Please let me remain a part of your life. You . . . you are all I have left now."

"Well, not all," Birch said. "Now, you've got Aida as well. We're . . . we're going to get some-kind-of-married, maybe at city hall, maybe just on a rock in Maine next week, but, well, we're in it for keeps."

"Oh, that's . . . it's just wonderful!" Glenda cried, rising and throwing her arms around the two of us.

"And that's not all," Birch went on, sounding like a game show host. "You've also got . . . or will have, anyway, in a matter of what, Aida, eight months? A grandchild."

"What?" she whispered, still hugging us. She kissed Birch's face, and then my own, and then placed her hand on my belly. "Congratulations," she said as a few tears fell to her cheekbones. "It's . . . it's just thrilling, isn't it? Have you told your father?"

"No. Just Aida's family so far," Birch answered.

"Are they as excited as I am?" Glenda asked.

My hand was halfway to my bruised face when Birch snatched it out of its flight pattern and held it between his own two hands. "I wouldn't go that far," Birch said.

Trying to smile, I added, "They're having a big problem with the fact that I'm pretty much abandoning Catholicism and that we're not married."

"But you've pledged yourself to one another. Any fool can see how in love the two of you are."

"Not the same thing as a gigantic Italian Catholic wedding," Birch noted.

"No, I suppose not. Birch, would you like me to tell Will?"

"No. I'll do it. I haven't spoken to him at all since that night. I need to."

Glenda had returned to her seat and her fingers danced aimlessly about her empty coffee mug for a moment. She was still looking at her hands as she laced her fingers together and asked Birch, "Would you like me to tell Thaddeus?"

As my hand was still enveloped by Birch's hand, I felt his fingers tighten around mine before he spoke. "I . . . well, do you two still keep in touch?"

"It's been a while, but I think he'd like to know that he's going to be a grandfather."

"It's up to you, Mom," Birch said softly. "Where is he these days anyway? Is he still in South America?"

"Well, it's rather . . . funny, I suppose, that you had mentioned running off to Maine."

"He's in Maine?" Birch's voice was getting a little louder. "What the hell is he doing there? What happened to the South American rainforests?"

"There's environmental work to be done everywhere, Birch. That's where he ended up. If you're interested in contacting him, he's in Bangor. I can give you the address and phone number."

"No! No, I don't think . . ." Birch trailed off, unable to finish. I listened to him take a deep breath.

"All right. I understand," Glenda said. "Well, I should be going. If you need any help at all with the pregnancy and getting ready for the baby, please let me know. I'd be happy to do anything at all. You probably have a doctor you're happy with, but if you're interested, I do know a doula—a natural childbirth coach. Let me know if you need anything. Either of you." Glenda then stood up, kissed both of us, and began to wrap herself in her coat and scarf. Birch helped her with her coat and held the door for her. "I love you, son," she told him as she stepped into the hall.

"I love you, too, Mom."

Chapter Eight

Having spent the morning deeply engaged in emotional discussion, Birch and I curled up on the sofa and napped for an hour, recuperating. When I awoke, I did not open my eyes. I listened.

Birch was no longer beside me and the apartment was quiet. I wondered if he had gone to his place to finally shower and change, or if he had felt pressed to be at the sanctuary. I knew it was hard for him to be away, and I had no idea how he would be able to get away to Maine. Time off was pretty much a foreign concept to him.

I put my hands on my abdomen and wondered when it would begin to swell and tried to imagine myself with a portly silhouette. I'd have to buy maternity clothes, I realized suddenly. And baby clothes. Maybe Yolanda and Sally would have a baby shower for me. Would any of my family come? How long were they going to be angry? I still couldn't believe my father had struck me like that, and that Marco had let him. And Nonna, too, I thought, fuming. I couldn't believe that they were all truly that disappointed in me. Surely my mother would have been more understanding. Of course it was easy to think that, when she couldn't contradict me. Either way, she wouldn't have allowed my father to raise his hand to me. She had always been my fiercest protector, and Marco's as well. While Pop had repeatedly threatened us with physical violence, Mom would always intervene, finding a more creative punishment for us. And where was Birch, anyway, I thought, opening my eyes and sitting up.

Wandering into the kitchen, I found a note on the table. "Went to shower, and in search of lunch. Be back soon. Love, B." While I waited for Birch to return, I began paging through the *Lonely Planet* guide to New England. I don't know why I was so fascinated with Maine, but I had always wanted to go there. Before long, Birch returned, holding a large brown paper bag.

"Hey, Love. I got takeout from Om Café. Sandwiches and fries. Is that okay?"

"Did you get coleslaw, too?"

"Yes. And pickles," Birch added gleefully.

I wrinkled my nose. "That's some sort of pregnancy myth. I have no craving for pickles." I sat down at the table and unwrapped my veggie club sandwich.

"Have you . . ." Birch began, then stopped abruptly. "Are you . . . ?" he tried again.

"What are you trying to say?" I asked him.

"Meat," he finally uttered.

"Oh. I wondered when you were going to ask me about that. I haven't had any since I found out I was pregnant. It just sounds awful right now. But, I was thinking, I can certainly live without it, if that's what you want for the baby."

"Really? You would do that?"

"Of course. It's your baby, too. And we can raise him vegetarian, or vegan if that's what you want. I mean, I have no ideological reason to eat meat, and you certainly feel strongly about *not* eating it. I just always have and haven't thought too much about it. I respect that you have actual beliefs about it. Although I can't promise to foreswear eggs and dairy as well while I'm pregnant."

"No, now probably wouldn't be the best time for you to become a strict vegan. And thank you for having thought about this all already. But what about work? What if you have to review a steakhouse or develop a new meatloaf recipe or something?"

"I'm sure I can manage to avoid it. Besides . . . I've been thinking about something else as well. As long as we have enough money saved, and you're making a decent amount, I don't want to go back to work right after the baby is born. I couldn't bear the thought of leaving him, or her, at least not for a while. And when I do go back, I want to try to work at least part-time from home."

"Whatever you want. We'll figure it out," Birch replied as he leaned over and kissed me.

"Maybe we shouldn't move, though. At least not for a while. To save money."

"You don't think it'll be too crowded?" he asked before taking a bite of his sandwich.

"Not at first. Not until the baby starts moving around."

"You're probably right," he agreed. "We just have to choose which apartment we'll live in."

"That's a tough one," I said.

"Not really. I can move in here."

"Really? Just like that? You're not going to fight for your place?" I asked, a little surprised.

"No. You're Italian. You're more attached to places than I am."

"The Irish aren't attached to places?"

"I don't know. But apparently I'm only half-Irish, remember? Who knows what Thaddeus is."

Frowning slightly, I put down the French fry I had been munching on. "Oh, right. I forgot. You could find out, though. In Maine."

Birch placed his sandwich on the brown, unbleached wax paper it had been wrapped in. "Can we please table

151

that topic for now and stay on task here?"

"Sure," I replied, contrite. I had no business pushing him to meet his biological father, just because I had some idealistic fantasy about Birch's original family trinity being made whole once again.

"How's this for an idea," Birch was saying. "What if we stay here in your place, but we redecorate, to make it both of ours?"

Wiping my mouth with my napkin, I leaned back in my chair for a moment, considering. I tried to picture what the apartment would look like with Birch's things and mine commingled under one roof. "It could work," I said slowly.

"Good. Good. We're getting a lot accomplished today."

"Now we just have to figure out how to get you out of the sanctuary for a week so we can run away together for a little while."

"I'll manage," Birch replied.

Birch and I spent the next few days sorting things out at our respective jobs, endeavoring to free up at least a week for the two of us to spend alone together. When I returned to work on Tuesday, Sally and Yolanda displayed great concern, not only for my purple lip, but for my general behavior over the past two weeks. I told them that I'd been sick, and that I had fallen, and that my father was having a difficult time as he always did around the anniversary of my mother's death.

"Well, what about Birch?" Yolanda was asking after work Thursday night. They had insisted we go out to dinner to get caught up, and of course they picked McFarland's. I prayed that Birch's father would rely on his manager tonight and not make an appearance himself.

"Birch is fine," I answered. "We're doing really well, actually. I've been talking to Dwight, trying to figure out how to get some time off next week. Birch wants us to get away together somewhere. Maine or something."

"Really?" Yolanda said.

"Do you think he's going to propose?" Sally chimed in.

Taking a sip of my water, I looked at them both for a moment before answering. "He . . . well, he sort of already has."

"What? When? How?" They were asking, excitedly stumbling over one another's questions.

I sketched them a quick version of Birch's proposal, such as it was. "I don't really care what we do, as long as it's not a big church wedding," I explained.

"Oh? Why not? It'd be beautiful, with you in a gorgeous white dress and roses everywhere," Yolanda breathed.

Sally, ever practical, cut in, "Get married in the spring. Daffodils will be in season. It'll be cheap. Then you can spend more on the food."

"That's true," Yolanda agreed. "But with your restaurant connections, I'll bet you can get the reception catered for a really decent price."

Listening to them plan the wedding I'd never wanted, I smiled. They sounded like my mother might have. I let them design my dress and debate the merits of various local bands before I repeated, "I'm not having a wedding." They both stopped chattering and glared at me as I insisted, "City Hall will be perfectly sufficient."

"Sufficient! Well, how romantic is that?" Yolanda cried. "Ideally, you're only going to do this once. Is that how you want to remember your wedding day?"

"Honestly, the marriage license, the city-hall ceremony, they're just formalities to me. I'll be happy with the two of us being alone together, promising to take care of each

other," I told them. It was the same thing I'd told Birch and
I mostly believed it. But the truth was that part of me was
just not prepared give myself wholeheartedly, and officially,
to something that might not last. It's not that I thought I'd
find someone better than Birch. That wasn't it at all. It was
a self-protection mechanism that would insulate me just a
little from the pain if it didn't work out; if he left, for whatever reason.

"Your family is pretty religious," Sally said. "Aren't they
going to be pretty upset?"

"That's putting it mildly," I replied as my tongue in-
voluntarily pressed against the inside of my swollen lip.

We finished eating and before long I'd managed to turn
the conversation in a different direction. Longing to make
an escape, I glanced at my watch and told them I needed to
get home. When I reached the exit and was preparing to
leave, I felt a hand on my shoulder. Turning around, I saw
the unsmiling face of Birch's father. "Mr. McFarland," I
stammered.

"Aida. Could you step into my office a moment?" he
asked, his eyebrows rising slightly when he saw my face.

"Well . . . I . . . was just leaving."

"Just for a moment," he said, spinning on his heel. He
apparently assumed I'd follow him. I supposed I had no
choice. We made our way to the back of the bar into an
oak-paneled room. As we passed Yolanda and Sally on the
way, I just shrugged in reply to their questioning glances.
Will closed the door behind me and motioned for me to sit
down. After he took a seat behind his desk, he looked at me
for a moment before he began to speak.

"How's Birch? What happened to your mouth?" he
began abruptly.

Swallowing my discomfort, I offered bravely, "I fell," I

lied. It was getting easier. "And maybe you should call Birch and find out for yourself how he's doing."

I watched his pale green eyes glance down at the desk before they flew swiftly up to stare at my face again.

"He's hurt," I said. When Will didn't answer, when he just kept staring at me, I could think of nothing else to do except to keep talking. "It wasn't fair of you to unload all of that and walk out the way you did. He has a right to feel the way he does. Just because he has doubts about the Church doesn't mean you failed him. He's not some faithless atheist, you know. And you know what, Mr. McFarland? Even if he were he'd still be a good person. He's the most decent human being I know, and you taught him that, you and Glenda, not the Church."

I stopped suddenly and looked away as my hand flew to my face, trying to hide the tears that threatened to fall. I wiped quickly at my eyes with the back of my hand and forced my gaze back to Mr. McFarland's stony face. Still he said nothing.

"I'm sorry, Mr. McFarland. I . . . I overstepped my bounds. But, well, I think you know I'm right," I said, clearing my throat as I rose from the uncomfortable wooden chair. I watched him nod at me.

"That's it?" I asked loudly. "Don't you have anything to say? Did you call me in here just for a status report? Look, if there's something you'd like to say to your son I suggest you get on with it."

"My son? I thought Glenda explained it all. He's not my son."

"And I thought I explained it all just now. He *is* your son. You raised him. And do you know what else?" I was talking so quickly now and seemed unable to stop myself even though I desperately wanted to. "In a matter of months he's going to be raising your grandson. Or grand-daughter. So you figure out how to make peace and you talk to him," I finished abruptly, collapsing back into the chair. What had I just done?

"What? You're . . . oh, my God. He's going to be a father?"

"He was planning on telling you himself," I said. At least that was my impression, I added to myself. "I didn't plan on seeing you, on telling you. I should go."

Feeling ridiculously awkward, I stood up again. I wasn't sorry for anything I'd said to him, but this was no way for him to find out he was going to be a grandfather. As I slipped out the door, Will did not try to stop me. I ran out the back entrance of the bar in order to avoid seeing my friends again. When I arrived home, Birch was in my living room, reading the paper. I gently pulled it out of his hand. I sat next to him, not looking at him.

"I'm an ass," I began. "I ran into your dad at the pub and he asked me to come into his office. He wanted to know how you were doing and . . . well, I got a little emotional, and I . . . I told him about the baby, Birch."

"Damn it, Aida! Why? What were you thinking?" he yelled.

I could only shrug. "Are you going to try and talk to him?" I asked, tentatively peeking at him.

"No. Not yet. I don't know. I just want to get the hell out of here for a while. We both need to clear our heads a little, don't you think?"

Nodding, it was then that I noticed the two plane tickets on the coffee table, waiting for their turn. "Birch?" I asked, picking them up. "We're going to Maine on Sunday?"

"If you managed to get next week off."

"I still have to finalize a few things with Dwight, but I think it'll be fine."

"I have no plans to look up Thaddeus, Aida, so stop looking like that. It's just that, you originally had your heart set on that rocky beach with the ocean on one side and the pine trees on the other, so . . ."

"Thank you," I whispered, throwing my arms around his neck and kissing him wildly.

On Sunday morning, Birch and I found ourselves flying east toward the morning sun, on a plane to Portland, Maine. From there we would rent a car and drive up the coast and find a place to stay. We chatted at first, then settled in with our own projects. I began reading one of the books Glenda had given me, and Birch pulled out the first of the letters from Thaddeus.

We hadn't spoken again about my conversation with his father, and as far as I knew, he hadn't spoken with him at all before we left. I had briefly considered calling my brother to tell him I'd be out of the state for a week, just so someone from my family would know I had gone, but I couldn't do it. I couldn't make the first move. None of them had tried to contact me, to see how I was doing. That made me sick to my stomach.

Glancing at Birch out of the corner of my eye, I saw him gripping a yellowing piece of paper with both hands. His face seemed tight, anxious. His jaw twitched.

I furtively returned my gaze to my reading. Abruptly, he stuffed the letter back in his knapsack, unbuckled his seat belt, and headed for the restroom at the back of the plane. Sighing heavily as the plane sliced through thick gray clouds, I resisted the urge to peruse the letter myself. I instinctively, irrationally, felt closer to Thaddeus than to Will, and found myself hoping that if Birch reunited with either of them, it would be with his biological father. Will, to me, seemed too much like my own family right now, in all the worst ways—unbending, heavy-handed, too Catholic. In my imagination, Thaddeus was a free spirit, an idealist, who had unfairly been denied the chance to know his son. That was what I personally had the hardest time forgiving Glenda for. I couldn't imagine having kept my baby a secret from Birch. It had been torture to keep silent for as long as I had.

After about five minutes, Birch returned to his seat, his eyes red, puffy. Reaching out to hold his hand, I opened my mouth to speak, but before words could emerge, Birch said crisply, "Don't, Aida. I'm sorry, but don't say anything about this right now. I promise you, we'll talk about it all, but please, just later, okay?"

Nodding, I withdrew my hand and pretended to go back to my reading. Birch folded his arms across his chest and closed his eyes, but I knew he wouldn't sleep. Feeling powerless to help, but desperate to ease his pain in some way, I sat in tortured, indecisive silence for a moment, tempted to press him to talk about things so that I could try to make him feel better. I hated it when he wouldn't let me in.

Instead of prodding further, I actually began reading the words in front of me, discovering line by line the individual, explosive, visceral spirituality of Walt Whitman. He placed as much emphasis on the body as the mind and the spirit. All were equally significant and vital to one's experience as a human being, a human being with a divine nature.

I finished his lengthy *Song of Myself* before we landed, and at the end of the poem, found a note scribbled by Glenda: "Aida, you'll find as you read the intro to world religions that there are parallels between Whitman's writing and Eastern religion, but his thought shaped it into something entirely unique. If you like Whitman, don't overlook the writings of the transcendentalists, particularly Emerson.

Keep reading with an open heart. Enjoy."

I smiled, thrilled at acquiring a whole new approach to spiritual perception. Poetry, essays, philosophy, all offering the opportunity for the scrutiny of an entire universe of inspiration. I relished the invitation to explore the flavor of each school of thought, rather than being force-fed a single view and being told all others were simply invalid. I felt myself opening, like one of those time-elapsed films of a ripening bud, unfurling itself petal by petal.

As we landed, I nudged Birch. He opened his eyes, raising his eyebrows as he noticed my face. "What are you glowing about?" he asked. "Were you thinking about the baby?"

"Actually, no. I've . . . I don't know. I was reading some of the things your mother gave me. Birch, she's given me . . . a new way to seek," I told him. "That sounds kind of strange, doesn't it?"

"Not at all," he replied. "It sounds like just the sort of thing she does to people." He paused for a moment, then added, "Myself included." Hoisting his backpack over his shoulder, he rose from his seat and we joined the stream of people exiting the plane. Walking through the airport to claim our luggage, I enjoyed the warmth and weight of Birch's hand on the back of my neck, and allowed myself the luxury of feeling lucky. I actually contemplated the possibility that we could be out walking someplace when we were in our eighties, and I'd still be smiling at the strong, warm hand resting gently on the back of my neck.

Before long, we'd slogged through the tedious details of collecting our luggage and renting a car and perusing the map, and finally, we were headed toward the coast in a rented Jeep. It seemed as though Birch was reluctant to drive anything else. "It's February. We're in Maine," he explained. "We're going to want something that can handle bad weather."

By early evening, we were checking into a bed and breakfast in Camden. Our room overlooked a small harbor to the right, and to the left, mountains whose foothills spilled gently toward the ocean. I'd read someplace on a sign as we drove into town: "Camden. Where the mountains meet the ocean." It was beautifully true. This would be the perfect place to say our vows.

After a late supper at a local brewpub, we retired to our room, complete with fireplace and claw foot tub. Birch made a fire, while I ran the bath water. It was late, and I was tired, but I couldn't resist soaking in that tub. We climbed in together, and I leaned back against Birch's chest and sighed. The warm gold cross he still wore pressed into my back.

"Aren't you going to ask me?" Birch asked.

"What?"

"About the letter I read on the plane."

"I figured you'd tell me about it in your own time," I said softly.

"How uncharacteristically patient of you."

"Well?"

I felt his chest expand as he took a deep breath before beginning. "It was the saddest thing I've ever read. It was Thaddeus' reply to my mother's letter telling him that she was pregnant, that he was the father, and that she was now married to someone else. He was devastated that she'd gotten married before she told him, forcing him into a position of home-wrecker if he tried to return for her, and me. Apparently she'd begged him not to do that. He demanded that she call him as soon as I was born. He insisted that she write, sending pictures and telling him everything about me."

Pausing for a moment, Birch cleared his throat. "He . . . Aida, he begged her to tell me about him, as soon as I was old enough to understand. He begged her to let him see me, to visit me as I got older. He wanted to have a relationship with me. I guess she'd said right from the beginning that she thought it would be too traumatic for me."

"God, Birch," I cut in. "I can't believe she waited so long to tell you. I wonder if she ever would have, if your father hadn't told you first."

"I don't know. She thought she was protecting me, I know. She thought she was protecting everyone. But, damn it, I don't know what I'd do if you ever tried to keep our baby from me, no matter what the situation or your intentions."

"I'd never do that."

"I know," he said, kissing the top of my head. "I wonder why Thaddeus never came back anyway, despite what my mother wanted. I would have."

"I don't know. But at least you know that . . . well, that you were wanted."

"You know what he said in that letter? He said, 'I don't know how it's possible for me to love someone I don't even know, but I do.' He loved me before I was even born. Now I know what that feels like," he said, placing his large hand on my belly.

"Have you changed your mind?" I asked. "About wanting to find him?"

"I'm still considering that. I think I want to get through the rest of the letters first."

"You know I think you should see him, right?"

"I know, Aida."

After our bath, I fell into bed, exhausted, and for a few moments before I fell asleep, I watched Birch's face as he sat in front of the fire, reading the letters.

Chapter Nine

Over breakfast the next morning, we didn't talk about the letters. We planned a day of exploring the small town. My nausea had nearly disappeared, and I was delighted that there was a chance I might not be vomiting for the first two or three months of my pregnancy, as I had read was common.

I had a hearty breakfast of oatmeal and fruit. Birch had the same, but had to request that it not be made with milk, that no butter be added. He didn't seem to mind having to double-check things and make special requests, but it seemed like a difficult way to acquire food. I was relieved that he hadn't expected me to give up dairy and eggs as well as meat. I didn't have a problem with a vegetarian pregnancy, but a vegan one would have been challenging for someone raised in a household where Parmesan cheese was served at nearly every meal. I was also perfectly happy to put off thinking about how to raise a vegetarian or vegan child until we got nearer to that reality. Although, I comforted myself, for Birch it would be second nature; I would be the one who needed lessons.

As we lingered over our coffee, I asked him, "Did you ever resent that your mother raised you as a vegan? I mean, you never really had a choice, did you? Did you think that was fair?"

Birch looked at me over the top of his mug for a moment before answering. As he took a sip of the steaming coffee, I wondered how often he'd been asked that same question.

"Well," he finally began, "when I was little, she simply told me that animals are our friends. That philosophy was just a part of everything we did. She never killed a spider in the house; we'd trap it and set it free outside. She was always taking in strays and finding them homes. Things like that. As I grew older, we talked about how all living things have their place in the universe. Now that I think about it, teaching me veganism was her way of teaching me her notion of religion—or spirituality, anyway. I can't remember ever wanting to eat meat. I always thought it was kind of gross that my dad did, but of course I never said anything to him."

Swallowing some of my sweet, milky coffee, I interjected, "That must have been confusing to have your parents maintain such different viewpoints."

Birch shrugged. "She didn't eat meat. He did. He went to church, she didn't. They disagreed about a lot of fundamentals, and we all just tried to respect one another. They were both pretty good at teaching me that. Anyway, when I was twelve or thirteen, I played a lot of basketball with a group of kids after school. They always stopped someplace for a burger on the way home. Of course I never did. The guys gave me a little bit of a hard time over it, but it wasn't that big of a deal. But it did get me to thinking that if so many other people were living their lives a certain way, then how could it be so wrong?"

"So, did you confront your mother?"

Nodding, Birch answered, "I did. What she said surprised me. She said that it wasn't wrong for everyone. She just knew it was wrong for her, and it was time for me to decide whether or not it was wrong for me. Determined that I should make a fully informed decision, and gauging that I was old enough to handle it, my mother decided to take me on a couple of tours. We went to a commercial dairy farm, and I saw firsthand the conditions the animals lived in. We went to a slaughterhouse, and I saw how cows were killed and turned into those burgers my buddies were eating. I'll spare you all the details, but we made several such trips. And I'm glad we did. I ended up making the same decision she did, and I probably would have even without our little field trips, but now I know I'll never second-guess myself, or her. My choices were not made in ignorance, and I'm grateful to my mother for that."

Looking down into my mug, I said nothing in reply as I thought of all the veal I had consumed in my life.

"Aida," his voice interrupted my thoughts. "Look, you do what's right for you. I'm sorry if I sounded preachy at all. I was just trying to be honest. You asked. I answered. We'll figure out together what's right for our child, all right?"

"Okay," I said, meeting his gaze at last. "You're right. We'll figure it out together."

After finishing our coffee, we bundled up and wandered the downtown streets of Camden before hopping in the rented Jeep and setting off for a drive. We meandered north, with the ocean on our right. Suddenly, Birch pulled onto a narrow drive that stretched toward a rocky beach. Picking our way over snow that slowly gave way to sand and stone, holding hands and only slipping a little, we stood with the ocean splashing just yards away. Birch stood next to me, smiling, and I turned around, noticing first the mountains rolling toward the coast, and then the stand of snow-covered pine trees across the drive. Pine trees, rocky beach, ocean. We had it all. The sun shone brightly overhead, and a frigid breeze swirled around us. But we were layered for the weather, and giddy in love besides, and I felt warm from the inside out. Returning my gaze to Birch's face, I grinned.

"Are you ready?" he asked me.

"I think so. You start," I said, blushing a bit. My legs felt loose and shaky suddenly.

"No, you first. This was your idea."

"Okay, okay," I said. I took a deep breath, struggling to remember the words of the vows I'd been composing in my head over the past few days. Holding both of his gloved hands in my own, I cleared my throat, and waited for the surging emotions inside me to be molded into words. Finally, as I stared into the earthy depths of Birch's eyes, I was able to begin. "I, Aida Angelina Benedetto, promise that I will always, always, love you, Birch Michael McFarland. I will feed you in every way, body, mind, and spirit. I . . ."

I faltered, stumbling over the riot of love and joy and fear in me. "I'll be faithful. I'll respect you. I won't hold grudges. I . . . I promise to trust you. To trust in your love for me." Looking down at my feet, I sniffled back a few tears. I had wanted to be so much more poetic, eloquent, sweeping. Feeling Birch's gloved hand on my chin, I looked up at his face. The sun teased the golden curls that escaped his red cotton hat. His eyes crinkled at the corners, and his mouth had burst open into a full, toothy smile.

"That was quite a formal speech, Aida Angelina Benedetto. Now it's my turn." He swept me into his arms and spun me in a circle, shouting to the pine boughs, to the ocean spray, to me, "I love you, Aida! I love you!" As I laughed from the pit of my stomach, he placed me back on the ground and sprinkled my face with whispered words and kisses. "You will never be alone. I will face the world, in all its glory and all its pain, by your side, forever and ever. Amen."

"Amen," I replied.

Over the next couple of days, Birch and I explored Maine's coast, spending a considerable amount of time enjoying Acadia National Park. We looked for whales, we watched the waves crash on the rocks, we talked about redecorating my apartment, about the future, our future.

One evening, as we were returning to Camden after another drive up the coast, I said to Birch, "So, besides this trip, we didn't really get each other any gifts for tying the knot, so to speak."

"Were you expecting something more?"

"No, but I had an idea. Tell me something about you that no one else really knows, or at least, something about you that I don't know."

"Hell, Aida. I think you know just about everything at this point," he said, rubbing the stubble on his chin with the back of his hand. He paused for a few long moments, then began, "Okay, I have something. But, it's nothing big."

"That's fine. What is it?"

"Whenever I'm driving on a toll road, usually when I'm headed out to see my Uncle Sean, I always stop at the manual toll booths instead of the automatic ones, even if I have change."

"Why? That's what the automatic lanes are for. Why take the time?"

"Purely for the sake of human contact, Aida. Just to look at another person's face and say, 'have a good day.' No one cares about just taking the time to talk to people anymore. It pisses me off."

"Yeah? I never knew that," I said, grinning.

"Now it's your turn. Tell me something about you that I don't know."

I shrugged. I didn't have anything good. I possessed a few little odd tendencies, but nothing with a moral purpose. "I don't know," I replied. "I need more time."

"No fair. I didn't get more time. Spill it."

"It's boring."

"I don't care, Aida," Birch said firmly.

"Fine. I crochet."

"You crochet? Like Nonna? I've never seen you crochet anything."

"I've never finished a single thing. My mother taught me just before she died. Every couple of years, I'll start a project then shove it back in my closet, half done."

"Well, why don't you ever finish anything? Make me a scarf or something?"

"I don't know. I just . . . I don't know," I finished lamely. It was the truth, though. I always wanted to make something, to be able to utilize the skill my mother had taught me. "I was never able to finish anything before she died. Maybe it's just easier to leave things unfinished. It's less final."

"You should make something for the baby," Birch suggested hopefully.

I shrugged. "Maybe," I said as I turned to look out the window.

"God, I can just see you in fifty years," Birch said through his laughter, "rocking in the chair like your Nonna, crocheting me a sweater."

"Knock it off," I told him, pretending to smile. The last thing I wanted was to end up like Nonna. She seemed so benign, creaking back and forth in the old rocking chair, crocheting a little red sweater for her great-grandson, but the whole time she was watching, judging, controlling. As the bare limbs of hardwoods whizzed by, I racked my brain for a change in subject. "So, it looks like you and your mother are going to be all right," I began. "What about your father? Or fathers, I should say."

Glancing away from the road for a moment, Birch looked at me with a small frown on his lips, and I knew he'd noticed my desire to shift the conversation away from myself. He turned back toward the road and answered, "I haven't made up my mind about Thaddeus yet."

"Well, I have," I said quietly. "How many times is he going to have to go through this? He was denied having a relationship with you. I think that Thaddeus should get to have a relationship with this baby." When Birch didn't respond immediately, I added gently, "It's not just your decision to make, you know."

"Oh, really?" Birch answered. "Just like it wasn't my decision to tell my dad about the baby, either. You're just taking matters into your own hands, aren't you?" he replied crisply.

"Somebody has to," I muttered, turning to look out the window again.

"What's that supposed to mean?" Birch was shouting now, shifting his attention between the road and me.

"Well, whenever anything comes up that you have to deal with emotionally, you just pull away from everything, from me especially. And I don't know what's going on in your head, but apparently you mull things over indefinitely, while everyone is left hanging. I think you're just waiting for it all to go away so you won't have to deal with it." Looking over, I saw that his lips were tight, his jaw clenched, but I continued, "Your parents are splitting up, and you've got two people with arguably equal rights as grandfathers to this baby. Maybe Will will end up being just like my family, stubborn and bitter. Who knows? But Thaddeus . . . he deserves a chance to be elated."

"Okay," he said briskly.

"What?"

"Okay. You're right. I've been stalling. We'll look him up tomorrow."

Surmising that my nod would suffice as the conversation's punctuation, I, with some difficulty, avoided opening my mouth again, and we drove on in silence back to our lodgings.

Later that evening, as Birch and I curled up together in bed, I asked him about the letters from Thaddeus. "Birch, were there a lot of letters? And when was the last time Thaddeus wrote to Glenda about you?"

"There were more than I expected. I didn't count. Some were addressed directly to me, some were to my mother. Judging from his familiar, friendly tone, I'm guessing that there were a lot of letters that he wrote to her that didn't concern me, that she chose not to show me. There are more from when I was younger, and then fewer as I got older. But he still corresponded regularly. The last letter is dated just last year."

"Really? What does he write about? Is it all just questions about you, or 'tell Birch this or that,' or what?"

"It's killing you that I haven't let you read any, isn't it? I'm surprised you've waited this long to pester me about them."

"Me, too," I grumbled. "I don't know why you have to keep everything from me."

He could be so reserved about things. I knew it was a private matter, but that was difficult for me to accept.

169

There were precious few secrets in my family. Everybody knew everything about everyone, and we didn't pretend things were different. The whole extended family knew that my cousin Carmine's second wife was cheating on him again, and she knew that we all knew. Years ago, when my mom's sister, my Aunt Beatrice, was being knocked around by the jerk she was married to, my dad and a few of his buddies paid him a very unfriendly visit, and husband soon became ex-husband. Everyone knew it was because he was afraid of my dad. Our family was brutally candid. I had always been sort of proud of that, but it occurred to me just then that fewer people got hurt in Birch's family. At least that's what I thought until I looked over and saw Birch leaning back against the pillows, staring at the ceiling, his face contorted with emotion.

"Birch, what is it?" I whispered, leaning over, caressing his cheek with my fingers.

He grabbed my hand and sat up. "It was never my intention to keep things from you. I've just been trying to keep them from me. I read the letters. But I'm trying to keep my distance, I guess. It's . . . Aida, it's just so confusing. I don't even know anymore where my loyalties should lie. I still don't know if I should be seeking out Thaddeus."

"Then why are you?"

"I'm not doing it for me. I'm doing it for the baby, and Thaddeus. Whether I like it or not, they're related. Family always counts for something, even in a mess like this, right? Isn't that what you've been trying to tell me?"

Not answering, I left it at that and we didn't speak about it again. The drive to Bangor the next morning was a quiet one. We arrived around noon and after some searching through a local phone book and map, we happened upon Thaddeus' modest home in an older part of town. It was a

170

small, old home sided with dark brown clapboard that looked as if it had been well kept. As we sat in the Jeep, a light snow began to fall. Thick, fluffy flakes plopped like dumplings onto the ground. They piled up into a clean blanket atop the soiled and trodden snow that already spread across the tidy yards of the neighborhood.

"Well?" I prodded quietly. "We don't have to do this now, Birch," I said when he didn't answer.

"I know."

I had been staring at the dark green front door of the house. An arched door, it had a circular window set near the top and I was watching it to see if anyone inside would notice us. Finally, though, I tore my gaze from the window and glanced at Birch's face. A few springy strands of hair peeked out from underneath his red snow hat and his prominent, square jaw seemed somehow softer than usual. With his lips tucked into a frown, he seemed to my searching gaze boyish and shy, afraid.

"Come on," I told him, reaching out to hold his hand. "It'll be fine. I promise. I have a good feeling about this."

He, too, had been eyeing the front door, and he turned toward me as I said this. "Really?" he asked quickly. He sounded unexpectedly hopeful. Birch placed a lot more stock in having a certain "feeling" about something than I did. I had gotten the reaction I'd hoped for.

"I sure do. Come on. Are you ready?" I asked him.

"No, but okay. Let's go."

Traversing the short front yard in several quick steps, we were soon standing on a wide white porch. Birch raised his hand and rapped three quick knocks onto the green door. It opened almost immediately. We were greeted by a tall, slender man with longish, wavy brown hair that was tousled but not untidy. His eyes were blue-gray. These features aside, I recognized almost instantly the distinctive set of the jaw, the angular chin, the arch of the eyebrows, and suddenly the smile that broke out across this stranger's face.

"I knew you would do it," the man declared in a warm, deep voice. "You found me, Birch. She finally told you and you found me." His voice broke here and there in the space of those short sentences, and his eyes were bright with tears. He leaned across the threshold and wrapped Birch in his arms. Birch, I noticed, received the embrace but failed to return it. Holding my breath, I waited to see what his first words to his father would be.

"He told me, not her," Birch uttered.

Thaddeus stepped back. "Oh, I see," he said softly. Then he turned to look at me. "You must be Aida. Glenda wrote me about you."

I smiled to think that Glenda would have written to Thaddeus about me. As I turned toward Birch and noticed the grim line of his mouth, I could only wonder what thoughts were tumbling through his head.

"Please, please come in and sit down," Thaddeus said as he escorted us into a small foyer that spilled into a cheery living room. Milky-white walls received the warm glow of the oak floor. A sage tweed sofa and chair were paired with a beautiful rocking chair with chocolate-colored upholstery. Inside a small fireplace, a fire crackled and spat. Having removed our outerwear, we shifted ourselves into the living room. I sank back into the cushions of the sofa, and Birch perched on the arm next to me.

As Thaddeus sat down in the rocking chair, he called out, "Nell? Nellie, we have company!"

Swallowing hard, I felt my heart ache a little. He was married. Part of me had been fantasizing that Glenda could somehow be reunited with the man I believed was her true love.

"Nell!" Thaddeus shouted once more. Just then, I heard a clicking on the hardwood floors and watched in disbelief as an enormous, soot-black Great Dane strolled into the room. She waltzed directly over to Birch, placed her mighty paws upon his shoulders and licked his face three times. One side of Birch's mouth jerked up into half a smile, and he scratched Nell behind her ears and cooed at her softly. The massive dog then casually sniffed and licked my hand before returning to her master's side. "I apologize if she is a bit forward," Thaddeus said. "She's usually much more shy."

"It's fine," Birch said. "She's beautiful."

Hearing Birch's voice now, I realized that Nell had softened him. With the dog in the room, he was instantly more relaxed. Birch and Thaddeus began an easy exchange centering on the dog, the shelter from which Thaddeus had adopted her, and Birch's own work with City Sanctuary back home. When that conversation dwindled to a slow halt, and Thaddeus had removed himself from the room to make some tea for us, I whispered to Birch, "Well? What do you think? You look a lot alike. And he's so sweet. Don't you think so?"

"Aida, I don't know what to think. Please don't look at me like that. I'm doing the best I can. I want to like him, too. I do like him. It's just that—"

"Just that what?" Thaddeus interrupted as he returned from the kitchen. He had padded as silently as a doe back into the living room, even carrying a tray laden with three mugs of tea and a bowl of sugar. Neither one of us had heard him approach.

Clearing his throat as Thaddeus handed him his tea, Birch faltered, "Just that . . . well—"

"It's quite all right, Birch. Feel free to be as candid with me as you like."

As I sipped my own tea, I listened to Birch sigh heavily before he began again. "I read the letters you sent to my mother, at least those she chose to share with me." Birch placed his mug on the coffee table, rose from the sofa arm and began to pace in front of the fireplace. "It really seemed as if you wanted to be a part of my life. What I want to know is why you never tried to meet me, in spite of what my mother said." Birch stopped pacing and faced his father. "Why didn't you ever come for me?" he asked quietly.

Watching his face, I saw him fight to keep his jaw taut. I knew he was trying not to cry, and with his lips pressed together, and brow furrowed, he looked to me like a little boy trying to be brave. I saw him as a five-year-old, asking the same question, and my heart broke to think of all the time that had been lost between them. I hoped fervently that Thaddeus had a good answer for him.

Now it was Thaddeus' turn to sigh. His eyes were cast downward and it seemed to be with great effort that he managed to lift his gaze to his son's face. "Nothing has brought me greater shame than the fact that I failed you. I should have forced my way into your life, despite your mother's wishes. I have my reasons—or excuses, anyway—as to why I did not.

"I told myself I was respecting Glenda's notion of what was best for you. She wanted you to have a stable, normal upbringing. I had nothing of the sort to offer a child. My life at the time didn't lend itself to the sort of stability that Glenda required, and that you deserved. But was the life she wanted for you better than the chaos of having two fathers? Maybe it would have been better for you to have known about me, and for me to risk jeopardizing the relationship between your parents. I thought that I had little to offer you personally. But I did have honesty, and love, and it's not always enough, I know, but it seems as if I should have tried to make it be enough. Anyway, I'm rambling now. I knew I'd never be able to explain it well enough. But you're here now. Why? She never told you? Was she ever going to, I wonder? How did you come to know about me?"

"My father . . . that is, Will, and I . . . well, we had a disagreement about the Church. He's a very staunch Catholic and raised me in the same manner. I'm sure my mother told you about all that. Anyway, I said some things that were, in his eyes unforgivable, and he basically just blurted out that I was not his son. Then my mother filled in some of the gaps."

Shaking his head, Thaddeus said, "That must have been painful. For all of you." He paused a moment and cleared his throat. He sipped some tea, and then asked, "And having learned the truth, you decided to come find me?" Thaddeus asked.

"Not exactly. It's . . . well, it's Aida, really," Birch stammered.

"I'm pregnant," I announced, "and we both agreed that as the baby's natural grandfather, you should know."

When I had finished speaking, I saw that Birch had turned to stare into the fire. Maybe he hadn't expected me to plunge in with the news, but, as I had told him before, this wasn't all about just him. He didn't get to make all the decisions. Thaddeus just stood staring at me, eyes wide, and he finally began to smile. I moved across the room to hug him, and as I did so, I whispered in his ear, "You deserve a chance at having a relationship with this child." I felt him smile against my cheek before I turned toward Birch, who was still facing the fire.

175

"Let's go," he said quietly, without looking at me. He then wrenched himself from his position in front of the fire and regarded his father. "I'm . . . sorry," he croaked.

"You've nothing to be sorry for, Birch. Not a thing," Thaddeus told him.

"Do you think it might be possible for us to meet again before we go back home? We only have a couple of days left out here, and I thought, maybe, that we could . . . catch up," Birch said, shifting his weight from one foot to the other.

"I'd like that very much," Thaddeus replied.

"I'll call you tomorrow, then," Birch said. He paused a moment, then stuck out his hand, which Thaddeus grabbed firmly and shook.

We left quietly and drove back through the snow to our hotel in Camden. Birch said little on the way back, but I was satisfied with the way things had gone. The two men had each let their guard down enough to reveal the pain of the lost relationship and the hope of a new one.

"Are you all right?" I finally asked Birch when we returned to our hotel room.

"You've done it twice now, you know," he replied, avoiding my question and confusing me at the same time.

"Done what?"

"Told my father about the baby before I got a chance to," he replied as he flopped down on the patchwork quilt covering the bed.

His face was unreadable.

"Are you mad?" I whispered, fearful and defensive. "Because you really shouldn't be. You hesitate so much. Truth is for telling, Birch."

He looked away from me and stared up at the ceiling, his hands clasped behind his head. After chewing his bottom lip for a moment, he began slowly, "You know what, Aida? You spent years jerking me around before you finally came to your senses and realized that we are made for one another. Then you started messing around with my faith, making me question things, or at least making me admit that I had things to question. Now, my parents are no longer together, probably for good, and not only do I have an extra dad, but I'm going to be one, too."

"What's your point, Birch? It's not my fault that your mom slept with someone else before she married your dad," I said, standing at the foot of the bed with my arms folded across my chest. It sounded mean, the way I said it, and I instantly regretted having opened my mouth. Maybe it was because I was so prone to guilt that I was hypersensitive to anything that sounded like blame. It made me lash out and I was appalled at my own lack of self-censuring ability.

"Stop being so defensive. None of this is your fault, Aida. That's not what I mean. It's just that . . . you're some kind of bizarre catalyst. Before we were together, nothing happened. Now, everything is happening. You make things happen."

"I make things happen?" I asked, my voice deadpan with disbelief.

"You have powers. Just like your Nonna. Mysterious Italian powers," Birch said, looking at me with furrowed brows.

I couldn't read his demeanor, couldn't tell if he was angry or anxious or just plain sarcastic. "I'm *not* like Nonna. Stop saying that. Anyway, was it so much better when nothing happened?"

"It was easier," he said, returning his gaze to the ceiling.

"Maybe," was all I could say. Where was he going with all of this? I wrapped my arms even more tightly around myself to avoid gesticulating wildly. I began speaking more quickly. "You don't get to back out of this now. You're scared. You finally talked me into embracing all this despite my fears, and now you're the one who is running scared. Birch—"

"Aida, Aida. Shhh. Slow down. I'm not running any-where," he said as he sat up and moved closer to me. "I'm not backing out. Everything just got so chaotic so quickly. I just was hoping things would slow down a little, that's all. I just wondered what else you have in store for me."

Swallowing deliberately, I took a deep breath and sat down on the bed, facing him. "I know things are crazy, but now at least you've got two more people in your life to love and who are going to love you back—Thaddeus and the baby. Even more if you count my family, who will all even-tually remember that they love you, once they calm down."

"More love? That's what I'm getting out of all this?"

I nodded, perplexed by the whole exchange.

He reached across the bed and pulled me down next to him. "So can I get a little more love right now? This is sup-posed to be our honeymoon, isn't it?"

Chapter Ten

Later that evening, I decided to call home and check my messages. No one in my family knew that I had been going away this week, and I wondered if anyone had tried to contact me.

Listening to my messages, I was surprised to hear my sister-in-law Rosie's voice saying, "Aida, please call here when you can. Everything has been a mess since the thing with your dad. Marco's not speaking to him at all and Nonna won't leave Marc alone about it. She's worried about Pop. Anyway, how are you doing? Marc's been worried about you. He thinks you're mad at him, so he won't even try to call. Anyway, I don't care about the baptism. Marco asked your cousin Sophie to be godmother at the last minute. Call soon."

"Shit," I mumbled as I turned off my cell phone. Birch had fallen asleep in bed reading after a late dinner and early bath. He stirred as I cursed.

"What's up?" he asked, sitting up a little.

"Marco's not talking to Dad because of what he did, and Nonna won't leave Marco alone. She thinks he can patch everything up."

"See. More chaos. What are you going to do?"

"I'll call Marc when we get back. I'm in no hurry to rush back into that mess."

"Just so you know, you're not going to your dad's without me. I'm not going to let him haul off like that again."

"Birch, come on. It was a one-time thing."

"I don't care. I'm coming. Anyway, it's getting late. Why don't you get some sleep and worry about it tomorrow. Speaking of which, are you coming with me to Bangor tomorrow?"

Shaking my head, I scooted under the covers next to him. "No, I think you should go by yourself. Besides, I have so much reading I want to do. I think I'll just sit by the fire and catch up."

"Okay. Don't forget to eat. I worry you're not getting enough."

Birch rose with the sun the next morning, kissed me good-bye, and headed for Bangor. I lounged in bed for a while, went out for a light breakfast, and returned to the room by ten a.m. to begin my day of study. I was halfway through the overview of world religions that Glenda had given me, and was fascinated with what I had discovered about ancient goddess religions, eastern religion and philosophy, and the early Judeo-Christian religious institutions. I wasn't sure if it would have made any sense to me if I had taken a course like Glenda's when I was in college, but now I devoured every word.

When Birch arrived back in Camden, he found me asleep in front of a dwindling fire, propped up on the floor by several fluffy pillows. After kissing me awake, he scolded me for not having lunch, and we left the hotel in search of dinner. Over steaming bowls of tomato soup and hunks of onion-dill bread, Birch and I discussed his visit with Thaddeus.

"He wanted to know everything about my childhood," Birch was saying, "but I was more interested in all the places he's lived, in the work he's done. When I finally got around to talking about the present, he seemed really impressed with what I've accomplished at the sanctuary," he said, with a small, closed-mouthed smile.

"Does it please you to have made him proud?" I asked.

Birch shrugged and sipped soup from his spoon. "I guess."

"So what's next for you two?"

"We're going to keep in touch," Birch said, dunking his bread in his soup.

"Did he ask about your mom?" I asked.

"A little."

"Do you think they'll try to see each other?" I prodded gently.

Birch placed his spoon in the nearly empty soup bowl. "Look, I'm not as eager as you are to see my parents split up. It doesn't seem right to think of her with anyone else. Although, having spent just a little bit of time with Thaddeus, I can see how things could have been different. My mom and Thaddeus have so much in common. I can't help wondering what it would have been like growing up in that household. But that doesn't matter. The reality is that she is married to someone else. Anyway, let's talk about something else for now, okay?"

Nodding, I gave in. It would do me no good to keep pushing him, and it really wasn't my business anyway. I'd gotten what I wanted. Thaddeus would be in this baby's life, and Birch's as well. I could only hope that Glenda could also be part of the Thaddeus equation. "Well," I stammered, trying to think of another topic as Birch had requested, "tomorrow is our last full day here. What do you want to do?"

What we ended up doing was sleeping in, wandering around Camden and the surrounding area, shopping, eating, and trying not to think of the mutual familial messes that awaited us back in Middleton. The day flew by, and we found ourselves flying home on Sunday, before we'd even realized a full week had elapsed.

Middleton failed to welcome us upon our return. It was bitterly cold, windy, and relentlessly gray, the sky a cruel shade of steel. The snow by the roadsides looked polluted and ashen.

"So, here we are," Birch commented uselessly as we approached the front door of our building.

"Yeah, I'm not thrilled to be back, either," I replied. We silently trudged our luggage up the stairs and stood outside the door of my apartment. Birch glanced up the stairs, in the direction of his own door.

"I don't want to go," he said.

"Just go toss your suitcase upstairs, grab whatever you need for work tomorrow, and come back to me. We'll figure out how fast we can get you moved in here."

"Okay. I'll be back in a few minutes."

Once inside my own apartment, I shoved my bags into my bedroom, poured myself a glass of water, sat in my mother's chair, and started listening to the messages on the answering machine. Two were from Rosie again, one was from my assistant at work, one each from Sally and Yolanda, and to my surprise there was one message from Nonna. I had never actually received a message from her before. Under normal circumstances, I saw her at least once a week, and she was not much of a phone talker besides. I replayed it for Birch when he returned.

"Listen. It's from Nonna," I said, as Birch flopped down on the sofa.

"Aida? This is Nonna. Are you there? It's Nonna. I'm calling to tell you to talk to your brother. He needs to make

182

peace with his father. You came between them. Now you have to fix it. And I'm praying for your soul and for your baby. I put you on the prayer line. *Ciao.*"

"Can you believe her? She couldn't care less about me, or my relationship with Pop. It's all about Marco. Always has been with her," I railed.

"I wouldn't go that far," Birch soothed. "She just doesn't understand you anymore."

"She never did."

"And she's worried about your dad. He was alone enough before. Now neither of his children is talking to him."

Frowning, I pressed my lips together and tried not to yell. "I would talk to Pop, but he doesn't want me anymore. He made that clear. And why should I care if Marco is pissed at him? I'd be mad if Marco *wasn't* pissed at Pop for what he did to me. But why isn't Marco calling me himself?"

"I don't know. So . . . what are you going to do? Are you going to talk to Marco?"

"Marco doesn't hold grudges. He's not going to stay mad at Pop. I'll just call Rosie and tell her that. She can tell Nonna whatever she wants to."

"That's your plan? Talk to the middleman?" Birch asked.

"What? What are you talking about?"

"Why let Ro be your intermediary? You need to sort this out with your father, your grandmother, and your brother. In person."

"You've got to be kidding. You're going to lecture me about this? None of them wants to see me. Nobody wants to work anything out with me," I explained slowly, as if he were a child.

"Who's holding grudges now? You know, Marco warned me about this, a long time ago. He said that nobody holds grudges like a Sicilian, and to watch out for you in particular. Anyway, don't you want to work things out with them? If not for you, then for the baby? Isn't that why you were so intent on my meeting Thaddeus?"

"This is different, Birch," I said, sighing in what I hoped was a dismissive manner. "Marco said that about me? When?"

"Don't change the subject, Aida. It's not different, and you know it."

"Damn it! Can't you just drop it?" I had started to yell and there was no stopping me now. I went on, louder and faster, "I wanted you to find your long-lost father because he missed out on your whole life, on you. My family has known me my whole life and now they wish I was the long-lost one. Get it?"

"You don't really believe that, do you?" his quiet voice seemed like a whisper in the aftermath of my tirade.

"Look, my family is a completely different kind of crazy than your family, all right? Stop trying to analyze them as if they could be made sense of. I'm going to talk to Rosie and if anyone else wants to talk to me, they know where to find me."

With that, I spun on my heel and stormed into the bedroom to call my sister-in-law. Luckily, Rosie had given me her cell phone number, so there was no chance that I'd have to speak with Marco. I left a message on Rosie's voice mail, saying that I'd been out of town, and to just give Marco time to cool off, that it usually doesn't take long. After I hung up, I returned to the living room to find Birch still sitting on the sofa. I plopped down next to him, but he didn't speak.

"Are you finished?" he asked me after a few moments.

"Finished what?"

"Running away."

In reply, I turned to him and raised an eyebrow.

"Seriously, Aida. The way I see it, we got married back in Maine. So your crazy family is now mine as well, and it's about time you let me in."

"Do you really want that? You know what they're like."

"I do know what they're like. They, you included, are loud and emotional. You *all* hold grudges, even if you pretend you don't. None of you is keen on outsiders, at least not at first. But beneath all the yelling and drama, you all care about one another deeply. You're all protective to a fault, and you know that enjoying a good meal with the people you love is just about the best damn thing on earth. Your family has a closeness that most people can only dream about."

"So why are they being so hard on me?" I asked, feeling my eyes grow warm with tears.

"I don't know. Maybe it's just because they've tied so much of what they believe 'family' is to what they believe 'religion' is. It's the same thing that my dad did."

"You know what?" I said, sitting up a little straighter and wiping my eyes with my shirtsleeve. "It's more than that. They're not just rattled that I don't believe the same things they do. They have no interest in understanding what I believe. Maybe it's not so much a lack of interest as a lack of capability. I don't know. To them, not being affiliated with a religion is the equivalent of being faithless and having no guidelines for personal morality.

"But I do have faith, Birch. I do have a moral compass. With or without the structures of organized religion, most people have gut instincts about what is right, what is good.

185

Don't you think so?" I went on without waiting for his reply. "But it's so easy to lose the ability to listen to yourself. You get told too many times by someone in a robe with a pious look on his face that you can't actually understand the most obvious moral truth without the help of the pious robed folk."

"Pious robed folk?" Birch asked with a smirk. "I'm still following you, but you're on the verge of not making sense."

"Come on, you know what I mean. It just seems to me that it is, in fact, possible for a person to experience something greater than oneself, just by being open to the perception of it. By meditating or reading or praying or sitting in the sun or running through the woods in winter and feeling a rush of pure, instinctively peaceful joy, just for a moment. And in that moment you *know* that every truth in the universe has been revealed, but then it's gone and it's almost as if you've forgotten. But you haven't. Not truly."

Birch leaned forward and kissed my forehead. "I'd like to be where you are," he said softly.

"What do you mean, Birch?"

"I mean, I've never felt that way. I guess I've been schooled out of it by the pious robed folk."

"Are you making fun of me?"

"Not in the least, Aida," he said gravely. "Not in the least." Birch paused for a long while, cleared his throat, and said, "Anyway, you might want to try explaining some of that to your family. And keep trying until they get it."

"Think they will?" I said, fighting to keep my face from yielding to the pull of the terror I felt at the thought of my family never understanding me.

"Maybe. Someday."

"Well, I could try calling my dad tomorrow. And Marco.

And . . . you could try calling your dad as well, you know. Will, I mean. You really need to start patching things up with him as well."

"I know, I know. I'll go see him. Soon," Birch promised.

Ambling through my Monday workday, I found I lacked the dedication to my work that I once possessed. Having once been so excited about my column, I was now obsessed with thoughts of the baby, my future with Birch, and how to make amends with my family. As Yolanda and Sally had known me for years, my restlessness was a glaring anomaly to them. They pestered me all morning with questions about my week in Maine with Birch. Over deli sandwiches in the *Middleton Daily Journal*'s cafeteria, I told them I was pregnant. Shock was stamped across their faces like the morning headline.

"You are kidding me!" Yolanda whispered loudly, stressing every word.

"How far along are you? When are you due?" Sally asked. "And congratulations!" she said, leaning over her Rueben to hug me.

Not wanting to be outdone, Yolanda jumped up, rounded the small table, and embraced me as well. "Of course. Congratulations."

"Well, let's see. I'm just eight weeks along. Oh! I have an appointment coming up. I wonder when you can hear the baby's heartbeat?"

My friends graciously allowed me to ramble on about Maine, Birch's moving in to my apartment, and my excitement about the baby. I was thrilled to have shared my news with people happy to hear it. Yolanda, who was divorced, had six- and nine-year-old girls, and she regaled me with stories about their births. Sally was single, and currently in between boyfriends, and listened patiently, smiling in what seemed to me to be all the right places.

After work, I stopped at the hardware store and picked up paint swatches for the kitchen, living room, and bedroom, and returned home to find Birch already there, in the bedroom. He was putting clothes away in his dresser.

"Moving in, huh? How the hell did you move the dresser down the steps by yourself?" I asked.

"I had help. Frank."

Our building was occupied by two men named Frank, the aging ex-marine on the first floor, and the computer programmer who lived in the fifth-floor flat with his partner, Raymond.

"First-floor Frank or fifth-floor Frank?"

"Fifth-floor. Have you ever been up there? They turned their second bedroom into an exercise room. They have a treadmill and a weight bench in there. Very cool."

"Yeah, I talk to Frank and Ray every once in a while. They do have a nice place. I wish we had a second bedroom here."

"I know. It's a weird building. Why are the fifth-floor apartments the only ones with two bedrooms?" Birch asked as he closed the bottom drawer of the dresser. "Where are we going to put the baby anyway?"

"In a bassinet in my—I mean, our room at first. After that, I don't know. Is this dumb? Should we just be looking for a house? Look," I said, pulling the paint swatches out of my bag. "I picked up these on the way home from work, but should we even bother painting, if we're just going to have to move anyway? I mean, we really need another bedroom. How are we going to fit your stuff, my stuff, and the baby stuff in this one room?"

Birch sat down on the floor and looked around. "Maybe

188

you're right," he said. "I guess we really didn't think this through very well."

We didn't think about it at all, I thought to myself. As soon as we had gotten back together, I got pregnant. What would happen if, despite all our vowing to trust in what we had and stay together this time, it still didn't work out? I would be raising the baby alone.

"Aida?" Birch's voice cut into my thoughts, mowing down the weedy phrase "single mother" before it had had time to fully sprout.

"Sorry . . . I was just thinking. Look, maybe we should just skip the painting. We'll get enough of your things moved in here so that you can live comfortably for a while. We'll figure things out from there."

"I think we should start house hunting right away," Birch said, suddenly eager. "Louis used to be a realtor in his pre-sanctuary life. I'll talk to him at work tomorrow. See if he can recommend anyone."

Nodding, I sat on the floor in front of him and put my arms around his neck. "Do you think it'll ever feel like we know what we're doing?"

"Come on, Aida. That would be boring," he said as he laughed and rolled me onto the floor, kissing my neck.

"Hey," I said, remembering something we had talked about the day before. "Did you call your dad today?"

"No," he said as he stopped kissing me and sat up.

"No? Why not?"

"Because I went to see him. At the pub," Birch said with a sigh.

"Really? How did it go?" I questioned eagerly. Sitting cross-legged in front of Birch, I held his hands in mine.

"It was strange. He seemed so different. Cold. I mean, he

was never that affectionate of a father, but he was so . . ."

"Distant?" I offered. "Like he was trying really hard to be distant toward you?"

"That's what was so horrible, Aida. It was as if he didn't have to try at all."

"Oh," I said, looking down at his hands, which I still clutched. I squeezed them softly. His fingernails were trimmed neatly, but very short. His large hands were covered with various scratches and scrapes and calluses, hazards of his job. These were the hands that would one day hold our child, confidently, carefully. Hadn't Will held Birch like that once? Still staring down at Birch's hands, caressing them, turning them this way and that, I whispered, "How can he? How can he act like he didn't father you, love you, raise you, teach you? How can he just dismiss you like this?"

Shrugging, Birch pulled his hands out of my grasp and stood up. "I think I'll go for a run," he said. "Are you up for it?"

"That's it? You're not going to talk to me about it? What about him? Are you going to try talking to him again?"

"What's the use?" Birch asked, stripping off his sweater and jeans and changing into his running clothes.

Watching the workings of his long, lean muscles as he changed, I said to him, "You don't know how powerful you are, do you?"

"What are you talking about?" he said, poised for flight.

"You. Your persistence. That's how you got me. Just don't give up on Will, even if it seems like he gave up on you."

"I'll see you in a little while," he said in reply as he strode from the room and out the door of the apartment.

The week passed quietly and on Saturday morning, Birch and I were curled up in bed, sipping coffee, and looking at house listings. We were trying to identify a few houses we could look at over the weekend.

"Have you spoken to your mom since we got back from Maine?" I asked him as I scanned the small print in front of me.

"Mm-hm," he replied vaguely, not looking up, either. "She was glad I looked Thaddeus up. She couldn't stop asking me questions about him."

"She misses him."

"How do you feel about the subdivision by the old train station?" he asked.

"Too far from any of the good markets. And don't think I didn't notice that you changed the subject," I said, letting it slide, at least for now. "Here's one," I said, reading from the paper, trying to get excited about the idea of buying a house. "Newly renovated nineteen twenty-five bungalow. Two bedroom—"

"We need three bedrooms," Birch interrupted without looking up.

"Three? How many children are we having?"

"Just one for now, but we could use an office. Anyway, the kids can share a room."

Laughing a little, I said, "Let's just take it one kid at a time."

"Fine," he replied with a smirk. "Unless you're having twins."

Gasping as I swatted him with my section of the paper, I attempted to propel the thought of two babies from my mind before I returned to examining the real estate listings. "Okay, what about a ranch? Although I think I'd really

rather be in something with an upstairs, wouldn't you?" I
began, then added, "Do I look fat yet? I'd be really fat by
now if I was having twins."

"What? No! I mean, no to the ranch, and no you don't
look fat. Forget about the twins. I was just joking."

"Even so, shouldn't I start getting a little round in the
tummy? I mean, I'm two months along. Things don't fit
comfortably anymore, but I don't look pregnant yet."

"Are you that eager to start wearing maternity clothes?"

"When do you think I'll be fat enough for those?"

"Aida, I don't know. We'll ask the doctor about it on
Friday, okay? Let's just stay on task here," he said. His en-
suing laughter was interrupted by the ringing of the phone.

"I'll get it," Birch almost yelled, even though I was sitting right next to him.

"Really? You want to get the phone? Here?"

"I live here now, don't I?" he said, as he reached over me
to grab the phone from the bedside table. "Hello?" he answered. "Lieutenant Alfano?" Birch said, and I watched the
smile that had only moments before played across his lips
straighten into a thin line. Handing me the phone, Birch
said quietly, "It's about your father."

"What?" I asked, the single word snaking its way around
my heart, which had suddenly lurched into my throat. Not
only was Victor Alfano, or Uncle Vic, one of my father's
closest friends, he had also been the officer on duty the
morning of my mother's car accident, the day she died.

"Aida? This is Uncle Vic. Don't worry. Your dad's fine.
He is in the emergency room at Middleton Mercy, though."

Birch and I were at the hospital in less than fifteen minutes. The lieutenant was standing in the ER waiting room,
sipping coffee from a paper cup. Over six feet tall and broad
shouldered, Victor Alfano was easy to spot in any crowd.

His hair was thick and gray, closely cropped. He must have been off duty when he'd found my father, and was dressed not in his navy blue uniform, but in jeans, a sweater, and a black leather jacket. Sprinting across the room, I attacked him with my questioning. "What happened? Is he okay? Where is he? I can see him now, right?" Birch stood behind me, his hand heavy on my shoulder.

"Slow down, Aida, slow down," Uncle Vic said, his voice quiet and deep. "I found him this morning, at the cemetery. I was on the way to my brother's grave. Your dad . . . well, Aida, he was drunk. It looked like he'd been there, at your mom's grave, for a while, maybe a few hours. Had a cut on his head, bleeding pretty bad, and I was worried about frostbite, too. It's a pretty cold morning. So I took him in to the ER. Don't worry. He's going to be fine. Bunch of stitches above his eyebrow is all. And . . . well, I'm not going to write him up, so, you just take him on home, all right?"

"Oh, Christ," I whispered. "What about my brother? Did you call Marco?"

"Marc wasn't home, but I left him a message. Ready?"

I nodded and asked as we began walking down the brightly lit hallway, "Is he sober now?" I'd never seen my father drunk in all my life. I'd never seen him drink more than a glass of wine at dinner.

"Sure is. Aida," Uncle Victor said as he stopped walking and turned to face me. "I don't know what's going on between you and your dad and your brother, but this is not the Salvatore I know, and shit, we've been friends since we were ten. Talk to him. Find out what's going on with him. Ask him about the Sunrise."

"The diner? Sunrise Diner on Third Street? That's where you guys meet for breakfast all the time."

"That's all you know about it? That we eat breakfast there a few times a week?" he asked me.

I nodded. "What else is there to know?"

"Ask him. That's all I'm telling you."

"But you haven't told me anything."

"That's right." He turned away and began striding down the hallway once more. Birch and I exchanged confused glances, then began following our mysterious leader once again. I didn't understand what the hell Uncle Vic was talking about. Before I could ponder it further, Uncle Victor turned right abruptly, opened a door, and suddenly from behind a partially closed gray-green curtain, I saw the crumpled old man that was, apparently, my father.

Glancing at Birch and Uncle Vic, I tilted my head toward the door, and they quietly backed out of the room.

"Pop?" I began, approaching the bed.

He sat with his legs dangling over the edge of the high hospital bed, in wrinkled gray pants, the burgundy sweater I gave him for Christmas about three years ago, and his heavy brown tweed overcoat, which was stained on the collar with dark blotches of blood. He looked up at me but said nothing.

Walking the few steps to him, I touched his arm. When he failed to respond, I moved closer and wrapped my arms around him for a long while before he finally returned my embrace. His arms locked around my frame and he rested his head on my shoulder. My hand smoothed his wavy black and white hair. He cried softly into my coat, and my own tears fell onto his neck and back.

"What's going on, Pop?" I asked, my hand still moving across his head. He didn't pull away from me.

"I'm lost, Aida," he mumbled into my shoulder.

"Why?"

"I've never stopped loving your mother."

"That's okay."

"I never knew how to put her to rest," he said as he finally withdrew from me. He sat. I stood in front of him. We regarded each other eye to eye.

"I know," I told him.

"I should have done a better job with you."

"Just me?"

"I understood Marco better. He turned out fine."

"And I didn't?"

Pop shrugged. "Who knows? I don't understand you. I don't know if how you are now is okay." His voice was tremulous and quiet, and set me to aching as I heard it.

"Okay with whom?" I asked, sticking out my chin.

"With your mother. And with God."

"You'll never know. But what about you?"

"Oh, Angelina," he said, his eyes crinkling in the corners and his mouth twisting into a grimace as he fought to keep from crying. After he sucked in a mouthful of air, his face relaxed. "Angelina. You are beautiful, and smart. You should hear how I have always bragged about you. You want to know something? When you were eleven years old, maybe ten, in catechism class, your mother and I, we got a note from your teacher along with your report card. It said, and I've always remembered this, 'Aida is one of my best students. Works hard and is not afraid of deep thinking.' "

The straightjacket around my heart loosened just a bit. "Not afraid of deep thinking? Sister Francesca said that?" I remembered her, a young nun with reddish brown hair and an easy smile.

My father nodded. "That's when I knew."

"Knew what?"

"That we were in for a world of trouble with you. You

always questioned our rules, wanting to know how we could know what was best for you. But you always went to church. Now, your deep thinking . . . well, look where it's gotten you. You didn't want to be Joe's godmother, you don't want to get married, you're leaving the Church, you're pregnant. I don't know how to just start thinking all of that is fine. And what you said about your mother. Do you know how ashamed she was of herself to be pregnant before we got married? I don't know about you, Angelina. You have no shame. I feel I must bear it for you," he said, bowing his head. I kissed his hair. I squared my shoulders. I took the deepest, fullest breath I had in a long while.

"I love you, Pop," I told him, wiping at the tears gathering in my eyes. There was nothing else I could say. I couldn't defend myself. I couldn't make him understand.

"Can you take me home now?" he asked, still not looking at me.

"Sure. Just give me one second, okay. I'll be right back."

Walking out of the room, I found Marco and Birch leaning against the wall on the opposite side of the hallway. They stood shoulder to shoulder, and appeared to be deep in conversation. Uncle Vic was nowhere to be seen. Marco and Birch looked up as I approached, and before I had finished crossing the hallway to them, Marco lurched toward me, throwing his arms around me. "Aida, I'm sorry about everything. We're okay, right? How is Pop? Is he all right? Birch filled me in."

Extracting myself from my brother's bear hug, I took a step back and replied, "He's . . . fine, I guess. Just emotional right now. This thing with all of us, the baptism, the baby, everything, really took a toll on him, you know?"

"I hadn't realized how bad it was until now. I shouldn't have stayed away for as long as I did," Marco said, his head hung low. "How was he with you? Did you two make up?"

My mouth twitched a bit as I tried to keep from crying again. "We . . . we're at an impasse, Marc. I can't be who he wants me to be, and he can't change his idea of who I should be."

"Oh," Marc replied awkwardly. "I see."

"But what's all this about the Sunrise?" Birch cut in. "And why was Lieutenant Alfano so vague about it all?"

"Uncle Vic wanted to tip us off to something, apparently, but he was evasive enough to avoid feeling like he's broken Pop's trust," I said, thinking aloud. "Let's get Pop back home, see if Nonna knows anything—"

"She won't talk even if she does know something. You know that," Marco interrupted.

Just then, the door behind me opened slowly, and my father lurched into the hallway, catching his balance before Marco and I reached him. "I don't know what's taking you all so long, but I'm ready to go home. I need a shower. Marco. Birch. Thanks, boys, for coming. But let's get the hell out of here. I hate hospitals."

Chapter Eleven

After loading my father into Marco's van, we drove back home, with Marco and Pop right behind us. My father immediately retreated upstairs to shower and change, while we filled Nonna in on what had happened. We were all sitting at the dining-room table, and had begged Nonna to sit down, but she insisted on shuffling around the kitchen, making an early lunch for everyone. "Nonna, let me help you," I said, getting up from the table and following her into the kitchen.

"No. I don't want you in here. Go sit down," she groused.

"But Nonna—"

"Go!" she said loudly.

My hands were already on my hips and I raised my eyebrows at her and opened my mouth to speak again, but she turned her back and opened the refrigerator door, dismissing me. Returning to the dining room, I sat down, reluctantly obedient.

As the rest of us talked, Nonna set down platters of our family's favorite Italian deli meats—cappicola, prosciutto, salamini—as well as a variety of sliced cheeses. Next came a platter of roasted, marinated red and green peppers, as well as fresh sliced tomatoes, pepperoncini peppers, and olives— big, fat green Sicilian olives and small oil-cured black olives, saltier than anything else I've ever tasted. Those were my favorite. After bringing out a basket of warm, sliced bread, Nonna returned to the kitchen to wash grapes, and we all began assembling sandwiches.

Appearing once more at the table with a large bowl of red and green grapes, Nonna sat down and tore off a small portion of the vine of red grapes for herself. She also selected a few slices of cheese, and some of the spicy cappicola, and nibbled as she spoke. "I saw Salvatore leave early this morning, around five o'clock. I had just said my rosary and was coming into the kitchen to make some coffee. He had on his coat already and I said, 'Hey, where do you think you're going so early?' and he said something about the cemetery and then off he went."

"Nonna, had he been drinking?" Marco asked.

"Your father doesn't drink at five o'clock in the morning. Who does that?"

"Well, he did it today," I said softly.

"Watch your mouth, Aida," Nonna said without even looking at me.

The old woman had it in for me today. She must still be fuming about me being a pagan unwed mother.

"Nonna, does he usually go to the cemetery that early?" Birch asked as he brushed his hand against mine reassuringly.

"What are you doing here? Why do you care so damn much where Salvatore went?"

I turned to look at Birch, saw his eyes widen in surprise at Nonna's venomous attitude toward him. She had always seemed to like him so much, but he had apparently fallen from grace.

"He's part of this family, now, Nonna," I told her.

She finally looked directly at me. "He's your husband? Are you married all of the sudden?"

"In a manner of speaking," I said.

"In a manner of speaking? What does that mean? Nothing, that's what. Child, I let you come in here, sit at my table, eat my food. Don't insult me by dressing up your sinful relation with this man as something of a marriage."

"This man?" Birch asked, quoting her. "You've known me for years, and you've been nothing but kind to me. Has that much changed?"

"You know it has," she told him, her lips setting into a deep frown after she had finished speaking.

"Okay, okay," Marco interrupted. "We're getting nowhere here. We're supposed to be talking about Pop, remember? Nonna, do you know anything about the Sunrise Diner?"

"Sure, Salvatore goes there to eat all the time. With Victor."

"That's it?" Marco asked swiftly.

"Oh, now you're going to take a tone with me?" Nonna said, rising from the table and shaking her head. She turned and walked into the kitchen.

"Well, that's it then," I said. "That's all we're going to get out of her. Where the hell is Pop?"

"He is taking a long while, isn't he?" Marco replied. "Should I go check on him?"

Just then my father entered the dining room, filling the entryway into the dining room with his broad frame. He stood with more confidence than he had displayed in years. His shoulders were squared, his spine straight. And he was smiling. Aside from the bandage above his left eyebrow, he didn't even resemble the man I'd seen just a short time ago at the hospital.

"Good, good. You're all still here. I want to talk to everybody. I've come to a decision," Pop announced in a loud voice. "Ma!" he yelled into the kitchen. "Please, come sit at the table with the family." After surveying the lot of us, he said, "Marco, please call your wife. She should be

200

here, too. Go on," he urged, as Marco sat there, watching him. Marco rose finally, went into the kitchen to use the phone, and returned moments later. "She'll be here in a few minutes. I called her when we were still at the hospital, so she's pretty much up to speed. Pop, what's up?"

"Let's wait for Rosie. Has everyone eaten?"

"We haven't finished, yet, Pop. Come on. Sit down. I'll make you a sandwich," I told him.

"Thank you, Aida. Don't be shy with the provolone, now, okay? Ah, *perfetto*," he said as he watched me assemble his lunch. "Come on. *Mangiamo*. Let's eat."

At least he had the decency to pretend as if everything was fine between us, but I was suspicious of his sudden change in demeanor since the hospital. I smelled no alcohol on him when I brought him his plate, so I dismissed the notion that he had suddenly become an alcoholic. I didn't understand what had happened at the cemetery that morning, but I had a hunch it was related to the announcement Pop was about to make.

In the approximately fourteen minutes we waited for Rosie to arrive, Pop ate, and Marco, Birch, and I finished the half-eaten sandwiches on our plates. When I wasn't staring down at my plate, I found myself glancing across the table at Marco. We used to do the same thing when we were kids. Pop would sit down and say something like, "so, who wants to tell me what happened?" and I'd look at Marco and raise my eyebrows, and he'd frown, or give the slightest shake of his head. Invariably, we would get our signals mixed up, and I'd end up telling Pop about how I'd used his good pruning shears to carve a fort into the enormous grouping of forsythia bushes in our backyard. Later, Marco had told me that he was going to take the fall for that one, since I had just gotten in trouble for not making it to dinner on time the day before. But I had failed to read his dinner-table facial code properly and had been forced to spend the next Saturday cleaning out the garage as punishment. It was worth it. The forsythia fort was the best place to be alone, to read, to think, to cry.

Shaken out of my reverie by the touch of Birch's hand on my thigh, I turned to look at him. He had a small, reassuring smile on his face. Meanwhile, Nonna's frown continued to etch itself further and further into the already harsh lines carved into her countenance.

"What?" Pop finally thundered as he finished his sandwich and started in on the plump red grapes. "Who died?"

"What?" Marco asked.

"Well, come on. You all look so serious. Lighten up. Everything is fine. Good sandwich, Aida. Thank you," he said.

Finally, we heard Rosie pushing her way through the back door and lugging the baby carrier up the back steps. Marco rushed to help. Joseph was sleeping, so Marco just took off his blanket and hat and left him snoozing in the carrier.

Rosie made her way around the table, kissing everyone as she said hello. "*Ciao,* Nonna. That's a pretty dress. Pop, you look well, considering. They did a good job with your stitches. Birch, haven't seen you for a while. Glad you're back at the Benedetto table. Aida! I haven't had a chance to congratulate you yet on the baby. Are you feeling okay?" As I nodded, Rosie hung up her trench coat on the back of a dining-room chair and sat down. "Okay, I'm here. What's going on?" Her dark hair had been hastily pulled back into a ponytail, with wispy strands framing her face. She looked a little tired, but more curious than concerned about Pop and his impending announcement.

202

"Rosie," my father said. "Thanks for coming so quickly. I wanted everyone to be here. Okay. So. I wanted you all to know something. I'm not sure why I haven't told you before now, but the time is right, I think. Aida, Marco, you two came to me this morning at the hospital without judgment, with no grudges even after all that happened. You reminded me how important it is to treat the people closest to you with respect, even when you don't agree with some of them," Pop said, glancing at me.

"Pop, please," Marco urged. "You're killing us. What do you want to tell us?"

"Okay, okay. What I wanted to tell you all is . . . well, I've been seeing someone." He waited for us all to stop gasping and shouting three questions each all at once before continuing. "Her name is Doreen Nickerson. She is a waitress and part owner of the Sunrise Diner, and we've been together for almost a year now. I . . . I guess I haven't wanted you all to meet her because . . . well, I haven't felt this way about a woman for so many years now, and I didn't want you all to think I was dishonoring your mother and—"

"Oh, Pop," I said, jumping to my feet, choking back tears, and hugging him. "I'm so happy for you! You've waited so long to find someone again. You deserve to be happy."

"Tell us about her. What's she like?" Marco asked.

"Pop, that's great!" Rosie exclaimed. "Good for you."

Birch grinned, and said, "Congratulations, Mr. Benedetto. I'm really happy for you."

"You know what we should do?" I asked, and without waiting for anyone to answer, I continued, "we should have her over for dinner. It'll be the perfect way to introduce her to the family. Birch, what do you think? Can we fit everyone at our place?"

"No," Marco cut in, before Birch could answer. "Your apartment is too small for all of us. We'll do it at our house."

"But make your manicotti," Rosie put in.

"Oh, that sounds good, and—" I began again, before Pop put his hands in the air to stop us all.

"Wait a minute, wait a minute," he said loudly. When we ceased our chattering, Pop went on, "Ma? You haven't said a word."

Suddenly, I turned my gaze to my Nonna's face. Her lips were pursed, her eyebrows furrowed, her gaze downcast.

"Nonna? You're happy for Pop, aren't you?" I pleaded.

"Well," she began brusquely, without looking at me. "A year, Salvatore?" she asked her son, fixing her steely black gaze firmly on him. "You've been with this woman for a year? None of us," she said, making a wide circle with her arm, "not one of us has met her. How can I, how can any of us, be happy for you without knowing what she's like? You made a mistake not to bring her home sooner, my son. You mourned your wife, and I know you always will. No one will fault you for seeking the company of a woman again. But you were wrong to keep this new woman from us for so long. There. I've said my piece," she declared, her face still looking rather dour.

Everyone, including my father, sat silently, biting their lips, or turning their water glasses aimlessly on the table, or toying with their forks, or staring at their plates. I caught Marco's eye, cocked my head toward our grandmother, and gave the briefest of nods, offering myself up, ready to defend my father. After all, Nonna was livid with me anyway. Marco gave one swift shake of his head, but I ignored him.

"And?" I asked Nonna, rising from my chair.

"What do you mean, Aida? And what?"

"So, you've said your piece. But what are you really trying to say? I can't believe you would actually fault Pop for not bringing this poor woman into our wolves' den. Look how we tore everyone to shreds before Marco finally brought home Rosie. And who knows what you all said behind Birch's back when I first brought him here. I know what you said to his face. You all ripped into him about what he ate, or didn't eat. 'What? You don't eat any meat? No cheese? You're crazy. Just skin and bones,' " I mimicked. "And that was just the beginning of the grilling he got. You all told me all the things you thought were wrong with him. His hair was too long. His mother didn't go to church. He wasn't Italian. 'Something must be wrong with him,' you said. 'Isn't he too smart to just be working at an animal shelter? What's he hiding?' "

Glancing over at Birch, I saw that his eyebrows had arched slightly above his sweet brown eyes, and his lips were puckered into something of a frown. "Sorry, Birch. You probably didn't need to know all that. Anyway, Nonna," I went on, glaring at her once again, "you're the most judgmental, the most unforgiving of us all. *That's* probably why Pop was drunk at the cemetery this morning," I accused, glancing at my father for confirmation.

His black eyes widened and his dark brows knitted together in silent fury. He would never publicly admit weakness; he would only shower rage upon me for having pointed it out. Ignoring him, I turned back to Nonna, "How could Pop even dream of bringing someone he cared about here? You never moved on after Nonno died. Why would my father have any reason to believe you'd understand him?"

Inhaling deeply, I realized that everyone, Nonna included, was staring at me, apparently in utter disbelief. I was a little shocked as well. I had never spoken with such raw candor to my grandmother before. Despite our differences, I had always tried to be respectful to her. But Pop needed her support right now, and her disapproval of his actions enraged me. Damn it, I thought. I shouldn't have brought up Nonno. Nonna was in her early seventies when her husband died, not middle-aged like my father had been when he'd lost my mother. That was out of line. Quickly sitting down, I gulped down some water. I had a habit of going just a little too far.

"Aida, that was too much," my father chastised, his voice a barely controlled growl.

"Sorry, Pop. I just—"

"*Basta,* Angelina. Why do I always have to tell you when enough is enough? Do you have anything to say to your Nonna?" Pop yelled.

"Nonna, I'm sorry. I didn't mean—" I began softly, trying to brave a glance at her face.

Raising her hand in the air to silence me, Nonna interrupted in a firm but quiet voice, *"Silencio."* Turning to my father she told him, "Invite this Doreen woman *here* for dinner next Sunday. *I* will make manicotti." Nonna then rose slowly from her chair and disappeared into the hallway leading toward the staircase. The steps creaked a bit as she slowly made her way to her room.

When we heard her door being closed, Birch let out a soft, low whistle, and exclaimed simply, "Wow."

Pushing away the plate in front of me, I slumped over the table, resting my head in my arms. Birch placed his hand lightly on my back.

"Damn, Aida," Rosie began, just as Joseph started to stir. "What were you thinking?" she asked, picking up the baby and rocking him.

"Yeah, Aida. That was just crazy. You knew she had it in for you when you got here. Why did you keep after her? Don't you know when to lie low?" Marco asked.

"Somebody had to stand up for Pop," I mumbled.

"Nobody needs to stand up for me," Pop replied. "You were out of line."

"So, I won't come next week," I said, sitting up.

"No, you won't," Pop agreed. "Not with things the way they are."

"Then bring Doreen to our apartment," Birch interjected into the fog of silence that choked the room.

"What?" I asked, turning to stare at him with narrow eyes and clenched teeth.

"Saturday," Birch went on, as if he were speaking to an ordinary group of people about ordinary dinner plans. "Mr. Benedetto, don't you want Doreen to meet Aida? I know you have differences, but won't it seem odd for her to meet everyone except your daughter?"

Pop frowned, and his gaze moved from Birch's face to mine. "She should meet you, Angelina," Pop said quietly, "but you cannot behave the way you have," he told me.

Feeling like a disobedient ten-year-old, all I could do was shrug, my excitement for my father's happiness having melted into resentment. I had only been defending him, yet he continued to treat me like an outcast.

"I think it's a great idea," Marco was saying. Rosie nodded next to him.

"Sure," she said. "Then Doreen can meet you and Birch without the usual . . . sparks that flare up when the whole family is together."

With my frown deepening, I pulled my hand away from Birch's as he reached out to me. I knew what they were trying to do. They all wanted to see Pop and me on easy, loving terms again. I just didn't know how that could ever happen.

"Okay. We'll come," Pop sighed.

"Good. Then it's settled. Aida, we should get going," Birch said before I could argue. "Maybe we can still see one of the houses on our list," he made the mistake of saying. Once Rosie and Marco found out we were house hunting, they provided an excess of advice. We were there almost another hour discussing the matter. Pop remained silent for a few minutes then retreated quietly into the basement, his expression sour.

When Birch and I arrived home, I crawled into bed for a nap, with Birch promising to call the realtor and set a few things up. Despite all the family drama to distract me, I found it hard to not think about being pregnant. I constantly wavered between nausea and hunger, and when I wasn't preoccupied with the state of my stomach, I found that I could barely keep my eyes open in the afternoon. Slumped across my bed, I fell asleep almost instantly, waking an hour and a half later when I heard Birch softly saying my name. "Aida? Hey, sleepyhead. Do you feel like looking at a house?"

Birch's question marked the true beginning of our quest for the perfect house. Over the next several days, in the evenings after work we looked at half a dozen houses and found nothing that felt like home to us. We were both eager for Friday, though. It held a lot of promise. We had a prenatal appointment, and from what I had read there was a chance that we might be able to hear the baby's heartbeat, and directly after the appointment we were supposed to be checking out a house that sounded like a good bet.

I managed to refrain from scolding Birch for inviting Pop and Doreen for dinner. I couldn't fault his intentions. I placed the blame squarely on my father's shoulders, and on my own. I had stood up for him, and he had reprimanded me for it. He had said that it was important for us to treat each other with respect, even if we didn't agree with one another. But that seemed challenging for both of us, and damn it, I wanted more. I wanted warmth and laughter, not distance and the semblance of respect. How could Saturday's dinner be anything but a disaster?

I woke Friday morning to a persistent, loud beeping sound. It was five a.m. I didn't need to get up to run for another hour. "Birch," I mumbled as I nudged his shoulder. "Turn it off." He did not stir. "Turn it off," I said with a more forceful shove.

"Hmmm," he grunted, turning over.

"Turn the damn thing off!" I shouted.

"Oh. Sorry."

Silence was finally restored to my bedroom, and I pulled myself into a ball, wrapping my arms around my queasy stomach. Today was not going to be a good day, I could tell already. Unable to get back to sleep and vowing to scold Birch later for not turning off the alarm right away, I stumbled into the bathroom and threw up. I hadn't done that for a while now. I pulled on my running gear, irritated that the pants felt so tight around my waist. Did they make decent outdoor athletic wear for pregnant women? In the living room I stretched my still-groggy limbs and forced my reluctant body through a set of push-ups and wondered if I should still be doing sit-ups. I did them anyway, thinking that I should at least ask Dr. Rodriguez this afternoon about acceptable prenatal exercise habits.

Closing the door softly behind me, I trotted down the steps and out the door into a frigid March morning. Just a short run today, I told myself as I headed down the block into the predawn gloom. Streetlamps, unaided by the meager glow of a quarter moon, lit the path before me with a bland yellowish glow. Slipping on a patch of ice, I caught myself before I fell, but in a panic, I slowed to a walk, wondering how I would ever be able to keep my baby safe from anything, including my own clumsiness.

Scanning the sidewalk ahead, I could see that for a good stretch it seemed well shoveled, so I picked up my pace again. The sharpness of the icy wind caused my eyes to prickle and tear, but I didn't bother to wipe my face and before long I was sobbing. I had been so focused on my physical symptoms for a long while, and then on the continuing turmoil in both my family and in Birch's, that I had ignored so many of the things I was feeling about being pregnant. Now, alone with my fears, I allowed myself the sick comfort of indulging each terror, hoping that by wallowing in my own emotional mire, I would expend those feelings and free myself from their filthy, choking grasp. Sometimes you had to get dirty to get clean.

Rounding the corner on which St. Benedict's stood like a gray tomb in the wan artificial haze of the streetlamps, I shook my head a bit, trying to clear it. My breath puffed out in front of me, and I felt just then a little like a colt, stomping, shaking, and snorting, skittish of too many things. I found that I was just as afraid that everything would go right as I was that everything would go wrong. Images of miscarriage, excruciating labor, episiotomy, emergency caesarian section, life-threatening infection, and horrific stillbirth afflicted me, and I was stopped dead in the tracks of my thought whenever these specters arose.

At the same time, I agonized that the pregnancy, labor, and birth would be perfectly normal and suddenly I would find myself at home with a newborn infant and would be expected to know how to care for it, whether or not maternal instincts had kicked in. There was the distinct possibility that having been given the gift of a healthy child, I would invariably find a way to ruin the poor thing's life, through my own ignorance and lack of ability. A line from a prayer we used to murmur aloud as a congregation flitted through my thoughts, something about having sinned in two ways, "in what I have done, and what I have failed to do." No matter what I do or fail to do, I thought, it seems inevitable that I'll fuck this whole thing up.

Running and weeping, I could not for the life of me envision what motherhood would be like for me. It occurred to me that the reason I was having such difficulty picturing myself as a mother was that it was a sign that something was dreadfully wrong, and that I would never hold my child in my arms. As this idea took hold in my mind, I forced my legs to move faster, felt the wind rushing against me with great fury, and prayed that speed, and wind, and tears would banish these darkest doubts from my mind.

After running for about twenty-five minutes, the last five or so in this state of terrorized sprinting, I reached my snug brick building, and facing the earth-colored bricks, I braced myself against the structure, stretching and catching my breath. Jogging back up my steps, I felt the blackest of my fears still nestled firmly in my chest, anchored to my heart. Birch was showering and when he emerged from the bathroom clad in a thick, fluffy pink towel that he clutched closed at his hip, I threw my arms around him. I clung to him in silence for a few moments, ignoring his questions, then I went into the bathroom to shower without speaking a word.

"Aida? Are you all right?" he asked me again. I heard him through the rain of hot water falling over my head, but

I didn't answer. "Hey!" he shouted. "Talk to me. I know you can hear me in there."

"I'm fine, Birch," I called to him. "Just freaked out a little. I'm sure it's just normal hormonal pregnancy stuff."

"Really?"

"Yeah."

"Okay, then. I'm going to go. I'll meet you back here and then we'll go to Dr. Rodriguez's together, okay?"

"Okay," I shouted through the water. When I emerged fifteen minutes later, Birch was gone. Wrapped in my bathrobe, I phoned my supervising editor. "Dwight? Hi. It's Aida. I'm feeling really lousy today, so I'm going to stay home."

"Really? Aida, I didn't expect you to be taking time off again so soon after your impromptu little vacation," he said sourly.

"I know, Dwight. But, I've got a few things I can finish up from here and I'll have the files to Ken by lunch. He knows what to do."

"If you're not well, I suppose . . . but you sound fine to me, Aida. What's going on?"

"Look, Dwight. I meant to talk to you in person, but I'm pregnant, and it's been a little . . . difficult."

"Oh," Dwight replied, clearly thrown. "Oh," he repeated, and paused a moment before continuing. "I want you in my office first thing Monday, Aida. We'll have to assess how to manage the column in your absence, and—"

"My absence?"

"Well, you'll be taking time off after the baby's born, right?"

"Oh. Of course. You're just thinking further ahead than I am, Dwight."

"That's my job. Get some rest. See you Monday," he said, then hung up.

Chapter Twelve

I wasn't even sure why I had taken the day off. Nothing felt normal any longer, and I was finding it increasingly difficult to carry on with my life as it had been such a short time ago, when it seemed that Birch and I were through, when I wasn't pregnant, when I was still telling myself I was a Catholic.

All I could do was mope around the apartment as the morning tumbled by. I tried going back to bed. I tried to eat an egg and a piece of toast. I tried to tidy up. I struggled with the writing I still needed to do for my column but managed to e-mail my work to Ken before noon.

Then I continued to dig myself deeper into my foul mood. I felt as if I no longer knew who I was supposed to be and, perhaps worse, I no longer knew my family. The united judgment and disdain being hurled at me from the only trinity that had mattered to me for a long time— Nonna, Pop, and Marco—was arresting. Their disapproval had stopped me in my tracks and I hated them for making it so hard for me to stand up for myself. They were supposed to believe in me and support me, not wither me. Marco was at least trying, but I knew things would never be the same between us. I had questioned things that in his eyes were unassailable. I sensed that he didn't know what to do with that part of me, and would prefer to just ignore it and keep things as peaceable, and as close to how they used to be, as possible.

As I sat at the kitchen table, I tapped a pencil on the

yellow legal pad in front of me, preparing to write a letter to my family that I would never send. I just needed to expel some frustration and blame and rage, because I didn't like the way those things were starting to take control inside my head. I stared at the blank page. I sipped some coffee. I couldn't begin, and in the middle of my not beginning, the phone rang. It was Birch.

"Are you okay? What are you doing home? I called you at work but you weren't there. I knew something was wrong this morning. What's going on?" he spoke quickly, his voice getting louder as he went on.

"Are you going to stop asking me questions so I can answer you?" I asked, a little irritated.

"Sorry," Birch mumbled.

"I don't know. I just didn't feel well this morning."

"You went for a run. You couldn't have felt too horrible."

"What are you? My father?" I shouted, instantly regretting it. I hated feeling so moody. He didn't deserve my abrasive attitude.

"Why are you getting like that with me?" Birch asked quietly.

"I don't know, Birch. I'm sorry. Everything is just too much for me right now. I'm falling apart. I'm not used to having my family hate me. I'm not used to being afraid so much. Being pregnant is terrifying, you know. You can't control anything. Do you know how many things can go wrong?"

Birch sighed into the phone. I wasn't sure how I should take it. "Your family doesn't hate you. And stop worrying so much. Everything is going to be fine. Aida, should we cancel tomorrow?" he asked.

"What? What's tomorrow?"

"Doreen. Your dad is supposed to come over tomorrow so we can meet her. You forgot?"

"Shit . . . okay," I said, trying to regroup. "It'll be fine. I'll run to the market before the appointment. I'll still meet you back here around three, all right?"

"Sure. Are you sure you're okay, though?"

"Yes! Look, we'll talk about everything later, okay?"

"Okay, Aida. See you later," he said, then hung up.

I turned the page in my notepad and began making a grocery list. After dressing in my roomiest pair of jeans and a warm sweater, I bundled up and headed to my car. Usually, grocery shopping involved just one trip to the supermarket, but for special occasions, like tomorrow's dinner, I spent the extra time and money to shop the specialty markets for the best ingredients. I traversed Middleton's uptown and downtown maze of streets to get organic produce, freshly baked Italian bread, and imported cheese and wine. I made it back to the apartment with enough time to put away all the food and take a short nap before Birch rushed in.

We made it to Dr. Rodriguez's office with time to spare. Paging through the parenting magazines that were strewn about the waiting room, Birch and I were too engrossed in articles on breastfeeding, diapering, birthing options, and colic to converse much. A young nurse with short brown hair called my name and while Birch waited in the examining room, I was weighed, had my blood pressure taken, and was asked to urinate in a cup.

Before too long, the doctor arrived and she and Birch exchanged introductions. As she measured my stomach and asked how I'd been feeling, we chatted briefly about morning sickness, my eating habits, and whether or not I was getting enough rest. Finally, Dr. Rodriguez said the words I'd been longing to hear. "All right. Let's see if we can hear a heartbeat yet. But don't be disappointed if we can't. That's normal. Sometimes it's hard to pick up this early."

After she smeared my belly with a cold, jelly-like substance, she placed the Doppler device on my abdomen and moved it slowly about. I listened carefully to the swishing noises and looked at the doctor's face hopefully when I heard a steady rhythmic sound. "That's you," she informed me. "I don't think we're going to get it today. That's all right. You should definitely hear it next time. Do you have any other questions?"

Birch shook his head and looked at me. "Well, actually, I . . . Birch, would you mind waiting outside for a moment?"

"What? Really?"

I nodded.

"Oh. Sure," he said, stepping out of the room and glancing back at me with a little frown before he closed the door behind him.

"Aida?" Dr. Rodriguez asked as she sat down on a wheeled stool. "What's up?"

"Well . . . I . . . This will probably sound strange," I fumbled.

"Trust me. It won't. I've been doing this a long time. I've heard everything."

"It's just that I have such a horrible feeling that something is really wrong. And we couldn't hear the heartbeat, and . . ." I trailed off, my eyes welling up with tears.

"Aida, it's perfectly common to have fears, even horrible fears, that there is some abnormality with the baby, or that something won't go right during the pregnancy or delivery. And it is true that things happen. I won't lie to you. People have miscarriages, babies are born with problems. But those are not things that you can control. You're young. You have a healthy lifestyle. You exercise, you eat right, and it seems as though you have a committed, loving partner. We have every reason to expect a completely normal pregnancy. Okay?"

"Okay," I said softly as she left the room. Birch didn't come back in, so I checked out at the front desk and found him in the waiting room. We walked back to my car in silence. As I started the engine and cranked up the heat, Birch asked, "Well? What was that all about?"

"Nothing. I didn't want to worry you just because I was feeling a little anxious about everything."

"Like what?" he asked, resting his gloved hand on my leg.

"Like . . . things going wrong. All the really bad things." I couldn't even say the words aloud, fearing that if I talked about the possibility of the baby not making it, I would somehow make it happen.

"Oh. I think about those things, too," he said as he stared at my face. "What did she say?"

"You do?"

"Of course. And I feel so removed from everything. It's all happening to you and I'm just powerless."

"Well, she said that it's normal to have some anxiety, but that my age and my lifestyle and having a committed partner like you are all good things. I mean, she did say that bad things happen, but we should worry less about what we can't control."

"Makes sense," Birch replied, nodding.

"I know. It's kind of hard to just assume the best instead of the worst, isn't it?"

Birch was silent for a moment and then said, "We

217

should go. We've got that house to look at, remember."

"Right. Where is it?"

Birch directed me as I navigated through the rush-hour traffic. Before long we found ourselves on the north end of town, a few miles past a large Catholic cemetery.

"There it is," Birch said suddenly, pointing just ahead. "Walnut Street. Turn left . . . Okay, we're looking for five eighty-two. There. The old farmhouse."

"Farmhouse?"

"Yeah. This whole area used to be cornfields."

The farmhouse was probably the oldest on the erratically developed block, which featured homes of varying ages and styles. The house we were looking at was a white two-story, with an L-shaped porch. It seemed clean and well kept. With an oak and a maple tree in the front yard, it was a welcoming place. Our realtor, Tracy Evans, was there already and she began showing us the vacated home. We commented on the red-brick fireplace in the living room, the beautiful woodwork throughout the home, and the adorable pink-tiled bathroom, which had been renovated in the 1950s.

Strolling through the kitchen, I was immediately able to see myself cooking here, preparing delicious meals for us. I could see Pop and Nonna milling about, offering unsolicited advice as I prepared our Sunday dinner. I could see Marco at the table with Joseph on his knee, and Rosie nearby helping me with dinner and gossiping about the extended family. I could even see Sasha running around the kitchen, looking for pieces of food that the children, my children, had dropped.

As I turned to Birch, he laughed as he saw my delighted grin, and just as I was nodding at him, indicating my willingness for us to put an offer on the place immediately, the realtor's phone rang. She swooped her long blond hair away from her ear with a toss of her head, and pressed the slim phone against her face. "Oh, I see," she murmured softly as she walked out of the kitchen and into the dining room.

"I want it," I whispered to Birch.

"Don't you want to see the upstairs?"

"Sure, but I've seen enough to know I want it. How about you?"

"I do love it," he was saying as Tracy walked back into the room. "We want to put an offer on the place," Birch told her.

Gesturing toward her phone, she said, "Sorry. You're too late."

"What?" I asked. "You didn't tell us there was already an offer on the place."

"Yes, she did," Birch said, frowning. "Just before the doctor appointment. I forgot to tell you. But Tracy, you said that we could put in our own offer if we were really interested."

"I know, I know. But the sellers went with the first offer. It was generous. The people buying the place must have really wanted to make sure the offer was snapped up. They must love it."

"Well, so do we," I mumbled to myself.

"We'll be in touch," Birch said to Tracy as we trudged out of the house.

All I could think on the way home was what a fruitless afternoon it had been. No heartbeat, no house. When we arrived home, Birch tried to strike up light conversations, but my responses were crisp and dour.

"What is wrong with you?" he asked as we got into bed that night. Snuggled with his pillow, lying on his stomach, he seemed curious, not complaining, which I found irritating. I would have rather he had snapped the question at me so I would have an excuse to fume. Instead, I found myself shrugging.

"We'll find a house. We have time, and we have enough money to get most of what we want. Don't worry so much, Aida."

"But we couldn't hear the heartbeat today, either. No heartbeat, no house. What if they're all bad signs?" I asked, looking up at the ceiling instead of at him.

"Signs? You sound like Nonna. Maybe if you say three rosaries on your knees tonight and take a plate of cannolis to Father Roberto tomorrow everything will be fine."

A rough, bark of a laugh escaped my lips in spite of my dark mood. I rolled across the bed toward him and kissed his smiling lips. "Thank you," I murmured. I fell asleep with Birch's large warm hand spread across the small mound of my abdomen.

The next morning, Birch rose early for a run.

"Do you really have to go?" I asked after he returned. He was showering, and getting ready to go to the sanctuary for a few hours.

"I have to go check on my girl," he told me as he turned off the water and stepped out of the shower.

"Sasha? She's still there?"

"She sleeps in my office, Aida. She cries when I leave. She was miserable when we were in Maine. I'm really pissed about the farmhouse. It had the perfect yard for her. Once we find a place, she's coming home with us."

I smiled. "Okay, go. I suppose you'll just be in the way here anyway, with all the cooking and cleaning I have to do."

After Birch left, I began scouring the apartment for our little dinner party, wondering to myself as I dusted and vacuumed what my father's secret girlfriend could possibly be like. After I finished making the apartment presentable, I made myself a light lunch of a handful of cherry tomatoes, ricotta topped with black pepper and fresh basil, and a slice of wheat bread. I ate quickly, suddenly very hungry, and then just as suddenly, completely exhausted. Curling up on the sofa, I planned on napping for only half an hour, but it turned into an hour and a half.

I woke with a jolt, looked at my watch and hastily rose. I still had plenty of time to prepare the menu for this evening, but I wanted to make sure I looked presentable before I began cooking. The time often got away from me in the kitchen. I freshened my makeup, tidied my hair, changed my clothes.

Having donned an apron, I then began one of my most treasured rituals, the making of the sauce, or *sugu,* that topped most of our family's dishes, and would be one of the primary components of my eggplant Parmesan. I used tomatoes that my father had grown last summer and that Rosie, Nonna, and I had spent a hot August day canning. I gently crushed the whole tomatoes in a large bowl with my fingers. I sautéed lots of garlic in extra virgin olive oil. Just before it browned, I added the tomatoes. Next came salt, pepper, and some sugar, a little more than my mother had used. Finally, I added a blend of herbs as unique to my *sugu* as my fingerprint was to me.

My mother had taught me the Russo family *sugu* that had been prepared in her family in the same manner for countless generations, and Nonna taught me the Benedetto *sugu.* Both tasted like heaven to me, and each had their own special subtleties. But when I made my own sauce, I added the tiniest of my own touches to my mother's recipe, borrowing a little as well from Nonna's version.

221

So rare were the occasions when I cooked for my father without my Nonna's domineering presence in the kitchen, I couldn't even remember the last time Pop had tasted my own tomato sauce. I hoped he would be pleased, and wouldn't be offended by the liberties I had taken. Once, when my mother was still alive, she had taken a weekend to visit relatives in Chicago, leaving my father's appetite in my care. I thought I would try something new and added a whole cup of chopped onions to the tomato sauce. The alteration was far too drastic, and Pop had been horrified. He could barely choke down the meal I had so eagerly prepared for him.

As the sauce simmered, I readied as much of tonight's meal as I could safely do in advance, preparing a separate pan of the eggplant with soy versions of the mozzarella and Parmesan for Birch. I then turned my attention to the vegan biscotti I was baking for dessert. As much as I loved the usual cacophony of family dinner preparation that was traditional at most of our gatherings, I savored with great reverence the silent progress I made alone in my own kitchen. I mumbled to myself the litany of ingredients and procedures. Nothing was written. All our most beloved recipes were transmitted orally. The sweet aroma of the *sugu* filled the kitchen and soaked in through my pores, steeped with the joy of memory. Inhaling that perfume, I chanted the myth of the biscotti, forming the dough into long, narrow loaves that would bake once, be gently sliced, then baked again.

Almost in a trance, I jumped at the sound of persistent knocking on my door. Wiping my hands on my apron, I scurried across the kitchen and opened the door to find Glenda standing there, her blond curls loose and windblown, her cheeks pink from the cold March wind.

"Glenda," I gasped. "I wasn't expecting anyone. Please, come in."

"Oh, Aida, I'm so sorry to barge in on you like this," she said as she entered the apartment. "Really, I am. God, it smells good in here. Birch wouldn't happen to be here, would he? Is he at work? I probably should have checked there first. You look stunning. Look at you! You're glowing," she said, reaching out to hug me.

"Thank you. And yes, he is at work. He should be back soon, though. Sit down. I'll make you coffee. Sit, sit," I told her, walking back to the oven to check the biscotti. "We're having company tonight. My father has been seeing someone for a year, and he's bringing her over for dinner tonight. He is still livid with me and barely speaking to me, so I'm not even sure why he's coming. Probably just wants to put on a good show for her with me, since she'll be meeting the rest of the family tomorrow. Anyway, the biscotti will be ready for slicing in a little while. It has to bake again, but I always eat the ends after I slice it," I rambled.

"I should go. I don't want to keep you from your preparations," I heard Glenda say, as I peered into the pot, stirring the tomato sauce.

"Don't worry about it," I told her. When I turned back around toward Glenda, she was sitting at the table, staring at me, her lips pressed together. I poured us coffee, and brought our mugs, along with milk, Birch's soy milk, and sugar to the table. "Glenda, are you all right?"

She shook her head slightly. "No. Not at all," she said, scooping a large teaspoon of sugar out of the cut glass bowl and stirring it into her coffee along with the soymilk she had already poured. "It's Will. He has finally filed for divorce. I didn't think he'd really go through with it, but he did. He did, Aida."

"Really?" I asked, not very surprised.

Nodding, she blinked quickly several times and cleared her throat. "Yes. It's official now. I thought he was just moving out temporarily, that he would cool down, and we would work things out. What is there even to work out, though?" she asked, pausing to sip her coffee. Before I could reply, she began again, "What I mean to say is, has anything really changed? It is not as if Will just found out he's not Birch's father. He knew all along. How can he be so angry with me? I didn't tell Birch, just as we had always agreed. Nor did I push Birch to question Catholicism. I did everything Will asked. So why is he doing this? I thought we loved each other. I just don't see what has changed."

"Well, have you been able to talk to him at all? Have you asked him those questions?"

"He refuses to discuss things, Aida. Just refuses, without explanation."

Not knowing what to say, I sipped my coffee. I fiddled with my spoon. I looked down at my hands.

"What is it?" she asked me, placing her mug carefully on the table. "You always get fidgety when you have something to say that you think is upsetting."

"What? I do not," I replied indignantly. "I . . . It's just that, well, I don't want to pry, Glenda."

"It's okay. Tell me what you're thinking," she insisted.

"What about Thaddeus?" I blurted.

"Thaddeus?" she repeated, her voice soft, her eyebrows slightly raised.

Inhaling deeply, I forged ahead. "It just seems to me that you two have so much in common. Aren't you interested in seeing if there is still something there?"

"Don't be naive. It's a romantic idea, but we don't even know each other anymore."

"But it doesn't have to be that way."

"I love Will. I don't want to lose him. I don't want to pursue a memory. Look, I made a choice thirty years ago between these two men. Yes, I loved both of them. I never believed that just one of them was my one true love. Different people bring out different things in the ones they love. No matter which path I chose, there would have been happiness and struggle, just different kinds. I can't just switch paths now, just because this one got a little rockier than I expected."

"Oh. I see," I said, not seeing at all. She was with the wrong person. Will was moody and prone to violent outburst; Glenda was the most centered, peaceful person I knew. I had seen Will be cruel and cold. He didn't understand Glenda—or Birch, for that matter.

"You're not convinced?" she asked me.

Leaning forward slightly and poking my spoon into the air in Glenda's direction, I said, "I met Thaddeus. In five minutes I knew he was more right for you than Will."

"Why is this so important to you, Aida? I know you're not pushing Birch's agenda. He would like nothing better than to see Will and me reconcile."

Just then the timer on my stove rang, and I rose, shrugging. I removed the loaves of biscotti from the stove and placed them on a cooling rack. Standing behind the counter, I replied, "I don't know. Maybe . . . maybe it's just because he's so much more obviously like Birch. Maybe that's why I connected with him. And I don't understand what you have with Will. From my outsider's perspective, he seemed positively vicious with both you and Birch that night. I feel . . . protective of you both. I admit to not knowing much about Thaddeus, just what Birch shared with me from the letters, just what I gleaned from our brief

visit with him. I don't know. Maybe I am just being naive,"
I faltered.

I watched her look into her mug, swirling the remainder
of its contents. She made a strange sort of noise just then,
and at first I thought she had laughed. Then she did it
again, and I realized that dry, throaty, raw sobs were
erupting from her unwilling mouth. I ran to her side and
held her while she cried. After an eternity of ten minutes, it
seemed her sorrow had melted into something controllable,
and she wiped her face on the paper napkin she had been
clutching in her lap.

"I apologize," she said, raising her chin slightly and
looking me in the eye once again. "This is not what I do."

I nodded. "I feel so . . . I'm just sorry, Glenda. I didn't
mean to . . ."

"It's quite all right. You are just forcing me to acknowledge the fact that I am as unresolved as I was thirty years
ago. I'm not sure what I should do with that. Quite honestly, I am utterly ashamed of myself. I should go. Thanks
for listening, Aida, and for all that you offered. I'll just . . .
I'll catch up with Birch tomorrow."

"No, wait, Glenda. Please don't leave like this. Sit. Let
me slice the biscotti. We'll talk a bit more. Please stay."

As she shrugged somewhat helplessly, I rose from the
table and returned to the counter to slice the loaves. Setting
aside the ends, I stood the slices on the pan and returned
them to the stove again to bake briefly. I brought the still-
warm, almond-flavored loaf ends back to the table, and as I
presented one to Glenda, I wondered how I could possibly
make her feel better. It just seemed cruel to let her leave
mired in so much pain, confusion, and self-doubt. For a
few moments, we munched silently on our cookies.

"Delicious," she mumbled.

"Thanks." Pausing for a moment, I chewed slowly, reaching for some level of common ground from which to approach Glenda's dilemma. "Look, Glenda. I know this is really none of my business. And it's true that I have no idea what it feels like to have such strong feelings for two men at the same time," I began, paying close attention to my fingers, which were pressing into the cookie crumbs on the table and dusting the crumbs off onto my napkin. "But I do know something about loving one man. And what I've learned about Birch is that even though people do change, there are some things about him that never have, and never will, and those are the things I love the most. He's a dreamer, but he's practical, too. He cares about so many things.

"I don't know. I feel like I'm just babbling. But I guess what I mean to say is that, do you really think that Thaddeus has changed so much? I'm sure you have more in common than you think. And maybe the fact that Will filed for divorce is a sign, that it's okay to at least talk to Thaddeus," I told her, my heart pounding in my chest. I finally raised my gaze to Glenda's face, and found her staring at me, eyes wide, jaw tense, brows furrowed.

"But isn't it horrible and wrong of me to want Thaddeus now?" she asked, speaking quickly and hurrying forward before I had a chance to respond. "Isn't it unfair to him? And to Will? And what would it mean for me to pursue him? In so many ways I feel as I did thirty years ago, even though so much has changed. I've built my life here. I'm a settler, he's a wanderer. What would it mean to my career, my life, to try and be with Thaddeus? I don't want to be in Maine, or anywhere else. My son is here. You're here. I'll have a grandchild soon."

I shrugged. I folded my napkin. Then I squared my

shoulders, lifted my chin, and began quietly. "I can't an-swer those questions for you, Glenda. But Will has made his choice known. And maybe it's possible that you're trying to talk yourself out of doing anything, because you don't want anyone, including yourself, to get hurt. But look how much this . . ." I paused, searching for the right word, "this stasis itself is hurting you. If I were you, and I know it's easier for me to say than for you to do, but I would at least talk to Thaddeus, and I would do it now. You've al-ready lost thirty years of loving him. I don't think I could live a day without Birch."

Just as these words were out of my mouth, the door flew open, and in walked Birch, accompanied by my father and Doreen Nickerson, whom I recognized instantly.

Chapter Thirteen

For the next several moments, the five of us exchanged greetings and questions. Birch opened the volley with, "Hey, look who I ran into outside," and then, "Mom? What are you doing here?"

Before Glenda could respond, my father stepped forward with Doreen on his arm, "Sorry, Angelina. We're early. This is Doreen."

Doreen and I were looking closely at one another. As she stuck out one thin hand for me to shake, the other flew upward, to brush strands of red hair away from her angular face. She was nearly as tall as my father, slender, and fair. Something about her smile and the red hair tugged relentlessly at my memory. I reached out to her, shaking her hand firmly and slowly, trying to remember. "I'm Aida," I said, "and I'm certain that I've met you before."

"You're right. I don't think it was at the Sunrise, either. That was my first guess when I saw your face," she replied.

As soon as I heard the soft, low tone of her voice, I knew. "The drug store. You were buying lipstick."

"And you were getting a pregnancy test, I remember now. So! Congratulations, then. Salvatore told me you were expecting. I knew you were pregnant," she said, leaning over to hug me.

The strange chaos of these greetings was interrupted by the timer on the stove ringing. "Oh! The biscotti!" I said, running to the stove to remove the slices from the oven.

They would grow perfectly crisp as they cooled. Placing them on the cooling rack, I stood behind the counter and surveyed the group assembled in the dining area of my tiny kitchen. The four of them were bunched together, hugging and chatting. I'm sure Glenda whispered something of an explanation in Birch's ear as they embraced, for I saw his arms clutch her a little more firmly, and noticed the way his head hung low for a moment, before he kissed her forehead and stood up straight once again.

"Glenda," I called from my position behind the countertop, "you'll stay for dinner?"

She nodded. Birch escorted everyone to the living room and returned to the kitchen to start pouring wine while I finished assembling the eggplant Parmesan and put it in the oven to bake. Hugging me from behind while I worked, he brushed aside my hair to kiss my neck. "How are you?" he whispered.

"I'm fine. Why don't you hop in the shower after you take everyone their wine, and I'll take out some olives and bread and cheese for everyone to munch on."

"Sure. How long was my mom here before we got here?" he asked.

"A while. We talked."

"About my father?"

I nodded, guessing that while he meant Will, I could still answer in the affirmative, even though we had mostly discussed Thaddeus.

"Is she okay?" Birch asked.

"Well . . . I think she will be. She just needs some time to figure things out."

Birch frowned at my reply, kissed me lightly, then departed with the wine. I ran my fingers through my hair, gulped a glass of water, and took a few deep breaths before picking up my tray of appetizers and setting out for the rather silent living room.

My father and Doreen were sitting on the couch, and Glenda was perched on the ottoman, which I had moved opposite the couch for extra seating. After placing the food on the coffee table, I sat in my mother's chair. She had always been such a gregarious person, always knowing just the right thing to say in every situation. Opening my mouth in an attempt to utter something innocuous like, "so, Doreen, you and my father met at the Sunrise?" I suddenly remembered the brief conversation I had shared with her and found that instead of my lukewarm conversation starter, what I finally expelled from my mouth was a loud guffaw. Three heads turned to me and stared.

"What? What's so funny?" my father asked.

Shaking my head, I continued laughing for a moment, and then said, "Doreen, you remember what we talked about, don't you? That night, at the drug store?"

She raised her eyebrows for a moment, then her head cocked slightly to the left, then to the right. She giggled quietly, then snorted, which set me to laughing even harder. "I do, I do," she gasped.

"What the hell is so funny?" my father bellowed. I stopped laughing, not because of my father's obvious irritation, which in fact added to the hilarity of the moment for me, but because I noticed out of the corner of my eye how uncomfortable Glenda looked.

"Oh, I'm sorry, I'm sorry everyone. It's really not *that* funny. I guess it's just that I walked in here and it seemed so tense, and then I remembered what Doreen had said, and . . . well, I guess I just needed a good laugh."

Glenda cleared her throat softly and said, "Aida? Are you going to share with your father and me what it was that inspired this mirth? You're not the only one who could use a good laugh."

My father nodded in agreement. "Thank you, Glenda," he said to her. "She's right, you know," he told me, "and this little insider joke has gone on long enough. That was rude of you, Angelina," he scolded. Doreen blushed lightly, having escaped my father's reprimand.

"Okay, okay," I began as Birch entered the room.

"What did I miss?" he asked, running his fingers through his damp curls. He sat on the floor, between his mother and me. "I heard laughing."

"I was just remembering talking to Doreen the night I bought the pregnancy test. She noticed what I was buying and said something about it being exciting, and I told her that my family—and Pop, I was thinking mostly of you—was a little old-fashioned and might not be too thrilled. And she said that she wished her boyfriend—you, Pop—was a little more old-fashioned, because she had been seeing you for a year and hadn't met your family yet."

I grinned broadly as I recalled the conversation, and Doreen smiled and nodded as I spoke. Glenda and Birch chuckled softly, and I felt a bit of relief that the story had offered at least a little amusement to this strange social circle. Then my gaze fell upon my father's face. His brows were crinkled into one dark, furry streak across his forehead. Glenda and Birch must have noticed his expression. Although I hadn't taken my eyes off of my father's face, I heard the room grow suddenly silent.

"Oh, Salvatore," Doreen chided him.

"Come on, Pop," I said. "It's a little funny. We were both talking about you, but didn't know it, and . . ."

"I get it, Angelina," he growled. "It's not that funny."

"Oh, sure it is! Now don't be cross. You'll spoil your

appetite," Doreen said. And then she did something that made me smile a little sadly, because Marco and I used to do the same thing when we were kids. With her finger she smoothed his furrowed brows. I missed that easy intimacy, being able to just reach out to him like that. Between us now hung a thick fog of disappointment, shame, guilt. Would there ever be enough sun to burn it off? Pop sighed and smiled, saying, "Okay, fine. I'm fine." Then he laughed and kissed her cheek.

"So," I said to Doreen, struggling for a feeling of normality, "Did he like the lipstick?"

She replied with another chorus of tinkly giggles. "Enough, you two," my father interjected. "You spend five minutes together in a drug store and now you're old friends? Angelina, go check the dinner. It smells like it's almost done."

Fighting a frown, I rose obediently, seeing that Birch's attention was not focused on me, or the cuddly exchanges between Doreen and my father, but rather on his mother. I gazed at her face as I passed, noticing the distant look in Glenda's eyes. This must be painful for her, having just been served with divorce papers. As I readied the dinner table, Birch wandered into the kitchen.

"Need any help?" he asked.

"No, thanks. How's your mother? Is she okay in there with just the two of them?"

"I think so. Your dad started asking her about work, so I'm sure she'll talk his ear off about the courses she's teaching this term. Did you get the mail today?" he asked, munching on a hunk of bread.

"No. I didn't get a chance to even run down to the lobby."

"I'm going to go grab it. I'll be right back." As I nodded, he was closing the door behind him. I felt slightly irritated that he had to get it right away, but maybe he was waiting to hear about a grant for the sanctuary. Retrieving the salad from the refrigerator, I heard footsteps and turned to find Glenda in the kitchen.

"I'm just grabbing another bottle of wine," she said, then added, "Thanks for inviting me to stay, Aida. It's good to be with people right now."

"Not just people, Glenda. Family. You're part of mine now, too, and what's mine is yours, grumpy Italian father and his girlfriend included."

She laughed lightly, inserting the corkscrew into the Chianti just as Birch strolled through the door. "I got a letter from Thaddeus," he said, looking down at the envelope and not realizing his mother was standing there.

"Really?" she asked.

He glanced up, nodded, and tore the letter open. Standing there with the door still opened behind him, Birch read the letter, eyes wide, lips silently mouthing the words. I walked over to him, closed the door, and touched him lightly on the back as he read.

"What's it say?" I asked.

Glenda stood at the counter, wine in hand, corkscrew halfway into cork. Her lips were pressed together and she had gone a little pale.

Birch cleared his throat, looked at me, then at his mother. "It's just a casual letter, at first, about work, the weather. But then . . . then he asks for my permission," he said slowly.

"For what?" Glenda asked, speaking the question already on my own lips.

"He's asking for my permission to see you. Just to catch up. He says he's not trying to come between you and Dad. Here," he said, holding out the letter.

Glenda's hands remained firmly attached to the bottle of wine and the corkscrew. "I . . . Birch, I don't . . ." she faltered.

She couldn't do it, I thought. She couldn't even take the letter, express interest in Thaddeus in any way, for fear of disappointing Birch. She tore her gaze from her son, and the letter, and focused all her attention on removing the cork from the bottle of wine, a task she performed slowly and deliberately.

My hand was still on Birch's back, and ever so softly, I pressed my fingers against the red cotton sweater he wore. After just a moment's pause, he walked over to his mother, laid the letter on the counter next to the bottle of wine, and placed his own hand on her back. Kissing the top of her head, he told her, "It's okay, Mom." Then he strode into the living room, and I heard the light tones of his conversation with Pop and Doreen.

Glenda's eyes were now fixed firmly on the letter. She finally released the bottle of wine and held the letter with both hands, scanning its contents. I watched as the thin, tight line of her mouth was eventually allowed to curve into a tiny smile. Folding the letter and clutching it to her chest, Glenda exhaled as if she had never breathed before. Her brown eyes crinkled slightly as they fixed upon me, and I replied with a tentative smile.

"Angelina!" my father yelled from the living room. "Are we ever going to eat?"

"Yes, Pop! Come on everyone," I called back. "Time to eat!"

Glenda stashed the letter in her bag near the door, and we all sat down. I watched my father take his first bite of my eggplant Parmesan, saw him put the fork down, lean back in his chair, and gaze up at the ceiling as he chewed.

"Angelina," he said, still looking toward the heavens. "Your *sugu*," he began.

"It's too sweet, isn't it? I always make it like that for myself, but it's not like Mom's, is it?"

"Sweeter than your mother's," he replied. "But it's good for the eggplant. Not bad," he said, as he recommenced eating. My father was fairly stingy with his culinary compliments. "Not bad" was at least a B+ in Pop's book. While I had been hoping for a more enthusiastic response, at least I hadn't repulsed him.

Glenda, Doreen, and Birch also complimented my cooking before our dinner conversation turned to family anecdotes, and then to local news and gossip, and finally to politics. I found Doreen to be congenial, well spoken, and more liberal than I'd expected of anyone involved with my father. By dessert, we had strayed to a topic I had hoped to avoid, thanks to Birch, whom I kicked under the table as he asked, "So, Doreen, do you go to St. Benedict's as well? I can't recall having seen you there. That is, when I attended regularly," he finished in a mumbly tone.

"Oh, I'm not Catholic," she said, sipping her coffee, which she drank heavily diluted with cream. "I'm Lutheran, but I don't attend with much regularity myself," she told us casually.

I raised one eyebrow at my father, who, having noticed my expression, suddenly took great interest in the way his biscotti soaked up the dark coffee as it was vigorously dunked into his cup.

Doreen went on, "Our church is a bit stuffy, and there are some things about the Bible that bother me, quite frankly. But my Bible study group is open to all sorts of viewpoints. I mean, that's the whole point, isn't it? Anyway, I don't know how else I'd stay on track, without

236

some sort of church activity, you know?"

Glenda was nodding, always deeply interested in people's spiritual motivations and beliefs. Birch, as usual, was smiling, able to see the humor in most of the situations involving my family. My father was still looking down at his now soggy biscotti.

"I think I know where you're coming from, Doreen," I replied. "You have to find what works for you, right?"

"Amen," she said with a grin.

"Ah, I wish I could be there tomorrow when you meet my Nonna," I told Doreen. Looking up, I saw my father glaring at me. Birch and Glenda were grinning in a nearly identical manner.

"I know. I wish we could all get together at the same time," she said.

My father cleared his throat and said, a little too firmly, "Too bad you and Birch have to be out of town tomorrow."

So, I thought. He hadn't told Doreen about the situation between Nonna and me. I thought about calling him out on his lie, but the look on his face told me I shouldn't dare. Birch must have noticed this silent exchange, as he wisely remained tight-lipped about our mystery plans to be gone tomorrow.

My father finally managed to change the subject, asking us about our house hunting, and the remainder of the evening was passed more or less pleasantly. It was nearly nine-thirty by the time everyone left and Birch and I had cleaned up. As we fell into bed together, we discussed the evening's exchanges.

"I'm glad your mom stayed," I said.

"I am, too."

"You did the right thing, Birch."

"What do you mean?" he asked, curled on his side, his

bare shoulder peeking out from beneath the covers.

"You gave her your approval. She couldn't—wouldn't—move forward without it. And I know it must have been hard for you. I know you really hoped she and Will would work it out."

"I know how impossible he's been to talk to. And I know how much she longs to be connected with someone. She and my father never interacted that way together, the way your Dad did with Doreen. Mom needs that, she needs to laugh. My father never made her laugh. I had hoped she would work things out with my dad, but . . ." He trailed off as he rolled onto his back to stare up at the ceiling. "But I guess that's not my choice to make," he finally finished. Clearing his throat, he began again, "So? How do you think things went with your father?"

Shifting my gaze from his bright eyes to the gold cross resting on his chest, I said softly, "Fine, I guess. Considering everything."

"What's everything?" Birch pressed.

"You've been around us. You know. He's ashamed of me. He's trying to at least be able to be in the same room with me, but . . . I don't know . . . I make him sad, and angry. And that leaves me feeling the same way."

"I'm sorry, Aida. But you guys are trying, right?"

I was thinking two things just then, but I voiced neither thought. I wondered if Birch and Will would even bother to try, and I wondered how long Pop and I could keep up the pretense of trying. When I didn't answer, Birch leaned over and kissed me, then settled himself back onto his pillow.

I watched him for a few long moments. His long golden eyelashes fluttered open and closed and I thought he might be falling asleep. I loved him so much in that moment that I almost stopped breathing. My chest felt tight, and inside my throat air was being blocked by a heavy thickness that must have been the commingling of joy and hope and pain and despair. Gasping audibly, I forced my breath into a regular pattern once again. Birch turned his head to look at me, but said nothing. Even though I had encouraged Glenda to consider Thaddeus, I found myself still wanting Will to be a father to Birch. It seemed unjust of Will to abandon Birch now, and I felt torn in half to think of Birch as suddenly fatherless.

"So," I said, clearing my throat and trying to feel sane once again, "what should we do tomorrow? Apparently we're supposed to be out of town."

"I know. I can't believe your father just lied like that. Why didn't he just tell Doreen that you and Nonna weren't getting along too well right now?"

"Well, that's a little embarrassing, don't you think? It makes us sound so childish." I paused, knowing full well that Birch probably thought we *were* being a bit childish. "Anyway, it's probably just not the first impression of our family that Pop wanted to show to Doreen."

"I suppose."

"Are you going to go to the sanctuary tomorrow? To check on Sasha? Can I come?" I asked.

"Really? Are you sure?"

I nodded eagerly.

"Okay," he replied, rolling toward me and kissing me. "We'll both go."

When the alarm rang at half past six, Birch and I readied ourselves for a run. Cold but sunny, Sunday morning smiled on us as we picked our way around a few downtown city blocks. I ran cautiously, trying to pay close attention to my footing. We kept the run short, and after we showered and were driving toward the sanctuary, Birch laughed and told me he could finally keep up with me.

We spent the better part of the day at the sanctuary. Birch made his rounds, conversing briefly with April and with the slew of volunteers there to help feed the dogs and cats and clean their cages. Sasha remained in Birch's office most of the time but rose to greet me whenever I entered the room.

"She really likes you, Aida," Birch told me. "How are you doing out there? I hope you're not doing too much."

"I've been brushing the dogs as the volunteers take them out to clean their cages."

"Leave that big black lab mix for one of the volunteers. He's really high strung, and I don't want him jumping all over you and knocking you down." I nodded as he continued, "Let me know when you're ready for a break. We'll take Sasha out, maybe walk down to Ophelia's for a snack."

After another thirty minutes of dog grooming, I went to the bathroom to scrub my hands, and returned to Birch's office. "Ready," I said.

He shut down his computer, grabbed a leash. "Sasha, want to go for a walk?"

Once outside, Sasha trotted obediently next to Birch, and I walked snuggled close to him, my arm looped through his. At Ophelia's, a small deli, Birch and Sasha waited outside, and I stepped in to buy some bread, a small wedge of cheese for me, and a couple of apples. We strolled down to a park by the river and munched our snack. I shared my cheese with Sasha, who sat on the bench between Birch and me. I looked over the dog's big head at Birch and said, "This feels right. She's a good dog." Sasha turned to me, nudging my hand for another piece of cheese. "Here," I offered. "It's the last piece. Don't ask me for any more."

"You must love her as much as I do, then," Birch said.

"You gave her your last piece of cheese."

I smiled, never before knowing what it was like to love a dog. I kissed Sasha's nose, and she kissed mine. I laughed.

Returning to the sanctuary, we remained for a couple more hours, and picked up a paper on the way home. We spent much of the rest of the day perusing the home listings, now more determined than ever to find a place for us, for our baby, for Sasha.

As the week unfolded, I met repeatedly with Dwight to develop a plan for turning my column over to Ken after the baby was born. I also wanted to whittle down my hours to a part-time position in the month prior to the baby's arrival so I would have time to get things ready.

Before long, March was finally over. I was getting a little thick in the middle. We were getting restless to find a house. Sasha needed a home. One Friday morning, after receiving a phone call from Dr. Rodriguez, I phoned Birch from my desk at work.

"Hey, it's me," I said. "Dr. Rodriguez had to cancel our appointment today."

"What? Why?" he asked, firing off the one-word questions rapidly. "I thought we were going to hear a heartbeat today," he said, more softly.

"Her office called this morning. She's delivering a baby. I rescheduled for next week."

"That's okay to do? Shouldn't we be staying on schedule?"

"They said it was fine. It's still pretty early in the game, Birch. I'm just thirteen weeks along."

"Seems longer," he replied.

"Tell me about it," I said. "But can you still get out early?"

"Sure, why?"

"I have a surprise. I'll pick you up at two."

That afternoon, I drove to the sanctuary, parked the car, and ran inside. "Come on," I said as I entered Birch's office. Sasha jumped up and ran over to me. I knelt down and let her lick my face. "Can Sasha come, too?" I asked him.

"I'm really not supposed to do that, Aida," Birch said.

"Come on, you're the boss."

"Not technically. No, she has to stay here until I can really adopt her and take her home. I'll see you tomorrow, girl," he said to Sasha.

I frowned as we left, but couldn't really keep it up. I was too excited. In addition to the call from Dr. Rodriguez's office, I had also heard from our realtor that morning.

"Where are we going?" Birch asked as I drove.

"You'll see," I told him, but as we got closer and closer to the farmhouse, he guessed.

"Why are we headed out there, Aida? Why rub salt in the wound? The new people are probably moving in as we speak."

"No, they're not," I told him gleefully.

"How do you know?"

"Because we're the new people," I answered.

Chapter Fourteen

"What?" he asked, jaw dropping.

"Tracy Evans called this morning. The other deal fell through. She didn't say why. I didn't care. She's meeting us out there now so we can take another look at it, but I told her we were still interested and wanted to submit an offer."

"I can't believe it, Aida! It's going to be ours," he said, leaning over to kiss my cheek.

When we arrived, we ran through the house like little kids with big ideas tumbling all over the place.

Tracy waited patiently for us to finish our tour, after which we followed her back to her office to draw up the papers.

"It's a good sign," I told Birch on the way home. He shook his head, laughing a bit. Then he looked out the window, and his expression changed. "Aida? Why are we headed toward my dad's pub?"

"Well, I'm hungry, and I thought maybe you could talk to your dad, tell him the good news."

Despite my instinct that Glenda should be with Thaddeus rather than Will, I remained convinced that since Will was the only father Birch had ever known, the two of them should try to pioneer some new kind of relationship, now that the lies of the past had been revealed. The truth was uncharted territory for them; I could only imagine how difficult it would be for both of them to find one another in it.

"No, Aida. I don't want to spoil it. I'll talk to him a different time. This day is too good to risk like that."

"Oh, come on. We're nearly there," I said as I turned the corner. Birch hung his head, sighing. As I pulled into the parking lot, I could not believe what I saw. A yellow sign with large black letters hung in the front window. "Commercial Property For Sale," it read. "Oh, my God, Birch," I whispered. "Look."

He raised his head and stared at the words on the sign as if he could not comprehend them. "Aida, let's go home now."

"But don't you want to try and talk—"

"No, I don't."

"But why would he sell it? It's his life," I wondered aloud.

"Don't you get it?" he shouted. "It's not just the pub he's through with, it's me. He hasn't returned any of my messages. I leave him several every week. I told you I went to see him. He's acting like a complete stranger. Selling the pub, well, there's a sign for you. Remember how he constantly used to pester me to go into business with him? He's not going to bother anymore, now is he? He's through with me. Let's get the hell out of here, okay?"

Nodding, I pulled out of the parking lot. That evening, after a chilly little dinner, Birch attempted to normalize things between us.

"I'm sorry I shouted at you in the car," he said as we flopped down on the sofa after putting away the last of the dinner dishes.

I waved off his apology with a casual swat of my hand through the air. "Forget about it," I said. "Shouting I can understand. It's when you keep everything inside and don't talk to me that bothers me. I don't care how you talk to me. You can yell and scream, you can whisper, you can cry, or you can just plain talk, but you keeping things, big things like this, to yourself . . . well, that will ruin us, I promise you. But you can make it up to me by rubbing my neck."

Birch bowed his head, listening to my sermon, receiving his penance. He dutifully placed his strong fingers on the back of my neck and began to gently massage it. "So," he began. "What color should we paint the baby's room?"

"I don't know. But do you know what?"

"No," he said softly.

"I love our baby," I told him, feeling my body tense with emotion despite the soothing motion of Birch's hands on my neck. "I don't know if it's a boy or a girl or what it'll look like or be like at all, but here I am, loving this little thing growing in me. We're always together, and I think about him, or her, all the time. Everything about being pregnant is so absolutely alien and I don't feel as connected with the baby as I want to, but I know that I want to feel that way. And when I think about saying something like 'I have a daughter,' or 'this is my son,' my heart goes all flip-floppy. I don't know. It's as much about what it will be as what it is. Do you know what I mean?" I asked, thinking he couldn't, not really, since I wasn't really sure if I knew what I meant.

"I think so," he answered.

We went on for a while about the house, the baby, and Sasha, continuing our discussion as we drifted off to sleep. On Saturday morning, Birch left for the sanctuary, and I headed out to run some errands. Later, I stopped at my dad's and told him about the house. To say that he was cool and reserved would have been an exercise in the fine art of understatement.

"I had always planned on giving you a down payment on a house as your wedding gift, Angelina," he told me tersely.

245

"But now . . . I can't do that. You're not getting married, I guess, and to make it worse, you're living with him in sin. And having a baby." He shook his head, eyes half closed, lips pressed together.

"I'm sorry I can't be her, Pop." I said, trying to cultivate a tone of distance in my own voice. Failing in that effort, I think I just sounded querulous.

"Who?" Pop asked, glowering at me.

"The woman you thought about when I was little. The one you thought I'd become," I told him. I felt the distance now. I didn't have to try to inject it into my voice. He still thought of me in terms of his expectations, rather than who I was. Maybe that's all a parent could do. Maybe that's all a child could do as well.

When I returned home, there was a message from Tracy saying that our offer had been accepted, but I'd had such a good feeling about the whole thing that I wasn't even surprised. That evening, Birch and I celebrated with Chinese takeout for dinner. I didn't tell him about my visit with Pop.

The next morning, we rose early, as was our custom, racing to meet the dawn. As our Sunday run slowed to a jog, I asked Birch, "Are you going to the sanctuary today?"

"Of course. I have to check on Sasha."

"Tell her she'll be coming home soon," I said, pleased about the prospect of having Sasha with us, and, at the same time, anxious at the notion of leaping into joint home ownership.

"What are you going to do?" Birch asked as we stretched our legs, bracing ourselves against the cold bricks of our building.

"Read, I think. I decided that Sunday morning is going to be my spiritual study time. Your mom gave me her whole course load of books, I think. There is so much I want to learn, Birch. Now that I'm not placing my faith in an idea of God that never really made sense, I feel as if there's hope, as if I might actually be able to believe in something again, or maybe for the first time. I'm finding that as I read, I'm really responding to the idea of a god that isn't an individual, and certainly not the traditional father figure. Damn, it sounds weird to say any of that out loud."

"It's weird for me to hear you say stuff like that," he said quietly. Pausing for a moment, Birch opened the door for me and we stepped into the entryway of the apartment building. As we sat on the steps leading upstairs, Birch began again, "Aida, doesn't it feel frighteningly less comforting to think of God that way? I mean, I like the idea that there is a some*one* out there, looking out for me."

"I like that idea, too, Birch, but it just seems made up to me," I told him flatly as I stared at his angular profile. He was gazing out the window, watching, I supposed, the gathering of clouds in a gunmetal sky.

"Not very realistic? Is that your angle? You can do without feeling comforted?" he asked, still not looking at me.

I shrugged. "What the hell do I know? Maybe comfort is the wrong thing to expect, or look for."

Birch turned to look at me. "You're really in a different place than I am, Aida." The statement closed our discussion.

As the day progressed, my plan to study gradually dissolved. I felt sick; I hadn't felt that way in a while. Worse, a tight, cramp-like feeling periodically seized my abdomen. When Birch returned from the sanctuary, I told him.

"Really? Should we call Dr. Rodriguez? Oh, this is from Sasha," he said and kissed me sloppily.

I couldn't help but laugh, and went into the kitchen to make Birch some dinner.

"What about you?" he asked. "You're not going to eat?"

"You know, it's probably just the Chinese food not sitting well with me. I had some of the leftovers for lunch. I bet that's all it is. I think I'm just going to go to bed, though."

"Let me know if you need anything," Birch offered.

I took a short bath, put on a nightgown, and snuggled myself under the covers, clutching my aching abdomen, eventually drifting off to sleep. I woke up at just after eleven p.m., when Birch was getting into bed. "Feeling any better?" he whispered in my ear.

"No, but not worse, I guess. The cramps kind of come and go. I don't know. I'll call Dr. Rodriguez in the morning if I don't feel better by then."

"Are you sure?" he asked.

As I was nodding, the phone rang. I clicked on the bedside lamp. When I answered the phone, I heard Victor Alfano's voice greeting me. "Jesus, Uncle Vic! It's not my dad again is it?"

"Um . . . no, Aida. I actually need to speak with your . . . that is, with Birch," his deep voice responded.

"Oh, I see," I said, handing the phone to Birch. My hand was shaking a little. "It's Victor Alfano. He wants to speak with you."

Birch's eyebrows knitted together instantly as he took the phone from my hand. "Hello? Oh, my God. Is it bad, Lieutenant? I'll be right there," he said, his voice cracking slightly.

As he tossed the phone on the bed next to me, I asked, "Birch, what is it?" His face had gone pale, and he was hopping out of bed and dressing hastily.

"I don't know. He said there was a break-in. At the sanctuary. That I needed to come right away. That's it, but he sounded so . . . I have to go," he said, sprinting back to the bed to kiss me.

"Go. I'm fine. Should I come?" I shouted at his back as he was rushing out the bedroom door.

"No!" he called back. "Lieutenant Alfano said you shouldn't. I'll call you!" he yelled to me just before I heard the door slam shut.

Sitting there in bed, I saw that he'd left his cell phone on the dresser. I couldn't imagine what could have happened. Who breaks in to an animal shelter? Doubting that I'd be able to get back to sleep, I turned off the light anyway, and scooted back into a horizontal position. As I did so, I noticed that something didn't feel quite right.

Damp, I thought. That's what it was. My underwear felt damp. I climbed out of bed and as I stood up the room spun a bit and I felt a trickle down my legs. Stumbling to the bathroom, I felt the strange, horrible warmth wetting my thighs, winding its way down my legs. Flipping on the bathroom light, I lifted up my nightgown and saw blood dribbling onto the floor.

"Oh, Jesus Christ," I whispered. "Oh, fuck. No, no, no," I chanted aloud as I raced back toward the phone, pausing to catch myself against the wall as another wave of dizziness made the world swirl in front of my eyes. By breath was coming in short little gasps. "No, no. Don't panic," I said. "Don't!" I shouted. Hearing the terror in my own voice, I forced myself to take deep breaths, to walk the rest of the way to the phone. Scooping it up off the bed, I knelt on the floor and dialed 911.

"Hello. This is an emergency," I said, thinking that I sounded quite calm now. "Okay. I'm thirteen weeks pregnant. I'm bleeding. It's kind of a lot. I've felt kind of crampy since this afternoon. I'm dizzy. I don't think I can make it to the hospital by myself," I said, gulping down air like water. I told the man my name, Birch's name. I told him my address. "I'm dizzy, too."

"We'll be right there, ma'am. Okay? You just hold on."

"My baby's going to be okay, right?"

"You just hold on," he said again.

"Okay," I said. I stood up, still clutching the phone, thinking that I should change my underwear, put in a pad so I wouldn't just be sitting on the floor, bleeding. I felt I should be doing something purposeful. I opened the drawer of my dresser to retrieve a fresh pair of underwear.

"Ma'am?" I heard the man's voice again. "You just sit down and stay put until they get there, all right?"

"Oh, you're still there," I said, a little surprised that I was still holding the phone against my ear.

"I'm going to stay with you until the paramedics arrive. Are you sitting down?"

"I'm just going to . . . to," I didn't really want to talk about underwear and maxi pads with him so I just sort of trailed off. I began to walk cautiously back toward the bathroom, marveling at the speckled red trail I'd left on the floor. The dizzy feeling returned, only this time, my ears felt hummy inside, there was some sort of whirring noise and there seemed to be darkness closing in on me from the left and right, and I felt the ground fall away from beneath my feet and suddenly my head hit the oak floorboards I had just been treading and then it all went black.

Waking up seemed to take a long time. My mouth was dry, my eyelids felt thick and heavy, and were reluctant to open. I ached, especially in my abdomen and my back. My head throbbed. Forcing my eyes open, the first thing I saw was the gray-green curtain encircling my bed. My hospital bed. I was wearing a white cotton hospital gown dotted with the faded cross logo of Middleton Mercy Hospital.

And there was Birch. He was seated in the mauve-colored vinyl chair next to me, his large, rough hands entangled his hair. His head was bowed. My memories awoke with a scream inside my head, but it was only the tiniest whisper of a sob that escaped my lips. Bits and pieces came straggling back into my consciousness, the blood, dizziness, falling, an ambulance. I had a gauzy recollection of my feet in the stirrups, and of gazing at a monitor displaying the inside of my uterus, and of a feeling of utter emptiness, in all senses of the word. "Birch," I whispered, my voice a hollow croak. "Tell me I just had a bad dream."

Slowly he turned his gaze upon me. His eyes were swollen nearly shut and shot through with scarlet. He shook his head.

"Aida," he said. His voice was quiet, hoarse, cracking miserably with each syllable. "They said you had a miscarriage. They told me they did a pelvic exam, and an ultrasound."

I nodded.

"I couldn't get here fast enough, Aida. I'm sorry. I should have been here with you. I should have been here sooner."

My head tilted slightly to the right as I looked at him. My eyes closed as they filled with tears. I opened them again and the tears trickled down my face, dripping onto the hospital gown with the faded crosses of Mercy on it.

In one motion Birch was at my side, kissing my head, crying into my hair. We sobbed together, wordlessly, endlessly, and I thought that I could easily die this way, wrapped in this warm, damp shroud that now held the hot tears of the raw pain of two would-be parents, who never got a chance to hold their baby, or stroke his soft newborn hair, or watch her latch on to her mother's breast for the first time, or hold his hand on his first day of school, or walk her down the aisle. It all seemed so cliché, thinking of those milestones, but that was what we, as prospective parents, had been bombarded with; these were the things we were supposed to look forward to, according to the magazines and movies. We never had our chance to learn about all the in-between moments, and how important they must be in their own right. We lost someone we never knew and we wept as if we had lost each other, and in a way, we had.

When at last it subsided, and we were through wiping away each other's tears with our useless hands, Birch asked, "Do you remember talking to the doctor?"

"Vaguely. Refresh my memory," I said. I heard my voice. It sounded monotone, robotic. I felt as if I had separated into two selves—the one who would have to appear as though she was dealing with this by detaching herself from the whole experience, and me, the one who was being seared alive in hot, fresh anguish.

"He said . . . he said that this was pretty . . . common," Birch was saying.

I winced. "What else?"

"That we could try again. That lots of people go on to have perfectly normal pregnancies," he said, his own voice barely able to struggle above a whisper. He tried to sit up a bit in his chair, but slumped over again as if a redwood was lashed across his shoulders.

"Oh." I paused. Try again? How could I ever? "Did you talk to our families?"

"I called them. Told them not to come."

"Can I go?" I begged.

"They want you to stay until morning. They want to watch for signs of infection, I guess."

"The sanctuary, Birch. What happened?" I asked, suddenly remembering the phone call from Uncle Vic and Birch's panic-stricken expression as he left.

"I can't. Not now. You don't want to know right now."

"Birch," I said, my voice low, quavering. "You tell me right now."

He stood up, turned away from me. "Jesus, Aida. Let it go."

"Look, I'm at rock bottom here. Tell me now while I'm in this fucking pit because if I ever manage to feel a shred better, if I can even come close to being a human being again, there's not going to be any way I can come back into this hell and ever get out again. So if it's that bad, you tell me now."

Birch turned back around to face me. Taking a deep breath, he looked at the floor and began speaking, shifting his weight from one foot to another. He reminded me of some sixth-grade kid giving a report to his class.

"Three kids," he began. "Teenagers. Like fourteen, fifteen. They're out looking for some trouble to get into, roaming the streets," he said as he began pacing the small space. "One of the sick fucks decides as they walk past the sanctuary that it would be an easy place to break into and wouldn't it be . . . fun . . ." Here, Birch virtually spat the word at the floor, ". . . to steal a cat to fuck around with. You always hear about kids like that, on the news, the ones who grow up to become serial killers, you know? Well, they manage to bust their way in. They trigger a silent alarm, but they don't know it yet. How stupid were we? A silent alarm.

"The cat room is locked. But there's my office, easy to

get into. And guess who's inside? Sasha. Curled up under my desk. If only I had . . ." He paused, shook his head violently, and then continued, "They go for my keys. Sasha comes at them. They panic. They kick her. The three of them, kicking the life out of her."

Birch stopped. He swallowed. I could only watch and listen in utter horror. "Then they . . . they pulled out a lighter," Birch was saying through his tears. I can barely hear him through my own cries. "When the cops get there, one of the kids had taken his coat off and was trying to smother the flames on her hindquarters. He panicked. Couldn't go through with it. He's the one who told the cops everything. The other two weren't talking. That was the first thing I noticed when I walked in was the smell. The burned fur.

"You want to know what the worst part is, Aida? Sasha . . . she survived. I can't even imagine the amount of pain she's in. Broken bones, burned, can't even fucking move when I get there and she just opens her eyes and gives me this look . . . I can't even describe it. April and Louis got there shortly after me. They did what they could for her then we got her loaded into April's van to take her to the emergency vet hospital. That's when Alfano pulls me aside, says he just heard over the radio that they're looking for me, that you're in the emergency room at Mercy."

Tears spent, throat raw from sobbing, I clamped my jaws together, clenching them hard for a moment as I swallowed the bile that had risen into my throat. After another gulp, I growled out through my gritted teeth, "Get me discharged, Birch, so we can get over there."

"Aida, you can't—"

"I'm going. We're going. Don't tell me otherwise," I said, sitting up.

After about an hour of paperwork, instructions to watch out for excessive bleeding and fever, and a million other things I had no desire to even think about at the moment, I found myself wrapped in Birch's coat, still dressed in the hospital gown, as my bloody nightgown and underwear had been discarded. Apparently, they couldn't force me to stay, but I was leaving "against medical advice."

I didn't care. Medical advice hadn't done me a whole lot of good up to this point anyway. Once home, I teetered like a fawn on shaky legs up the steps to the apartment, leaning heavily on Birch. He helped me shower and dress, forced me to eat a piece of bread and drink some water, and then we were on our way again. Before we departed, I carefully folded the hospital gown and placed it on the top shelf of my closet.

Headed south, we drove silently in Birch's Jeep for several long miles before Birch croaked, "What the hell are we doing, Aida? After what you've just been through? Aren't you in pain? We should be home. You should be trying to get some rest. It's the middle of the night. You just had—"

"Birch!" I screamed at him. "Don't! I can't think about it yet. I can handle the pain. I want to feel it."

"What? Why?" he bellowed back at me.

Because I deserve it, I thought to myself. And because it was mine, and it was all I had left. "It helps . . . to focus on the pain instead of what happened," I mumbled.

"That doesn't make any sense, Aida," he said. I could tell he was trying not to shout but was scarcely able to restrain himself.

"No."

We didn't speak at all until we arrived at Middleton Emergency Veterinary Hospital. Birch opened the door for me and helped me out of the Jeep. "Come on," he said. "We'll go in the back. They know me here. We work with these guys a lot."

Once inside, Birch was greeted warmly by the staff. He held my hand tightly. The place retained the antiseptic quality and odor of any other hospital, but was additionally perfumed with the musky scent of animals hot with fear.

We were led to the room where Sasha was being held, and found her snuggled on a multicolored blanket in a clean, spacious cage. All the air that was in my lungs rushed out of my mouth when I saw her, as if a booted teenage foot had landed in my midsection as well. She was so heavily bandaged that little of her fur was even visible. Birch began to sob softly. We both knelt by the cage, sticking our fingers through to touch the soft fur of her muzzle. As Sasha opened her eyes, her singed tail thumped only once and she whimpered a little.

"She was lucky," said a voice behind us. We turned to view the speaker, an elderly black man with white and black hair. "As far as the burns go, anyway."

"Gordon," Birch said as he rose and shook the man's hand.

"Louis and April left a little while ago. They stayed while we treated Sasha. The burns were relatively minor, Birch," Gordon began. I listened quietly, stroking Sasha's nose, while Gordon described the extent of Sasha's injuries, which included cracked ribs and a broken leg. The two of them reviewed x-rays and discussed Sasha's rehabilitation. I sat on the floor next to Sasha and sang her the firefly song in Italian, the one my mother used to sing to me.

Sasha opened her eyes again, looked at me, flicked her tongue out between the bars to lick my hand. "Sasha," I whispered to her. "I broke tonight, too." Her tail thumped again, and I thought about something that Birch had said earlier, that the worst part was that Sasha had survived. I knew what he'd meant. I knew that Sasha had been abused before, and that she didn't deserve this, and that even if she could handle the pain she'd be in for so long she would be scarred forever by fear. Maybe Birch was right, I thought as I rested my head against the bars of Sasha's cage. Maybe it was better to not survive.

Chapter Fifteen

When Birch and I arrived home, we crawled into bed. We clung to each other, wordlessly, and I felt as if I could utterly dissolve.

I knew at that moment that people were praying for me, for Birch. I no longer idolized the type of god that could be prayed to, but I ached with the feeling that words, as feeble as they were, should be said about what had happened. The Hail Marys and Our Fathers that were being chanted for me by well-meaning relatives could really only soothe the one who was praying, not the one for whom they were praying.

More than anything, I sought not comfort for myself through prayer, but rather, simply, acknowledgement. So I began, "Something." I whispered into my pillow, "Something left me today. Not just my baby. But the . . . life force . . . the spirit . . . that was in her, or him. It was here in this world, in this body, for just a very short time, but it changed me, it made me want things, seek things I had been too afraid to find before. And I'm grateful for that. But I'm terrified for that innocent little soul. I don't know what will happen to it now. So, if there is any mercy in this universe, I pray that the spirit of my baby may find peace. Amen."

Birch stirred next to me, and I wondered if he had heard. I turned onto my back, wiggling into the mattress, then rolled to my other side, facing Birch. Comfort continued to elude me. But after an hour or so, I finally fell asleep with my head on Birch's shoulder.

When I woke the next morning, I was alone. In a blissful

moment between sleep and wakefulness, there was no memory, but as I slowly sat up, rubbed my eyes, the ache of reality posited itself inside my being once again. Wandering into the living room, I smelled coffee, and saw a notebook, Birch's address book, and the phone on the kitchen table.

As Birch emerged from the kitchen, he looked at me, and I swallowed grief once again, trying to force it back down inside me. I couldn't cry anymore, not yet; but seeing Birch's face, the struggle not to weep left me weak.

Of course he hadn't shaved and a scraggly beard roughened his appearance. Smudges of midnight blue marred the usually sunny skin of his face, beneath his eyes. And his eyes. The lids were still puffy, the whites bloodshot, and the look in them was one of raped innocence. He had always been the everything's-going-to-be-okay optimist. He could always lighten my mood just by his bright and hopeful presence. Now his spirit was forever changed, shot through with a dark stain that the rest of us who had already experienced some sort of horror or death already possessed. He was one of us now, and I hated everything and everyone that had helped do him in, myself included.

"Morning, Aida," he said softly. "Why are you awake? You should be resting."

"So should you," I told him, walking toward him. I stopped in front of him, touched his cheek with my hand. "Did you sleep at all?"

"A little. Sit down. I'll get you some coffee."

I obeyed. He brought me a cup of coffee the way I had preferred it up until yesterday, sweet and very milky. Sipping it slowly, I cringed.

"Too sweet? Too much cream?" Birch asked.

"No. It tastes fine. Still, I think I'll go back to the old

way. Isn't it strange that a cup of coffee can taste like a different life?"

"Oh, I forgot. That's just the way you liked it when you were . . . It's hard to believe that you're not anymore," he said, sitting down at the table.

"What are you doing?" I asked him, gesturing toward the materials on the table.

"Making some calls. I talked to Dwight Bukowski. You've got at least the week off. You can decide after that if you need more time. You have an appointment with Dr. Rodriguez for a follow-up tomorrow. As for Sasha, she's drinking water but hasn't wanted to eat yet. I've got to go down to the police station today about the . . . break-in at the sanctuary. And I have to meet with the triumvirate, too. They'll probably want to fire me."

"No, they won't. And thank you for talking to Dwight for me," I told him quietly.

"As for you," he continued, "I want you to take it easy today. Rosie's coming to help out after I leave."

I shook my head. "I don't want to be around anyone."

"And I don't want you to be alone right now," he said, glaring at me.

"Why? I'm fine."

"You're not fine. What if you have problems from the miscarriage? An infection or something? What if you start bleeding again? They said that could happen, you know. I want someone to be able to take you to the hospital if I'm not here. I should have—" He stopped abruptly. He closed his notebook. He dragged his hands through his hair.

"Should have what, Birch? Should have been here when it happened? Guess what? It still would have happened. There was nothing you could do. You needed to be where you were."

He spoke again, his voice gravelly. "I couldn't do anything for Sasha, either. I was useless to you both."

"Useless? What are you talking about, Birch? You—"

"Aida!" he cut in with a shout. "Knock it off. Don't try to make me feel better. I let you both down. If I had listened to you maybe they could have stopped it. You said you were having cramps. Why did I just think everything would be fine? And Sasha. If I hadn't been so stupid, none of this would have happened to her. Letting her sleep in my office. It was arrogant and indulgent to think that she was so attached to me she'd be miserable and desperate in a cage like all the other dogs."

"Birch, she would have been, and you know it."

"Well, at least she would have been in one piece! And maybe you would have been, too, if I'd been doing my job."

Withering with grief, I felt my face twitching with the effort of trying not to sob. "Is that what you think of me? That I'm broken, now? And there's nothing you can do to fix me?"

"Aida, come on," he said as he knelt in front of me. "That's not what I meant. It's just that—"

"You're right, you know," I interrupted. "I don't feel whole. But they wouldn't have been able to stop it, Birch. They said there was probably something wrong with the baby. That's why this usually happens at this stage. Of course they never even called it a baby. It was just a fetus to them. Anyway, I don't really believe what they said. Maybe you couldn't have stopped it, but maybe I could have prevented the miscarriage from starting in the first place. I shouldn't have kept running. I should have eaten better, slept more, worried less. Something."

"It's not your fault. I think you know that. Dr. Rodriguez will tell us the same thing tomorrow. I think we're both just

261

trying to figure out the best way to deal with it."

"Guilt. The Catholic's first line of defense, right?"

Nodding, with a frown pulling at his lips, he shrugged and stood up. "I have to get going. My Mom might be stopping by to see you today, too."

"Jesus, Birch. I just want to be alone."

"They want to take care of you, Aida. Let them. I'll be home around five or six. I'll bring dinner." After Birch kissed my forehead, he put on his coat, opened the door and stepped out. I saw him in the hall, looking down the steps. "Hi, Rosie," he called out. "You brought Nonna," I heard him say. He turned to look inside the apartment at me. "She brought Nonna," he repeated.

Holding the door open for the two women, Birch mouthed "Sorry," at me then disappeared into the hall, the door closing softly behind him. Still sitting by the kitchen table, I just looked at the two of them. I could think of nothing to say, wishing that neither of them had come.

As it turned out, I didn't have to say anything. Rosie rushed to my side, bending down to hug me, stroking my hair. "Oh, Aida," she whispered. "I'm so, so sorry that this happened to you. Why are you sitting here in this uncomfortable chair? Come. Come into the living room," she said, hauling me up as gently as she could and guiding me to the sofa. She covered me with Nonna Anna's afghan. "Here. Aren't you chilly? Have you eaten yet? No? I'll go make you some toast." As Rosie disappeared into the kitchen, I saw that Nonna had proceeded directly there as well, avoiding greeting me at all. Why had she even come?

After a few moments, Rosie reappeared with a plate of lightly buttered toast, and Nonna trailed behind her, holding a steaming mug. I still had not said a word. "Here," Rosie said, handing me the toast. I nibbled off one corner then placed the toast back on the plate and the plate on the coffee table. Frowning, Rosie sat across from the couch, on the ottoman.

Nonna stood in front of me and thrust the mug in my hands. "Drink this," she ordered. After I had taken the cup, she sat in my mother's chair.

"It smells awful," I told her, as my nose hovered above the cloudy brown liquid.

"It's my special tea. It takes away pain. Brings back color to your cheeks. Relaxes the body."

"I don't want it," I said, furrowing my brows. My whole face was yanked into a vicious grimace.

Nonna looked at me with her eyes wide, then turned to Rosie. "Then why?" she asked, arms extended, palms facing upward. "Why did I come?"

"I didn't ask you to." My scowl deepened.

"No, no you did not, Aida Angelina, but still I am here, because no matter what came before this day, you are my granddaughter and you need me. Now, drink the tea and listen to me."

Already I was so tired of the old woman sitting in front of me. She spoke as if her sense of familial duty ought to be viewed by me as a generous favor for which I ought to be grateful. I wasn't. But maybe if I drank her foul tea she'd leave. I looked at Rosie. She nodded at me, smiling softly. "It's not that bad, Aida," she told me. I wondered if she meant the tea, or having Nonna here to lecture me. I took a sip. It was strong, a little bitter, but left a clean taste in my mouth after I swallowed. I think there was fennel in it, but I couldn't isolate the other individual flavors.

Nonna nodded deeply in my direction, almost bowing. Her thick white hair, still streaked through with black, was pulled back into a loose bun, and a few strands escaped as she straightened herself. Tucking the rebellious locks behind her ears, she exclaimed, "There! Finally! Write it down, Rosie. Aida listened to her Nonna."

Raising my eyebrows, I felt my jaw clench. I glanced at Rosie again. She was shaking her head softly. "Nonna," she said quietly. "Please. You were the one who told me you wanted to come. Why must you bait her, especially after what she's been through?"

"*Basta,* Rosie. Enough," Nonna said without looking at Rosie. She stared straight at me, but still seemed to be addressing Rosie. "What she's been through? That's what I wanted to come to talk about. Aida," she said, finally speaking directly to me. "You lost a baby. I came to tell you that I know what that is like. But I didn't lose one baby. I lost three, Aida. And no miscarriages, either. After your father was born, I had one stillborn. A boy. Marco. That's who your brother was named after. Then there was your Aunt Frannie. And after her, your Uncle Niccolo. Then, another girl, Viola. Oh, Frannie was so excited to have a sister. But my little Viola died when she was seventeen months old. She was sick. Finally, one more time, I became pregnant. I had twins. Your Uncle Enzo, and another girl. Her name was Angelina. My little angel. The last child to leave my womb. She died when she was just three months old. Frannie never got her sister. See? In a way, Aida, you are lucky. Imagine how much more it hurts to lose a baby after you bring it forth into the world, after you come to know her. My prayer for you is that you never know what that is like."

Rosie's muffled sob broke the quiet that followed Nonna's speech. "But why?" my sister-in-law whispered. "Why did so many die?"

Nonna shrugged. "Back during that time, it wasn't uncommon to lose several children when they were very young. Lots of sickness. They didn't have all these shots that babies get today, no modern cures for anything. Some just were not strong enough to survive. It was God's will, I suppose. Just like for you, Aida. God took this baby from you for a reason. Maybe there was something wrong with it. Maybe God thought you weren't ready to be a mother yet. I always thought that God took my children to punish me for my sins, even though Father Roberto told me that wasn't true. But, it hurts so badly. How can you think otherwise?"

As I placed my mug on the table, I swallowed hard, fighting my fury. I wrapped the afghan tightly around my shoulders. I sat up a little straighter and looked my grandmother in the eye. "Go," I told her. "Get out of here. How can you come in here a day after I miscarried and talk to me this way? It's true that I can't imagine the pain of going through what you went through, and I'm sorry that you had to go through it. I honestly am. But why tell me all this now? Just to show me how much worse you had it? I just skinned my knee, but you lost a leg, is that it? I should just brush it off? And all this about 'God's will.' Maybe there was something wrong with the baby, like you said. That's what the doctors said, too. But telling me that God punished me because I wasn't qualified to be a mother, that my sins are so great he needed to take my baby from me?

"How could you, Nonna? Is this the great maternal wisdom you have come here to impart? Have you fulfilled your duty now? Please, just go," I said as I scrambled to my feet. "Rosie, thank you for coming. I do appreciate what you tried to do. Give my love to my brother and Joseph. I'm going back to bed." I turned and trudged away from them both, closing my bedroom door behind me.

As I sat on the bed, I could hear soft mumbling and then

Nonna's shrill shout, "*Andiamo!* Let's go. Take me home." A few moments passed, but there was no corresponding closing of the door. I waited. Following a short rap on my bedroom door, Rosie's voice melted into my room as she cracked the door open. "Aida? Nonna's waiting in the kitchen. Your father is coming to pick her up. I'm going to stay with you."

"No, Ro. Just go on home. Thanks, though."

"This is non-negotiable," she informed.

I curled into a ball on my bed, still clutching Nonna Anna's afghan. Why couldn't Nonna Anna have been the grandmother who had come to comfort me? She was so much more gentle. But she'd moved back to Sicily ten years ago. She'd been diagnosed with some life-threatening liver ailment and had said she was going back to the old country to die. Except she hadn't. She was still managing the almond orchard her relatives had kept running during her absence, and was healthier than she'd ever been. Nonna Anna always wrote to those she'd left behind in the States, saying it was the magic of being in one's true home and rightful place that had healed her. I wondered what it was like to have such a place. I needed one now.

Rosie entered, sat on the edge of the bed, stroked my hair for a moment.

"That woman has always hated me. She blames me, you know," I told Rosie.

"Why? For what?"

"She was at our house the day my mom died. She was always there, even when Nonno was still alive. She heard me arguing with my mom. If you asked her, I'm sure she'd say that I drove my mother to her death."

"You don't really believe that do you? That she thinks that?" Rosie asked, her hand still on my hair.

266

I nodded. "She tried, for a while, to be kind to me. But then, there was the whole baptism thing, and then I got pregnant, and all of that. That's why she always says how disrespectful I am. She's not just talking about now, about my leaving the Church, and getting pregnant and not getting married. She's talking about how I was with my mother."

"You were a teenage girl, Aida. You fought with your mom. It was a completely normal, even healthy thing to do," Rosie said.

"Healthy? That's going a bit far, don't you think?" I questioned, raising my eyebrows.

"Don't you pay any attention to popular psychology, Aida? Teenagers need to break away from and challenge their parents. It's a violent, angry process because it's so painful to both parent and child, but so necessary if the child is ever going to be able to be independent."

"Oh," I answered, pausing to consider this explanation. "That makes sense, I guess. I didn't know you knew so much about child psychology, Ro. You're good at this," I said. I hesitated a moment, before continuing with a bit of a grimace on my face, "I guess that's why God let you be a mother."

"Shut up, Aida," she said, the softest of smiles on her lips. "This is no time for your dark, sarcastic anti-Catholicism nonsense. Anyway, I'm always reading a lot of parenting books. But none of it really helps when you're actually in the trenches and you're trying to figure things out as you go along. And Joseph's just a baby. I can't imagine how difficult it's going to get when my sweet little baby boy is an angry teenager, shouting at me and breaking away."

We talked for a bit longer before I remembered Nonna in the kitchen. "What is she doing out there, Ro?"

"I don't know. If she liked you better she'd probably be making lasagna. She's probably just cleaning out your sink."

"What?"

"Oh, she doesn't like me all that much, either. Every time she comes to my house, I find her cleaning something. Like I'm not tidy enough for her grandson or something. Marco thinks it's hilarious. I find it insulting."

"I never knew she did that."

"I know. We don't talk as much as we should," Rosie said, looking away from me, toward the bedroom door.

"I'm sorry," I replied. "We do things," I pleaded, remembering just then that we had never gotten together to make the cannolis. "I just figured that you've got all those sisters. You seem pretty close to them."

She shrugged, looking back at me. "There's always room for one more, Aida." Just then, I heard the apartment door open, and my father's voice. It sounded as if he was trying not to yell, but I could still hear him say loudly to his mother, "Ma? What did you say to her? You couldn't just come and talk? Try to make her feel better? She needs a mother right now."

"I tried!" Nonna shouted back. "She doesn't want to listen to anybody. Just like always. Take me home now. Rosie's going to stay."

Rosie and I had been staring at the half-opened door, listening to the exchange. "Ro," I said to her, nudging her elbow. "Get my dad before he leaves. I want to see him."

She nodded and jogged out of the room. "Dad," she said. She had been married to Marco for something like five years now, and I still thought it strange to hear her call my father "dad." "Wait," Rosie called. "Aida wants you." I sat up a little straighter in bed and waited.

A moment later, my father peeked his head into my bedroom. He looked down at the floor as he spoke. "Aida? You wanted to talk to me?"

"Come on in, Pop. Weren't you going to even say 'hi' to me? Come and check on me?"

He shuffled into the room, glancing at my face. "I didn't know if you'd want more company," he said. "And . . . I just don't know what to say, Angelina."

As he stood there, halfway between the door and me, calling me Angelina, I recalled what Nonna had told me, and I felt my cheeks flushing with anger at how much always went unsaid between us. "Pop, why did Nonna and Rosie come without you? Did you really think I wouldn't want to see my own father? And why didn't you ever tell me that I was named after Uncle Enzo's twin sister? And that you had a brother Marco who died when he was born, and a little sister who died when she was a year and a half?"

"What? This was the comfort your Nonna brought you? Telling you all that? What else did she say, Angelina?"

"Pop, it doesn't matter. I didn't expect comfort from her. I expected it from you." I wanted him to rush to my side and hug me and at least try to make me feel better, but still he stood there, shifting his weight from one foot to another.

He cleared his throat before he spoke again, his words finding their way slowly out of the straight line of his mouth. "I thought, that since your mother isn't here, that you'd rather have Nonna, and Rosie, too, to talk to."

"Because this is woman stuff?" I asked him, half joking.

He nodded, tearing his gaze from my face and returning it to the floor.

"Don't you know by now that since Mom died, *you* are the closest thing I've had to a mother? Not Nonna."

269

As my father raised his face once more, I saw that tears were streaming down his swarthy Sicilian cheeks.

"Pop," I said. "Get over here already."

He stumbled to my side, wrapped his thick arms around me tightly. My arms were folded in an 'x' across my chest, allowing me to be completely enveloped by his embrace. "I'm sorry about the baby," he whispered in my ear.

"Me, too, Pop. Me, too," I said, sobbing into his shoulder. I'm not sure how long we sat there like that, but finally we pulled ourselves apart.

"Will you stay?" I asked him.

"Nonna. I've got to take her back. And you have Rosie here. She really wants to help out, Angelina."

I nodded. I could see how hard Rosie was trying, and actually, how hard she had always tried to be my friend, my sister. "Well, I've got to see the doctor tomorrow, but maybe you can stop over later this week?"

He kissed my forehead, shrugging a little. "Soon," he said. "I'll see you soon." He walked toward the door, then glanced back over his shoulder at me. "You're strong, Angelina," was all he could manage to say.

I nodded. "Thanks." I watched him walk out of the room. Our grudges had not evaporated, but at least they had been placed out of sight for a moment.

Rising slowly from the bed, I wandered back out into the living room and found Rosie on the couch, eating my toast and reading my Tuscany travel guide. My father and Nonna were gone. As I sat next to her and adjusted the afghan over my lap, I nodded at the toast in her hand. "I'm hungry now," I said.

"Sorry. I'll make you more. Or something else, if you want. Are you and Birch planning on going to Italy?" she asked, gesturing toward the book in her lap. "Marco and I always talked about going, but now we'll have to wait for Joseph to be a little older. Oh, that reminds me. I should call my mom and see how he's doing over there."

"We'll go someday," I said. "Call your mom. Check on Joseph. I'll make myself something."

But Rosie protested, propping pillows behind me, tucking me in, and promising to return in a few minutes with some nourishment. We spent the better part of the morning trying to keep my mind off of what had happened, and were successful at least some of the time. Inevitably, though, the raw pain of the miscarriage, as well as the abuse Sasha had suffered, seeped into my thoughts and into the conversation.

Rosie bore it well, but by early afternoon was called upon by her mother to pick up an inconsolable Joseph. She kissed me good-bye, left, and returned moments later with a large bouquet of flowers she had intercepted from the deliveryman. The flowers—mums, daisies, and carnations— were from Sally and Yolanda, and I placed them next to my bed and curled up under the covers, praying for the amnesia of sleep to envelope me. Aching physically as well as emotionally, I felt as if the whole of my being was simply throbbing, and I could find no peace.

I sat up again. I wondered how Birch was coping today. As I struggled with the possibility of making sense of all that had happened, I found that the path of coherence and logic was blocked. Other people, I knew, would turn to prayer at this point. They would seek comfort and understanding. They would shoulder what they believed was their fair share of blame. And finally, just as Nonna had, they would accept their life and all its events, their fate, as God's will.

Lacking the ability to cope either intellectually or spiritually, thanks to the useless religious toolkit I had acquired through years of Catholic tutelage, I did the only thing I could do. I read. I poured over the books Glenda had lent me, seeking answers in other faiths, philosophies, unstructured spiritual ramblings. At the very least, even if I failed to glean any awareness or understanding, I had found another activity that would prevent me from simply lying in bed and weeping.

I discovered that about two hours of this type of reading had a blissfully soporific effect, and I finally nodded off in the midst of a summary of philosophical thinking on the problem of evil and suffering. After dozing for a short while, I awoke with my face in a small puddle of drool on the pages of my book, and I rolled over onto my pillow, glancing at the clock as I did so. It was nearly half past three, and I wondered as I drifted off to sleep again when Glenda might be coming over. Waking again just after five p.m., I stumbled to the bathroom, washed my face, yanked a brush through the thick tangles in my hair, and made my way to the kitchen, in search of a real cup of tea. The floral aroma of Earl Grey smelled like heaven in contrast to the brackish brew my nonna had served me.

Settling onto the sofa, I flipped on the television, staring at the images on the screen, hearing the sound, but not really ingesting anything. Just then, Birch walked through the door, shoulders slumped, looking even worse than he had this morning. "Hey," he mumbled. "How are you doing? Where's Rosie and Nonna? Where's my mom?"

"Nonna and I fought and Pop came to get her. Rosie left a while ago. She needed to pick up Joseph. I haven't heard from your mom yet," I responded from my position on the couch. "Come here," I told him.

"No, I need to shower first. I bounced back and forth between the sanctuary and the hospital today. I smell."

Shaking my head, I said, "Birch, I don't care. I've never cared about that. Come here. Tell me about Sasha. Tell me about you. How are you doing?"

"Shit," he said, still standing just inside the door. "I forgot to bring something for dinner. I'll be right back."

"Forget about it," I called after him, but it was too late. He was already gone, and I could feel him pulling away, just as he had when he found out about his father, when Will told him the awful truth and stormed out, and I could feel myself crumpling inside in reply. As much as I hated to think it was the case, the fact was that Birch and I were stronger together than we were apart. That's why we had spent three years finding each other over and over. It's not that we couldn't manage on our own. We brought out each other's strengths, and what we really needed to do was recognize that and embrace it. But if that was all true, then what would happen to both of us if we had to go through all this without each other? In fact it felt like that was what Birch was gearing up for. He'd been gone all day and left again as soon as he'd arrived home.

After about half an hour, Birch returned with a paper sack from the deli, and we sipped our vegetable noodle soup in silence. Birch ate quickly, and when he had finished, he reached into the bag and handed me an enormous oatmeal chocolate chip cookie. Touching my head softly, he disappeared into the bathroom. Nibbling on the cookie, I absently picked at the crumbs that clung to the fuzzy yarn of my worn afghan and waited for Birch's reappearance. I finally heard the bathroom door open, and listened to him pad softly to the bedroom. I waited, thinking that he'd slip into some sweatpants and return to me. I rose from the couch, cleared away the dishes from the coffee table, and wandered back to the bedroom to find Birch face down on the bed.

"Birch? Are you okay?"

"Of course not, Aida," he groaned into his pillow.

"But I thought you were coming back out there. I thought we'd be able to talk," I heard myself whine.

"Why?"

"Well, what do you mean why? How's Sasha doing?" I pressed.

"She's stable, which is more than I can say for me."

Sitting down next to him, I ran my fingers through his curls. Reaching for comforting words, I found only useless clichés, which I knew Birch would despise. Lying down by his side, I grasped his hand. He allowed it to be held. I heard a knock on the door. "It must be your mother," I said.

"What?"

"At the door." I let go of his hand reluctantly, and left the bedroom to let Glenda in.

"Hello, Aida," she said, embracing me. "I wish there was something I could say," she began, "or do, or . . . something. I'm so sorry about what happened to you and Birch, and to Sasha. Everything all at once," she said, shaking her head softly. "How are you coping? How is Birch?"

"We're . . . lost," I told her, the crumpled feeling returning.

Glenda reached out, brushed my hair away from my face. "Come on," she told me, grabbing me by the hand and leading me to the living room. She pushed aside the coffee table, making room in the middle of the living room floor. "Sit," she said. "I don't think you'll be that comfortable on your stomach right now, so just sit."

I obeyed, and she sat behind me and began to gently rub my neck, my shoulders, my back, gradually applying more pressure. I moaned, feeling the tight ache that had gripped my body begin to release itself, like a python uncoiling from its prey.

"What have you been reading?" Glenda asked.

"Philosophy of religion. The problem of evil and all that," I said with a sigh.

"A bit academic for you right now," she replied. I nodded as she continued, "But it can't hurt, unless you're trying to escape what you're feeling."

"Escape is bad?" I asked suspiciously.

"Well, it just means that you're taking a very circuitous route toward getting through all this. You're too practical for that, Aida. The direct route would be an immediate exploration of what you're feeling. You know—plow through, look it in the eye. But I understand that there is only so much a person can bear at one time. Anyway, if you need a break from philosophical treatises, try some poetry. Whitman might be uplifting, or the English Romantics, who really embrace and examine their emotions. Where's Birch, by the way?"

"In the bedroom."

"He's here? Is he coming out?" The octave of her voice increased just the tiniest bit.

"I don't know. I can barely get him to look at me, let alone talk to me."

"He learned that method of coping, or avoidance rather, from his father," Glenda said.

"What about you?" I asked. "And Thaddeus?"

"Oh, Aida," she said, her hands working quickly now. "We don't need to talk about that now."

"I've embraced and explored my pain enough for today, Glenda. Take my mind off of things. Tell me something good," I said, turning to face her.

She held my hands in her own, and we sat there for a

moment like schoolgirls. Her pink bow of a mouth wound itself into a small smile. "Well," she started. "After that letter, you know, where he asked Birch about me . . . well, I called him. I told him what Birch had said. We talked for hours, Aida, hours."

"Really?" Leaning forward, I hugged her. "I'm so happy for you. Are you going to see him?"

"No. I don't know."

"Why not?" I asked her. "Why, Glenda?"

She shrugged. "There's Will. We spoke recently. I can't tell if he's softening or not, but I'm so uncertain about giving up on the life I chose, the man I chose. I don't know. Duty, love . . . they blend a bit after a while, you know? No, of course you don't. Anyway," Glenda said, touching my chin gently with her long, pale fingers. I looked up at her as she asked, "Are you feeling all right? Physically, I mean?"

I shrugged. "I guess. Have you ever . . . ?" Glenda nodded in response to my unspoken question. "When?" I asked.

"Birch was five. I miscarried when I was about eight weeks along. It was . . . devastating. Will and I had tried for a long time to conceive. We didn't try again after that. I mean, we could have, but his heart wasn't in it anymore. He said it was a sign. Catholics are so superstitious. Not everything is God trying to tell you something. You don't think that, Aida? Do you? That this was some kind of indication that you and Birch should not have children?"

I thought about everything that Nonna had said. It didn't feel true, that this was a sign that God didn't want me to be a mother. I half shrugged, half shook my head. "I suppose not. But I don't know if I want to risk going through this again. Do you know what I mean?"

"I know."

Just then, Birch trudged into the living room. "Hi, Mom," he muttered, kneeling down beside us. He kissed her cheek, placed his hand on my back. "Are you helping my girl feel better?" he asked Glenda.

"Oh, I don't know about that," she said, smiling sadly. "You have to feel a little worse before you can feel a little better, I think."

Birch frowned, sitting back on his heels. "I don't know if that's possible."

I reached out to hold his hand. "Your mom was telling me that maybe we shouldn't try to avoid what we're feeling. That we have to explore it before we can move past it."

Birch raised his eyebrows, gazing first at me then at his mother. "That's all I've been doing, trying to figure out why all this had to happen to us, how I could have prevented it."

Glenda grasped Birch's other hand. "Perhaps those are the wrong questions," she said softly. "What have I always told you, Birch? The past can't be undone. Some things are simply beyond your control, but not your fault."

Birch snorted a bit, releasing our hands and standing up. "Thanks, Mom, but I'm not one of your starry-eyed students, seeking out Glenda the Good Witch for vague spiritual guidance." I winced, wondering if Birch had intended to wound both Glenda and me with his comment, which implied that I was one of those misguided students.

As I stared at Birch's face, I heard Glenda gasp a bit. "I should be going," she said.

"Don't leave on my account," he said as he headed for the door. "I'm going for a run."

"But, Birch," I began. He was dressed only in sweats and a long-sleeve t-shirt, not his winter gear. He ignored me, tied his shoes, and slipped out the door. Glenda and I, both still seated on the floor, stared at one another.

"He's gone," I finally said. "I've lost him, and I don't know why. We should be pulling together right now, leaning on each other, and he just keeps wrenching himself further from me, and I don't know why, Glenda." I wanted her to put her arms around me and tell me that it was one of those things that was beyond my control and not my fault, and that Birch would come back to me as he had always done, but she said nothing. She kissed my forehead and held my hands but said nothing.

Chapter Sixteen

When Birch returned about an hour later, Glenda had gone and I had showered and climbed into bed to read. He said nothing to me, proceeding right to the bathroom to shower.

When he entered the bedroom, he was wrapped from the waist down in one of my pink towels. He held it closed at his hip with his right hand. As he stood in front of me, I watched the tensing and releasing of muscles across his chest. The gold cross hanging there glinted in the lamplight, flickering as he inhaled and exhaled. Birch hadn't been to church since he found out the truth about his father. Wondering why he kept wearing the necklace, I brought my gaze to his face.

"So what was that all about?" I asked him. "With your mother, I mean."

"Look," he said. "I'll go with you tomorrow to the appointment, but after that, I have to go. I can't be here for a while."

Tossing my book aside, I straightened, stiffening. "What? What the hell are you talking about? What do you mean, you can't be here? Where are you going to go? How can you?"

"I'm going to stay with my uncle Sean. It'll take me a while to get to and from work every day, but I need to get away from here."

"From me, you mean?" I accused.

"From everything."

"But why, Birch?"

With his free hand, he raked his fingers through his wet hair, looking away from me for a moment. "I have nothing, Aida. No way to deal with all of this. When you left the Church, you gained a mentor in my mother. She never counseled me in that way. I suppose I never sought it out. Catholicism, as it was offered to me by my dad and St. Benedict's was all I had. Then you . . ." he paused, and stood there staring at me and clenching his jaw. Then he looked away again, and continued, "And now, I don't even have that. I've tried to pray, Aida, I've tried, every second of every hour since I found out about Sasha, and then the baby. It's as if the comfort I used to derive from the familiarity of those words has completely evaporated, as if there isn't anything behind them anymore."

"Oh, my God, Birch," I said, finally getting it, finally understanding why he was so rigid and cold and telling me he was leaving. "You blame me."

"Of course I don't blame you, Aida. The miscarriage was not anybody's fault—"

"No, no," I said, crisscrossing my arms in the air in front of me. "Not the miscarriage. You blame me, for having nothing, as you said. For losing faith."

I watched him press his lips together, heard him exhale heavily through his nose, nostrils flaring. He glared at me, and I knew I was right. Barely opening his mouth as he spoke, his teeth gritting, he began, "If it wasn't for you, I wouldn't have questioned things I had no business questioning. I'd still have two things that could provide some comfort right now: a father and a faith."

It was my turn to look away. My eyes stung with salty tears. I tasted blood in my mouth and realized that I had been biting my lip. Clamoring out of bed, stumbling and raging, I made my way to him. "Grow the fuck up," I spat as if each word was poison being expelled from my mouth. "Stop thinking that you always have to find a way to feel better. Nothing is going to make you feel better! What happened to us was horrible! What happened to Sasha was horrible! Nothing—no amount of praying or philosophy or poetry—is going to make either of us feel better. There is no comfort to be had, goddamn it! So stop fucking blaming me because you don't feel any! If you keep looking for ways to feel like everything is going to be all right, you're going to be disappointed. That's a fantasy. Bad things, the worst things, happen with stunning regularity," I proclaimed.

"Good things, the best things, do, too, Aida. At least I used to believe that. I want to believe it again. You don't even want that anymore," he said with a small shake of his head.

"Well, what's the use of wanting that?" I shot back. "Just when things get good it's all knocked out from under you!"

"That's the difference between us, Aida," he growled. "It's all so bleak with you. You just keep getting more and more bitter. I want to get better."

"Oh, that's poetic," I said, my face contorted into a sneer. "You know what? Don't wait until tomorrow. I'll go to the doctor by myself. I want you out of here tonight. Go to your uncle-priest. See if he can make you better. I sure as hell can't."

"No, you can't," he said flatly.

"Get the hell out!" I screamed at him, exhausted by his take on me.

He threw the towel on the bed, standing there, naked except for his cross, his damp hair tangled, his mouth an angry gash across his face. I looked at him for a long while it seemed, feeling my breath come in and out of me in hasty, hot little gulps, wondering if this would be the last time I saw him. I watched him as he hurriedly dressed, grabbed a duffel bag out of the closet, threw some clothes into it, and left me without a backward glance.

After hearing the door slam, I sat on the bed and shrieked a lifetime's worth of fury and grief into my pillow. When my throat was raw and I was still shaking and sick with emotion, I tripped into the kitchen, dragged a chair in front of the stove, and rummaged through the cupboard above it. My grasping hands finally found purchase on a half-empty bottle of whiskey left over from New Year's Eve. I poured half a juice glass full and gulped down most of the searing liquid. It burned inside my throat and stomach. I sloshed a bit more into the glass and dragged myself back to the bedroom, staring at Birch's dresser.

Two drawers hung open, socks and t-shirts spilling out over the edges. After a few swallows of the whiskey, I placed the glass on the bedside table, strode toward the dresser and slammed the drawers shut. On the way back to the bed, I stopped. I stood in the center of the room. I looked at the pink towel Birch had tossed onto the bed, knowing it was still damp, maybe even still warm from his body. He was gone.

Dawn screeched into my bedroom the next morning through unveiled windows; I had neglected to close the curtains the night before. The morning sunlight seemed brighter than it had a right to be in a Middleton April. Glancing at the clock, I saw that I only had half an hour to make it to my appointment. My body ached. I brushed my teeth, washed my face, combed my hair, and applied a little makeup. Rushing from dresser to closet, I managed to find something to wear and proceeded to my car.

Sitting alone in Dr. Rodriguez's office, I did my best to

ignore the parenting magazines strewn about the other chairs, the adorable baby pictures grinning at me cruelly from every cover.

"You're alone today?" Dr. Rodriguez asked me in surprise after she entered the examining room.

I could only nod. Wearing a paper gown, I placed my feet in the stirrups obediently, staring up at the ceiling and trying to imagine what it was like in Tuscany right now. The images of cypress trees that my travel guide had implanted in my brain could not distract me from Dr. Rodriguez's probing, however.

"Everything looks as good as it can, Aida," she was saying. "I see no signs of infection. You're going to be fine." She went on to talk about when it would be safe to start trying again, telling me the feelings it was normal to be experiencing at this time. I found myself nodding a lot, wishing I could leave but not wanting to go home, either.

When it was finally over and I found myself back in my car, I drove aimlessly, listening to the radio, and changing the station every five minutes or so. Eventually, I turned the radio off. I started thinking of church songs, the ones they always play at funerals. Singing "Amazing Grace" softly to myself, I stopped at a red light. I listened to the words. I wondered where I was. As the light turned green, I continued driving, disoriented. "Amazing grace, how sweet the sound, that saved a wretch like me," I whispered tunelessly. Those were really the words. There was a nicer version, "that saved and set me free," but a lot of churches still used the version that emphasized one's wretchedness. "I once was lost, but now am found, was blind, but now I see," I finished, shaking my head. I had always been lost in the Church, had left it, and was still without sight, intuition, or instinct.

Before the miscarriage, before Sasha, I had believed that making the break from the Church was an enormous first step for which I should be congratulated. I had believed that I was finally headed in a direction that made more sense, a direction that allowed mistakes to be made without judgment, that allowed the freedom to explore other ways of apprehending faith. I had believed that I had all the time in the world to pursue the wealth of materials Glenda had loaned me, texts that would lead me in still other directions. But now, that luxury of leisurely exploration had evaporated. I had lost the baby and apparently Birch as well. Birch had said that I had left him without a faith, while I had gained the hope of Glenda's guidance. But without him, I doubted I could even muster the desire to be guided.

Shaking my head forcefully, trying to focus on a road now wet with a slushy sort of Midwestern rain, I realized that I was only a few miles from the animal hospital. I proceeded in that direction until I could see the parking lot from the intersection. Birch's Jeep was nowhere in sight, so I parked my car and traipsed inside, speaking as little as possible to the staff.

Sitting at the door of Sasha's kennel, stroking the fur on her face, I cooed at her softly. She opened her limpid blue eyes and gazed at me, offering me a brief thump of her tail. My heart pinched with pain, I sang to her. I tried to forget everything, imagining rain washing away my memories until there was nothing left but light, the simultaneous emptiness and fullness of light. Thinking only of light, I pictured it traveling through my fingertips to Sasha, imagining it exhaling with my breath and onto Sasha.

Just be something good for her, don't bring her more grief, I told myself. I sat there just breathing for almost an hour. I bent down and kissed her nose. "I love you," I whis-

284

pered. "I'll be back tomorrow. And you'll be coming home soon. To a big white farmhouse with a yard to run in. I promise, Sasha."

I walked out to find that the slushy rain had turned to snow. I hated April. Just when you thought you'd seen the last of the snow, there was always one more storm before you could start believing it really would be spring again. Glancing at my watch, I found that it was almost three in the afternoon. I had no recollection of where I had actually been for most of the day. Exhausted, I couldn't bring myself to return to the apartment. I drove to Marco's instead.

When I pulled into the driveway, I was surprised to find Marc's car there, but not Rosie's. I knocked on the door. I waited. After a few minutes, Marco opened the door, holding a sleeping Joseph with one arm. I took one look at the two of them and burst into tears.

"Aida? What are you doing here?" he asked, holding the door open with his free hand. "Get in here already. Shouldn't you be home, resting?"

I shrugged, wiping the tears away with both hands. "I guess. I don't know. What are you doing home anyway?" I asked, calming myself with some effort. Standing in the foyer, I bent down to take off my shoes and coat, and then followed my brother to his living room.

"I come home early on Tuesdays so Rosie can have some time to herself," he explained. "Did you want to talk to her? I can call her."

"No, no. That's okay. I'm glad you're here. I was just . . . driving. I went to the doctor this morning, and—"

"By yourself? Where was Birch?"

"He . . . he . . . he left, Marc," I said, sobbing again.

"But why? How could he leave now? Doesn't he know how much you guys need each other at a time like this?

285

Damn it, Aida, where is he? I'll go talk to him." Marco was whispering, so as not to wake the baby, but was as fierce as he could be in such hushed tones.

"I don't get it. He's . . . he just can't deal with it all, I guess. He has no way to deal with it, and he blames that on me," I tried to explain.

"What? Why? That's so unfair."

"Well, it was sort of all my questioning about the Catholicism that prompted him to acknowledge his own . . . doubts, I guess. And then he was arguing about it all with Will, and he found out that Will isn't really his father, and—"

"What? What the hell are you talking about? I heard that Will and Glenda were splitting up, but I didn't know all that."

"It's all kind of a long story, Marco. I didn't think he'd want me telling everyone. Anyway, I was sort of the anti-Catholic instigator, and now he feels like he doesn't have anything at all to help him through this, and he's probably right, and—" I paused to fish a tissue out of my pocket and blow my nose, but Marco interrupted before I could continue speaking.

"Aida, he's a grown man. He made his own decisions. He can't blame you for any of that. He's just running away." Marco shook his head. "I thought he was a better man than that. I really did."

"Don't. Don't say that. I can't blame him for leaving, if he feels even half the hell I do. The thing is, I don't have anything, either. I don't know how to find my way out of this," I said, hot tears spilling onto my cheeks again. "I'm lost, Marco."

"No you're not," he said gently, putting his arm around my shoulders, and softly shifting Joseph in his arms as he did so. "You found your way here. Don't say you don't have anything. You've got family."

Frowning, I thought about Pop and Nonna. I didn't have them at all. As I leaned on Marco's shoulder, he whispered in my ear, "Although I don't think a rosary would hurt, either."

I felt my mouth jerk into a thin smile. "Shut up," I told him softly.

Marco pulled his arm away, and nodded his head toward Joseph. "I'm going to go put him down. I'll be right back." I watched him cradle his son in both arms and walk gingerly up the staircase. Swallowing the lump that had risen in my throat, I felt a little crazy, wondering if I had a right to be so grief-stricken over a baby I had never even seen. Maybe Nonna was right. At least, if I was to lose a child, I hadn't held him, or knew him. Surely this was the easier burden to bear. But it was still my baby whether I knew him or not, touched him or not. There had been some kind of life in me that Birch and I had created and now it was gone and hadn't I earned the right to grieve like any other mother?

When Marco returned, he found me slumped in a ball on the chocolate-colored sofa, my face wet and puffy. "Hey, hey, come on," he said, sitting me up and leaning me on his chest as if I were a doll.

"Seriously," he began. "You can always come back to the Church, you know. I mean, it's the only way I was able to get through Mom's death, knowing that she was at peace, feeling like God was there for me, to help me, to help us all through it."

Shaking my head, I stiffened against him. I sat up and glared at him. "You're so self-righteous, Marc. And forgetful."

"What are you talking about?" he asked, the volume of

his voice rising as his aggravation with me sparked.

"It wasn't just God who helped you through Mom's death. It was . . . oh, hell, what was her name? She was a senior and you were a freshman in college and—"

"Cut it out, Aida," he spat, his voice a low warning growl. "One thing had nothing to do with the other."

"You don't really believe that, Marco," I announced.

"Anyway," he went on, shooting me another glare, "How did you manage then? To get past her dying? Didn't you find any comfort? In anything?"

With tremendous force of will I granted him the change of subject and tried to answer his question. "Honestly, I can't remember. I don't know how I got through it. It sounds ridiculous, but running helped. It was the only way I could ever clear my head. I just ran as fast as I could for as long as I could."

"How could that help?" he asked, frowning a bit.

I shrugged. "It was just a little relief, to just not think. It was all about what my body was doing, until I wasn't really aware of my body at all, for a few moments anyway. And then it was just . . . clear."

It had been nothing and everything together, and still was like that from time to time. Running and sex and cooking, I thought as I shook my head a little. Pathetically, these were my meditations, my prayers, my escapes from conscious thought, my glimpses at the mysteries of the universe. They all allowed me access, in different ways, to a very grounding, nurturing sort of energy. I wondered if people who really knew how to pray felt the same way, and I wondered how they would feel about the way I equated such mundane and profane activities with sacredness. Walt Whitman wrote a lot about the physical and the spiritual, their union, their equality. Maybe I knew more about that than I had thought, but I found it impossible to make good use of any of that information now, when I really needed something to make sense.

Marco and I had been sitting side by side on the sofa, and I felt him stir quietly next to me. "I must sound a little crazy, huh?" I asked him.

"Everyone is a little crazy," he answered. We just sat there for a while after that, listening to Joseph moan softly on the baby monitor. Finally, Marco said, "Okay, so do you want to hear something really crazy?"

"What?"

"I told Dad that if he and Doreen got married, Nonna could move in with me."

"You're kidding! You did not," I gasped, staring at his face, trying to determine if he was joking.

"Hey, you're the one who doesn't get along with her, not me. And it'll be great to have her here to help out with Joseph. She adores him."

"What does Rosie think? What will Nonna think?"

"Ro and Nonna get along pretty well. And she likes the idea of Nonna and Joseph spending more time together. Rosie said it will be good for everybody, and give her a chance to get back into her painting."

"She is good," I said. "It must be hard to have been away from it for so long."

"She told me about what happened yesterday, between you and Nonna," Marco said.

I shrugged. "Nonna and I . . . I don't know. We can't seem to find a common language."

"You'll figure it out," Marco said, looking at his watch. "Hey, I've got to get started on dinner. Care to help me out and stay to eat?"

Thinking about how much I hated the idea of my Birch-less apartment, I nodded. "Thanks, Marc. I don't really want to be at home."

"Well, why don't you just crash here tonight? Or, for as long as you like."

Before he had even finished the sentence, I was hugging him. I did spend the night, then returned to my apartment in the morning to gather a few things. I spent the next few days alternating my time between Sasha and Marco's. I never ran into Birch at the animal hospital.

He did a good job avoiding me. Glenda had given me the phone number at Birch's uncle's place. I left a couple of futile messages, but received no replies. Once, the priest answered. The conversation stumbled on for a moment or two. Father McFarland had said that Birch was trying to reconnect with God. "Oh," I had responded stupidly, wishing Birch would spend a little time trying to reconnect with me. I don't even know if Birch had been told that I'd called.

At Marco's, I spent the days talking with Rosie, playing with Joseph, rocking him to sleep. Being with him seemed to help me a lot more than it hurt, much to my surprise. When Marco arrived home from work, we'd make dinner together. I'd forgotten how much I liked being with my brother, how funny he was, in a dry, sarcastic way. It helped to be with them, but I cried myself to sleep every night.

On Friday evening, Marco revealed that he had invited Pop and Doreen over for supper. I groaned in reply. "Really, Marc?" I whined. "Why did you do that? Pop and I . . . God, Birch, we haven't been able to have a normal conversation since I told him I wasn't going to be Joe's godmother. And then the whole pregnancy thing, and him hitting me . . ." I trailed off. The strain between my father and me was more than I wanted to deal with right now.

"I know it's rough, right now, Aida," Marco began as he

opened the oven to prod at the roast browning inside. I hadn't eaten meat since I'd found out I was pregnant. Now, with the baby gone, the prospect of a cut of roast beef remained unappealing. I watched him poke at the dark flesh, saw the juices running out, a little pink and pooling in the bottom of the pan and studded with glistening splotches of fat. "Anyway, it's too late. They're on their way," Marco informed.

When Pop and Doreen arrived, we exchanged awkward hugs and gathered around the kitchen table. Marco had a formal dining room, but it was only used for large holiday gatherings. As we ate, I finally told them all about the house.

My stomach knotted with tension, I nibbled on mashed potatoes and salad.

"No roast, Angelina?" my father asked me. He had expressed his views about the house situation when I had visited him before the miscarriage, so he had little to say on the topic now.

"I'm not that hungry, I guess," I answered quietly.

Pop raised an eyebrow in my direction. "If Birch can make you not eat meat, why can't he make you go to church?" he asked gruffly.

"Pop, come on," Marco tried weakly to intervene.

"Really, Salvatore," Doreen added, her voice subdued. "She's going through enough right now. Don't pick a fight."

I saw Rosie's glance dart nervously between Pop and me. Looking down at my plate, I said meekly, "I can't even get Birch to talk to me, Pop." I wanted to argue with him about the Church and why no one, not even Birch, could get me to go back, but I couldn't muster the energy. "And we're supposed to be buying this house. They accepted our offer before all this happened, before he left and now . . . I just don't know what to do. I don't know if I can get out of it now. We're supposed to close in a couple of weeks, but with Birch . . . gone, I just . . ." I trailed off, lost.

"Well, call him," Rosie urged. "Just call him."

"I tried. He made it clear before left that he doesn't want to have anything to do with me right now. I've left him messages at his uncle's place, but he won't call me back. How can we buy a house together when things are like this?"

"Things won't always be like this," Rosie offered. "You two will get through this."

My father waved his fork in the air, saying, "You want me to go talk to him? I'll go talk to him. He can't treat you like this, Aida."

Dropping my fork, I slammed my hands on the table and stared at my father. "Pop, what the hell are you talking about? One minute you're riding me about not going to Church or telling me how because I'm living in sin you decided not to help with the down payment on the house—which I never asked for, by the way—and then the next minute you're offering to help me. What is it? Are you on my side or not?"

"What are you talking about? Sides? I want you in Church because I know it's what's best for you. I don't know why you want to be with Birch. I don't understand him most of the time, either. But he'll come back to church, I think. Maybe that's why he's out there with that uncle of his. He's a good priest, I hear. He'll get Birch's head on straight. And with Birch back in church, well, that'll be good for you, Angelina. I only want what's best for you," he explained, speaking slowly and deliberately as if I were a child.

"But you only want one thing. Church, church, church," I stated, exasperated.

"It's the best thing for you!" he yelled. "Aren't you listening to me? Once you come back to church, everything else will make sense again!" He looked at everyone else at the table, shaking his head a little, as if to say, "Can you believe her?"

Doreen placed her hand on his arm and whispered his name, Rosie cleared her throat loudly, and Marco, the master subject-changer, was at it again. "Look, Aida. Can you make the house payments on your own, without Birch's salary?"

I nodded in reply, and then added, "But it's going to be tight."

"Don't worry about it," Marco said. "Sign the papers, whether Birch is back in the picture or not. We'll help if things get tough until you two work it out, right, Ro?"

"Of course!" she agreed, nodding enthusiastically at her husband, then at me. "Of course, Aida. You and Birch are going to be fine."

"You seem to have a lot more faith in Birch and me than we do ourselves," I told them.

"Maybe that's what the problem is," Doreen said quietly, meeting my gaze for just an instant.

I opened my mouth, but closed it again when my brain failed to expel any useful reply. Still, my neck and cheeks prickled with the heat of indignation. I liked Doreen. I really did. But her candor came a little too early after her introduction to the family for my taste. I cocked my head to the side and looked at her for a long moment. She had spent the last several minutes quietly trying to reign my father in on the religion issue, and now here she was, bent on her own attack, one whose aims mystified me. "Doreen," I began, leaning forward a bit in her direction, "I don't think you've known me, or Birch, long enough to have a say in this." Admittedly, my tone was a little condescending, but I wanted to insure that my meaning was clear.

I heard my father clear his throat pointedly, but I did not take my eyes off of Doreen's face.

She tossed her head a bit, red hair bouncing. "It's just my opinion, Aida. I'm sorry. I didn't mean to upset you," she said so casually that it infuriated me further.

I paused a moment, my teeth toying with the inside of my bottom lip. I knew I should just drop it, but I was as irritated with her backing down as I had been with her speaking up in the first place. She should at least follow through if she did indeed have an opinion.

"Well, what the hell did you mean anyway? That we have no faith in each other? What do you know about it?" My voice grew louder, word by word, seemingly of its own volition. I hadn't wanted to attack her, but there it was, and I felt myself spiraling. I had just commented myself on the lack of faith between Birch and me, and here I was railing at Doreen for what? Agreeing with me? I felt again the sense of myself divided, only now the detached robotic voice was silent and it was the angry, agonized me who was doing all the talking.

"Aida!" my father admonished sharply. "What's wrong with you?"

As Rosie put her hand softly on my back, Marco caught my eye. "What are you doing?" he said quietly. I turned my eyes back to Doreen, who just sat there, eyes wide, mouth slightly open, apparently in shock.

Closing her mouth and clearing her throat, Doreen took a deep breath and then began, "Aida, please don't be upset with me. It's just that, over the past year, your dad talked a lot about you. Not just you, the whole family. Anyway, he mentioned that you and Birch had a habit of splitting up and getting back together. And from what I've seen, and I know it's only been a little bit, you two seem really great together. All I meant was that maybe you were . . . I don't know, afraid, I guess, to trust what you had. But what do I know, right?"

I was breathing quickly now, and I honestly wanted to tell her to go to hell, but I wasn't sure why. It wasn't as if anything she had said was news to me. Of course I was afraid. Birch had always known it, too. I spent years getting close to him and then running away before I completely lost myself. I was afraid of giving myself over to something unquestionably finite. If he didn't find a reason to leave me, then he'd die. Whether or not we'd been together three years or thirty, one of those two things would inevitably happen, and I truly didn't think I'd survive. And I thought Birch deserved a woman who could love him wholeheartedly without being gagged and bound and blindfolded by fear. But when Birch had told me he needed to be away from me, instead of finding some way to convince him to stay, I grew angry, resentful that the leaving had come so soon, and when I needed him so desperately. And I was still angry. And he wasn't here for me to spit fire at. But Doreen was.

"Right," I finally said. "What the hell do you know about relationships? Look at the one you're in." Without looking away from her, I jerked my head in my father's direction. "He kept you in the closet for a year because he was too afraid, ashamed, embarrassed, or whatever, to have you meet his family. And you put up with it. He was so freaked out by the thought of coming clean with us all about you, maybe just by the thought of being with you, that he wound up drunk at his dead wife's grave. What does that say about you? How desperate are you?"

Doreen pressed her lips together and tears welled up in her big blue eyes. My father rose from his chair. "How dare you?" he roared.

I sucked in my breath, choking on regret. Of course Doreen hadn't deserved the rancor I had hurled at her. "Shit," I mumbled.

"Maybe you have a lot to be angry about, Angelina. But who do you think you are taking it out on her?" Pop boomed at me. Doreen had been rendered silent by my attack and remained completely immobilized, staring down at her hands.

"Well, what about you?" I wailed back at him as I rose from my chair. "Can I take it out on you, then? Don't you deserve it? Of course Birch left me. I expected him to. Hell, I drove him to it! What do I know about sticking it out with anybody? After Mom died, you fell apart. So did I, but you didn't even notice. You didn't notice Marco falling apart, either. He just kept on disintegrating, especially after he left for college, but you didn't notice. He—"

"Aida!" Marco shouted at me, his voice tinged with panic. "Don't," he pleaded.

It was too late, though. Reason had abandoned me. Rage was my only companion and I clung to it like a best friend as I went on. "Do you know what, Pop? Marc got *married* while he was away at school!" I blurted.

"What?" Pop yelled. "Marco, is this true?"

Shoulders slumped, Marco was looking at his wife through terrified eyes. "Rosie," he cried. "I was young. I was nineteen. It was a crazy college thing. It . . . damn it, Aida! What the hell is wrong with you?" he snarled as he turned to me.

"Why didn't you ever tell me?" Rosie asked quietly. "I

keep waiting for you to say that it didn't mean anything, or that you had it annulled, or . . ."

"Tell her, Marco," I insisted, still drunk with my own demons. No one ever came clean in my family, not about the things that mattered, not about how devastating Mom's death was, and how it affected all of our relationships from then till now. Marco remained silent and inert.

In his silence, I continued, "You loved her, Marc. I only met her twice, but I could see that. *She* helped you work out all the pain of Mom's death. Maybe the Church did, too, but it wasn't enough. And of course you were young, and of course you thought it would last. She was a senior and graduated and left you after you'd been together only a year.

"Of course Birch left me. Everyone always gets left somehow, some way. That's life, right? People die, grow up, move away, whatever. But damn it, Pop, and you, too, Marc. Maybe if you both had talked to me about what was going on with you, I would have been able to understand how to get through it all. But no one ever let me in. Of course I drove Birch away. The only person I was ever taught to be was the one standing there, alone, after someone leaves," I told them all, my tone was one of pleading desperation. I had to make them understand me just a little.

"Aida, that's not fair," Marco began quietly. His glare had softened a bit, but his brows were still furrowed, and he was frowning. "You have no right to blame us. We were dealing with everything, too, you know."

"But we should have been dealing together, not so painfully separately. Alone," I replied.

"I didn't think I was alone. I had God," he said. "But we've covered this ground before."

"I know, I know. You had God and you didn't need another living soul to help you. I get it," I stated in defeat. Marco just sighed and shook his head. Nodding toward Rosie, who had left the table and stood near the kitchen window, I mumbled, "I'm sorry, Marco. I thought you had told her."

"You had no right," he said again, averting his gaze from my face.

"That's right!" Pop agreed in his usual bellow. "No right at all to talk to us this way. Marco had God to help him through when your mother died, and when this other woman left him, too. A man's secrets are his own for as long as he chooses to keep them, Angelina. You were wrong to bring that up. Anyway, I didn't think you were going through anything alone. I thought your faith would see you through as well. But all I hear now is that you never had any. All you do now is remind me how much I failed. You should go," he said gruffly. "Every time you open your mouth lately someone gets hurt."

Turning quickly, I sprinted for the foyer, shoving my shoes on, grabbing for my coat. No one stopped me as I left. Why would they?

"She should go back to church," my father said loudly, "and pray for forgiveness."

Chapter Seventeen

What I needed, I decided as I drove back to my apartment, was to run. I raced up the steps of the building and through my door. I shed my clothes and dug through my dresser for my running gear. This early in April, it was already dark, and tonight was cold and cloudy. I didn't care. I wasn't sure if I should be running yet. But the doctor said that my miscarriage had been a "complete spontaneous abortion," that it had expelled all of the "pregnancy-related material." If there had been anything left, I'd still have heavy bleeding, a fever, an infection. I was fine, apparently.

So I ran out into the night. I headed for the path along the river. It was fairly well lit. I'd avoid the woods. As my muscles warmed to the task, I lengthened my stride, inhaling deeply the frigid night air. Clouds obscured the moon; I had no companion. I thought of Sasha, wondering when she'd be able to run again, and I screamed hate into the wind for the beasts who had maimed her. Cold drops of rain began to pepper the path in front of me, splattering my face, marrying my tears. I wept for my baby, wondering if it had been a boy or a girl. We hadn't even picked out any names. Nameless, faceless, pregnancy material. My baby. Birch's baby.

Birch. Birch. Birch. My feet pounded his name into the puddles on the ground as I ran, hard, fast, steady. Trying to reconnect with God, his uncle-priest had said. God. Fuck God. Fuck the God Birch was looking for. We had found it already and he had thrown it away. *We* were God. He should know that by now. I sobbed harder as the rain washed over me, as I ground my feet into the earth, trying to ground myself. Hell, maybe I was just trying to bury myself. Doreen was right. I was afraid. I was terrified that I was losing everyone I ever loved, myself included.

And Birch was right, too. I just kept getting more and more bitter, as if I were consciously seeking it out. And I was aware of it. I think I might have always been aware of it. But the self-knowledge seemed useless. Splashing my way toward home, I rounded the corner at which St. Benedict's stood, a cold, stony mountain rising from the earth at the intersection of Fairview and Monroe.

I stopped at the front steps, staring up at the cross atop the steeple. What was the use, I thought. I felt small, hollow, futile. I was nothing compared to the power the Church wielded in the lives of the people I loved. It's not that I felt that they were choosing the Church over me, but it seemed as if they all wanted to make sure that I understood that I was missing out on something, that I would forever be empty without the thing they had.

But it wasn't that I was empty without the Church. That wasn't it at all. The thing was, I was empty without my people. I had lashed out at them but wasn't completely sure why. I kept blaming them for everything. My family and the Church, the twin roots of so much of the pain in my life. Why couldn't I weed out all the anger and misunderstanding, and nurture the connections that still must exist between my family and myself? At the moment, however, this seemed to be a garden that could exist only in myth. In reality as I knew it, I could not exist as a nonreligious but spiritual entity that was separate from, yet still connected with, my Catholic family.

Walking the rest of the way home, soaked to the skin, I

felt my legs shaking with fatigue, wishing my heart and mind could be as easily shut down as my body. I dragged myself up the steps and checked in vain to see if there were any messages on my answering machine.

After peeling off my clothes and soaking in a warm tub, I slipped into a bed that without Birch seemed two sizes too big, and begged for sleep. When it wouldn't come, I got up, threw on jeans and a sweatshirt, and drove to Glenda's house. She seemed to be the only person who vaguely understood me anymore. As I pulled into her driveway, I was relieved to find lights on in the house.

I rang the doorbell. I waited. I tried to collect my thoughts so I could do more than just cry on her shoulder. Following the passage of a few long moments, I heard footsteps. The door opened, and I reached out, collapsing into her wiry arms. "I'm so sorry," I mumbled into her shoulder. "It's late. I just couldn't be alone. And you're the only one who's talking to me."

"What? Why? Come in, come in. Into the family room, I have a fire going. Sit," she told me. Her hair was pulled back into a ponytail. She wore pink long johns and a faded gray UC-Berkeley t-shirt. "I'm getting wine," she said, retreating into the kitchen.

She returned a few minutes later with two glasses of deep purple wine, one of which she handed to me. "Drink up," she said, talking a gulp out of her own glass. "Okay, what's going on, Aida?"

I told her about what happened with Doreen, and Pop, and Marco, about what Father McFarland had said about Birch. I talked about my mother for a long time. I talked about the baby. Glenda listened. She was a good listener, I thought, asking all the right questions in all the right places and not saying much else.

"It just keeps coming back to this Church thing, Glenda. It's like they all keep clutching their faith like it's a piece of meat and I'm a starving dog. I mean, they think I'm starving. But I'm just starving for them, not religion. I don't need the kind that they have. And they don't get that. I keep pushing them away and then chasing them down."

"Why?" she asked patiently.

"I feel like I'm constantly on the verge of losing what I love, unexpectedly, you know, like my mom. So I don't want anyone to get too close, but I don't want to lose them, either. And I simultaneously blame both the Church and myself for my mom's death. I know I do. I've always known it."

"Is that why you have such hostility toward the Church? Is that why you didn't want to be Joseph's godmother?" Glenda asked.

"No. I don't know. I guess, subconsciously, that was part of it. The godmother thing was a springboard for me. It gave me a pressing reason to think about what I believe. Then it just kind of snowballed, and I'm just kind of admitting to myself that a lot of how I feel about a lot of things comes back to my mom's death. Birch said that I just get more and more bitter. I think he's right. The more I think about things, the more bitter I get."

"About religion?"

I nodded. "Not just religion, though, Glenda. With everything that's happened, it feels like it's spilling over."

"What do you mean?" Glenda asked, sipping her wine.

"Well, after the miscarriage, and Sasha, Birch was obviously having a hard time dealing with everything. Of course he was. I was, too. But he felt that I had pushed him to question things he wouldn't have questioned otherwise. I don't know if that's true or not. But he felt that he was lost without Catholicism, that he didn't have a way to cope with all that had happened. I was so furious that he blamed me for losing it, and furious with how much he wanted it back. That's what I mean by spilling over. I've become hostile toward him for wanting something that I rejected.

"I guess that's what happened with my family, as well. Every time they seem to be reveling in their religion, like with the baptism, it becomes so easy for me to turn my back on them. And tonight, with Doreen. She said that I didn't have faith in Birch. That really got to me, because I thought, or at least I hoped, that it was one thing that I did have faith in. But it hurt so much because I think she was right. I don't know. Maybe she wasn't. Maybe it's just that he doesn't have faith in me.

"And then I turned on Pop, and Marco. I was hurtful, but honest, too. I needed to get some things out of me, I guess. But they don't want *my* truth, just the version they've told themselves for so long, just the one that makes them feel better. And everything just seems hopelessly muddled together—love and faith and family and religion and . . . everything.

"I just want some breathing room. My family doesn't know what to do with me anymore. It's as if they suddenly can't relate to me at all. So I'm not Catholic anymore. I'm still part of them. I'm still Italian. We've all shared the same experiences and traditions and history, and not *everything* was tied to religion, but maybe that's just how I saw things. I don't know."

I was speaking hurriedly, in confusing little eddies and spirals that I wasn't sure Glenda could even follow and I stopped abruptly, lost in my own muddy head.

"Aida," I heard Glenda saying. I felt her hand on my leg. "Aida," she said again, and I opened my eyes. I hadn't even realized I'd closed them. "Boil it down for me. What is the most essential nature of the conflict? Let's try to focus. You'll never figure things out if you can't focus on the heart of the problem."

For a few moments, I just listened to the sound of my breath, trying to calm down, trying to allow the truth of the situation to rise to the surface so I could skim it off and examine it more closely. "I think," I began tentatively. "I think that I'm in a position in which I have to chose between existing as part of my Catholic, Italian American family, or existing within an entirely self-constructed, individual framework," I explained, feeling as though I had to adopt her academic language in order to turn the problem into something that might be made sense of. "I can't simultaneously be who I am and who they want me to be. And they seem to not want to have a relationship with the person who I feel I really am."

"And does that person want to have a relationship with her family as she perceives them to be?" Glenda asked, ever-prodding.

"It doesn't matter, Glenda. They don't know how to interact with me unless I'm behaving only in ways that make sense to them!" I protested.

"But, hypothetically, if they could accept you, could you accept them? Or are you doing the same thing they are, and expecting them to join your camp?"

"No, they'll never do that," I told her. "And I don't want them to, Glenda, I really don't. I can honestly say that I have no desire to convert anyone into whatever I am. I just want them to let me be a part of them again. Can't they just ignore what they don't like about me?"

"I don't know, Aida. I don't know your family that well," she replied. "I do have to challenge you on something, though. You said you didn't want to convert anyone. But what about Birch?"

"Well, what about him?" I asked, stiffening a little. "Aren't you glad he at least started questioning some of the things he didn't believe in?"

"That's irrelevant, Aida. I think you're a great influence on him. But that's not the point. It's not fair to try and convert someone who doesn't want to be converted," Glenda said. Somehow, though, she managed to not sound like she was admonishing me. I loved that about her.

"All I did was question him about some of his beliefs, Glenda, I swear it. We were talking about hypocrisy. And I never encouraged him to leave the Church. In fact, I did just the opposite. I told him I thought he should stay and just try to change the things he thought should be changed, to be an activist." I tried not to be defensive. I honestly had never tried to purposefully pull Birch away from Catholicism, even though I would have been perfectly happy to have him on my side.

"Okay, okay," Glenda was saying. "The issue of my son aside, you've made it fairly clear what your dilemma truly is. If everything really is as stark as you have painted it, then all you can do now is somehow decide which is easier to lose: yourself or your family."

"Oh, Christ, Glenda," I groaned. "I don't . . . I can't . . . how does anyone ever figure anything out? I need some time to—"

"Aida," she cut in, perhaps growing impatient with my indecision, my ignorance about myself and my place in my own life. "No one gets a time-out. I know that everything seems out of balance right now. But I truly believe that harmony does exist. There is some sort of equilibrium between what we characterize as good and that which we view as bad." She was leaning forward, speaking with great urgency. I, however, remained unconvinced about the validity of this "balance" theory.

"Don't look so skeptical," she went on in the absence of my verbal response. "Open that narrow, pessimistic mind of yours for a moment."

"What?" I asked. "I'm not narrow-minded. Pessimistic, yes. I think I have reason to be. But narrow-minded? That's not fair, Glenda."

"Oh, Aida," Glenda sighed. "The two go hand-in-hand, romping around like dismal little lovers. You've been trained to think the worst—you're bad, everyone is bad. They've told you all your life that there is only one way to escape this badness, there is only one road to salvation. And you've been trained to lust after this salvation, the gleaming prize of a life lived in service to a fiction of faith, constructed by power-hungry men two thousand years ago. You've been spoon-fed so many rules about how to think and pray and be and act that you've been stripped of the ability to see for yourself the beauty in each simple moment of this existence.

"I know, I know. I'm rambling. I apologize. Look, Aida, religion works for some people and when it does, it can be satisfying and inspiring for them. But when the discordance of religion with reality is apprehended by someone listening, like you, a struggle begins. I know Birch has struggled, but he has never wanted to discuss these things with me, and I promised Will as well that I would keep my views to myself. But you came to me, Aida. And I don't know much, just that in truth, there are no answers, not really, just approaches. So, anyway, maybe you should try to unlearn your very linear, 'if-then' approach. It's a hopeless way of looking at things, don't you think? And besides, it's not working for you."

Looking down into my wine glass, I felt stupid, like I'd

been led around on a leash all my life by an institution afraid of letting me think for myself. Hell, to be honest, *I* had been afraid of letting me think for myself. And based on what I'd been led to believe, I'd extrapolated a view of life so morose and devoid of light that it was no wonder Birch had called me bleak, no wonder he had left.

"Tell me what to do," I begged.

"Damn it, Aida," Glenda whispered to me. "You know I can't do that. The only thing I can tell you is, now that you've started thinking, really thinking about things, don't stop. You can't stop now. You don't have to figure everything out. You just have to trust yourself. You know more than you think you do. You know everything I'm telling you already, I don't know why I keep going on and on. Oh, and stop being afraid of everything you think you might lose. You have absolutely no idea of what you could possibly gain," she offered as she emptied her glass.

"I'm not sure if I'll be able to do that," I said.

"Well, you're not the only one who needs to do it," she declared.

"You mean Birch?" I asked.

"Definitely Birch, but I need to as well. I've been foolish, Aida, stubbornly clinging to something that was gone a long time ago, all for the sake of . . . well, for the sake of a lot, I guess. But a little less fear of loss will do me some good as well." She shook her head softly then said, "I'm sorry, I didn't mean to change the subject."

"No, no. It's fine. We did me. It's your turn," I said, perfectly willing to put my own excavation on hold for a little while. I had a lot to think about, but I was spent with questioning, digging, examining, solving and dissolving and resolving. "Are you talking about you and Thaddeus?" I asked her.

Glenda nodded. "I believe I have a chance to be happy again, Aida, to be with someone who is truly happy to be with me. Shouldn't I take it? Shouldn't I release myself from my dedication to tradition and duty? It was noble once, but, now . . . it can no longer lead me anywhere. I can't be whole with Will. Even if he still wanted me I couldn't do it. I tried and tried. And I don't regret the trying. But, you were right. I need to stop being afraid, and get on with living."

"Me, too," I murmured, not sure how one went about doing that.

"Stay here tonight. It must be lonely at home. I know it's been lonely here."

I nodded. We talked well into the night, drinking wine and munching on the odds and ends we pulled out of Glenda's fridge and cupboards. Finally, at around two in the morning, we trudged upstairs, and Glenda made up Birch's old bed for me.

I'd seen the room before, but I'd never slept here. When Glenda had redecorated it into a peach-colored guest room, Birch had been horrified, or so the story went. But it was still his bed, his room, and as I curled up under the covers, I smiled to think of him sneaking a high school girlfriend up here and making out with her on this bed. It made me miss him, and the anger and frustration retreated a bit.

Hugging the extra pillow that Glenda had given me, I thought about all we had talked about and tried to comprehend my place in the new world I found myself in. It was a world of voids. No Birch, no baby. There was no family now, either, apparently, as we had purposefully and mutually estranged ourselves from one another. They had alienated me through their rigid requirements regarding my faith and my behavior, and I had driven them away as well through my defensiveness and fury, through my inability to escape my own resentment and indignation, through my failure not only to adhere to their stringent guidelines for morality, but to even understand why they insisted on my compliance with those mandates.

Pulling the covers up to my chin, I thought of Birch again and realized that he must feel the same tangle of emotions, discarded as he had been by his father, as well as betrayed by his mother. I wondered if I could help unsnarl things for Birch a little. The whole situation with my family seemed to be the definition of hopeless, as I couldn't afford to lose them, nor could I sacrifice myself and my own beliefs. But maybe, even if I couldn't have my family, I could try to help give Birch's family back to him.

Awaking the next morning, I slowly opened my eyes. My muscles tightened just a bit. I glanced around, disoriented. With my mind still muddy with sleep, I struggled up the slick slope of memory, trying to identify this unfamiliar setting. I closed my eyes. I opened them again as I clutched the covers around my body. I smelled Birch and smiled. "Oh," I muttered aloud, remembering everything in an instant. Birch used the same herbal, animal-friendly detergent that his mother used. That's what I smelled. I was at Glenda's.

After pulling on my clothes, I trotted downstairs, glancing around for a clock. Glenda was already in the kitchen. She smiled at me as I made my appearance and handed me a cup of coffee. "I only have soy creamer," she informed me.

As I sat down at the kitchen table, I nodded, stirring in a heaping teaspoon of sugar into my coffee, and pouring in a generous portion of the soy creamer. I'd had it before. It was pretty good. "Thanks. What time is it?"

"Ten," she replied, sipping her coffee.

"Wow. I slept so soundly. I haven't done that in a while."

"Guess who called this morning," Glenda said as she peered into the refrigerator. "I have nothing for us for breakfast."

"That's okay. Was it Thaddeus?"

"No. It was Birch," she said, closing the refrigerator and turning to face me.

"Really?" I placed my cup on the table and leaned forward. "What did he say? Is he coming home? Why didn't you wake me?"

"He didn't know you were here, Aida. And when I told him you were, he asked me not to wake you up."

"Oh. I thought . . . I thought maybe he had called here looking for me."

Glenda shook her head, her unrestrained hair tumbling around her shoulders. "I'm sorry. He did ask how you were doing. That's why he didn't want me to wake you. He knows how hard this all is, and that you need all the rest you can get right now."

Slumping over my coffee cup, I asked, "How did he sound?"

"Horrible. I don't know what he expects to find out there, but so far, he hasn't found it. I understand that he needs to be alone, to figure things out, but I don't think he's being fair to you, and I told him so."

"Thanks, Glenda, but you don't have to stick up for me."

"I'm entitled to my opinion. I'll go out there and try and talk some sense into him if you want me to."

"That's not how I want him," I mumbled into my cup.

Glenda's lips tightened. She cleared her throat and sighed. "I know," she finally said.

We silently sipped our coffee for a few moments. Then I rose, running my fingers through my hair. "I have to go, Glenda. Thank you for everything."

"It was my pleasure. What are you going to do now?"

"I've got some people to see," I told her as I left. We said our good-byes and I drove home, showered and ate a late breakfast. Munching on some toast, I noticed the flashing light on the answering machine. Pressing the "play" button and praying it was Birch, I heard the real estate agent saying, "Hi, Birch and Aida. Good news. I know you two are eager to move in, so we were able to negotiate a closing date in two weeks. You can take possession upon closing. Call me, and we'll go over all the details."

"Shit," I said aloud. I wasn't ready to deal with this now, and definitely not without Birch, but I didn't know if I even had a choice. I saved the message and told myself I'd figure it all out later. Now, I was headed to the animal hospital. I'd been missing Sasha. When I arrived I found her in good spirits. I was told she would be able to leave within days, provided someone could be with her all day. Birch would probably take her out to Sean's place, I assumed, and then I wouldn't have either of them.

After leaving Sasha, I forced myself to pursue the path I'd decided upon earlier that morning, and steered the car in the direction of Will McFarland's pub. Unsure of what I would say, I explored a dozen different scenarios in my mind, but nothing seemed right. I only knew that much of the conflict between Birch and Will had been generated, however unintentionally, by me. As I pulled into the parking lot, I noticed the "for sale" sign again. The last time I'd seen it, I'd been with Birch, and I had been trying to convince him to talk to his father. It was right after we'd found out we'd gotten the house, and I was sure now that it had happened in a different life.

Sitting in the car, I took a few deep breaths before I got up enough nerve to go inside. "Is Will in?" I asked the hostess, who was helping ready the restaurant for the lunch crowd. I knew her. Her name was Jenny and she had worked at McFarland's for years.

She nodded. "Sure. He's in his office. Just go on back."

I walked slowly across the polished oak planks of the floor. A few patrons were munching their early lunches, and I suddenly missed Sally and Yolanda. I was actually looking forward to going back to work on Monday and seeing them. Doing something that seemed normal would be a good thing, a healthy thing, I thought as I approached the door of Will's office. It was cracked open slightly, and I rapped on it twice and waited.

"Yeah! What is it?" Will shouted.

Pushing the door open, I cleared my throat. Will's dark head was bent over the papers on his desk. When he didn't look up, I asked, "Are you really selling the place?"

"Aida," he said, his voice a near-whisper suddenly. As he rose from his chair, his beefy hands clasped one another, fell away, and found each other once again. "I was so sorry to hear about the baby," he mumbled.

"Thank you," I said, looking down at my feet.

"Have a seat."

I sat down obediently, waiting for him to answer my question. When he just looked at me blankly, I asked again, "You're selling the pub?"

"Oh. Um . . . Is that why you came?" he asked.

"No. I was just . . . wondering," I said as I waited again for his reply. He still didn't answer the question, and I began to gather that he had no intention of doing so. Having no choice but to pursue my original course of action, I continued, "I just came to talk. About Birch. Have you heard from him?"

"Not directly. But I spoke with my brother Sean. Birch is in good hands."

I bit my lip. My hands were good hands. We were supposed to help each other through this, and Birch hadn't given me a chance. I shook my head slightly, trying to clear it, attempting to remain focused. "Anyway, I just wanted you to know that I'm sorry."

"For what?" Will asked, leaning forward.

"I never meant to . . . to pull Birch away from the Church. To have that be something that came between the two of you. I want you to know that. Look, we don't really know each other that well, even though we've known each other for years now, and anyway," I continued, taking a sharp, deep breath inward, trying to stop just blathering incoherently. "I know things are different for you and Birch now that he knows everything, but that doesn't change the fact that you raised him. I've realized that since the day you told Birch you're not his father, I've been slowly building up this grudge against you. I admit it's a bit unfair, but you hurt him so badly, Mr. McFarland. I understand that he hurt you, too. But simply having different beliefs about the Church just doesn't seem like a big enough reason to . . . disown him. He's your little boy, Mr. McFarland, and he needs you."

I felt my eyes grow warm with tears at the thought of Birch as a young child, doing everything in his power to win his father's approval. Blinking a few times to clear my gaze, I continued, "I don't know what he'll come away with when his . . . pilgrimage . . . to your brother's place is over, but he'll always need you and you'll always be able to . . . to help make things . . . better. You're still his people, blood or no blood, and—"

"Aida," Will said loudly, putting his hand up in an apparent effort to stem the onslaught of my words. "Stop. Please, just stop. You're right. We don't know each other very well. So I don't know why you think you have the right to come in here and tell me things that you really know nothing about. Come on, Aida," he almost whined. "Who do you think you are, anyway? Look, I'm sorry you lost the baby. But you and I have never been close; we both know that. And when we have discussed things in any detail, it's been clear that we don't see eye to eye on most things. Why do you think I care whether or not you've been holding a grudge against me? And I can't say that I'd really give a damn if you and Birch never patched this one up. I think you've been a bad influence on him, and the longer he stays away from you the better. He needs a good Catholic girl. I thought that was a sure bet with an Italian girl, but I guess I was wrong. You're both better off without each other. Wasn't a good fit."

My eyes opened a bit wider and I suddenly noticed how dry my mouth was. I stared at him.

"Anything else?" he grumbled. "I've got a lot of work to do."

I shook my head, rose quickly and strode toward the door, ready to run away from him as fast as I could, but something made me pause. The weight of his contempt for me made my shoulders slump, my head bow, but I bore it, especially since I hadn't expected much else. So I stood there, stooping under the load of his disdain and tried once more to reach out, desperate for Birch to not feel fatherless.

I stopped at the door and turned back to look at him. "I hope you decide not to sell, for Birch's sake. And I *am* sorry, about everything." I closed the door behind me, left through the back and sat in my car. My all-encompassing apology, I finally admitted to myself, had included my pushiness regarding Glenda and Thaddeus. I had been so repelled by Will's treatment of Birch that I had developed an unwarranted attachment for his stranger-father, Thaddeus.

Even so, Will's anger, his irritation, it all had to be a front. Maybe his bitterness toward me was genuine, but it was unnatural for him to dismiss Birch the way he had. Will needed to stop being so sanctimonious and start acknowledging how he really felt about Birch. I don't know if Birch was going to find religion again or not, but I prayed that whether Birch emerged from his uncle's care a Catholic or not, Will would start treating Birch like a son again.

Grabbing my cell phone, desperate to undo damage I might have unwittingly wrought, I dialed Glenda's number. "Glenda," I said urgently when she picked up. "Look, I'm sorry I was so adamant about you and Thaddeus. I . . . I've just realized that I don't really know enough about him to keep trying to push you in his direction. I—"

"Aida," Glenda cut in. "What is this all about? Look, are you at home? Do you need to talk? I can come over."

"No. I'm not home. I'm at the pub. I was talking to Will."

"What? But why, Aida?" she asked softly.

"I don't know. I was trying to make things right with him. To apologize, but to try and make him see that . . . that Birch is still his son, no matter what. Birch needs him, doesn't he, Glenda?"

I listened to her sigh. "Who knows? What does it matter if we need people who don't need us?"

I wondered if she was talking about her and Will, Birch and Will, or Birch and me, or maybe all of us. Ignoring her question, I pressed on. "Well, anyway, after I spoke with Will, I realized that maybe it was my anger with him for

315

how he treated Birch that made me so insistent about you pursuing Thaddeus."

"Maybe," she said steadily, apparently nonplussed by what I had said. "But I think there's more to it than that. Anyway, my decisions are my own, Aida. Whatever decisions I may have made about Thaddeus have been arrived upon through my own careful deliberation, your own biases notwithstanding."

"Oh," I replied, a little hurt that my "biased" advice was so easily dismissed. "But what do you mean about there being more to it?" I asked, confused and just a little suspicious of her now.

"Well, you said yourself that Thaddeus reminded you of Birch in many ways. Couple that with your history with Birch, and it is easy to understand why you wanted to see Thaddeus and me together. Aida, I think that maybe, in your eyes, Thaddeus and I are sort of surrogates for you and Birch."

"So you think I wanted to see you and Thaddeus together as some sort of . . . affirmation that Birch and I could make it?"

"Something like that," Glenda told me.

I paused, swallowing my initial defensive response, thinking.

"Aida?" I heard her say. I didn't answer.

"As far as Thaddeus and I are concerned," she went on. "I've made my own choice to find out if there is anything still there. I know what I'm doing, Aida."

"Okay, Glenda. Hey, I have to go," I stumbled.

"Well, call me if—"

I hung up before she could finish and tossed the phone into the passenger's seat. Once again my "history" with Birch was thrown back in my face, and I was more than a little irritated, especially since this time *he* had left, not me.

After sitting and thinking for a long while, I realized there was no place else to go but back to the apartment. I couldn't even call it home anymore, not without Birch. As I walked in the door, I tossed my keys on the table, took off my shoes and coat, and just stood there.

There was so much to deal with. I had to patch things up with Doreen and my family, try to convince my father once again that I was a worthwhile offspring. I had to figure out what to do about the house. I ached with the need to be with Birch, but I was utterly devoid of any inkling of how to bring us back together. And most urgently of all, I had to learn how to not be completely undone by the loss of my baby.

And I was so tired of everything. I couldn't grasp the right answers. I didn't know how not to ruin things. How could I mend things I'd never had right in the first place? I stood there, weeping, filling up the gaping empty spaces inside of me with tears. While my Wonderland was a bit more hellish than hers, I felt like Alice, unable to get it right, too large to get through the door, then suddenly too small to reach the key, then gigantic with grief.

Collapsing into my mother's chair, I huddled there, wishing fervently to be a child again, for it to be easy again, to receive love as effortlessly as my mother had given it to me, and to give it back again. And give it to my baby, my baby who was gone forever. I was sickened by how unfair it was that I didn't get to have her, that I didn't get my chance. It couldn't possibly be true, as Nonna had told me, that I didn't deserve that chance. I wasn't that horrible.

"I would have been good to you," I whispered to the nothingness that was my child. "I would have. Why didn't I get my chance?" I fell asleep there, sobbing into the worn upholstery of Mom's chair, knowing only that somehow, I had to put my baby to rest.

When I awoke, moonlight was softly whispering its way into the room. I breathed it in, feeling calmer now. People who lost those close to them had funerals, memorials, wakes. Mom had had a hell of a funeral, I recalled, my cheek resting on the back of the chair. I still found myself trying to smell her in the fabric.

Every long-lost relative had been at the house when Mom had died. They'd brought lasagnas, and manicotti, and baked ziti. Our freezer was overflowing. They wept at the funeral, threw red roses on her grave, looked at me with pity, stroked my long hair and wailed for the motherless child.

Now, I was a childless mother, and who was there to wail for me now? Why did I feel as though I wasn't allowed to grieve for my baby? As though I needed to just shake it off, put it behind me, try again? I felt as though I needed to make known that my pain was real, that my sorrow was justified. I needed to leech it out of myself so it didn't eat me up inside, and everyone else needed to let me do it. What I needed to do was commemorate the passing, to simply say, "This happened."

I loved this little one, this child who wasn't. He or she deserved to be acknowledged. My life had changed because of the baby. My faith had changed, had shattered, had rebirthed itself, and much of that was due to the little life inside me that I hadn't wanted to betray.

Rising slowly, I made my way into the kitchen, turning on lights as I did so. I pulled bread and cheese and an apple out of the refrigerator and ate them as I stood by the counter. I drank some wine. After I'd finished, I made my way to the bedroom and rummaged about in the closet for some yarn, and I began to crochet a baby blanket.

My fingers remembered their choreography, miraculously. I had lots of yarn to choose from, having planned many projects in the past that never made it past infancy. I selected a butter yellow that was once intended for a shawl for Nonna, a mossy green that would have been Birch's scarf, and white that had been destined for my hat. A little reluctant to use Nonna's yellow, I included it because for better or worse, she would have been part of the baby's life, too. Working well into the night, I finally set aside the project and crawled into bed when my eyes were drooping mid-stitch. I'd begin again in the morning after I called my father.

Chapter Eighteen

In the light of day, it seemed better to speak to Pop in person, rather than calling him. I knew well the family routine. They'd be getting home from eight o'clock mass around nine-twenty. After showering, I stopped at the grocery store then made my way to my father's house. I let myself in and began preparing an asparagus and mushroom frittata and hash browns. Thick slices of crusty, rustic Italian bread waited to be toasted as well. I washed and sliced a heaping bowl of fresh strawberries, my father's favorite. Out of season, they'd been shipped from a warmer climate and had lost a little of their punch along the way, so I sprinkled them generously with sugar.

As I finished setting the table, I heard a car in the driveway, and then another. Marco and Rosie must have come as well. That was fine; there was plenty of food, and I owed everyone an apology. The back door jiggled open. "Aida?" I heard my father's voice calling. I peered down the short flight of steps between the kitchen and the back door landing. My father was stepping in, with Doreen in tow. "What are you doing here?" Pop growled.

"Making you all breakfast," I told him. "Come in, come in," I said, helping to hang up coats and hats as Pop, Doreen, and Nonna tumbled into the house. Doreen looked at me blankly as she walked past. Nonna just glared. My father came up the steps, shook his head. "Please, just give me a chance," I whispered to him.

"Go on everyone. Sit down, I'll get the coffee," I instructed as they hovered uncertainly in the kitchen. I proceeded to greet Marco, and Rosie, taking Joseph's carrier from them so they could remove their outerwear. Joseph watched me with wide dark eyes as I took him out of the car seat and nuzzled his neck. "Hey, Joe," I said softly as I handed him back to Marco.

"What's going on, Aida?" Marco asked, scowling at me.

"Just go sit down. I made breakfast. I'm just trying to make things right, Marc."

His frown deepened as he proceeded into the dining room. Rosie hugged me lightly but wouldn't look me in the eye. I poured them all coffee then stood at the head of the table, at my father's right shoulder. Looking down at my hands, I realized I was rubbing them together absently. I stopped, forcing them to just grasp one another. I cleared my throat. I tried to smile.

"Okay," I began. "I know you're all wondering what I'm doing here. Well, I made you all a wonderful breakfast, first of all. And," I paused, my gaze darting toward the floor briefly.

I hated this. It was abhorrent to me to have to apologize when I felt that, to some extent, I had a right to be angry with them. But I supposed that whether or not my enmity was justified, it was not fair or appropriate for me to insist that they all confront the past, with its demons of both the recognizable and disguised variety. For that matter, it wasn't right for me to assume they hadn't already dealt with such devils in ways concealed from me. So I inhaled from the top of my head down to the pit of my churning stomach and began.

"I want to apologize for the way I behaved. I *do* wish that as a family we had handled things differently, more openly after Mom died, but I should not have attacked you all."

Pausing, I swallowed. My throat felt dry and gritty. Scanning the table, I observed dark eyebrows, furrowed and unforgiving; angular chins thrust into the air, challenging and defiant. While I judged my apology as dignified but thorough, I could tell they wanted more. I tried again.

"I was wrong," I continued, "and I hope you all can forgive me. I know that we don't see eye to eye on a lot of things, especially religion. But . . . I don't know. I just want you all to know that what we have as a family means a lot to me. It means a lot more than just Catholicism. It doesn't matter that much if we have different views, does it? And I'm not trying to change all of you. And if you can manage to not keep trying to change me, we can get through all of this, can't we?"

Before anyone could shift their disapproving demeanor, or whether they even had an inclination to, I went on, speaking at breakneck speed, trying to get it all out, "Look, I'm sorry about everything, okay? I know everything that I've been saying and doing must be really shocking to you all. It is to me, too, but that's only because I've been so good at lying to you and to myself for so long. Anyway," I hesitated for a moment, trying slow the chaotic merry-go-round in my mind, "I'm sorry."

I waited. Their expressions had changed little. "Well," Nonna began. "Nothing has been made right between you and me. And I heard about all that was said at Marco's. You have only pretty words for us, but no right behavior." Nonna leaned forward, pressing her hands together as if in prayer, "Be a good girl, Aida, we all beg you. Come back to church. Go to confession. Try to do *something* right," she pleaded.

"I am trying, Nonna," I answered quietly. "Just not in the way you want me to."

"I don't know, Aida," Marco said. "You have changed so much. We don't even know how to be around you anymore," he said, his lips puckering into a frown.

Pop cleared his throat loudly. He looked straight ahead, right over Nonna's head instead of turning his gaze to me. "Your brother is right, Angelina," he said. "I don't know what to do with you anymore."

Still standing at my father's side, I glanced down at him, and then saw Doreen reach over and place her hand on top of my father's. "I really wish we could have gotten off to a better start, Aida," she said, her eyes on Pop's face, "but I have to stand by your father, you know."

All their forces were aligning against me. Rosie was the only one who had not yet spoken.

"Rosie?" I whimpered.

"Oh, Aida," she sighed. "You were really out of line the other night. But I know that you're going through a lot. There's no bad blood with us," she told me.

Nodding gratefully in her direction, I heard the disapproving clearing of Nonna's throat. Ignoring it, I proceeded with the rest of my speech. "Well, there's one more thing, if any of you care," I said, nearly muttering. "I'm going to have a little . . . memorial, I guess, for the baby, and—"

"What?" Nonna croaked. "You didn't *have* a baby, Aida. Babies who are born and then die get baptisms and funerals. Like my little angels who died so young. You betray their memory with this . . . this ridiculous idea."

Blood rose swiftly to my face. I felt hot, but I continued as if I hadn't heard her. "And I'd like it if you would all come. I know it's unorthodox, but I really think it will help me to deal with this. The baby was . . . well, he, or she, was just . . . *real*, and—" emotion knotted thickly in my throat and as I tried to swallow, I heard Rosie's voice.

"Aida, you don't have to explain," she said, saving me. "Of course we'll come. Well, I'll come, anyway." As she spoke, I noticed that Pop's mouth twitched a bit, as if he were biting the inside of his lip. His eyebrows pulled together angrily once again, and both he and Marco remained silent.

"Thank you, Rosie." There was nothing else I could say. The food I had prepared was ready, as awkward as it would be to share a meal with them all at this point. "I'll get breakfast."

Turning back toward the kitchen, I brought out the platters of food and served everyone, and then seated myself next to my brother. With the exception of Joseph's cooing, the only noises at the breakfast table were those of forks clinking against the plates and the occasional clicking of Nonna's dentures. Finally, my father cleared his throat, carving the air with his butter knife, gesturing absently as he spoke. "So, what about the house?" he asked me abruptly.

"I think I'm still going to get it, Pop," I answered. "On my own."

"You haven't heard from him at all?" Marco asked, speaking of Birch.

Before I could answer, Nonna wiped her mouth on her napkin and then said, "He's coming to his senses."

"Excuse me?" I gasped, certain I hadn't heard her properly.

"I heard he is returning to the Church. I talk with Serafina, my cousin, almost every Saturday, after confession. Her sister-in-law, Mary, goes to church at Father McFarland's parish. It's a very small parish, St. Luke's. When someone visits, Father McFarland introduces him to everybody. Yesterday I saw Serafina. At confession. She

324

told me something that her sister-in-law Mary told her. Father McFarland has been bringing a young man with him every day this week for morning rosary. A young man with a strange name and wild blond hair. Well, when Serafina described the man that Mary saw, I knew it was your Birch, Aida. So," Nonna concluded, placing her fork precisely on the table just to the right of her plate, "he's coming to his senses. He's going to church. He's saying rosaries." She picked up her fork and pointed at me with it. "See? You haven't undone the poor boy altogether. So, Aida," Nonna said, her voice lowering a bit, "faith is thicker than lust after all, eh?"

Nearly gagging on the asparagus in my mouth, I barely managed to swallow my food.

"Ma!" I heard my father thunder. *"Basta!"*

Enough, he had told her. But it was never enough with her. She always had one more jibe. I watched as she put her palms out in front of her, yielding to my father. I bowed my head, placed my hands in my lap, stunned into silence. She thought I had lured a good Irish Catholic boy away from the Church and his family with sex. Shame and dread washed over me, and I felt like a teenager caught on the sofa with her boyfriend's hand up her shirt. How could I look Nonna in the eye again, knowing she thought so little of me? How could she have said that in front of everyone? My father? My brother?

"Nonna?" I whispered, my gaze still fixed on my hands, which remained folded in my lap. "Are you calling me a *puttana*? Is that what you think of me?" She thought I was a whore.

I heard her grunt in reply. I raised my eyes, my gaze darting furtively around the table. Doreen stared helplessly at my father, lost in this horrid Benedetto drama. Marco and Rosie were exchanging worried expressions, and my father glared at his mother. Nobody could even look at me.

"Once," I began, regarding my grandmother again, "not too long ago, you told me I was a good girl." My voice quavered and I hated myself for letting her make me feel timid and meek, like a mousy child.

"You were a good girl once," she said loudly. "Then you got pregnant. Then you left the Church. Then the poor Irish boy followed you in your sinful path. You moved in together. And the whole time all of this was going on, you grew more and more bold in your disrespect for me, for this family." She put her hands up in front of her, palms facing me as if she were physically pushing me away. "I could not hold my tongue any longer."

"Any longer!" I gasped loudly, astonished. "You've never held your tongue. You . . . you . . ." I stopped there, my insides writhing. Talking to her was an exercise in futility. I stood up, and began collecting the dishes. Silverware clanked against ceramic plates. Feeling all their eyes upon my flushed cheeks, I tried to make the table clearing as noisy of an activity as I possibly could. As I turned to stomp into the kitchen, no one spoke. I was certain that Doreen was regretting having ever been introduced to the family, or at least to me.

After depositing the load of soiled dishes into the sink, I slumped over the counter, my head in my hands. Trying to ignore what Nonna had said about me and focus instead on her report about Birch, I wondered how I could ever reinstate myself into his life. I couldn't compete with the Church. I shouldn't have to. Yet I knew that Birch felt I had played an instrumental role in the deterioration of his attitude toward Catholicism. Maybe Nonna was right about that. Maybe I had dragged the poor boy with me.

Of course I would be pitted against the Church in his mind. Me versus the familiarity of ritual, the promises of salvation, and heaven, and life everlasting, and eternal comfort. I didn't stand a chance, not with my "maybe you can catch a glimpse of truth and peace in a moment of transcendence" philosophy, and all my talk of the "pious robed folk" ruining your chances of real spiritual understanding. It was hopeless. Resting my cheek against the white-tiled countertop, I could smell the bleach Nonna used to keep the grout clean. She was meticulously thorough in the way she ferreted out dirt.

"Aida?" I heard Rosie say. I stood up, straightened my black blouse, rubbed my face with my hands. I opened my mouth to reply, then closed it again with a sigh.

"Don't listen to a thing she says, okay? You know how she is. She doesn't know how not to judge. It's in her blood," Rosie said.

All I could do was nod.

"Have you tried calling him?" she asked, stepping toward me to turn off the water I had left running. The sink was nearly spilling over with soapsuds and water.

"Lots of times," I said, staring absently at the soap bubbles.

"Try again. And again. Until it works."

Shrugging, I said, "I don't know. Maybe it's over. Maybe Nonna's right and he's coming to his senses."

"Oh shut up, Aida," Rosie snapped. As I glared at her, a little surprised at her tone, she continued, "Don't be stupid. Nonna is blinded by her sense of piety. No one has ever defied her sense of what's right as much as you have."

As much as I wanted to just roll over and give up and wallow in Nonna's characterization of me, I tried to

327

summon a little strength. "You think that's why she's so hard on me, Rosie?"

"Of course, Aida. And as for Birch, I won't forgive you if you give up on him. You can't do that to him again. Stop being afraid to be happy with him."

I clenched my teeth, stuck out my chin. "Damn it, Ro. Don't be like that. Haven't you seen how miserable we can manage to make each other?" I asked, turning away from her, and leaning my back against the counter again.

"Aida," Rosie said as she stepped toward me and grabbed my hand. "Life can be miserable. You know that. You've known it since you were sixteen. And if Birch didn't before, he knows it now. But what you two manage to do with each other is amazing. You give each other the courage to not pretend that the answers are all there. You're helping each other figure out your own way through everything, on your own terms. Do you think just any man can walk that path with you? There are a lot of cowards out there, Aida, and Birch isn't one of them."

I stood there, looking at her, my hand squeezed tightly by her urgent grasp. "Rosie, I've always known that he was more than worth my effort, and I've often questioned whether or not I was worth his, but . . . together . . . Well, we're a completely different entity together than we are apart. It's that 'the whole is greater than the sum of its parts' thing."

"Yeah, I know a little about that," she said, looking over her shoulder, back into the dining room toward Marco.

"It doesn't seem very . . . well, very modern, I guess," I told her when she had turned back to me. "I feel as though I'm supposed to be a whole person on my own. I don't want to depend on Birch for my identity, my happiness."

"That's not it at all, Aida. Look, people need each other.

What's so wrong about that? I know who I am, individually, without Marco. I just know that I am a better person with him than without him. And the same goes for him. It's worth fighting for, Aida, no matter if you label it old-fashioned or not. I don't care about any of that. People can help make each other better people."

"I know, Rosie," I answered, my head hung a little low. While Rosie had the experience with pop psychology about child rearing, I, as the single one, had felt bombarded by all the talk shows and paperback self-improvement books about how you need to feel complete on your own before you can expect to find happiness with someone else. While on the surface of things it wasn't a bad theory, it seemed to me that it was just a lot of "you don't need a man" talk. I had not yet gotten to that point where I feared that I would never find someone, I hadn't begun all the "what-iffing" yet, but still, having your mindset not be a little tainted by all that stuff seemed unavoidable. But people needed each other. What was so wrong with that?

"Then do what you need to do," Rosie urged. "As soon as you help me with these dishes."

I smiled a bit and we turned and started on the dishes. As I washed the plates clean and Rosie began wiping them dry, she said, "I'm glad you brought up Marco's first marriage the other night, Aida. He and I talked a lot about things after that. I . . . you gave me the chance to understand him a little better than I did before. It made him seem more vulnerable to me, vulnerable in a good way, to know that he needed more than the Church to get him through your mom's death. Obviously the two things were related and he did finally admit that."

"He did?" I asked, scrubbing at the egg and cheese that clung to the plate in my hand.

Rosie nodded, taking the plate from me after I'd rinsed it. As she dried it she said, "He can get a little self-righteous about religion, you know. Must run in your family. Anyway, it was good for him to see that there are chinks in the Catholic armor."

Nodding, I answered, "I don't know why it's so hard for all of them to admit that you need more, that you need your family at least as much as you need faith. I guess they can all do without me, though, can't they?" I asked, pulling out the drain cover and watching the soapy water tornado down the pipe.

"Probably not for long, Aida. Don't worry. They'll come around. I know Marco will," she replied.

I smiled weakly, then kissed her cheek. "I'll be in touch."

"Go on. Get out of here," she told me, nudging me toward the door. "And don't mess it up with Birch this time. I'm guessing you're about out of second chances."

Unsettled once again by her frankness, but knowing she was right, I left the house with my breakfast sitting in my stomach like a brick. I drove home under a gray April sky heavy with unspilled rain. By the time I reached home, a downpour was imminent, but I managed to step into the building before it all let loose. Inside my apartment, I removed my outerwear, then decided to change into more relaxing clothes than the slacks and blouse I had worn to my father's house. I slipped into some soft gray sweatpants and one of Birch's college sweatshirts. It was frayed at the cuffs and neck, and despite my prayer, the smell of Birch had faded from the worn cotton.

Getting comfortable on the sofa, I dialed the number at his uncle's. Hopefully, Father McFarland would have some sort of social engagement following the morning masses.

The phone rang. I held my breath until I heard Father McFarland's voice on the answering machine. "Um . . . this message is for Birch," I mumbled. "Please, just call me." I hung up. I took a deep breath, dialed again, and left another message, and a few moments later, a third.

I put the phone down, wandered around the apartment, crocheted a little of the baby's blanket, then picked up the phone again. When the answering machine picked up, I began, "Birch, it's me again. Please . . . if you would only . . ."

"Aida." It was Birch. He'd picked up. He'd been there all along and he'd picked up finally. For a moment, as I heard his voice again, the earth seemed to stop spinning upon its axis. But with the words he spoke next, my world lurched into sickening motion once again. "Please stop calling," he was saying. "I . . . I just need to focus right now. I need time."

"No, Birch," I began, trying to will the trembling out of my voice. "You don't need time. What you need is me. And I need you. We can get through this together better than we can apart," I pleaded, trying to sound strong and confident.

"I'm trying a different approach right now. Please try and understand that. Just because Catholicism doesn't work for you doesn't mean it can't work for me. I'm trying to find a way for it all to make sense again, Aida."

"Well, can't you come home and still find your way? Go back to St. Benedict's. Father Roberto has known you all your life. I'm sure he can help you. Not that your uncle can't. But you can be in touch with him from here. Just come home."

"I don't even know what home is anymore," he told me. He said it easily, just as if he were giving directions. But it hit me like a boot in the chest.

"But what about the house?" I asked, ignoring the thick, aching knot inside me.

"We can still get out of it. I think we should get out of it." He spoke in such a matter-of-fact way, his tone devoid of intimacy.

"You don't mean that, Birch, do you?" When he didn't reply, I went on. "But, I . . . it's just that . . . what about us?" I mustered, completely thrown off balance by the way the conversation was going.

"Aida, I should go."

I paused, trying to buy time. I didn't want to stop hearing his voice, even if he was reading our death sentence. "I wanted . . . I thought we should have a memorial. For the baby," I finally told him.

"For the . . . but Aida, why?" he asked softly.

"What do you mean why?"

"Well, we never . . . we never had our baby. How do you have a memorial, a remembrance, of something that never really happened?"

"Is that what you're telling yourself?" My voice rose half a dozen decibels. "That it never really happened? I don't know about you, but it fucking happened to me, Birch!"

"You don't have to talk to me like that. I don't want to get into an argument with you. That's not what I meant. It just seems . . . unusual, unnatural. Since we can't really have a funeral or anything like that, since the baby wasn't . . . Aida we don't even know when it happened. We never heard a heartbeat."

"Why are you doing this?" I shouted into the phone. "Why are you trying to undo it all? Is this how Father McFarland is counseling you? Are you supposed to be able to cope better by thinking of it as a miscarried pregnancy rather than a dead baby? Because, you know, if I'd had an abortion instead of a miscarriage, you can be damned sure I'd be accused of killing my baby!"

"Aida, calm down. It's not like that," he said.

He sounded so . . . placating. He wouldn't even get mad at me. He was so distant. I couldn't engage him at all. "What the hell happened to you, Birch? You used to yell with me. You used to meet me halfway. And then we'd work through things. Why are you being so cold?"

I listened to him sigh before he answered. "I'm just trying to manage my emotions better. It's easier to focus, to pray, when you're not all wound up with all sorts of emotions. I'm just trying to focus," he repeated.

"What's the matter with *emotion* all of a sudden? How is that living? Who wants to live without feeling?"

"After everything that happened, I could do with a lot less feeling. Couldn't you?"

"I . . . I . . ." Forced to pause by the reasonable nature of a question I couldn't answer, I changed tactics. "He's brainwashing you," I told him simply.

"Aida!" Birch finally snapped, shouting my name at me. I gloated in a miserable, smallish way, grimly relieved that I could still stoke his ire. "Aida," he said again, his voice more restrained now. "I have to go."

"No, please, Birch, just listen—"

"Good-bye, Aida."

"Birch, please. I love you."

"I know. And I will always love you. It's just . . . too much. I have to go," he said again, just before he hung up.

I slammed the phone down on the coffee table. This couldn't be happening. I couldn't be losing him. Not really. Not forever. Throwing on my coat and sneakers, I grabbed my car keys, ran around the building to the parking lot, slipped soaking wet into my car, and headed for Elk's Run and Father McFarland's farm.

With the April rainstorm slowing my progress considerably, it took me well over an hour to reach the farm. I knew the general route and had called Glenda on my cell phone for specifics. Pulling up to the small, stout brick home that stood near the front of the property, I found that Birch's Jeep was nowhere in sight. I ran through the rain, up the steps of the covered front porch, and knocked loudly on a wooden door, which was painted white but pockmarked with chipped paint.

A round man whom I recognized as Father McFarland swung open the door after a few long moments and looked at me blankly. His reddish brown hair was thin and receding from his circular face. He looked quite unlike his brother Will, except for the eerily pale green eyes, and the strong, straight nose. He wore a cabled cream-colored sweater and jeans. "Can I help you?" he asked, obviously not recognizing me.

"Hi, Father McFarland. I'm Aida Benedetto. Is Birch here?"

"Oh! Aida, Aida. Come in, come in. I'm so sorry for not recognizing you. It has been a while, hasn't it?" He ushered me into a modestly furnished living room that had the feel of a woodland cottage. The room was dimly lit; a fire lay dying in the hearth. Pine-framed furniture wore green-plaid cushions. "I was just trying to revive my fire," he said, hurrying over to the hearth. "Please, sit down," Father McFarland instructed as he seated himself on a rough-hewn, three-legged stool.

Perching on the edge of the sofa, I asked about Birch once more. "I just spoke with him about an hour ago. Is he here?" As I finished my sentence I heard a sound I hadn't expected—a dog barking. Not just any dog. "Sasha? That's Sasha. What is she doing here? I just saw her yesterday. They said it would be a couple of days before she could leave, and—"

"Slow down. Birch brought her back here yesterday evening. He said he'd be able to care for her from here, especially with me being home much of the time to help out. Anyway, he just stepped out. He needed to go pick up a few things for Sasha."

My heart thumped in my chest like a hounded rabbit. I had just missed Birch, and Sasha was here. A riot of emotion washed over me, and I took a deep breath then stood up. "Where is she?" I asked as I began following the sound of Sasha's intermittent barking.

"Aida, please wait. I really don't think we should excite the poor animal," Father McFarland was saying to my back.

Ignoring him, I wandered into a small dining room, to the left of which was a white kitchen with pine cabinets. To the right of the dining area was a small hallway leading to two rooms; one door was opened, the other closed. Peeking into the room on the right, with the open door, I saw an oak dresser and a small, antique table with a white enamel-coated metal top that seemed to serve as a desk. It was piled with notebooks, a Bible, and a few other texts. There was a single bed dressed with a patchwork quilt, and on the quilt lay Sasha. Her tail wagged and she barked again when she saw me, and I ran to her side, sat down on the bed next to her, and scratched her behind the ears.

"Hey, Sasha. It's good to see you out of that cage," I whispered. "Look at you, lucky girl. You get to curl up with him at night, huh?"

Footsteps at the door drew my attention away from Sasha's sparkling blue eyes. Father McFarland cleared his throat. "Aida? I understand that you came to see Birch, but I have no idea when he'll be back. Is there any way I can help? I'd be happy to pray with you," he offered earnestly.

I shook my head, uncertain as to what I should do next. Looking back at Sasha, I kissed her nose. "Get some rest. I'll see you again soon. I promise," I told her. After I had hugged her again, I reluctantly followed the priest out of Birch's room. It was the closest I had been to him in a week.

"How are you coping with everything that's going on in your life right now, Aida? That is, if you don't mind me asking," Father McFarland questioned as we returned to the living room. I sat back down on the sofa, and he returned to his station by the hearth.

"Well, I . . ." I was startled by the question, not expecting him to take an interest in me or how I was feeling. My hair was damp from the rain and I pulled the clinging strands away from my face as I thought about his question. While I made an attempt to answer honestly, I suspected that I probably wouldn't make much sense to him. "I've just been trying to recognize the truth of things, you know? To not run away from . . . from how I really feel, how things really are."

Father McFarland was looking at me and nodding. "And how are things?" he asked.

"Sad. Painful. Terrifying."

"Have you found no comfort?" A frown tugging on his thin, pink lips as he questioned me.

I shrugged. "I find the love of my family reassuring. Well, I used to. I'm not sure if they're still speaking to me, actually," I trailed off in a mumble. After clearing my throat, I began again, "Anyway, I'm not looking to be made to feel comfortable. Comfort is a bit of a shroud, I think."

"I don't follow," the priest asked, poking at the struggling logs in the fireplace with an iron rod. "What is it that you think comfort is hiding?"

"Well, truth, Father."

"What truth is that?" he prodded.

Pausing, I bit the inside of my bottom lip and stared at the glowering cinders in the fireplace. Exhaling raggedly, I struggled to respond with a precision that would end his curious examination. "That more of life than we care to admit is pain."

As Father McFarland leaned forward, the stool creaked under his bulk. "Everyone experiences sadness and suffering from time to time. Everyone does," he insisted in a hushed but urgent tone. "But prayer and faith can alleviate it a bit."

"I'm saying that maybe it shouldn't be alleviated," I responded quickly. "Maybe we should just go ahead and experience our sadness and suffering and accept it as part of our existence. I mean, you can be one of those people who believe there is a lesson to be learned from it, or you can be someone who feels that somehow you must deserve it, but no matter what, everyone has to deal with it. Looking for comfort just seems like a way of trying to escape it."

"That's rather bleak," he replied.

"Well, then, so be it," I said, irritated. "Look, I don't think that there is anything in the entire universe that can make me feel better about what happened to Birch and me. Honestly, I don't want to find a way to make it easier to get through. I don't think that's possible. I just want to deal with it . . . No," I paused, interrupting myself. "Not just *deal* with it. I want to acknowledge it and *respect* for what it is. I think that is the way to survive it."

"I see, I see," he answered, nodding as he straightened his back and looked up at the ceiling for a moment. For whatever reason, he let the issue of human suffering and my opinions about it drop for the time being, and asked, "And what of this . . . memorial you want to have? Birch mentioned something about it before he left."

"He did? What did he say?"

"Just that you wanted to have some sort of service for . . . for the baby," he explained as he looked into the fledgling flames. "I have to admit, Aida," Father McFarland said, still gazing into the fire, "I told Birch I thought it was a bad idea."

"What? Why? Why would you do that?" I shrieked, flying from my seat.

Hearing me rise, he turned to me once again. "He asked me my opinion. Please, sit, child. Come now, sit down . . . That's better. I simply explained that this type of response to what you experienced seemed peculiar, and in its overly dramatic nature, perhaps unhealthy."

"What do you know about it?" I shouted at him.

"Please lower your voice. I have actually counseled a good many couples who have gone through the same thing. The best way to handle things seems to be through prayer, to ease the suffering. Then a sincere attempt should be made to move forward, to put it behind you."

"Put it behind me?" I growled, trying to keep my voice quiet. "That's what you do with a bad day, not a dead baby, Father McFarland."

"With all due respect, Aida," he said, straightening his back slightly, "it was a miscarriage. I've counseled parents who have suffered the death of a child and it is another matter entirely."

"I'm certain it is, to *them,* but right now, this is what it feels like to me, and this is how I'm choosing to handle it," I declared, my entire frame rigid with outrage.

Shrugging his round shoulders, Father McFarland only sighed in reply. "Have you considered at all the possibility of returning to the Church?"

I swallowed. I glanced down at my wet sneakers and then back up at the priest's round face. "I . . . well, no. That's not something I can honestly say that I've considered, Father."

Rising from the wooden stool, he took a step or two toward me, forcing me look up at him instead of across the room. "I care about my nephew. It always troubled me that my brother Will got so little support from his wife in Birch's religious upbringing. And now, Birch tells me that Glenda has been tutoring you. Frankly, that troubles me."

"I don't understand," I said simply. I wished he would make his damned point.

"Right now, the last thing Birch needs is the two most important women in his life teaming up against Catholicism, the one solid thing Birch has found to cling to in this time of turmoil."

I raised an eyebrow at him. "You've got to be joking," I told him. Father McFarland's fuzzy reddish brows knit together in one long, disapproving line across his forehead. His pale lips pushed themselves into a frown once again. Gathering that he lacked the ability to make a joke, I replied, "We're not teaming up against anything. I want to learn about other religions, different types of spiritual philosophy. I never even knew how insightful poetry could be. Glenda's teaching me a new way of examining spirituality. I fail to see how that's wrong."

"I believe that's the problem, Aida," he replied, his tone low and stern and cross.

"Oh, come on, Father. I can't understand why Birch ever told me you were so liberal," I said, shaking my head, truly mystified. *This* was the man Birch had wanted me to talk to when I first started expressing my doubts about the Church? "We're not deconstructing the Bible or studying the way the early Church violently eliminated the natural spirituality of every culture it encountered. There are plenty of anti-Catholic avenues I've chosen to bypass. You know what? I'm tired. I'm tired of blaming Catholicism for everything. I just want to find a different way for myself."

"Even if it means dragging Birch down that path with you?" Father McFarland asked quietly, his head shaking slowly.

He had dressed himself in pity and sorrow for the poor, hapless, good Irish Catholic boy I'd had the audacity to corrupt. He sounded just like Nonna and Will. If Catholicism was so great, and Birch was such a good boy, why were they all so afraid I could tease him away just by expressing different thoughts?

I yelled at Father McFarland, "I'm not dragging him anywhere! He has a mind of his own, you know."

The portly priest turned his back to me and wandered back across the room to his perch near the fire. He sat down and returned his gaze to my face. "Well, now. You have a point there," he agreed. "He *is* using his mind these days, isn't he? He realized that he could never be the Catholic he wanted to be in the atmosphere you were creating. So he left. He came here."

Sitting there on Father McFarland's sofa, looking at the self-satisfied face of a happy Catholic, I let myself sink into the lumpy cushion I sat upon. I put my head into my hands and closed my eyes. I was definitely missing something. Nothing seemed to add up anymore. Why were the positions Birch and I occupied mutually exclusive?

"Father, there is something I need to know. Will you please answer me honestly? Can you forget about Birch and me for the moment and just try to be . . . objective?"

I watched him stiffen a bit, saw both eyebrows rise slightly and his lips purse, and I couldn't tell if he was suspicious of my new line of questioning or just irritated and disgusted with me. Finally, he nodded. "Yes, Aida. I will try to be truthful and unbiased with you, as I try to do when anyone in my parish comes to me with a spiritual question. Please, proceed."

Taking a deep breath, I attempted to organize my thoughts before continuing. "Okay," I began. "Is an examination of the value of other faiths, other approaches to . . . to God . . . compatible with, or, allowable within the framework of Catholicism? Can such an exploration ever be justified? Why is it considered such a threat? Why isn't it encouraged, even, within the religious education setting? Because if I had been brought up in the faith that way, instead of indoctrinated—"

Father McFarland raised a hand to stop me. "I thought we were leaving you out of this for the sake of objectivity," he said.

"Fair enough," I answered, waiting for him to continue.

"In my personal opinion, simply as a Catholic, not as a priest, not as an officer of the Holy Church, there is an incredible amount of value in such an undertaking—"

"Thank you," I said. "I knew there was a reason Birch thought so highly of you. When I first started discussing my doubts about the Church he said I should talk to you."

"I wish you had, Aida. But please, allow me to finish what I was saying."

"Of course. I'm sorry," I murmured.

341

"Now, there is great value in the analysis of other faiths, *provided* that the objective of the study is to create a deeper understanding of and appreciation for Catholicism. Jesus tells us that only through Him can we be saved, Aida. Now, does that mean that individuals born and raised Jewish, or Muslim, or Hindu, for example, are damned? Of course not. I don't believe so. The Lord recognizes that everyone is born into a given culture and taught a specific path to God. The truth is that God is love, that he inhabits all individuals. Therefore we are all connected."

I nodded, understanding a little better Birch's desire to seek out his uncle Sean.

"But, Aida. To be blessed enough to be raised with the knowledge of Jesus, our savior, and to subsequently engage in the study of other forms of spirituality only to *reject* him, rather than more fully embracing him, now, *that* I find un-forgivable."

"Oh!" I gasped, deflated. Stupidly, I hadn't seen that coming. He had really started to seem open-minded, to offer a cogent rationale for broad-based spiritual explora-tion. Only as long as the objective remained the Catholic God could my quest be justified. And that wasn't the case at all. I wasn't embarked on a journey that possessed any recognizable destination. Apparently, my questioning could only be sanctioned as long as the maze perpetually ended with Jesus. Now I understood why my future with Birch was perilous, at least in Catholic terms. If I had no intention of ever reconfirming my own Catholicism, then I diverged too radically from the path Birch was on. If we were together, he would be joining his life with someone whom he had to believe was damned. If Birch bought Catholicism part and parcel, then he would have no hope of meeting his beloved again in the afterlife. We were, simply put, doomed.

Rising from my seat, I strode across the room to where the priest remained. The fire now blazed in its little brick altar. I offered my hand to Father McFarland. "Thank you for your time, Father. I . . . you helped clarify some things for me."

He shook my hand. "You're welcome, Aida. I'm glad I could be of service."

"Will you please tell Birch that I was here?"

Sean McFarland's response was a simple nod, and I trudged back to my car, head bowed against the rain, tasting the acrid tang of defeat inside my mouth.

Chapter Nineteen

Once home, I rummaged through my near-empty fridge and cupboards, finding little to sustain me. I boiled some pasta, and prepared it with olive oil and Parmesan and peas. I sat at the table, feeling the thickness of silence.

Picking up my bowl of food, I trudged into the living room, plopped myself on the sofa, and ate in front of the babbling television. I had to go back to work tomorrow. Maybe work would be more distracting than watching television.

After washing my dishes, I soaked in the tub, sipping a mug of warm milk and honey. I always thought that breast milk must taste something like this to babies, warm and sweet and soothing. It usually made me feel nurtured, but it didn't help much tonight. As I snuggled into bed and hugged Birch's pillow, I thought of Birch and Sasha stretched out on the little bed in Father McFarland's guest room.

What was he thinking about before he drifted off to sleep? I wondered if he felt lost and bewildered, or if his faith in the Church had been renewed by Father McFarland. The priest had helped me, anyway. He had cemented my certainty that I was doing the right thing by leaving the Church. He had told me, essentially, that I was going to hell. And I knew he was wrong because I was already in hell. The only thing that death could bring was an end to longing, for truth and peace and knowledge. Either I would possess those things, in some fashion, or all spirit and consciousness would disappear and it wouldn't matter. But hell, well, that was my current existence. Recalling Father McFarland hulking victoriously by the roaring fire as I left, the notion that I had lost a crucial battle resurfaced. I felt suffocated, disoriented as I slipped into a world in which I was the only outsider.

All I could do now was channel all of my emotion into this bizarre commemoration I was planning for the baby. Fighting the temptation to call it all off, I hoped that by staring down my loss, instead of pretending it never happened, I would be able to start to recognize myself once again. With everything that had transpired between Birch and me, and my family and me, I began to believe that the picture of myself I carried around inside my head, the one with Birch next to me and my family surrounding me, would have to be altered. It occurred to me just then, as I writhed uncomfortably in my bed, that the memorial I was having might be a laying to rest of many things.

Rolling over on my back, I turned my mind with great effort to work. Tomorrow, I would have to go back. I had to find something to write about. Maybe a series on comfort foods. That seemed appropriate. First, Italian, of course—lasagna winning the top slot. Then, similar dishes from other cultures. Recipes would be included, and letters from readers. I would emphasize that comfort foods are comforting because the recipes have been in our families for generations, because these dishes are layered with love and care. We are as much nurtured by the food itself as we are by the memories of our mothers or fathers or grandparents or aunties preparing the dish for us when we were children. So I finally slept, with this innocent and silly little purpose in my brain, something small and within my control and unable in any way to trip me up. I'd been stumbling enough, and the thought of just a little stability was an enormous relief to me.

I rose early on a frigid, cloudless Monday morning, stripping off my pajamas and throwing on my running clothes. After about half an hour of crisscrossing the short blocks in my downtown neighborhood, I found myself approaching St. Benedict's. I strode past, my steps swift and steady, surprised for once by the lack of emotion I felt as I passed the cold, gray edifice.

The Church was what it was. It could not change its requirements for its faithful any more than I could change my requirements for my own sense of spiritual integrity. I nodded a greeting to Father Roberto as he exited his residence next to the church. He waved at me, pausing on his doorstep, but I did not stop.

"Aida!" he called after me.

Why? I asked myself. Why couldn't he just let me keep running? I slowed my gait and turned to jog back to him. Standing in front of him, I tried to slow my breathing a bit so I could speak more comfortably. "Father?" I asked, still panting a little.

"I'm sorry to interrupt your morning run, dear," he told me, his voice a little scratchy at this early hour.

"That's all right," I lied. I jogged in place a little, not wanting my muscles to cool so abruptly.

"I just wanted to extend my condolences. I understand you've been through quite a bit recently. You know your Nonna put you on the prayer line."

"Did she?" I asked, not really caring. She was always having people pray for me.

"She cares for you very deeply, Aida. At any rate, I wanted to wish you luck," he told me.

"Luck? Why?"

"Well, your father and I have spoken extensively about you since you suddenly decided not to become little Joseph's godmother. Like your father, I pray that someday your spiritual journey will lead you back to us," Father Roberto told me softly.

I stood there, no longer warming my muscles, and shrugged a bit in reply before I flatly asked the priest, "Aren't you going to tell me I'm going to hell?"

"No! Of course not, child. God is for finding. Who am I to tell you how to go about it? I mean, I've been telling you for years how to go about it, and it's not working for you. I suppose I'm just glad you're doing something, instead of giving up, like some people do."

"Really?" I asked. Even this slight bit of encouragement was not what I expected from Father Roberto. I would have thought he'd be as strictly pious as Father McFarland.

He nodded. "Maybe we can talk about it sometime. Don't worry. I'm not going to try to lure you back to the Church. You'll come back if it's right for you, in your own time. Although, I wouldn't mind picking your brain a little about how to keep things interesting and relevant for St. Benedict's parishioners."

As I tilted my head to the side, I cocked an eyebrow. "Father, you'll excuse me if I seem . . . surprised."

"You seem suspicious, not surprised," he told me.

"Well, this is not how you normally sound in church, or even at my dad's house."

"To be honest, Aida, I've lost a few more parishioners than I'm comfortable with. I don't want to say folks are leaving in droves, but . . . well, the pews are becoming increasingly deserted of late. I'm asking for help. I don't want to lose all the young people. I'm thinking of starting a class for people who have left the Church, for all of our brothers and sisters, like you, who have somehow fallen away. It would be more for me to learn from them than the other way around. You know something? I've even heard some people calling themselves 'recovering Catholics.' As if it was a disease. It saddens me. Anyway, I'll at least be seeing you from time to time at your father's house, won't I?"

"That's up to him, I suppose, Father."

Now it was the Father Roberto's turn to shrug. "Maybe not as much as you think, Aida," he offered.

I knew he was implying that it was as much up to me as it was to Pop, but I also knew what I'd have to sacrifice to stage a return to my father's good graces, and I wasn't willing to start singing the Church's praises again for the sake of familial peace. Glenda had asked me what was easier for me to lose, my family, or myself and I suppose I had made my choice.

"Father Roberto? Can I ask you something?" I asked. Now that I was no longer moving, I was growing stiff and cold as the frosty morning closed in on me. I noticed Father Roberto wrap his black coat more tightly around his lanky frame.

"Yes, Aida. I have a few minutes. But can we at least step inside? It's freezing out here," he said as he turned back to his front door. I followed him inside. Two high-backed wooden benches faced each other in the small foyer, and the priest and I took seats opposite one another.

"What is it, Aida?" he asked, studying my face.

"Well, Father . . . it's just that you were the last person to talk to my mother before she died. She never regained consciousness at the hospital. You know that."

He was nodding his silvery head. "And you would like to know what we discussed?"

I bit the inside of my bottom lip, not sure if I even had a

right to be asking him about this. "I know you can't talk about anything she said in confession, but can you give me any clue as to how she was feeling about me? I mean, we had just had a horrible argument, and . . . I don't know, Father. I'm sorry. I shouldn't be bringing this up with you."

"Don't apologize. I understand. Your mother and I spoke in an 'off the record' sort of way before she asked me to hear her confession that morning. She told me about the disagreement the two of you had just had. Aida, she was upset with the way you had spoken to her, and extremely disappointed in herself for having struck you. But I promise you that what the two of you were going through was pretty typical of the mother-daughter dynamic as far as I can understand it. And believe me, over the years I've had countless mothers expressing similar frustrations with their teenagers."

Looking away from his face and down at my running shoes, I said quietly, "But Father, if I hadn't been so cruel, maybe she wouldn't have left to come see you. Maybe she'd still be alive."

Reaching across the narrow foyer, Father Roberto grasped my hand. "We can never know what *would* have happened, Aida. Things simply happened the way they did, and we don't know why."

That's all he said, and I suddenly respected him for it. He didn't tell me not to blame myself, that it wasn't my fault, but he didn't make any accusations, either. I had to bear responsibility for the choices I had made, as did everyone else, my mother included. And he didn't say anything about "God's will." It was useless to wonder how things could have gone differently. They hadn't. And it was just as fruitless to magnify what did happen. Perhaps I'd played some role in putting my mother in the wrong place at the wrong time, but hadn't everything in her own life led her to that point as well?

I could only shrug, a little unwilling, after all this time, to let myself off so easily. I didn't know how else to feel about my mother's death except at least partially responsible. That guilt was an integral, familiar part of me, and in its familiarity was much easier to cope with than feeling the full spectrum of the pain of my mother's death. My guilt had always been my shield. If I lost that, I'd lose the little part of my mother that I kept alive as I relived our argument—the last words we'd spoken to each other—over and over again since I was sixteen. As Birch and the rest of my family were plummeting away from me, it seemed an unacceptable loss right now.

Rising, I cleared my throat and tossed my head a little, trying to shake away some of the confused emotions rioting in my mind. "Thank you, Father. I have to go."

"You're welcome, Aida. Good-bye," he said, following me out, and closing the door behind us. "I have to get ready for the morning rosaries."

"*Ciao*, Father," I said over my shoulder as I began to trot away, befuddled, stiff, groggy. I jogged home and got ready for work.

Walking toward my desk, it seemed as if I had been away from the office for a year instead of a week. Everything in my life had completely changed, but things hummed along as usual here at the paper.

Yolanda grabbed my hand and squeezed it as I passed her desk. Sally waited until I had seated myself then came over, whispered "I'm sorry" in my ear and hugged me. She crouched over me, and I waved Yolanda over when I noticed her watching us. I hugged them both.

"Thanks for the flowers, you guys," I told them.

"Are you okay?" Sally asked.

"Of course she's not," Yolanda admonished. "Do you realize what she has gone through? But she'll be fine before too long."

Sally frowned at Yolanda, then turned back toward me. "And Birch? How is he doing?"

Shrugging, I answered, "I'm not so sure. He left."

"What?"

"He didn't!"

When some of the others in the office started glancing over at us, I gathered my friends and led them to the conference room where we could close the door. I told them most of everything that had happened over the past week. "I'm really feeling just kind of numb," I told them. "At least today, right now, anyway. I'm still going to close on the house—which reminds me, I have to call my real estate agent this morning."

"Really? By yourself? You're still going to get the house by yourself?" Sally asked.

I nodded. "It'll be the closest thing to a fresh start that I can muster right now. I need to do it."

"And what about Birch?" Yolanda asked.

"He said we should get out of the house deal. But I'm not going to do that. And if he ever changes his mind about us, well, he'll always have a place to call home, right?" I told them, I felt my mouth smiling, but a frigid stiffness had taken over behind the ridiculous façade of my happy face.

Clawing my way through the rest of my day, I managed, with my assistant's help, to begin to find my place again. I met with my supervising editor, Dwight, ironing out a plan for the column for the next few months. I phoned the realtor, and after a series of calls with all the other pertinent

351

parties, we arranged a closing date of Friday, April 24th, in just a couple of weeks. I would take possession of the house upon closing.

The next week or so was spent in much the same grasping manner, scratching the smallest bit forward, searching for where I had left off in my regular, daily life before everything happened. Although I went about the ordinary business of living, it was without the usual amount of talking or laughing or eating or sleeping. I spent some time with Rosie and Joseph. Marco and Pop seemed to have agreed to remain polite with me, but the absence of warmth and tenderness in our cursory exchanges didn't go unnoticed. I avoided Nonna all together. I left a couple of messages with Glenda to give her details about the memorial, but hadn't heard back.

As I crocheted the tiny baby blanket, I silently composed a eulogy of sorts. I'd decided to have the memorial at the new house, the Sunday after I closed. I tried several times to contact Birch, to give him the specifics, and I left messages both with Father McFarland and on the answering machine. I even sent a letter, determined that Birch not miss this chance to try to lay to rest the worst of the pain. I never heard from him.

Over and over, the phone did not ring. Over and over, I didn't hear his lovely, deep, steady voice. And over and over I fell asleep without his beautiful arms wrapped around me.

As the days wore on, I was reminded repeatedly that the business of buying a house was complicated enough for two people. The constant phone calls and details like inspections and paperwork were too irritating for me handle on my own, but I had no choice. I muddled through and tried to pack. Yolanda and Sally followed me home from work on Tuesday and Wednesday to help. I had until the end of the month to move out of the apartment and Marco agreed to borrow Rosie's brother-in-law's moving truck, as well as Rosie's brother-in-law, on the 30th to move all of the furniture and whatever remained of the boxes. It was all worked out.

I kept telling myself that everything would go according to my well-laid plans. I would close on the house on Friday, spend Saturday cleaning and preparing for the family to be over on Sunday. Whether or not anyone would come was another story. But I would at least have the kitchen and dining room set up so that we could eat and visit. Marco was going to help me move the table and chairs on Saturday.

On the Thursday evening before I closed on the house, I tried Glenda once more. When her answering machine picked up, I almost hung up, feeling slighted by her continued absence. The last time we had actually spoken was when I called her on my way to Father McFarland's for directions. I had promised to call her back later that evening but had failed to do so. Deciding to leave her another message, I began, "Hi, Glenda. It's me again. I just wanted to remind you about the memorial on Sunday morning. You head north on Cumberland, past St. Patrick's cemetery, to Walnut Street. It's—"

"Aida," Glenda's voice cut in. "Aida, I'm here. Sorry, I couldn't get to the phone right away. I just got back into town this morning. I was going to call you."

"You were out of town?" I asked.

"Yes. We're on spring break now. So I . . . well, I drove out to Chicago. To meet Thaddeus. He had a conference there, and we decided to meet there, since it was only a few hours drive for me. Less than that really."

"You . . . and Thaddeus? Really? You've been in Chicago with him? How did it go?"

"Actually, he's still there. He's going to stay on another week so we can spend a bit more time together," she said a little breathlessly.

"So, I gather it went well?"

"Oh, it's so strange. I was truly expecting things to just be awkward, stilted, and . . . I don't know, strange, I guess, after all this time. As it happens, it was none of those things."

"It seems sudden, Glenda. But I'm happy for you," I told her. And I really was, too. I had never been sure she'd be brave enough to act on her feelings, but she'd gone ahead and done something. I used to be certain that this was the right course of action for her. But having seen Will, having questioned my own motives for wanting Glenda and Thaddeus to be together, I wasn't sure anymore. Of course, it didn't matter at all what I thought about the whole thing anyway.

"Well, it was difficult you know, to actually take a step toward Thaddeus. As I've told you before, I loved Will. I will always love him. Even so, all throughout our marriage, though we had some truly exceptional times together, things were typically . . . uneasy between us, at best. There was always this unspoken tension between us, and we both knew it was all tied up with Thaddeus, and—"

"Glenda," I interrupted, sensing her guilt. "It's okay. You don't have to explain anything to me."

"No, it's not that. It's just that you are the first person who knows about this, and . . . I don't know. I suppose I'm practicing, in a way. For when I tell Birch."

"Oh," I said softly, knowing that it would be a hard speech for him to hear.

"Anyway, the instantaneous connection that I felt with Thaddeus when I first met him . . . well, it is still there. It was there throughout our relationship at Berkeley, and it was there when we met again at Michigan, and it is just as broad and deep and . . . thick as it ever was, and that is as much a source of joy to me as it is one of sorrow. It's difficult to imagine that when I was so young and inexperienced that I could have chosen to do things differently than I have, and it is equally impossible to look back over the past thirty years and feel regret. But at the same time, I have to acknowledge that I lost something of myself by not being with Thaddeus for so long."

In the stillness of my apartment, I heard Glenda swallow over the phone, and then a small sniffle. I had no idea what to say, and so I said nothing. I could make no judgments. I felt no compulsion to. A few seconds passed and I opened my mouth, determined to somehow cut into the quiet, but Glenda did it for me.

"Anyway . . . how are *you* doing, Aida? Have you had any luck with that mixed-up son of mine? I spoke to him briefly before I left, and he sounded just as lost and forlorn as ever. Although, honestly, I didn't expect him to get much help from Sean. He's a sweet man, Sean really is. And I know he truly means well, but . . ."

"I know exactly what you're talking about. I went out there, to talk to Birch. He wasn't there, but I spoke with Father McFarland for a long while. As far as I was concerned, he vacillated between concern and condemnation. He was very protective of Birch. I guess he'd be the right person to talk to if you wanted someone to scare you into returning to the Church, though."

"So, no contact with Birch, then?"

"We spoke once. It didn't go well. He has really dug his

heels in. The only thing I've ever known him to be this stubborn about was getting me back. Now he's doing all he can to push me away."

"Aida," she sighed. I waited for her to tell me that Birch would come around, that before long we'd be back together. Instead she said, in a quiet voice, "I just don't like the position he has taken. I wish he would realize that he can have you *and* Catholicism, if that's what he even wants. The two things are not mutually exclusive. I know your family thinks so, but I thought Birch would be able to see through all that."

"Did he tell you that? That he doesn't know how he can be Catholic and still be with me?" I asked, my own voice cracking mid-sentence, suddenly getting it.

"I gathered it from the way he discussed things the last time we spoke," she replied.

"Christ, Glenda," I said through clenched teeth. My grip on the phone tightened. "Of course he would think that. Why wouldn't he?"

"What do you mean? I don't—" she stopped suddenly, and I heard her suck in her breath. "It's because of Will and me, isn't it?"

I didn't really need to answer her. The silent clash between Glenda's brand of nonreligious spiritual philosophy and Will's hard-line Catholicism had played second fiddle only to Thaddeus in generating tension in the Fallon-McFarland marriage. If Birch decided Catholicism was the best spiritual route for him, he certainly would view his parents' marriage as a telling example of serious incompatibility.

"Aida, I—"

"Don't, Glenda," I interrupted. "It's fine. If Birch can't see that his decisions about him and me have to be based solely on the two of us, then there's not much to hope for anyway, right? Anyway, let me tell you how to get out to the new house."

"Sure, Aida. I think the memorial is a beautiful idea, by the way. Please let me know if I can help in any way," she offered politely. I declined, gave her the directions.

"Shall I mention the memorial to Will? Or have you already?"

"No, I hadn't thought about that. The last time he and I spoke, he seemed to have no interest in being part of my life, or Birch's for that matter. You can tell him if you want to, though." We said our good-byes, and I hung up. After a bath and a mug of milk and honey, I heaved myself into bed, waiting for sleep to erase reality, just for a little while.

Chapter Twenty

Friday just sort of happened to me. The day pushed me from one task to the next, and I bumped obediently along, wrapping things up at work around half past four and then heading to the realtor's office for the closing. I signed an infinite number of papers, attempting to make sense of all the forms and numbers and percentages and legal terms, feeling only halfway competent to be going through this process. I shook hands. I received keys.

Returning to the apartment, I gathered the items I would need for the weekend, including the hospital gown I wore the night I miscarried and the baby blanket I had finished crocheting during my lunch hour that afternoon. I placed the two items into a faded pink silk hatbox I had begged my mother for when I was thirteen. Grabbing my suitcase and a bag full of cleaning supplies, I tucked the hatbox under my arm and managed to grasp the handle of a small cooler. Somehow I made it to my car without dropping anything.

Driving out to the farmhouse, my new house, the house that would insure that I lived in perpetual debt until I died, I felt innumerable emotions tugging away for dominance inside of me. Pulled in a thousand directions, I felt positively eroded by the time I turned down Walnut Street.

Before long I was parking the car in my driveway. After depositing my gear on the front porch, I plunged my hand deep into my coat pocket and retrieved the key. "Damn it, Birch," I whispered aloud. "You're supposed to be here."

It was *our* house, and he was supposed to be with me

when we walked into it for the first time as its owners. He was supposed to carry me over the threshold and swing me around the room and laugh. A sob ripped through me and I wiped the tears onto the sleeve of my red spring coat, the one with the big shiny red buttons. It always reminded me of the coat my mother wore in the black-and-white pictures of her and my dad when they were dating. She never told me what color it was. I just always imagined it was red. Maybe because she always looked so good in red. Today, it was actually too chilly for the red spring coat. I had been trying to feel hopeful when I had put it on this morning.

I unlocked the door, pushed it open and peered inside. "Hi, honey, I'm home," I mocked myself as I walked in, the heels of my dress shoes echoing throughout the empty house.

After setting up the cot in the living room, I placed the suitcase on it, opened it, and took out a t-shirt and sweats. I changed my clothes, then wandered throughout the house, remembering the first time I'd seen it and all the daydreams I'd had in an instant. I plugged in the refrigerator and closed its gaping doors. I had purchased the old appliances along with the house. They were all dated but would be replaced before too long.

I scrubbed out the downstairs bathroom first, knowing I'd want to shower before I went to bed. Then I turned my attention to the kitchen. It wasn't filthy by any means, but I had to make it mine, which meant erasing as much of the residue of the previous owners as possible. Top to bottom, I told myself, and climbed onto the countertop so that I could begin scouring the tall cupboards.

By midnight, I was only halfway finished with my siege on the kitchen, but I couldn't push my scrub brush one more inch. I took my first shower in the new place and stood there under the rain of hot water, aching, exhausted, spent. It felt good to have completely expended myself in such a productive effort. I slipped into one of Birch's t-shirts and some pajama bottoms, then draped the cot with crisp white sheets and Nonna Anna's afghan. I fell asleep listening to the quiet of my new neighborhood.

I awoke the next morning to the sunlight that was trumpeting through the uncurtained windows and to the sound of my cell phone chirping insistently. Half blind with sleep, I fumbled through the purse I had tossed on the floor the night before and found my phone.

"Hello?" I croaked.

"Aida! Where the hell are you?" Marco yelled.

"What? What time is it?"

"It's eight-thirty. You were supposed to meet me at your apartment half an hour ago so we could load up your table. Remember?"

"Shit. I'm sorry, Marc. I'll be there in twenty minutes. And I'll take you out to breakfast."

"Just get over here," he sighed, hanging up.

Tripping off the cot and onto the bare wood floor, I shivered. We were going to need an area rug in here. Funny that I kept thinking of the things "we" would be doing with the house, when as far as I could tell, I was now just a "me." After I'd rummaged through my suitcase for jeans and a sweatshirt, I wandered through the dining room and kitchen to the bathroom, noticing the way the morning light filtered through the maple leaves on the east side of the house and into the kitchen window. One day, breakfast would be pleasant here.

After I'd washed my face, thrown on my clothes, and brushed my hair, I raced out the door to meet Marco. When I arrived at my old apartment building, he was leaning against the brick wall, scowling at me.

"I'm sorry, Marc," I offered again as I approached him. I kissed his cheek and hugged him briefly while he endured my greeting. "Well, come on then," I said as we entered the building.

"Aida, what the hell are we doing this for anyway?" he asked, climbing the stairs alongside me.

"What do you mean, Marco? I need the table for the memorial. I'm going to get movers for the rest of the big furniture later, but I at least need the table and chairs for tomorrow." We'd reached the door to my apartment and as I unlocked it, with Marco behind me, I heard him sigh heavily, purposefully. We walked into the apartment and he slouched into one of the chairs we'd soon be moving.

"What?" I asked, replying to his sigh. My eyebrows were raised and my hands had already made their way to my hips as I geared up for a fight I didn't want to have.

"Well, come on. You don't really think anyone is going to come, do you?"

"You're coming, aren't you? And Rosie? She already said she'd come." I tried to keep my voice at a normal octave. "And maybe Pop and Nonna will realize how much it means to me. How much *they* mean to me. I've really tried to make amends, you know."

Marco was half slumped on the table and from this position he somehow managed to shrug. "I guess you have. We're all just so tired of trying to understand where things went wrong with you."

Crossing my arms over my chest, I shook my head a little. "So that's it, huh? You're all just washing your hands of me? Fine then. Don't come tomorrow, not even if Rosie threatens you with bodily harm if you don't. I don't want you there if that's your attitude. Just help me move this table and you're free of me, okay?"

Marco straightened a little in his chair. "Don't be like that, Aida . . . Are you still going to make breakfast?"

Stamping my foot, I marched angrily into the kitchen. Of course I would still make him breakfast. I was programmed to provide food for all hungry males, and he knew it. I fried a few eggs and made some toast. After I'd removed the eggs from the pan, I threw some garlicky roasted green peppers into the pan to warm them, then served them alongside the fried eggs and toast. Marco liberally ground black pepper over his eggs, then tore off a hunk of toast and jabbed at the egg yolk until the yellow seeped out. I attacked my own breakfast with a little less vigor.

In between bites of pepper and egg, Marco said, "So, you probably haven't heard about Pop and Doreen, have you? I guess they figured I'd tell you."

"What are you talking about?" I asked, mopping up egg yolk with my toast.

"They're getting married," Marco answered, smiling broadly. "Can you believe it? Pop finally finding someone after all these years? And Doreen's great, too, don't you think?"

My eyes widened at the news and I had difficulty swallowing the food in my mouth. While I tried to sort out how I felt about the whole thing, I found myself nodding. "Um . . . yeah, Doreen is . . . she seems good for Pop. I'm happy for them," I said, nodding again.

"Really? Because you seem a little . . . reluctant."

"No. It's just that . . ." Just that however great Doreen had seemed when I first met her, she had shown no support for me when I had offered my big family apology. I suppose I had no right to expect her to, but it still stung a bit. "I guess I just wish Pop had told me himself," I finally finished.

Marco sipped some coffee, then peered into his mug rather than look me in the eye. "I know. Things just aren't how they used to be."

We didn't say much after that. I cleaned up the dishes and Marco began hauling the chairs downstairs. Together we carried the table outside in two pieces, both of which he loaded into his van, along with two chairs. I slid the other two chairs in my Golf. Marco followed me out to the new house, and as we were setting up the table in the dining room, I told him, "Well, if Pop and Doreen and Nonna decide to come, bring your card table and chairs, okay?"

"I wouldn't get my hopes up if I were you," my brother replied as we slid the two halves of the table together and fastened the underside latches. "But I'll bring them if you need them."

"Thanks. Marco, has Nonna said anything about me? Or about coming to the memorial?"

Marco rubbed his hands across his face and said, a little impatiently, "No. I don't know. Look, I hate being the middleman between you and the rest of the family, okay?"

"You just don't want them to start questioning which side you're on, do you? That's why you're so pissy about helping me today, isn't it? You don't want them to think you're sympathizing with me? Fraternizing with the enemy?" I accused. While I was being a little melodramatic about it, I knew we were both feeling a little that way. What he hated was not being on Pop and Nonna's good side. He liked being their golden boy, and they liked having someone they could beam about.

"Is that how you see yourself? As the enemy?" Marco said quietly, shaking his head. "God, Aida." He took a step toward me then, put his hands on my shoulders and kissed the top of my head. "I have to go. Thanks for breakfast." As he turned to walk away, he called out over his shoulder. "I like the house. It's really you."

The heavy wooden door shut solidly behind him, sealing me inside where I found it a little hard to breath suddenly. I had always liked being alone, but it was far more enjoyable when I knew the condition was temporary, when I knew that on Sunday I'd be at Pop's house, having dinner with everybody and hanging out in the kitchen afterward with Rosie and Nonna, listening to all her stories about the "old country." She used to tell those a lot, and I remember listening with great interest about how she grew up not too far from the sea, and a respectable distance from Mount Etna.

While I didn't expect Nonna to come tomorrow, I had to admit that despite our differences, or rather, because of them, it would have meant so much to me to have Nonna here, to have her reach out just a little, to understand me just a little, to nurture and comfort and . . . mother me just the tiniest little bit. I had to laugh to myself, though, at the ridiculousness of hoping for such a gesture from her. Far too many hurtful words had been exchanged between the two of us, and I realized just then that it wasn't even fair of me to expect much from her.

She had tried to reach out to me, in her own way, when she visited me after I had the miscarriage, but her approach had been so distasteful to me that in the immediacy of my anguish, I had failed to see the genuine concern behind her misguided effort. Things had gone too far with us, and I knew she'd written me off, and I really couldn't blame her for that.

Could it really be that everything, all my relationships, had gone awry the moment I allowed myself the luxury of disbelief in the Church? It was as if everyone in my life was so snuggly fettered to the spiritual moorings of Catholicism that once I had unknotted myself, I was set adrift and those moored did not have the ability to retain any ties to the drifter. I had lost my place. In some ways, being lost suited me a bit more than being found. But at the same time, I grieved for the connections I had, however unwillingly, relinquished.

When I finally stretched out on the cot that night, I knew I had prepared as much as I possibly could for the dismal day that awaited me tomorrow. At the very least, I could close a little door, though, and leave behind me, hopefully, the most jagged edges of my sorrow for the lost, lovely being that had been, for the shortest while, my child in my womb. A new chapter could begin, the one in which I settled into my new home, the one in which I rededicated myself to my work.

While I longed to dream that my new life would include Birch, I tried to make myself face the fact that he, and whatever we could have been together, might be closed behind that little door along with all the rest of it, if he didn't come. But how, I asked myself over and over, how could he not come? All night long I asked myself that question, sleeping only in short bursts, only to wake again and again, with an ache in my chest, with anxiety eating holes through my insides.

I rose before the sun that Sunday, the last day of this part of my life. I moved the cot against the wall, draping it with the earthy afghan Nonna Anna had made, and piling it with pillows I had stolen from the couch back at the apartment. I hauled my suitcase, my sheets, and my bed pillow upstairs and piled everything in the master bedroom. I dressed in a long black skirt and a red silk blouse.

In the kitchen, I brewed coffee. I prepared a wild mushroom strata and returned it to the refrigerator where it would wait to be baked. A substitute vegan strata prepared with tofu and soy cheese awaited Birch, if he chose to attend. I washed strawberries and raspberries. Everything was ready. On the dining-room table stood the uncovered hatbox. It contained my hospital gown, the baby blanket, and a letter to my unborn child I would read if and when the family had gathered.

As I wandered around the house, trying to breathe, I sipped coffee. Despite my efforts, I couldn't help but imagine Sasha galloping around the living room and up and down the stairs, and Birch on the porch with the paper and a cup of coffee, with the sunlight tickling his curls, with his bare feet propped up on the porch rail. Ripping my mind away from the scene in my head, I refused to envision curly-headed toddlers bouncing around their father's legs. Before my gathering tears could fall, I heard a car in the driveway. It was time.

Opening the front door and stepping onto the porch, I watched as Marco parked his van. He got out, opened the door for Rosie, and then retrieved Joseph's car seat from the backseat.

"He's sleeping," Rosie said quietly as they approached. "He always falls asleep in the car."

"Do you want to leave him in the car seat, then? You can put him in the back bedroom. Anyway, we'll leave the door ajar so you can hear him, but he'll be enough out of the way so he can sleep as long as he likes," I offered.

"That should work out fine," she said. She hugged me. "How are you?"

I sighed. "Don't ask," I told her before I turned to Marco. Rosie took Joseph from him, and Marco and I shared a brief embrace. He kissed my cheek.

"You came?" I asked. "Why?"

"Because you're not the enemy. You're my little sister, and I wanted you to know that," he told me.

"Thank you," I whispered.

Marco cleared his throat. "I'm going to get the card table and chairs out of the van. Pop and Doreen and Nonna should be here any minute."

"What?" I asked, my mouth dropping open. "They're coming? I don't believe it."

"Catholic guilt, Aida," Marco explained as he turned to head back to the van. "Never underestimate its powers."

I shook my head as I watched him descend the front porch steps. Catholic guilt must have been more powerful a motivator than I had previously imagined if it could overcome Sicilian stubbornness.

As Marco was setting up the card table and I was bringing Rosie a cup of coffee, Doreen and Pop came through the door, followed by my sour-looking Nonna. I hugged them all, but I felt Nonna stiffen in my arms. "I'm glad you came," I whispered in her ear. Without replying, she backed away and eased herself into one of the dining-room chairs.

Pop and Doreen had wandered into the kitchen and I followed them. As they stood there discussing the cabinetry, which either needed to be stripped and restored or freshly painted, I said to them, "It means a lot to me that you both came."

While Pop shrugged and looked around the kitchen, avoiding my gaze, Doreen explained, "Marco stopped by while we were having dinner last night. You have a very devoted brother, Aida. You should be grateful."

"I am," I replied, smiling to think that Marco couldn't help but fulfill his role as the family peacemaker, or at least

367

make an attempt to do so on my behalf. "Oh! I almost forgot," I said excitedly, rushing over to hug them. "Congratulations on your engagement."

Pop mumbled, "I was going to tell you myself . . . it was just that . . ." he trailed off.

"I understand," I told him, kissing his cheek. "I'm happy for you, Pop."

Before long everyone was sipping from steaming mugs of hot coffee. No one spoke much, but it seemed fine that way. Glancing at my watch, I realized I had told everyone we'd be starting around nine. By ten minutes after the hour, the five us were milling around the living room when we heard another vehicle. Glenda or Birch, I thought, waiting to see whose face would appear at my front door.

My breath caught in my throat for an instant. It was Will. Setting down my mug on the card table, I opened the door. "Mr. McFarland. Please, come in. Thank you for coming. I really . . . I didn't think . . . Thanks," I finished lamely, caught off guard by his appearance. He knew everyone except Doreen, whom I had the presence of mind to introduce as my father's fiancée, however strange it sounded when the word rolled off my lips.

"Glenda phoned me," Will explained as I looked up at him. "It seemed . . . I realized that maybe I should come, that maybe you were right, Aida, about Birch and me. He's not here, though?"

I shook my head. "No. I'm glad that you are," I said, still shocked. As I turned to look at the assembled group, I heard the slamming of a car door, knowing it must be Glenda, but still praying for Birch to fly to my side, where he belonged.

When I opened the door to greet Glenda, I felt my mouth drop open. I closed it, and tried to swallow, but my throat had gone dry. "Thaddeus," I managed to utter. "Glenda, you brought Thaddeus," I stated, despite the obvious nature of my observation.

As the couple walked in, a triangle thirty years old reformed itself. Will stared at Thaddeus, his dark eyebrows arching high above his green eyes. His gaze then shifted to Glenda, and I was suddenly aware of how confused my own family must be. I looked at Marco, who had to be putting the pieces together from the little I had told him. I watched as he grabbed Pop and Doreen by their arms and led them into the kitchen. Nonna trailed behind them, looking positively befuddled. I hoped that Marco would be able to debrief them with the small amount of information he possessed.

Thaddeus extended his hand toward Will and said, "Hello, Will. Glenda didn't expect you to make it today. I would have stayed behind if I had known you would be here. I apologize. I . . . I should leave." His arm was still stuck awkwardly in the space between him and Will.

Not breathing, I watched the twitching of Will's face, the clenching and unclenching of his right hand. Finally, though, he raised his now-relaxed palm to Thaddeus'. They shook briefly, pulled away. "No," Will said. "You have a right to be here. Whether I like it or not, you are part of this, by blood." His voice was low, a little gruff, but not menacing.

Thaddeus nodded. "Thank you," he offered. "Not just for that. But for everything."

Glenda's eyes flitted back and forth between the two men. Her mouth opened slightly as if she were about to speak, but she closed it again when Will spoke once more.

"Look," Will began. "We were young back then. We all thought we were doing the right thing. Glenda, we gave it a great shot, and it's not through lack of love that we have to call it quits. I think we both know that."

"Oh, Will," she sobbed, stepping toward him, into his arms. I took a step back, feeling as though I should just disappear, but knowing it would draw even more attention to my presence at this point. "We tried," she said. "And I do love you, you know I do."

"I know, Glenda, I know," he said softly, his hand pushing a few strands of blond hair away from her face. "And I love you. It . . . it just wasn't enough. Sometimes it's just not enough. We tried to make a good thing, and we did, here and there, but . . . ."

As he trailed off, she nodded. "It wasn't enough," she repeated.

"I want you to be happy, damn it, in that big, forever, everyday kind of way that we could only catch sight of once in a while. I know that can't happen with me. And I know you know it, too."

Glenda nodded again, and stepped back. Will regarded Thaddeus now, and there was no more face twitching or jaw clenching. "I don't know if things will work out with you two or not, but no matter what, be good to her," Will ordered.

"Of course, Will," Thaddeus replied.

Thaddeus' responses, I noticed, were clipped, precise. He made no speeches. I realized just then the tremendous regret he must have shouldered at having refrained from being a part of Birch's life. He was here now, not for Glenda or me or the baby, but for Birch.

"That goes for Birch, too," Will went on, "but you're going to have to share him with me. I thought . . . I thought that maybe I should just kind of disappear from his life. I actually thought that maybe if he thought about it long

enough, maybe he wouldn't want to bother with me anymore. But, even if he doesn't, well, it's too damn bad. I'm
still his old man."

"I know that, Will. I would never do anything to come
between the two of you. You'll always be his father. I'm
only hoping to go from acquaintance to friend."

Will cleared his throat, then turned to look at me, and I
tried to look as if I hadn't been standing there, watching all
this, and trying not to cry. "So where is he, then?" he asked
me.

Then I really started to weep. Looking at my watch, I
saw that it was nearly half past nine. "I don't know," I
croaked. "He's not coming, I guess," I said slowly, the reality settling down around inside me like a choking cloud of
dust after a building demolition. "I don't think he's
coming," I repeated.

I was gazing down at my feet, at my shiny black dress
shoes and tears splashed on the toes of those shoes for a few
long moments before Glenda rushed to my side and encircled
me in her arms. Accepting the embrace for a moment, I
took a deep breath, wiped my eyes with the heels of my
hands. I looked up, but found I couldn't make eye contact
with Birch's family gathered around me, so I turned away,
only to see Nonna, planted in the doorway between the
kitchen and dining room. She bowed her head and turned
to hurry back into the kitchen.

"Well, then," I announced a little too loudly, "let's get
started then."

Glenda retrieved my family from the kitchen and we all
gathered around the dining-room table. One by one, everyone stole glances at the front door, still believing Birch
would magically appear. "Stop it!" I yelled at them.
"Forget about it. He's not coming." I breathed deeply,

then said more quietly, "He's not coming."

"Anyway," I said, trying to shift myself from despair to the purpose at hand. "I want to thank you all for coming today," I began formally. "I wanted to have this memorial, because even though this baby was never born, he, or she, changed my life in powerful ways. So, I just want to take a moment to read a letter I wrote." I cleared my throat, and removed the paper from the box and unfolded it.

"My dearest child," I read. "We never had our chance to know each other. I'm not sure why it had to be that way, and I will forever be saddened by what you and I were denied. But you helped bring me closer to being the person I'm supposed to be. You made me see how important truth really is. I spent years lying to myself, but I knew there was no way I could ever lie to you. So I want to thank you, for giving me back to myself. Even though we never met, I will always love you, and so will your father. We can only hope that your spirit knows peace. Good-bye, little one."

I sniffled. Hot tears rolled down my cheeks. Nonna handed me her handkerchief, which I grasped tightly in my fist. I put the letter back in the box and closed it, then raised my eyes to the people gathered there with me.

At some point, they had all grabbed one another's hands and were only now letting go. Eyes were wiped, noses dabbed with tissues, throats were cleared.

"That was beautiful, Angelina," my father said. Heads bobbed in agreement.

We all stood there in silence for a long while until Nonna slapped her hand forcefully on the table. "Aida Angelina Benedetto!" she wailed. "*Why* are you still here?"

"What?" I asked her, stunned and confused.

"There are many, many things that you and I will never, ever agree on. Things will never be the same with us. That's life. *Così va il mondo.* We both know that. But *basta,* enough about that," she said. At this point she thrust her finger in my direction, saying loudly, "You and that boy are supposed to be together. I can see that now. God have mercy on your souls if you both don't come back to the Church. But even an old fool like me can see that you belong with him. Maybe I couldn't see that before, but I am blind no longer. Now," she continued, nodding in the direction of Glenda and Will, "now I know a little better the people that he comes from, which is important. Are you blind, child? *Go,*" she told me.

She was always telling me to go, but this time, it made sense. I stood there, nodding. *Così va il mondo.* That's life, it meant. That's how the world goes.

"*Sì,* Nonna," I said, bewildered that the two of us were finally in agreement. "*Sì,* I'll go."

"Go on," my father was saying. "Go to him. Shake him up. Make him see. Sometimes a man must be made to see," he said as Doreen smiled a little.

"Um . . . okay. I'm going," I looked around, suddenly wondering what I should do with all of them. "Ro, can you manage the food?"

"Of course, get out of here already," she told me.

And suddenly I was running to my car, hatbox in hand. I drove ten miles above the speed limit, at least, racing to Elk's Run. On the toll road, however, I did the strangest thing. I drove through the manual booths, handing my change to people who seemed surprised that I didn't breeze through the automatic lanes on a Sunday morning with no traffic. "Thanks," I told them. "Have a good day." It's what Birch would have done and it suddenly mattered.

Pulling up to the old brick house, I gleefully recalled that, this being Sunday morning, Father McFarland would be at mass. I could only pray that Birch hadn't gone with him. Then I saw Birch's Jeep parked under an enormous elm tree by the barn, a hundred yards off from the house. Throwing my car into park, I ran up to the front door of the house, knocking furiously. There was no sound from within, not even the sound of Sasha barking. As well as I could in my dress shoes, I sprinted to the barn, hatbox under my arm, and peered into the dark interior. Sunlight needled in through the gap-tooth red planks, but it took my eyes a moment to adjust to the diminished light.

And then I saw him. Birch was sitting on a bale of hay, with Sasha at his side. He was feeding a large brown cow some sort of grain from his cupped palm. Sasha saw me first. She actually limped over to me, and I crouched down, feeling her warm, wet tongue on my cheek.

"Aida!" Birch called. "What are you doing here? I thought the memorial was today."

When he didn't get up, I walked slowly to him, Sasha following close behind. I got close enough to touch his cheek, prickly with a couple of days' worth of unshaven beard, but I didn't do it. He looked tired, but peaceful.

"You didn't come," I said.

He shook his head, golden curls bouncing. "I was going to come later. I couldn't face you again, all of a sudden like that, with everyone there. Something happened to me, Aida, and I wanted to talk to you. I just thought I should wait. What's that?" he asked, gesturing toward the hatbox.

"It's from the memorial." I opened the box, showed him the blanket I made, revealed the hospital gown underneath. "Here's the letter I wrote," I said, handing it to him.

As he held the soft blanket between the fingers of his left hand, he grasped the letter with his right. Reading it to himself, he began to cry, then folded it back up and put it in the box. He was still holding the blanket and he lifted it up, unfurling it with both hands. "You finished something," he said. "It's beautiful."

"It was time. So what happened?" I asked, sitting next to him. Our shoulders touched, as did our thighs. He felt warm and solid, a familiar stranger.

Reaching across my leg, his hand found mine, and our fingers knit themselves together. The cow grumbled a little and nudged Birch's knee. He patted her head. "No more, Maple," he told her softly. "It was so strange, Aida. I happened to walk in on my uncle yesterday. He was praying, in his room. His door was open and I was walking to my room and I heard him praying softly, kneeling down beside his bed. He didn't hear me and I found myself watching him because he had this look on his face that I'd only seen once before. On my mother."

"Your mother? She was praying?"

"No. I couldn't go to church with my dad one Sunday when I was eleven or twelve or something, because I was sick. I went to look for her and found her in the room she had set up in the basement to do yoga. She was sitting there, cross-legged, meditating, and had the same calm, peaceful look on her face. I asked her what she was doing, and she told me that sometimes, she got this feeling, of incredible fullness, she had said, but emptiness, too, as if she were everything and nothing all at once, but it made her feel perfectly content with everything, just as it was.

"She said that there was the space in consciousness, before your intuition is translated by your brain into words. You just *know* things there, in that space. She taught me a little then, just that once, about clearing my mind, and listening, and stillness. Anyway, my uncle had just the same look on his face when I saw him praying."

375

I had been watching his eyes closely but looked away just then, knowing what was coming. I knew he wanted to achieve that same feeling, that his uncle would teach him how, through prayer, that he had chosen Catholicism, and that I didn't fit into that world. I recalled the exchange I had witnessed between Glenda and Will earlier that morning, about love just not being enough. Why didn't I know that by now, I wondered. A heaviness settled upon me and I squirmed a bit underneath the weight. I waited for him to continue.

"Are you okay?" he asked me. "You look pale all of a sudden."

"I'm fine," I lied, gazing just above his head at the darkness above us. A few rays of light broke through the tiny spaces between the slats of barn wood, but for the most part, the musty space was as cool and dark as a mausoleum.

"Well, you know something?" Birch went on. "In thirty years as a Catholic, I have never once felt that way. That look has been absent from my face all my life. And I thought, why do I keep doing this, trying the same thing over and over, expecting to get different results? It's insanity. But never once have I tried things her way, or even your way. You've experienced that feeling. You've described it to me. Don't you get it sometimes, when you run?"

I nodded, shrugging a little at the same time. "Sometimes I can stop myself from thinking, and everything turns quiet, sometimes it's when I'm running, but I've felt it settle on me at other times, too. Strange times, like when I'm baking biscotti, or even when I'm with you, when we're . . . together. And then suddenly it feels perfect that everything is exactly what it is. But it doesn't happen very often. And anyway, it doesn't really mean anything. It's not really

376

like praying, or meditating. I mean, I can't get that feeling by going after it. It just happens. It's not like I'm *seeking* anything, like enlightenment or answers."

"Maybe that's what makes it like true prayer, or meditating. Maybe it's the *not* asking for anything that's important," he replied. "Anyway, I tried it. I tried meditating, the way she taught me. I know it takes practice, so I didn't expect much. And I didn't get much, either. So I ran. I mean, I really ran, just tried to run away, to get away from everything. Aida, I truly wanted to just dissolve, to just disappear and be done, you know? Anyway, I ran for quite a while before everything went warm and just kind of blank and I stopped, and I found myself in this grove of trees—maples, pines, oaks—on the edge of the property. I'd never come that far before. It was beautiful, silent, and it seemed as if I had run right out of myself, just for the smallest of moments as I stood there, in that space after you sprint but before you really start breathing again.

"It hit me, like I'd been kicked in the gut it hit me so hard, that everything, *everything* was as it should be, full of pain, yes, but joy as well, and not as fractured as I thought, but simple, whole. And then I lost the thread of my thought, but it wasn't so much thought, really, as just a feeling, an intuition, like my mom had talked about, but it all gets sort of twisted when I try and put it into words—" he stopped abruptly and swallowed, then sighed. "That doesn't make any sense," he finished.

In a moment that seemed to last an eternity, the thick weight locked in my chest dissipated, and I nodded, slowly. "It's . . . it's amazing, for lack of a better word, isn't it? We . . . I want to figure out how to live a little longer in that space. It's as if you're suddenly freed of the burden of having to evaluate everything as good or bad or in between. It's just all there, waiting to be accepted."

Nodding, Birch agreed. "That's exactly it. Does it seem strange to you to get that feeling from the physical exertion of running, instead of kneeling down and praying or sitting and meditating?"

I shrugged and began slowly, discovering my meaning only as the words left my mouth. "Maybe it's not so strange. I mean, isn't the point of meditation and prayer, too, to learn how to dismiss all the clutter, the distractions in our brains? Maybe you and I just need a more visceral approach than some people. We need to feel as if we're physically shedding what we think we see so that we can really see. Maybe thinking it all away is something we have to work up to. And maybe understanding it all better comes with time, too."

Birch nodded again, and we sat there for a long while in the semidarkness of the morning barn, listening to the cow rustling about and Sasha sniffing at something under the straw on the floor.

"Aida?" Birch asked in a whisper. "May I add something to the baby's box?"

"Of course," I told him. I opened the box, confused and waiting. My eyes widened as I saw him reach behind his neck and unclasp the golden cross that had hung there for as long as I had known him. "Birch?"

"A part of me died when our baby died, Aida," he said. He dangled the cross above the blanket I had made, then gradually released the chain in a silent ritual meant only for him. Taking the lid from my hand, he placed it securely onto the box. "But a part of me came to life as well. Do you understand what I mean? It seems strange to me, feeling on the one hand as if I'm turning my back on something that I thought meant a great deal to me, but running toward something more meaningful, toward . . . what I can make out of truth, and toward you. I don't know . . ." he trailed off, looking down at the pink silk cover of the hatbox.

"Yes, you do, Birch," I told him, a small smile, a real smile, tugging at my lips for the first time since I didn't know when. "It's called evolution. *Così va il mondo.*"

"Cosi what?" he asked, laughing a bit.

"*Così va il mondo.* That's life . . . that's how the world goes," I translated.

"Yeah? What about us? Our life? Our world?"

"What do you mean?" I asked warily, wondering if we could possibly still be tripped.

"Are you going to accept that I'm just the kind of person who needs to believe that everything is going to be okay? That's something that always seems to be coming between us," he said.

"You mean my bleakness?" I asked, only a little sarcastically.

He shrugged. "I need to hope, Aida. I can't resign myself to thinking that there is no 'okay,' no comfort to be had, as you said that night."

Sighing, I looked into his brown eyes, dark as the soil just outside the barn. Good things would always spring from him. He was that kind of person—hopeful, bountiful, and I truly wanted to be a part of that.

"I think," I began cautiously, "I think I'm starting to redefine what it means to believe in . . . well, anything and everything, I guess. It's all worth the risk of losing. I mean, I've lost a lot and . . . I've survived. And to keep gaining, and growing, well, it's compensation, in a way," I concluded, concentrating on not losing this thread. "Compensation," I repeated.

Yes, that was it. That was what I meant. There was always compensation. "Not as something to seek as if you were owed, just something to be recognized, accepted, and embraced." My brows had been furrowed together as I concentrated on unearthing my newly discovered philosophy on life. As I finished speaking, Birch brought his hands to my face, and with his thick thumbs he smoothed each eyebrow into relaxed submission.

Throughout the next several weeks, Birch and I completed the move to the new house. The process was bittersweet, as our history together had begun in those two little apartments in the old brownstone. But before long, we were ready to host our first Sunday dinner, with both of our families. And rather than our usual pasta, we had decided to try something new. Glenda was going to teach me how to make a vegetarian loaf-type entrée, in the style of meatloaf with gravy. We were also going to serve mashed potatoes, and green beans, and Doreen was going to make the cucumber salad she was apparently famous for with her own family. I had baked a loaf of rye bread the day before.

Birch and I woke with the sunrise that May morning. It was chilly but sunny, just as Midwestern days ought to begin in early May. On the front porch, we regarded the dawn and prepared for our run.

"So, is your mom bringing Thaddeus today?" I asked Birch as we stretched our legs on the porch railing. I watched the sunlight brighten his hair as he leaned his long body over his leg. He grabbed hold of his foot and I smiled, watching him wince a little. Sasha whined behind the screen door.

"Are you coming with us today, Sasha?" I asked as I opened the door for her. Her tail wagged, and she trotted off the porch and began pacing in the front yard. Only a ghost of a limp still haunted her. Her recovery had been thankfully swift.

"No," he said to me as he relaxed into the stretch. "He couldn't come out this weekend. I'm not sure how long they're going to do this ridiculous long-distance dance."

"Do you think he'll move out here eventually?"

Birch straightened himself and shrugged before repeating the stretch on the other leg. "Probably. He'll have to find some kind of work, though. My dad's not coming, either. I think he's still not quite comfortable being my mom's ex. I mean, they both agreed it was what they wanted, but still . . . It's just so awkward for them both."

"And for you, too," I added, bending myself toward the gray slats of the porch floor. I grabbed the back of my ankles and pressed my face toward my knees.

"You're so limber, Aida. You'd be great at yoga."

"Really? Did your mom ever teach you?"

"I know a thing or two," he told me. "Watch this." Hopping over the porch railing, he found a spot in the grass. On all fours now, he placed his elbows on the grass, cupped his hands, and placed his head on the ground, braced by his hands. He then straightened his knees, and pivoted his legs up over his head, grinning, upside down, in what seemed to me to be a perfect headstand.

"Show off!" I shouted at him as I ran past. Before long he was on my heels and we ran side by side for about an hour.

"Well?" Birch asked me as we ran. I was getting used to his chattiness on our morning excursions. "Do you feel different? Since Friday, I mean."

On Friday we'd had our ceremony at the city hall. We were as married as we were ever going to be, despite the lack of a church wedding. "I'm pissed off," I answered.

"What?"

Smiling at his confusion, I explained, "At Nonna. For not coming. Even your dad came."

"Yeah, both of them," he replied. "But did you really think Nonna would show?"

"Yes. She came to the memorial. I thought it was a start. But I suppose some things will never be made right between us," I said, leaping over a muddy puddle from last night's rain. "I wonder if she'll come to dinner today."

"I wouldn't count on it, Aida," Birch answered. "Maybe you should let it go."

"No!" I shouted over my shoulder as I sprinted ahead. Birch quickly caught up and we ran on in silence for another fifteen minutes. After we had slowed to a walk, I continued where I had left off. "I don't expect her to start understanding me. I don't really even know what to hope for where Nonna's concerned. It just doesn't feel right to give up on her altogether."

"Maybe," Birch began, "maybe she's doing the same thing. Her protesting the way you're doing things is her way of trying to show you what she believes is a better way. She still wants to save you, Aida. Maybe she's not giving up on you."

"I guess. I still want her to come to dinner, though." We left it at that and finished our journey home.

As I headed upstairs to shower, Birch wandered out to the backyard. From the window of our bedroom, I watched him climb up into the apple tree, to sit amidst the flower buds. He hung his legs on either side of a thick branch and leaned back on it. He'd been performing this ritual a few mornings a week for the past couple of weeks now. I asked him about it once and he said he was trying to meditate. "Aren't you supposed to sit on the floor and chant or something," I had asked him. I had been meaning to get a few lessons myself from Glenda.

"I'm trying that, too," he had replied, "but this feels more right to me."

We came together again for a light breakfast of bananas and my homemade granola. It would be the last moment we would have to ourselves before Glenda and Doreen arrived to help me with the meal.

As he fed Sasha a bit of banana, Birch said, "Don't you think this house is kind of quiet, Aida?"

"Without the noise of neighbors above and below us you mean? Are you missing the apartment?" I asked him, sipping my coffee.

"No, not at all. I meant . . . I meant with just the two of us here. Well, and Sasha."

Lowering my head, I looked at the pattern left by the few remaining bits of oats and nuts at the bottom of my bowl. "Too bad you can't read granola like tea leaves," I told him.

He laughed a little, the sound dying in the back of his throat. "Why? Do you need a sign to know if you're ready to start trying again?" he asked me.

Looking up at him, I stared into his eyes. I could see little of the fear that still lingered in me. I could think of nothing to say.

"Aida, it's useless to wait until you're not afraid anymore," he said, knowing me too well. "We'll always be afraid that it will happen again. But you know what? It might not."

"I know, Birch," I said, rising and walking over to him. I stacked my bowl inside his, and bent down to kiss him. "I've got to get started on dinner, okay? Your mom told me to soak some lentils." I turned toward the sink, hoping to avoid the topic, at least for a little bit longer. As I turned on the water to rinse the bowls, I heard his footsteps leave the kitchen.

Glenda arrived shortly after, followed by Doreen about half an hour later. Sasha greeted them with a few short barks before flopping down on a patch of sun on the living-room floor.

"Where is Birch?" Doreen asked as she began peeling potatoes.

"At the sanctuary," I told her. I was chopping celery.

"You two will end up with a house full of dogs before long," Glenda warned.

"That's what I'm afraid of," I said. "Okay, Glenda. What's next?" As she began her lesson in vegetarian cookery, something occurred to me. "When did you become a vegetarian anyway?"

Looking up from the pot on the stove in which she was stirring the lentils, she said with a small, proud smile, "When I was fourteen. Didn't Birch ever tell you?"

I shook my head, peeling my onion. The strong smell of it, along with the peppery scent of the cooking lentils filled the kitchen, and I thought how odd this collection of aromas was for a Sunday. I looked over at Doreen, seated at the kitchen table. Her potato peeling had slowed as she focused her attention on Glenda, preparing to hear the story.

"Well, I grew up on a farm, in upstate New York, and—" Glenda began.

"I didn't know you were from New York," I interrupted. "Or that you lived on a farm. Birch has never mentioned it."

"I don't talk about it that much. It was a long time ago," she replied quietly. "Anyway, we raised chickens. We sold the eggs, and some of the birds were raised for meat. Every spring, though, we sold some chicks as pets at Easter time. I never understood why people bought them. I suppose they thought it was a charming idea for their children to have real chicks as pets for Easter, but inevitably they ended up as meat. We also had a couple of cows, and a few horses."

"What a way to grow up," Doreen commented, her potato peeling now completely halted. "I lived in Chicago all my life, until I moved out here a dozen years ago. After a big city like that, Middleton seemed so rural to me, but it's nothing compared to what you experienced."

"It was an interesting childhood, and I had freedoms that I've never known since. But it was also very brutal to be surrounded so regularly by the presence of death. So one morning, I marched into the kitchen where my mother was cooking breakfast. I remember it so clearly. My best friend Margie had raised a pig named Daisy who had just been to the state fair. Well, Daisy hadn't won anything, but my father bought her from Margie's father anyway and had her butchered. And that was what my mother was frying for breakfast that day. Bacon and eggs. I had had enough. It had bothered me all my life, the way we lived, the way we consumed these creatures I had lovingly helped to raise. And that's pretty much what I told my mother."

"What did she say?" I asked.

"She said nothing. Nothing at all. She slapped me across the mouth and went back to cooking breakfast, then relayed my speech to my father when he came in from his chores. I feared a more sound beating than the one my mother had given me, but instead he actually tried to explain, or defend, the way of life he had inherited from his own father. But I couldn't be swayed, and from that day forward I felt like an outsider in my own home. I left when I was seventeen. We've exchanged polite contact over the years, but we've never been close."

Birch had mentioned his maternal grandparents only once or twice since I had known him. Now I knew why.

"That took a lot, to stand up to your folks that way,"

Doreen said. Glenda only shrugged in reply and turned back to her lentils. Without looking back at me, she said, "Aida, when you're through chopping the onion, sauté it with the celery."

"Did you get along well with your mother before that?" I asked her.

Not looking up from the cooking pot, Glenda replied, "Not really, not once I reached the age of eleven, or twelve. She was extremely attentive and nurturing when I was a small child, but seemed to feel so irritated with me as I grew older. I suppose I questioned a lot of things. She never understood that."

Remembering something Rosie had said about children needing to break away from their parents, I asked, "That's part of growing up, though, isn't it?"

"Of course," Doreen answered. Glenda had drained the lentils. I took her place at the stove and sautéed the vegetables in olive oil. No one spoke for several minutes, and before long, the onions and celery, now warm and fragrant, had been lightly cooked. I slid the pan off the burner and turned to look at Glenda, who was standing at the sink, washing a couple of pots and knives. "What next?" I asked her.

Wiping her hands on a yellow-and-white-striped towel, she handed me the bowl of cooling lentils and a fork. "Give these a nice mash," she said. I sat at the table next to Doreen, sprinkling salt and pepper into the lentils and pressing them into the bottom of the bowl with the fork.

"I went through the same thing, you know. The same arguments and endless conflicts," Doreen said.

"You did?" I asked. "How did your mother handle it?"

"Oh, actually I was thinking of my daughter and me, but I suppose my mom and I went through it, too."

"You have a daughter? Pop didn't tell me that." I was stunned by how little I knew of these women. I stopped mashing the lentils for a moment and looked from to Doreen to Glenda, realizing in that instant that they were both now mothers, of sorts, to me. Doreen would become my stepmother when she married my father, and Glenda was now my mother-in-law.

"I have one daughter, Colleen. She's in graduate school, getting her MBA from Northwestern."

"Impressive," Glenda noted. I nodded in agreement.

"We didn't always get along as well as we do now. We battled constantly, about everything, from the time she was twelve to the day she left home for college. It wasn't until she started finding out who she was that she began appreciating me—as another woman, that is, not just as her mother."

Leaning over my shoulder, Glenda told me what seasonings to add, and as I crushed dried herbs between my fingers, she stirred in the sautéed onions and celery. Doreen had finally finished scraping the skins off the potatoes and was now chopping them, but her head was cocked to the side and she was chewing a little on her bottom lip. I imagined that she was still thinking about her daughter.

"I never had a chance to do that," I told them. "To get past the battling and start understanding my mom in another way."

"You would have gotten through it, too," Doreen said softly. "Everybody does. But it must have been especially hard for her to pass away when you were at such a difficult place in your own life. Being a teenager . . . I don't know. It must be one of the toughest parts of anyone's life."

"Birch had a rough time of it as well, but he seemed to save most of his conflict for his father. He went easy on me.

It must be different with mothers and daughters. Maybe it's because you have to figure out what kind of woman you want to be, and one of the only ways to do that is based on what kind of woman your mother is. Inevitably you'll reject some part of her."

Doreen was nodding. "Yeah, daughters can be bitches sometimes," she said with a broad smile.

Glenda laughed as hard as I had ever heard her laugh, and I did as well, grateful to Doreen for lightening the heavy mood.

"My mother would have liked you two," I told them, thinking about that morning fourteen years ago, our last morning. After all this time, I finally realized something—that my mother thought I was a little bitch that morning, too. I laughed a little to myself. I had been horrible, and I had earned the slap, and talking with Doreen and Glenda gave me permission, in a way, to feel all right about what had happened with my own mother. Marco, Rosie, and Father Roberto had all in their own way told me the same thing, that what my mother and I had been like with each other on that morning was normal. But it felt different coming from the two of them, my two new mothers.

Just at that moment, Birch entered the kitchen through the back door of the house. Hearing the three of us laughing together, he said, "Uh-oh. A hen party? Should I go?"

"Oh, stop," his mother told him, greeting him with a hug and a kiss.

Doreen smiled at him. "Hi, sweetie," she said.

I sat there with the bowl of vegetarian meatloaf mix in front of me, flanked by Glenda and Doreen, and I looked at Birch and smiled. "I might just take you up on your offer from this morning," I told him.

His sandy eyebrows arched above his eyes, which

sparkled with surprise. "Really? Well, we should get started right away, don't you think?"

Laughing, I winked at him and returned to my work.

"I'm going to hold you to that, Aida," he said as he strolled out of the kitchen.

"I'm counting on it!" I called after him.

Later that evening, after everyone had left, Birch and I lounged on the living-room floor. The evening was cool enough for us to have a fire in the fireplace. It would likely be our last this season.

"So, you were right," I began, as I listened to the pop and hiss of the burning logs. "Nonna didn't come."

"I know. Are you disappointed?" he asked quietly.

Shrugging, I answered, "A little. I'm not surprised, though. I can't make things be the way they used to be. And she can't accept how they are now. At least Pop and Marco see now that even though they can't change me, they can change how we relate to each other. It's going to take a while, though, before we can redefine what 'normal' means for us. Anyway, we've all become a bit more pliable since the memorial. It helped in a lot of ways."

"How so?"

I moved into a cross-legged position across from Birch and leaned toward him. "Well, I needed it in order to acknowledge, in a public way, that the baby was a real and true force in my life, not just a fetus that didn't make it. I didn't want to just put it all behind me. The baby changed me and in return I wanted to honor that little spirit. Anyway, I think for my family the memorial helped them to understand not just what I went through with the miscarriage, but that I still have something that they can recognize as faith. Pop and Marco are beginning to respect that, I think. And Nonna . . . well, she was moved by something that day. Something made her push me back to you. I mean, I really felt as if the only thing important to her, just in that moment, was my happiness. I love her for that. But without the Church in my life, I think she sees me as a little of a lost cause. That's why she didn't come to the wedding Friday. That's why she didn't come today. It hurts more now, her not coming, now that I understand how much she really does love me."

Birch had been reclining on the floor, propped up on an elbow, and now he pulled himself up into a sitting position across from me. "Do you think you'll ever go back?" he asked, as his fingers brushed a few strands of hair away from my face. "To church I mean?" he finished.

Grasping his hand, the one that lingered by my face, I told him, "I have a new church, a new faith. It's me, and you, and us, and all the rituals of every day that connect us to each other, that bring us peace and clarity. It's making love to you and it's a Sunday run at dawn and it's preparing food for our families and it's you up in the apple tree. And you know what else? It's that little pink hatbox on the top shelf of my closet.

"Birch, there is so much that is sacred right in front of us. Divinity right at our fingertips. It's always been that way. It's just taken me thirty years to finally recognize it. Catholicism clouded all that for me. It's a distraction from the truth, for me, anyway. I know it's not like that for everybody. But for me, I feel like I'm evolving, into a better version of myself. And I don't know if I could've gotten to this place, this place that I'm ecstatic to be in right now, if we hadn't gone through everything that we did."

Birch nodded in a small way and smiled a little. "Compensation, right? Like you were talking about before, in the barn?"

"Exactly," I whispered. "And what about you? Will you ever go back to church?" I asked. "I mean, I know that it once meant a lot to you. Maybe you can still get something out of it?"

He shrugged a bit. "I don't know. I just know that I'm not going to rule it out." Pausing for a while as he stared at me, Birch's smile widened as he began again, "So, were you serious before? About trying again?"

"Yes," I replied, nodding. "I'm serious. Uncertain, too. And terrified of little pink hatboxes. But serious." I sighed, shaking my head, and with the force of a smile silenced my inner worrier for a bit. "So, come on," I told him, leading him to the bedroom. "Let's go pray."

About the Author

Catherine DiMercurio Dominic was born and raised in Michigan. She graduated with distinction from the University of Michigan with a Bachelor of Arts degree in English literature with an emphasis in nineteenth-century British literature. After college, she went on to secure an editorial position with a major reference publishing company and began dabbling with an idea for a novel. Later, when her husband David's job drew them to Illinois, Catherine worked as a freelance editor. At that time, she also moved from dabbling to actually writing her first book. The novel she created then never made it to print, but the process of having written that unpublished novel served her well when she began writing again after returning to Michigan. The result of this effort was _Amazing Disgrace_. From her home in Ferndale, where she lives with David and their children, Margaret and Grant, Catherine is working on her next novel and has plans to complete a screenplay as well.